DIRECTIONS FOR

ALSO BY NIKKI COPLESTON

THE DI JEFF LINCOLN SERIES

The Price of Silence
A Saintly Grave Disturbed
The Shame of Innocence
The Promise of Salvation
A Strange and Murderous Air

DIRECTIONS FOR MURDER

NIKKI COPLESTON

A JEFF LINCOLN NOVEL

COPPER SMITH PRESS

Published in 2025 by Coppersmith Press
www.nikkicopleston.com

ISBN 978-0-9569594-1-6 (paperback)
ISBN 978-0-9569594-2-3(ebook)

British Library Cataloguing in Publication Data
A CIP catalogue record for this book is available from the British Library

Typeset by Shakspeare Editorial

To Harvey, 2008–2025,
who lives on in 'Tux'

TUESDAY 24TH OCTOBER

CHAPTER 1

Chris Darbyshire settled back in the passenger seat of the car, tension easing thanks to the Italian food and the wine – and the hour spent in bed with Leanne. He glanced across at her, but she was concentrating on her driving, craning forward to peer through the rain-swept windscreen.

He rubbed a clear patch in his window as they drew up at traffic lights, a hooded cyclist pulling up alongside. Christ, who'd be out on a bike on a night like this?

'Everything's misting up.' Leanne rubbed the window with her sleeve while she waited for the lights to change.

'It'll clear.' His eyelids felt heavy. It would've been so easy to drift off to sleep after hours spent staring at screens, but this was the part he liked best, the research, the speculation, the probing behind the headlines to get at the underlying story. Everything was falling into place at last.

The car moved forward and he opened his eyes. Rain gusted across the windscreen as the lad on the bike stood up on his pedals, forging ahead. He must be soaked through.

Leanne smiled across. 'Not long now.'

The lights along this stretch of road seemed farther apart than in the town centre. Away to the left stretched the unlit expanse of Coronation Gardens, the river tumbling through the darkness at the foot of sloping lawns. Beyond the Gardens, the towers of Barbury Abbey rose, ominous and forbidding, silhouetted against the night sky. Chris shuddered and looked away.

And then –

'Oh God!' Leanne braked as a slight figure – a child? No, a girl – was suddenly there in front of the car, slamming her hands on the bonnet, yelling, her hoodie sodden, her face slick with rain.

'Help me! You gotta help! Someone's in the water! Come quick!'

Chris shoved his door open as Leanne swerved into the side of the road and turned the engine off.

'No,' he shouted as she started to get out. 'Stay where you are. Call for help.'

'But I –!'

He didn't wait to hear her words. He jogged after the girl, who was fast disappearing into the darkness, heading for the river. He wished he'd stopped to grab his overcoat, but it was too late to worry about that now. Someone was in trouble and needed his help.

Heading for the river, he rushed down into the darkness.

WEDNESDAY 25TH OCTOBER

CHAPTER 2

'Didn't get to Caldey Island, then?' Mike Woods retrieved something from the printer and sat down again.

'Too rough.' Detective Inspector Jeff Lincoln pushed himself away from his desk, abandoning the backlog of emails that had accumulated while he'd been away. 'And then, of course, we had to come back because of Ted's accident.'

Woody, his detective sergeant, tutted. 'At least it was a clean break. Reckon it's his dignity that's hurt as much as his arm. You'd think he'd know better than to leave a rake where he could trip over it.'

'Accidents happen.' Lincoln grabbed his mug and crossed to the filing cabinet, where the kettle sat next to a jar of coffee and various packets of tea. Why was the kettle always empty? Why did no one fill it up for the next person if they'd emptied it? Refilling the kettle in the cloakroom, he glanced at the mirror over the sink. He looked more in need of a holiday than ever, his greying hair untidy, the shadows under his eyes still dark.

Yesterday, he and Trish Whittington had been enjoying their fourth day in Tenby, a holiday they'd promised themselves for months: time alone together, make or break. A brisk walk out onto Castle Hill, a pub lunch in town and a stroll on the beach afterwards.

But then her mobile had rung. She'd ducked out of the wind to take a call from Suki, her sister. His first thought had been a selfish one: was Tux okay? Suki had agreed to feed his cat while he and Trish were away and now he held his breath, braced to hear that Tux had been run over or had run away.

The call ended and Trish began to stride back towards the town as she put her phone away. 'It's Dad,' she said. 'He's had a fall on the allotment and broken his arm. I've got to get home.'

'Suki and Woody will make sure he's okay, won't they?'

'But you know how Suki fusses and Dad hates a fuss. If we leave now, we can be back by four.'

So much for not making a fuss…

The much-needed holiday had been cut short and here he was, back at Barley Lane police station as if he'd never been away. Still, the change of scene, brief as it was, had done him good. Lincoln always loved being by the sea, even in October.

He leaned back against the filing cabinet, arms folded, as the kettle came to the boil. 'Okay, so what have I missed?'

'Not a lot,' said Woody. 'Some lads got into a scrap outside Sainsbury's, damaged some cars. And an old chap went walkies from that care home near the abbey, but they found him in one of the outhouses. He said he had to get out for a bit cos he felt like a prisoner. Lucky they found him before it got dark. He'd have frozen to death out there in pyjamas and slippers.'

'No fun getting old.' Coffee in hand, Lincoln sat at his desk again. The shrilling of phones, the clicking of keyboards, the banging of desk drawers… The familiar sounds of Barley Lane police station made the tranquillity of Tenby seem like a daydream. 'I'd better let the DCI know I'm back.' He called his boss at Park Street nick.

DCI Claire Connors sounded surprised to hear his voice. 'Sorry you had to come home early, Jeff,' she said after he'd explained why he was in Wiltshire, not Wales, 'but it's lucky for me.'

'Lucky for you, ma'am?' Uh-oh. What had she got lined up for him? She wasn't going to ask him to work out of Park Street again, was she? He'd had enough of that in the summer, sweltering in an office with air conditioning that was on the blink, trying to manage an unfamiliar team that was either obstructive or defensive or both.

'A young guy's been reported missing, not seen since he left the Brewery Tap last night. His name's Ritchie Payne, twenty-five, from Barbury Down.'

In a town built on five rivers, a boozy night out all too often ended with someone in the water. If they were with friends who could raise the alarm, all well and good, but if they were on their own…

'Uniform are doing a search as we speak,' she went on, 'but could one of your team have a word with the family?'

'Can't uniform do that too?' Why was she involving investigators at this stage? The lad would probably turn up safe after sleeping rough all night or else he'd turn up, drowned, on a riverbank.

'Before he left the Tap, he had a bit of a clash with Garvin Steele.'

'The bloke who walked away from a murder charge last month?'

'The very same. A bit of a coincidence, don't you think?'

'What's that about?' Woody asked as Lincoln put the phone down, but before he could tell him, the door flew open and DC Pam Smyth rushed in. When she saw Lincoln, she stopped short, her cheeks flushed.

'You're back!'

'Rather sooner than I wanted to be. Did I miss anything else apart from a scrap outside Sainsbury's and a pensioner making a dash for it?'

She pulled her cycle helmet off and ruffled her cropped blonde hair into shape. 'You did. Breezy's got engaged!'

'Breezy's engaged?' Lincoln drove out of the yard behind Barley Lane and set off towards Barbury Down, the huge housing estate on the western edge of the town. The thought of the unruly DC Dennis Breeze getting married took some getting used to.

'He met some woman on the internet,' said Woody. 'Turns out she's local.'

'She knows she'll have to house-train him first, does she? So, Ritchie Payne – what's the address?'

The Paynes lived in a ground-floor maisonette in one of Barbury Down's scruffier roads, where most of the properties were still rented. The front door opened by slow degrees, dragging on the floor as if it was swollen with damp or had dropped on its hinges. A face peeped round, gaunt and deeply lined, with an unhealthy pallor.

'Mr Payne?' Lincoln identified himself and asked if he and Woody could come in, talk about Ritchie.

His wife came bustling through from the kitchen, where a kettle or pan was producing enough steam to fog all the windows. 'Have you found him?'

'Not yet,' said Woody. 'We need to ask a few questions about your son, get an idea of what might've happened.'

'Ritchie's our grandson,' she said. 'June, his mum, died when he was twelve. He'd got no dad, so we brung him up.'

'And he was at the Brewery Tap last night?' Lincoln sat down at the table under the window. The sill was swimming in condensation.

'He went out after he'd had his tea.' Mrs Payne sat down across from him, while her husband plodded quietly across to his armchair. 'We had the television on and he stuck his head round the door to say he was off out. When he wasn't back at his usual time and wasn't answering his mobile, Bert phoned the Tap, see if he was still there. He's never out past eleven. He's not a big drinker. Drinks more lemonade than beer.'

'Could he have gone to a friend's house, stayed the night if it got late?'

'He wouldn't do that without letting us know. He's good like that.'

'He always goes to the Tap,' her husband put in, 'even though it's all the way down into town. Darts, you see. He loves the darts and they've usually got a game going on. Lots of places don't even have a dartboard these days.'

'Bert taught him to play, didn't you, Dad?' Mrs Payne beamed at him.

'Fella at the Tap said Ritchie left after a bit of argy-bargy with the Steele lad. That's what got us worried. Garvin Steele's a nasty piece of work.'

'He used to bully our Ritchie when they were at school. Even now he never misses a chance to have a go about his mum. June took her own life,' she added softly.

'I'm sorry.' Lincoln paused for a moment. Then, 'Does this bullying ever get violent? Have Ritchie and Garvin ever got into a fight?'

'Ritchie's too soft for that, and with Garvin, it's all talk. Mind you, he's a big lad, isn't he, Dad? I wouldn't want to be around when Garvin loses his temper.'

'When did you last hear from Ritchie?' asked Woody. 'Did he phone you or text you while he was out?'

'Doesn't bother,' Bert said. 'He knows she turns her phone off when she's indoors.'

Mrs Payne looked across at the little clamshell mobile that sat on the table next to the sauce bottles.

Lincoln stood up. 'Mind if we take a quick look at Ritchie's room?'

She led them along a short corridor past the bedroom she shared with her husband. The instant she opened the door to Ritchie's room, a powerful smell rushed out: grainy, animal.

She gasped. 'Oh, he's forgotten to clean out the mice!'

A small cage sat on a tea trolley below the steamed-up window. With a rustle of paper and a flick of their tails, Ritchie's pet mice dived for cover under the torn newspaper lining their cage. Black pellets of mouse droppings had fallen from the cage onto the tea trolley, along with shredded paper and sawdust.

'My boys are always pestering me to let them have a guinea pig or gerbils,' said Woody, poking the bars of the cage, 'but I know who'd end up looking after them.'

Lincoln cast his gaze over Ritchie's bedroom, his only private space in this small, claustrophobic flat: a rumpled, unmade bed; an old-fashioned wardrobe with cardboard boxes stacked on top; a small table with his laptop open on it.

'That's for his games, mostly.' She nodded at the laptop. 'He spends hours on his games when he gets home from work.'

'Where does he work?'

'Tesco's, the one in town. He's on *replenishment*.' She said it with a flourish, though Lincoln was pretty sure it simply meant he filled shelves. 'He works funny shifts, night-time mostly, but he doesn't seem to mind. If he can't get the bus he walks, whatever the weather. Likes to be out and about.'

'He doesn't drive?'

'Can't. He's epileptic. They put it down to the tablets his mum was taking when she was expecting. For her nerves. He manages,' she said brightly. 'He's never known any different and he's on medication to control the seizures now he's older. That's why he doesn't drink much. Doesn't mix with his tablets. Oh Lord!' Her face fell as she looked across at the window sill, where a plastic tray of blister packs sat in a puddle of condensation. 'He hasn't got his pills with him.'

Woody moved the tray to a drier spot. 'How long can he go without them?'

'He has to take them every day.'

Another reason to find him as soon as possible.

On a pinboard next to the wardrobe were a list of upcoming darts matches, an advert for a coach trip to Belgium next March, and a photo, cut from a magazine, of an actress Lincoln vaguely recognised.

'A Sherilyn fan, is he?' Woody pointed at the photo and grinned at Mrs Payne.

'Oh yes, he's always loved Sherilyn,' she said. 'She's local, of course. Her dad lives on Folly Hill.'

They got back in the car, subdued because they could foresee the outcome of Ritchie Payne's departure from the Brewery Tap: something bad had happened, by accident or design.

'Reckon no news is good news,' Woody said as he checked his phone for updates.

'So where is he? Why hasn't he come home or called his parents – *grand*parents? He must know everyone's looking for him.'

'He's probably crashed at a mate's, overslept, not looked at his phone.'

'Or Steele's gone after him. Who's this Sherilyn woman?'

‘Sherilyn Croft. She was in that TV series, the one about the kids who run away from home to find out who killed their mum and dad. Something Hollow. Then she was in *Eastenders*. Or was it *Emmerdale*? One of the soaps. Of course, you don’t watch that sort of thing, do you, boss?’

‘I haven’t got a television and I don’t plan on getting one.’ Though Lincoln supposed that if, at long last, Trish and her daughter were to move in with him…

‘Whatever it was,’ Woody went on, ‘they sacked her after some nude photos turned up on Instagram. She’d modelled for the lads’ mags before she got her Equity card.’

Without further comment on the lissom Sherilyn, Lincoln started the car.

‘Let’s go and see what Garvin Steele’s got to say for himself.’

CHAPTER 3

Annie Darbyshire's mobile rang as she was going into a lecture on the impact of smartphones on teenagers' emotional health. A few seconds more and she would have turned it off for the duration of the talk, but when she saw who was calling, she hung back in the lobby and answered, juggling coffee cup, document case and phone.

'Jessica? I'm about to…'

'Have you heard from Chris?'

'No. What about?' Annie hadn't spoken to her husband in weeks and was surprised that Jessica Hale, his partner, had her number.

'He was away overnight and now he's not answering his phone and it's not like him, and…'

Actually, love, that's *exactly* like him, Annie felt like telling her. How else do you think he got away with cheating on me for so long?

'Where's he supposed to be?' she asked instead, edging towards the door of the lecture room. She didn't want to get shut out.

'In Barbury, of course. He had to be there early for that meeting about the arts centre.'

What meeting about the arts centre? Why the hell did this stupid girl think Annie knew anything about Chris's plans these days? He'd walked out on her months ago and moved into Jessica's place near Tisbury. Their separation might not be official yet, but for all practical purposes, they were living separate lives.

'Sorry, Jessica,' she said. 'I've got to go.'

The lecture began but the speaker's voice was so

monotonous, Annie struggled to concentrate. Her mind kept drifting back to Jessica's call. This was how Chris's cheating had started, with overnight stays "because the meeting starts really early".

For the last few years, he'd been one of the key people behind the project to create the Paragon, a new theatre and arts centre for the town. But then last year, not long before its official launch, the scheme had been summarily scrapped by the council amid allegations of corruption. Was Chris involved in plans to revive it? Or was "a meeting about the arts centre" simply a lie he told Jessica?

In the comfort break, Annie hurried out into the lobby to get more coffee and to check her phone for messages from her young cousin Molly, who was feeding the cats while she was away.

There was only a text from Jessica:

I called the hotel. He didn't check in.

She tried not to feel smug. Chris had probably never intended to stay at the hotel, had probably never even made a booking. He was sleeping with someone.

This, Jessica, is how it starts.

But instead of texting back, she slipped her phone away, poured herself some coffee and grabbed a chocolate chip cookie. She couldn't suppress a feeling of *schadenfreude* over Jessica's predicament.

Now you know what it feels like to be cheated on, love.

CHAPTER 4

Garvin Steele was leaning against the wall of his house when Lincoln and Woody pulled up outside. He threw his cigarette down and went back indoors, pointedly slamming the door when they were only ten feet away.

A young woman answered their knock: pale skin, dull blonde hair in bunches, no make-up. Her jeans were tight, torn at the knees, topped off by a thick black jersey several sizes too big. Maybe it was one of Garvin's. He was easily twice her weight.

He came up behind her and steered her out of the way. 'What's this about?'

'It's about Ritchie Payne, last seen drinking with you in the Brewery Tap. Any idea where he is now?'

'How would I know where he's got to? And I wasn't drinking *with* him. *I* was in the bar, *he* was in the bar. *He* leaves. *I* stay. Nothing suspicious about that, is there?'

Lincoln shook his head. 'Not at all. Can we come in and talk? A bit more private?'

Garvin hesitated, then stood back, waving them in past a clutter of trainers and work boots in the hallway, into the living room and towards the sofa that stretched the length of it. Air freshener had been sprayed round, perhaps at the sound of their knock on the door. A baby was mewling somewhere and the air freshener couldn't quite mask the smell of soiled nappies.

'You fell out over something, we understand.' Lincoln sank down into the low seat. He moved a stained baby bib from the arm of the sofa and laid it carefully on an adjacent six-pack of Thatcher's Haze.

'He slopped his drink over me, the stupid cunt, that's all.'

Woody stayed standing. 'You weren't arguing?'

'Okay, so I was winding him up a bit because he didn't have the balls to chat up the girl behind the bar. No reason for him to go off on one the way he did. I told him to grow some and he threw his drink over me. He's twenty-five, for fuck's sake, and he's still living with his nan!'

'Did you see him leave the pub?'

Garvin, perched on the edge of his chair, shrugged again. 'Seen him leave, but I couldn't tell you when exactly. He never stays late. Between half-nine and ten? Expect he likes to be home in time for a bedtime story.'

'And what time did *you* leave the pub?' asked Woody.

'Half-ten, eleven? Iris'll tell you.'

His girlfriend drifted in at the sound of her name.

'What time was I back last night, Iris?'

Her gaze darted from her boyfriend to Lincoln, to Woody and then back to her boyfriend. 'Half-ten?'

Garvin clapped his hands. 'There, see, I told you. Yeah, half-ten.'

'You didn't follow him when he left?' Lincoln knew there was no CCTV footage to corroborate or contradict Garvin's account: they'd have to take his word for it.

'Nah! And I had his fucking beer all over me. Stinking I was when I come home, wasn't I, Iris? Had to wash my clothes.'

Iris nodded dumbly.

'Hasn't turned up yet, then?' Garvin's concern didn't sound authentic.

Lincoln got to his feet. 'Not yet. Let's hope he turns up safe and well, eh?'

Lincoln stood at the whiteboard in front of a blurry photo of Ritchie Payne, downloaded from his Facebook page. A page that hadn't been updated since March 2013, when he'd created three posts and made four friends.

'West Ham supporter.' DC Graham Dilke nodded at the shirt Ritchie was wearing in the photo.

'What about CCTV?' Pam asked.

'Town centre security are sending over anything they've got,' said Woody. 'Not many cameras round the Brewery Tap, but we should be able to pick him up once he gets nearer the Market Place.'

A mugshot of Garvin Steele joined Ritchie's photo on the whiteboard.

'Trouble is, he's on meds for his epilepsy,' Lincoln said, 'and he's left them at home. He could have a fit if he's without them for long.'

The CCTV footage arrived and Lincoln pulled a chair up to Woody's desk so he could see the screen. The first camera picked Ritchie up at nine forty-one, heading away from the Brewery Tap and towards the town centre.

Cameras tracked him across the deserted Market Place, hands deep in the pockets of his jacket, the fluorescent flashes on the heels of his trainers rhythmically catching the street lights.

He was hurrying somewhere, somewhere definite, head down against the drizzle. And he was on his own. Where was he going? The bus stop, probably, to catch the 53 up to Barbury Down and home. He disappeared through a gap between the shops.

'Should pick him up coming out onto Spicer Street,' Woody predicted, switching to footage from a camera above the bus stop.

Sure enough, Ritchie emerged from the shadows and

crossed Spicer Street, looking towards the single-decker bus that was waiting there. But as he began to walk towards the stop, a white van drew up alongside him. When it moved off again, less than thirty seconds later, Ritchie was nowhere to be seen.

'He must've got in the van,' said Woody. 'Shame we can't see the registration.'

Lincoln shunted his chair back and returned to the whiteboard. 'At least we know he didn't fall into the river last night. That van must belong to a mate the Paynes don't know about – or it could be something more sinister. With any luck, there's a camera on the other side of the street that might have caught the reg.'

'Why's the DCI so concerned about Garvin Steele?' Dilke asked.

'Because of that case the team at Park Street handled back in the summer. Remember the lad who was fished out of the river?'

'Black kid celebrating his exam results? Alfie Corrigan? The DCI was worried it was a racial attack, but she would, wouldn't she?'

'Whether he was black, white or brown, Graham, Alfie Corrigan shouldn't have ended up in the river. And Connors would've been concerned about a racial motive regardless.'

Still, Alfie's case must have resonated with her because of her own background: her African Caribbean grandparents had arrived in England in the fifties and she was the most senior black officer in the Wiltshire force. And in a Wiltshire market town where black and brown people were very much in the minority, it wasn't hard to think the worst.

'So how was Garvin Steele involved in Alfie's death?' Pam asked.

'He was drinking in the same bar as Alfie and his mates. Something was said, there was an argument and when the group left, Steele went after them. There was some pushing and shoving according to witnesses, but then Alfie and his mates went their separate ways – except Alfie never got home. Some kids found him below the weir next morning. He'd drowned, but the post-mortem showed he'd been badly beaten up before he went into the water.'

'But Steele denied attacking him?'

'Of course he denied it, but there's always been a suspicion that he caught up with Alfie in town, beat him senseless and pushed him in the river. No way she could pin anything on him, though – certainly not a murder charge. But now, with Steele having a row with someone else who's gone missing…'

'You want us to look for a camera that might have clocked the van's registration?' Dilke was already picking up his jacket and phone.

'Yes. Check along Spicer Street and the routes out of town. We need to know where that van went after Ritchie got into it.'

As Dilke and Pam were leaving, DC Dennis Breeze arrived, accompanied by the distinctive aroma of fried chicken. Dumping a greasy carton on his desk and wiping his fingers, he took his leather jacket off and pulled out his chair.

'Fucking hell, it's nippy out there!' He stopped short when he saw Lincoln. 'You're back early, boss. Wales too wild for you?'

Woody saved Lincoln the effort of explaining again. 'My father-in-law, Ted, had an accident and broke his arm. Trish thought she'd better come back to make sure he was okay, help Suki out.'

'Sisters!' Breeze picked his chicken up again and took another bite. 'Wish my fiancée's sister was that supportive. Don't think she approves of me.'

'Why's that?' Lincoln didn't really want to know.

'Because of my job.' Breeze peered down at a blob of grease on his T-shirt, brushing at it ineffectually with the back of his hand. 'Thinks Rosie could do better for herself. But Rosie, of course, doesn't agree.' The detective constable, his fingers shiny with chicken fat, grinned.

Lincoln strode back to the whiteboard and tapped it smartly.

'We've got a missing person, Dennis. Ritchie Payne. Left the Brewery Tap last night and hasn't come home. And Garvin Steele's in the picture again.'

'Like with that black kid that went over the weir?'

'Yeah.' As Lincoln reached for the phone to update her about the white van, the DCI rang him.

'There's been a development down by the river, Jeff,' she told him grimly. 'We've got a body.'

CHAPTER 5

Lincoln's first thought was of the Paynes, Ritchie's grandparents: Bert in his scuffed slippers, his wife embarrassed by the cage of mice in their grandson's room.

'You'd better get down there,' DCI Connors told him. 'Coronation Gardens, near the play park. Uniforms are at the scene and the pathologist's been called. Keep me posted.'

'Was he in the water?'

'Half in, half out. That's all I know.'

Lincoln and Woody arrived at Coronation Gardens twenty minutes later. Word of the body's discovery had evidently spread: an outside broadcast van was already waiting at the entrance, and a presenter wearing too much make-up was practising talking to camera.

They strode down the path into the sprawling riverside park. To their left, half a mile away, beyond the sloping lawns and the water meadows, Barbury Abbey thrust its battleship-grey bulk into a sky that was almost as grey. Behind them loomed Ebbesbourne House, formerly Barbury's Victorian hospital but now converted into flats. No other buildings overlooked the crime scene and even Ebbesbourne House was some distance away across the road.

The footpath crossed the river by way of an ornamental bridge, but council notices warned that dredging operations would be blocking it off until October 31st.

Lincoln turned to the constable who was trying to keep the nosy onlookers at bay behind the cordon.

'DI Lincoln, DS Woods, Barley Lane,' he said. 'Is the pathologist here yet?'

'Yes, sir, she's just getting suited-up.'

Woody's eyebrows went up. '*She?*'

'Must be Ken's replacement. Let's hope she's as easy to work with.'

Long-time pathologist Ken Burges had recently retired to nurse his wife, who was terminally ill. He'd be a hard act to follow.

The two detectives donned the obligatory white coveralls, though Lincoln was in no hurry to set eyes on Ritchie Payne's body. He kept thinking of the cage of mice on the tea trolley in the young man's bedroom, the pinup of Sherilyn Croft, the abandoned blister pack of pills.

Ken's successor, in her paper suit, was crouching on the riverbank, blocking their view of Ritchie's head. With her face obscured by mask and hood, her age was hard to estimate, but Lincoln guessed she was a lot younger than Ken. She moved back and –

He gasped. 'That's not Ritchie Payne!'

She peered up at him over her shoulder. 'Who's Ritchie Payne?'

'He's been missing since last night,' said Woody. 'We assumed this was him.'

She stood up. 'And this is definitely not him?'

As soon as Lincoln caught sight of the body, a strange sensation crept over him. The man lying stiffly on his back on the riverbank was about his own age, late forties, with a similar build. His wet hair clung to his mud-smeared forehead, and where it had begun to dry, it looked like Lincoln's, brown going grey. Even his clothes were oddly familiar: a sports jacket over dark trousers, a shirt and loosely knotted tie.

'Is this where he was found?' he asked the constable.

'More or less, sir. That gentleman over there was walking his dog, saw him lying behind those bushes there, head first in the water. He dragged him out, turned him over in case he was still alive but… That was about an hour ago.'

The uniform jerked his thumb towards an elderly man sitting on a bench overlooking the river, a foil blanket draped over his shoulders. A grizzled Jack Russell terrier sat obediently at his feet, ears pricked.

'You've taken a statement?'

'A brief one, sir, yes. He didn't see anyone else around. Thought the guy had slipped and fallen in. The bank's very muddy along there.'

Lincoln introduced himself to the pathologist.

'Are you the SIO?' she asked.

The DCI hadn't actually told him he'd be Senior Investigating Officer on this one, but with DI Rick Nevin on sick leave, he supposed he must be. There was no one else more senior on her team.

'Yes,' he said. 'And you are… ?'

'Antonia Yardley. And he didn't drown, even though he was found with his head close to the water.'

She peeled back one flap of the sports jacket, which was heavy with moisture and smeared with mud. The front of his shirt, too, was plastered. Then Lincoln saw what she was getting at: under the mud, a bloodstain had spread through the wet fabric. The source was a ragged tear in the material. There would be a ragged tear in the man's flesh, too.

'Stabbed?'

She nodded. 'And here.' She lifted the other side of the jacket to reveal similar damage: an incision two or three inches above the waistband of the man's trousers.

'Not accidental, then.'

She pulled her mask away. 'Unlikely.'

He looked around, surveying the scene in search of clues to what might have happened. 'He was killed here?'

'I'd say so.'

'Approximate time of death?'

'Rigor's set in pretty much, so I'd say at least twelve hours ago.'

'Late last night, then.'

'At a guess.' She returned to her inspection of the body, diligently searching through the dead man's pockets: keys, a wallet, loose change, a spectacle case, a felt tip pen. 'Phone.' She held it up, but didn't pass it across to him, instead laying it down in a plastic tray with the rest of his belongings. 'It'll need to dry out.'

Lincoln stooped down to retrieve the damp wallet, which bulged with bank cards and cash.

'Reckon if this was a mugging, they came away empty-handed,' said Woody.

'Christian Darbyshire,' Lincoln read, then flipped through the business cards until he found one with Darbyshire's phone number and address on it. 'The Old Farmhouse, Hyperion Avenue.'

Antonia chuckled. 'Hyperion Avenue? I used to practise three-point turns up there and reversing round corners. It's very quiet. All the driving schools use it.'

'You grew up in Barbury?'

'No, but I learnt to drive here. Late developer.' She nodded towards the body. 'No sign of a weapon. Hard to know what they've used on him, but it could be something like a kitchen knife. Can't tell you much more until I get him to the mortuary.'

'Did he fight back?'

With some difficulty because of the rigor, she lifted

Darbyshire's left hand, crouching closer to inspect the palm for defence wounds. His wedding band glinted. She checked his right hand too.

'No obvious defensive wounds,' she said, 'but until I get this mud cleaned off him, I can't be sure.'

'We need to search the area for any other belongings. This time of year, a rainy night like last night, he'd have had a mac or an overcoat, wouldn't he?'

'Maybe he was driving,' Woody suggested, 'got caught short and stopped here, left his coat in the car.'

Lincoln shook his head. 'No car key.'

'Could still be in the ignition,' Antonia said, 'or he's got one of those push-button cars. He probably thought he'd only be a minute or two. How long does it take the average man to pee?'

Lincoln took her question as rhetorical. He looked towards the road, but the only vehicles parked there now were a BBC Wiltshire van and the ambulance. The mortuary van would be along soon.

'We need to inform his next of kin,' he said. 'Get a positive ID. You'll let me know what else you find?'

She nodded and returned to her examination. The police photographer arrived and prepared to document the scene.

Back on the path, Lincoln studied the dead man's business card again. The name wasn't familiar. 'While I call on the family, can you start looking into Darbyshire's background, Woody?'

'Going on your own?

'I'd like to take Pam with me. Where is she?'

'She went with Graham to check on traffic cams that might've picked up the white van last night.'

'I'll get Graham to drop her here and you can go back to Barley Lane with him.'

Half an hour later, Lincoln drew up outside the Old Farmhouse in Hyperion Avenue.

'I used to drive round here when I was having lessons,' Pam said. 'Not much traffic so you could do three-point turns without holding anyone up.'

'Antonia said the same.'

'Antonia?' She frowned at him over the roof of the car as they got out.

'Yardley. New pathologist.'

'Right.'

They approached Christian Darbyshire's house, the biggest in the road and clearly the oldest, a rambling former farmhouse in red brick, with a slate roof and tall chimneys. Lincoln wondered when it had last been a working farm. Developers must have bought its fields to build the executive homes that now threatened to engulf it.

Pam rang the doorbell and they stepped back to wait. The door swung open and a girl of maybe sixteen or seventeen stood before them. Plump and with short but unruly dark hair, she was casually dressed in jeans and a zip-fronted sweatshirt, a smartphone clutched in her hand. Was this Chris Darbyshire's daughter?

Lincoln showed his ID and asked for Mrs Darbyshire.

'Annie's not here,' said the girl. 'I've been feeding her cats while she's on a course. I'm her cousin, Molly Bancroft. Has something happened?'

Before the start of the afternoon lectures, Annie went up to her room to take some painkillers for the headache that had been sneaking up on her all morning.

Turning her phone on, she saw that Jessica had texted her three more times. For God's sake! Why did she think

Annie knew where Chris was or that she cared? He was all Jessica's now, and good luck to her.

Then she saw that Molly had called her several times in the last half hour. She feared something must be wrong at home. She hoped not. She rang as she went back down the stairs.

'Hi, Molly. Everything okay?'

'There's a policeman here. I'll hand you over to him.'

A policeman? She stopped on the half-landing. The back of her neck prickled. Her arms tingled.

'Mrs Darbyshire? My name's Jeff Lincoln. I'm a detective inspector at Barley Lane police station. I'm afraid I've got some bad news.'

Her hands were tingling now. She wasn't sure she could hold onto the phone. She leaned against the wall of the stairwell. 'What's happened?'

He told her Chris had been the victim of an attack in Barbury. She knew from the tone of his voice, that professional regretfulness, that practised sympathy, that Chris was dead. She caught her breath, heart thudding, fixing her gaze on an engraving of Winchester Cathedral that hung, crooked, on the half-landing wall. She reached up to straighten it.

'An attack? What sort of attack?' She had a vision of a fight breaking out at this morning's meeting about the arts centre. A nervous giggle threatened to escape.

'He was stabbed,' he said. 'At this stage, we think he was mugged. Can you get yourself back here as soon as possible? I understand you're in Dorset right now.'

'Hampshire. Winchester.' As if it mattered. An hour's drive. But she'd need to pack her bag, find someone to explain to. She might need to get petrol on the way. 'Where do I go when I get there?'

'The hospital. Presford General.'

When he said that, she had a wild thought that Chris was still alive, that he was only injured, but then he said, 'We'll need you to identify his body. I'm sorry, having to tell you like this. Are you sure you'll be okay to drive?'

As if she wasn't capable of driving back on her own! Her head swam. Maybe she wasn't. 'I'll be fine,' she said. 'I'll be fine.'

Somehow, she climbed back up the stairs to her room and mechanically packed her bag. She checked and double-checked the bathroom, the cabinet drawers, the wardrobe, was halfway out of the door before she realised she'd left her phone charger plugged in next to the bed. She yanked it out and bundled it into her bag.

Chris was dead. She was on her own.

Had they rung Jessica, she wondered, as she went downstairs to tell someone she was leaving? Chris must have had Jessica's number on him. The police had probably rung Jessica first. Except that she, Annie, was his wife. His widow.

She found one of the lecturers in the bar, the one who'd droned on about digital devices and the danger they posed to developing brains.

'I have to go home,' she said. 'A domestic crisis. Please pass on my apologies.'

She didn't need to fill up with petrol after all, but she stopped anyway, pulling into a layby on the A30. She pressed her forehead onto her hands, which were gripping the steering wheel as if they couldn't let go. No tears came. It wasn't supposed to end this way. No chance now that Chris would realise his mistake and come back to her.

She started the car and continued on her journey. Soon after three, she arrived at Presford General, bracing herself for what would come next. Outside, the afternoon was damp and windy. Without hurrying – what was the point? – she slipped her coat on, grabbed her bag and went towards the entrance.

CHAPTER 6

The hospital café was the closest place for Lincoln and Pam to take Annie Darbyshire after she'd identified her husband's body. Although she walked briskly along the corridor from the mortuary, apparently unaffected by what she'd had to do, she suddenly swayed, slumping against the wall beside a lurid abstract painting entitled *Grief Transformed Into Joy.*

Lincoln held his arm out for her to lean on. 'Come on, Annie, let's find somewhere to sit down.'

'I'm okay. It's the shock, that's all.'

He guessed she was in her early forties, slim and attractive, with wavy auburn hair and fair skin.

He left her with Pam at a corner table while he went up to buy two teas and a coffee. Ravenous, he was tempted by a cheese sandwich in the chill cabinet, but it would have been crass to eat it while he was talking to Annie and it was too big to hide in his pocket for later.

Annie shook her head, despondent, as he set the drinks down. 'Whatever did they do to him? All those bruises…'

With the mud cleaned off him, it was obvious that Darbyshire had been hit in the face before a knife was driven into him.

'We don't yet know the circumstances,' Lincoln said. 'He was found lying near the river in Coronation Gardens.'

'Coronation Gardens? Why was he there, of all places?'

'Can we go back a bit?' He pulled his chair closer to the table. 'You and your husband live at the Old Farmhouse, Hyperion Avenue?'

'Yes. No. We … we're separated. We've been living apart since December last year. *I* live at the house, *Chris* lives with his girlfriend.' She watched as Pam started to take notes. 'Jessica Hale. She lives on a farm near Tisbury.'

The leather lace-ups Darbyshire had been wearing didn't seem rugged enough for a farmyard.

'Do you have the address?' Pam asked, pencil poised. 'A phone number?'

Annie hesitated as if she didn't understand the question. Then she reached for her bag and pulled her phone out. Her hands, as she brought the screen to life and thumbed through her contacts, were trembling. She found Jessica's number and read it out.

'Where did Chris work?' Lincoln already knew from the business cards in the dead man's wallet that he was a script consultant, whatever that was, but he didn't know where.

'From home, mostly. He's a writer. Part of a team, so he goes up to London or Bristol quite often, depending on the project. Drama. Drama documentary. *Went*. He *went* up to London or Bristol. He rented a flat in London. Nothing fancy. A *pied à terre*, he called it, somewhere to shower and sleep whenever he was staying up there overnight.'

'Do you know where he was going last night?'

She shook her head, the red glints in her hair catching the light. 'I only know what Jessica told me, that he was staying in Barbury last night because he had an early morning meeting there today. When she couldn't get hold of him this morning, she phoned the hotel and they said he hadn't checked in.'

'Could he have been on his way to your house last night?'

'Coronation Gardens is nowhere near there. He'd be going out of his way, driving along Cranbrook Road. And before you say anything,' she added, holding her hand up as if to fend him off, 'I've heard all about those Gardens being a rendezvous for dodgy sex, but I can assure you my husband was never into anything like that.'

'Perhaps he was caught short,' Lincoln suggested, swerving thankfully away from the topic of outdoor sex, gay or straight, with friends or with strangers. 'Maybe he stopped the car and nipped into the Gardens. He wasn't wearing a top coat when he was found, despite the weather.' An image of Darbyshire's body flickered in his mind's eye: a shape not unlike his own, even the same style of clothes if, probably, more upmarket.

Maybe Annie, too, was imagining her husband left out in the rain all night. She stared into her tea in silence. At last, she looked up again. 'Is his car still there?'

Lincoln shook his head. 'His attacker could've taken it. What car does he drive?'

'He got a Ford Focus not long after he moved in with Jessica, but I can't tell you the registration.' She pushed her tea aside. 'You'll be speaking to her next? She'll have the details.'

'We'll need to talk to you again,' Lincoln said. 'Someone will come to the house…'

'Okay, fine.' She cut him off, grabbing her bag and getting unsteadily to her feet. 'I need to go home now, make some phone calls.'

'Are you sure you're okay to drive? I can get someone to…'

'I'm fine. I just need to get home.'

They left Christian Darbyshire behind in the hospital mortuary while his wife, his widow, drove home.

'What did you make of her,' Lincoln asked Pam. 'A bit cold?'

'Still in shock, I'd say. She's just lost her husband and even if they've been living apart, she must still have feelings for him.'

They were driving west towards Tisbury, a large village on the Wiltshire/Dorset border. Standish's Farm, Jessica Hale's home, was a mile outside the village, and although Lincoln could have sent Woody, Dilke or Breeze to call on her, he wanted to see for himself where Darbyshire had been living since his marriage to Annie broke down.

'I meant to ask if Annie and Christian had any children,' he said. 'Although, if they did, they'd probably be away at college or whatever. Let's hope she's got family to give her the support she needs.'

'Molly's there now, her cousin, so she's not on her own.'

He thought back to the ungainly teenager who'd opened the door to them. 'Yes, but she's only a kid.'

The clocks would be going back at the weekend and it was already dark once they left the lights of the main road in search of the farm. The sat nav threatened to take them down an impossibly narrow lane, but luckily Pam spotted a sign to Standish's Farm in time for him to turn off.

It wasn't a farm, not as he knew it, but a mishmash of prefabricated outbuildings around a floodlit concrete yard, with a brick-and-flint cottage at one end. This must be where Jessica lived and from whence Darbyshire had driven away yesterday in his smart leather shoes. Not a dollop of horse dung or a single cowpat in sight. A farm repurposed as an industrial estate.

The young woman who came to the cottage door was heavily pregnant, leaning back as if to ease the burden she was carrying. With long, curly dark hair and a softly rounded face, she was sheathed in an ankle-length black dress, a multicoloured cardigan over the top.

'Where the hell have you been?' she cried out when she saw Lincoln. 'I've been worried sick!' But then, realising her mistake, she clapped her hand over her mouth. 'Oh God, I'm so sorry. In silhouette, in the doorway, you look just like Chris, my partner. I should've put my glasses on.'

Lincoln introduced himself, introduced Pam. That's all he needed to say, because Jessica sank back against the door frame.

'Oh God, something's happened to him, hasn't it?'

Lincoln took a step forward. 'Can we come in?'

A man appeared behind her and she introduced him as her brother.

'What's this about?' he demanded, putting his arm around her shoulders and letting her sag against him.

'It's Chris, Toby,' she managed to say. 'I knew something was wrong.'

They sat around the pine table in the kitchen, a room made cosy by a Rayburn stove set into the old hearth. When Lincoln told her, as delicately as possible, that Darbyshire had been found dead, Jessica pressed her fist against her mouth and shut her eyes.

'He was mugged?'

'We think so,' said Pam. 'When did you see him last?'

Jessica – in her twenties, Lincoln guessed, about half Darbyshire's age – tried to pull herself together. 'Yesterday morning. He had to be in Bristol for work so I drove him to the station here so he could get the nine o'clock train to Barbury and then the train to Bristol.'

'He didn't have his car with him?' That would explain why there was no car key on the body. Lincoln kicked himself for overlooking the obvious.

'No, it's here, in the garage. He always takes the train if he's going to Bristol. He can get some writing done on the way.'

'Assuming the trains are running,' Toby put in. His sister cast him an angry look. 'Sorry,' he murmured. 'I'll put the kettle on.'

'And when he'd finished in Bristol?' Pam looked up from her notebook.

'He was getting the train back to Barbury, staying overnight at the Black Swan. He had a breakfast meeting this morning, wanted to be there nice and early.'

'A breakfast meeting?'

'At the theatre.' She glanced away, her eyes filling with tears. 'He tried calling me last night after he'd caught the train from Bristol, but I didn't hear the phone so he texted me instead.' She picked up her glasses from the table and put them on, snatched up her phone and searched it frantically. 'Look, twenty thirty-one.' She held it up to show them the screen.

On the train. Just leaving Temple Meads.

'Chris was working in Bristol, you said?'

'He's a writer. A scriptwriter.'

'Script *doctor*, more often than not.' Toby again. 'Rescuing other writers' crap screenplays.'

'He works here most of the time, but he goes up to Bristol quite often. He and Fred August share an office there. They write a lot of stuff together.'

Lincoln made a note of the name. 'And the meeting at Barbury Theatre this morning?'

'There's a campaign to get the arts centre project restarted. It's a cause close to Chris's heart. BACC,

Barbury Arts Centre Campaign.'

'Were you expecting him to call or text you once he got to Barbury last night? His train would have got in from Bristol at, what? Half-nine?'

'About then, yes. I go to bed early. I get so tired.' She swept her hair back wearily. 'But he usually sends me a WhatsApp last thing, even if we don't speak.'

'And last night?'

'I fell asleep about ten. This morning, when I saw he hadn't messaged me or tried to call before he went to bed, I rang him, only he didn't answer.'

'What time was that?' Pam asked.

'Eight o'clock?' Jessica looked to her brother for corroboration. He was plucking mugs out of the dishwasher. 'Toby?'

'I was already up and out by then.'

'When he hadn't phoned by lunchtime,' she went on, 'I called the hotel and they said he hadn't checked in.'

And now you know why, Lincoln thought sadly. Darbyshire must have been walking from the station to the hotel when he was attacked, taking a route into town that was quieter, if less well lit. A route that took him past Coronation Gardens…

'Was he wearing an overcoat yesterday?'

'Of course. It was cold and wet all day.'

'And a bag?'

'Yes, his overnight bag.'

'And a briefcase?'

'No, he put everything into his bag. Oh God, they must have taken his coat and his bag. It had his laptop in it.'

'Can you describe this bag?'

Toby chose that moment to put mugs of coffee in front of them, but it gave his sister time to think.

'Khaki canvas,' she said. 'Leather handles.'

'Was he often away overnight?' Pam asked.

'Maybe four or five times a month, depending on what project he was working on. You've spoken to Annie?'

'Yes,' said Lincoln. 'And she's identified him formally.'

'But he's been living with *me.*'

'Yes, but Annie is officially his next of kin.'

Jessica looked put out but then asked, quietly, 'Can I see him?'

'Can you get to the hospital first thing tomorrow morning?'

'I'll be there.'

Lincoln drove away from Standish's Farm feeling concerned for Jessica and guessing Pam felt the same. Darbyshire had left behind a young partner with a baby on the way, her world now turned upside down.

'Do you really think he was mugged?' Pam said as they wound their way back towards lighted roads. 'Didn't you say his wallet was still in his jacket?'

'Yes, and you'd think a mugger would know to check the jacket pockets, not just make off with his top coat. And why knife him? He'd beaten him too badly to worry about him coming after him to get his stuff back.'

'You think he was followed from the station?'

'Possibly. We need to check the station CCTV. Why the hell didn't he take a taxi from there to the hotel?'

'Must be tough for Jessica, not being his next of kin officially. What rights does she have if he's still married to Annie?'

'Bugger all unless they've made provision, a cohabitation agreement or some such.'

'Funny the way she swore at you when she opened the door.'

Lincoln snorted. 'At a quick glance, I suppose Darbyshire and myself could look a bit alike. And she hadn't got her glasses on.'

'Should've gone to Specsavers!'

'What?'

'You must've seen the adverts on the telly, boss. Oh, no, I suppose not.' She cleared her throat. 'I hate having to do these death knocks, don't you?'

'It was stupid of me to assume he was driving. When I saw he wasn't wearing an overcoat, I thought he must've got out of his car.'

'Whoever attacked him must have taken his coat off him after he'd been stabbed.'

'Not easy to do once he was lying on the ground. Strange. They went to the trouble of taking his overcoat off him but didn't bother to go through his jacket for a wallet.'

'Supposing there were two of them? *Two* attackers.'

'Two knife wounds, two knives?' Lincoln whistled through his teeth. 'The DCI's going to be over the moon, a duo of knife-wielding muggers at large.'

Pam groaned. 'And the press will have a field day.'

'Still no sign of Ritchie Payne, boss.' Woody nodded towards the whiteboard, where photos of Ritchie and Garvin Steele stared out into the incident room. 'His phone must be turned off and it's not set up for voicemail.'

'Doesn't mean it can't be tracked if the tech team get onto it.'

'And so far,' said Graham Dilke, 'we haven't been able to pick up that white van on any traffic cameras.'

'Still no index number for it, then.' Lincoln sighed. That van – and Ritchie Payne – could be anywhere by now, assuming he was still travelling in it.

'And his nan keeps phoning,' Breeze added. 'I told her, any news, love, *we'll* call *you*.'

'We need to concentrate on our murder case for now.' Lincoln strode across to the kettle and switched it on. 'Park Street can keep a look out for Ritchie.' He shook the communal biscuit tin in the hope that there was something in it, but the soft rustle suggested nothing more than crumbs. When he prised the lid off, though, he found two Maryland cookies of dubious vintage and half a bourbon cream. He was too hungry to be picky.

'You in charge of this one, boss?'

'The DCI hasn't much choice, Woody. Rick Nevin's off sick, Orla Cook's transferred to Hampshire and her replacement's only been a DS a few months. Okay, so what do we know so far?' Biscuits in hand, Lincoln headed for the whiteboard. 'We've spoken to Darbyshire's wife and his girlfriend and we can put together some sort of timeline. The girlfriend drops him off at Tisbury station yesterday morning so he can get a train to Barbury and then another one to Bristol, where he was working all day. Twenty thirty-one, he sends her a text to say he's leaving Bristol Temple Meads. He should've got into Barbury at twenty-one thirty-five.'

Breeze grunted. 'Assuming it was on time.'

Lincoln nodded. 'We can check that later, Dennis. He was staying overnight at the Black Swan because he had a meeting at Barbury Theatre today, quite early…'

'He could've driven in from Tisbury this morning, couldn't he?' Breeze interrupted. 'Why shell out for a hotel?'

Lincoln turned back to the whiteboard. 'Whatever his reasons for staying at the Black Swan, when she hadn't heard from him this morning, Jessica phoned the hotel and they said he hadn't checked in. She…'

'Would they, though?' Dilke twirled his pen between his fingers. 'Data protection and all that. The Black Swan wouldn't give out that kind of information over the phone. She's not even his wife. She could be anybody, checking up on him.'

'Okay, so let's call them when we're done here. Maybe Jessica misunderstood what they told her. Last night, he's walking from the station, passing Coronation Gardens about quarter to ten. Someone jumps him, pulls him into the Gardens. He puts up a fight, but he's stabbed, twice, possibly by two assailants. They take his overcoat and his overnight bag, then dump him face down on the riverbank with his head nearly in the water.'

'Leaving his wallet in his jacket,' Woody put in. 'Left his bank cards, a lot of cash and his smartphone too. Reckon they could've been interrupted.'

'So there could be a witness,' said Dilke. 'Someone who didn't realise what was going on.'

Breeze snorted. 'Or someone who didn't want to get involved.'

They all stared at Chris Darbyshire's photo.

'If it was just a mugging, why kill him?' Dilke scratched his head with the end of his pen.

'Muggers are often addicts,' said Lincoln. 'Addicts get desperate. He may have put up a fight and things got out of hand.' His mind flipped back to the dead man lying on the riverbank, his mud-plastered face, the glint of his wedding ring. 'Background checks on Darbyshire, Woody. What did you find?'

'He was forty-seven, married to Annie who's a teacher. Started out as an actor, turned to writing instead. Co-wrote several hit TV drama series over the last ten years with a bloke called Fred August.'

'Jessica mentioned Fred,' said Pam. 'They shared an office in Bristol.'

Woody carried on. 'Darbyshire also works as a script consultant. I had to look that up, but it's mostly tidying up scripts that other writers have been working on.'

Lincoln sighed. 'Not the sort of job in which you'd make enemies, surely? Dennis, you and Graham check the CCTV from the station, see if he was tailed after he got off the train. Pam, check the Black Swan.' He glanced at his watch and picked up the phone. 'I'd better update the DCI.'

'If you don't need me,' said Woody, turning his lamp off again, 'I'd best be getting off. Suki's been round at Ted's all day, so I reckon she could do with my help this evening.'

'How's Ted doing?' Lincoln punched in the number for DCI Claire Connors.

'Fine, just keeps saying what a bloody fool he is, tripping over a rake.'

'Typical Ted. Yeah, you get on home. Thanks.'

'What's the latest, Jeff?' Connors sounded as weary as he was beginning to feel.

'The attack on Chris Darbyshire looks like a mugging gone wrong, ma'am. We think he was walking into town from the station when he was attacked.'

'How d'you mean, "gone wrong"?'

'The level of violence seems excessive.'

'I've had media relations onto me already.' No wonder she sounded fed up. 'He was a well-known writer, apparently. Did you know that?'

'Not that he was "well-known". How did the press get hold of it?'

'A tip-off, apparently. There were tributes on social media even before there'd been a press release.'

'Tributes? Who from?'

'Celebs he'd worked with, people who'd been in his series. The socials will need monitoring in case there's anyone else we should speak to.'

More avenues to explore, more precious resources tied up…

'And on top of this, we've got another missing person,' she went on. 'Sherilyn Croft, some sort of local celebrity.'

Lincoln shut his eyes, visualising Ritchie Payne's messy bedroom, a big photo on the wall: Sherilyn, actress and sometime soap star.

Ritchie Payne was still missing and now his idol had gone missing too.

CHAPTER 7

On the station concourse, Graham Dilke and Dennis Breeze waited until the crowd of commuters had thinned. As soon as they could get through, they crossed the ticket hall in search of whoever was in charge of the CCTV.

'Is this to do with that young fella that's gone missing?' The security officer led them into a dim room where a bank of monitors glowed and flickered.

'No,' said Breeze. 'It's a bloke who got mugged last night after he got off the train from Bristol Temple Meads. The train that gets in about half nine.'

'What, mugged outside the station?'

Dilke shook his head. 'On his way into town past Mill Close and Coronation Gardens.'

'The scenic route. Not very well lit, is it? And that park can get a bit unsavoury after dark.'

'We need to watch him leaving the station,' Dilke went on, 'see if anyone follows him.'

'Got a picture of this guy? A description?'

Dilke produced the only photo they'd got, a head shot downloaded from LinkedIn.

'Tall, short, fat, thin?' The security man looked at them expectantly.

'Six foot, well built,' said Breeze. 'Late forties, wearing a top coat and carrying an overnight bag.'

Security Guy pulled out his chair and sat down. 'Twenty-one thirty, you said?'

They watched Tuesday night's footage, a small crowd of travellers emerging from the underpass and dwindling to a few stragglers.

None of them was Chris Darbyshire.

'You're sure about the time?'

'He sent a text to say he was on that train.' Dilke sensed a gap opening up between the text Darbyshire sent to Jessica and the evidence in front of them.

'Anywhere else he might've got off?' Security Guy sounded peeved.

'He caught the nine o'clock from Tisbury yesterday morning,' said Breeze, 'so he could pick up the Bristol train from here.'

Security Guy had a suggestion. 'Let's try and pick him out of the crowd yesterday morning when he arrived from Tisbury. That shouldn't be difficult. Then we'll know what we're looking for.'

Minutes later they were watching camera footage of the train's arrival.

'That's him,' said Dilke as a tall man with broad shoulders and untidy hair stepped down from the train. Darbyshire looked about him as if to check which platform he needed for the Bristol train. Then, his overnight bag slung over his shoulder, he loped along the platform towards the camera.

'That's weird,' said Security Guy. 'The Bristol train comes in on the other side of the same platform – but he's heading for the underpass and the exit.'

Breeze peered closer. 'Where's the bugger off to?'

'What do you mean, he didn't go to Bristol?'

Lincoln stood at the whiteboard, marker pen in hand, trying to make sense of what Dilke and Breeze were telling him. It was nearly nine, it had been a long day, and he wasn't sure how much more they could accomplish without a break.

'Darbyshire got off the train from Tisbury yesterday

morning,' Dilke explained, 'but instead of waiting for the Bristol train, he headed out of the station and walked towards town along Station Road.'

'And he wasn't staying at the Black Swan on Tuesday night,' Pam put in. 'Jessica must have misheard the receptionist when she phoned to ask if he'd checked in. They told her he hadn't *booked* in.'

Lincoln sighed. 'Which makes me think he was up to something. He tells Jessica he's off to work when he's actually meeting another woman.'

'Or another man. Sorry, boss,' said Breeze, 'but you're the one who's always telling us not to assume anything.'

'Yes, Dennis, you're right. Another woman *or* another man. So, what was he doing in Coronation Gardens last night if he wasn't walking from the station like we thought?'

Breeze sniggered. 'I stand by my previous remark, boss. We all know what those Gardens have got a rep for – cottaging.'

Lincoln recalled how hastily Annie Darbyshire had headed off any suggestion that her husband was in Coronation Gardens for illicit sex. He'd never been interested in "that sort of thing", she'd insisted, but they couldn't rule it out.

'Let's assume he wasn't walking after all. He got out of a car by the Gardens. Not his own car – that's still in the garage at Jessica's place – but he could've been a passenger in someone else's car. He gets out, leaving his coat and bag behind. Goes into the Gardens, gets attacked. The car drives off. But who's the driver?'

'The woman – or man – he met in Barbury instead of going to Bristol.' Pam frowned at the whiteboard, the original timeline now in doubt. 'But why haven't they come forward?'

'A bit obvious, isn't it?' Breeze waggled his eyebrows. 'They were both playing away and his lover doesn't want to be found out.'

'In the morning, we can try and track him on his way into town,' said Lincoln. 'There'll be more cameras along Station Road that will have picked him up. They should show us where he went and we can start to build up a picture of what he did during yesterday.'

'And there's this Fred August guy that he worked with in Bristol.' Dilke waved at his screen. 'He may know something. Darbyshire's trending on Twitter. #ChrisDarbyshireRIP.'

'Yeah, but if August's in Bristol, he'll come under Avon and Somerset, won't he?' Lincoln didn't welcome the prospect of having to liaise with another force at this early stage, dealing with detectives he didn't know.

'I Googled him. He lives in Bradford-on-Avon – and that's Wiltshire.'

'Well done, Graham. That's an action for tomorrow then.' Lincoln took one last look at the whiteboard, capped the marker pen and went back to his desk. 'The DCI tells me Sherilyn Croft has gone missing.'

Dilke looked blank but Breeze's interest was piqued. 'You're kidding! Where from?'

'She was visiting her family in Folly Hill, apparently. But while we've got this murder on our hands, Park Street can deal with her.'

'Like they're dealing with Ritchie Payne's disappearance.' Dilke sounded cynical. 'Who is she, anyway?'

'Actress,' said Breeze. 'Actress and nude model. She was in that series about nuns. Ironically.'

'I thought Woody said she was in one of the soaps.'

'Oh, that's right. The nuns came after *Emmerdale*.'

Breeze grinned. 'And then the glamour shots came to light. Not connected, though, is it, her going off and Ritchie Payne disappearing?'

Lincoln sat at his desk, keen to wrap up for the day, get home, have something to eat. Something to drink. 'I'd say it's unlikely. He is a fan, though.'

Breeze laughed. 'What lad wasn't, back in the day? She was big about ten years ago, when he'd have been fifteen. An impressionable age.'

'When's the PM?' asked Dilke.

Lincoln thought of Jessica Hale going to the hospital to view her partner's body. 'I need to confirm that with Antonia Yardley, Ken's replacement.' He rang the number that used to be Ken's and she answered after only two rings.

'I'm out of the office,' she told him. 'At least, I'm *in* the office, but I'm about to go home. Can't it wait till the morning?'

'Chris Darbyshire's partner wants to see him before the autopsy. What time are you doing it?'

'Ten o'clock.'

'I told her to be there early.'

'Can't she wait till after?'

'It's a courtesy. His wife did the formal ID, but it's Jessica he's been living with for nearly a year.'

'Okay. Will you be coming along?'

Nothing he liked better than an autopsy after breakfast… 'Of course.'

'Are *you* still on duty?' She sounded less concerned than disapproving.

'Only for the next few minutes. It's been a long day.'

When he got home to the Old Vicarage, Lincoln wished he'd got round to putting up more outside lights so the driveway wasn't half in darkness. One more thing to add to the list of potential improvements. He'd bought this place when it was semi-derelict and it was taking all his spare time, energy and money to put it to rights. But he had no regrets, even if the house had become an ongoing project, like a hobby.

The house was cold, but he couldn't be bothered to investigate why the central heating hadn't kicked in. He dumped his coat in the hall and headed for the kitchen, turning on lights as he went. A soft thud announced that Tux had woken up and jumped down off the bed. In a moment or two, the little cat would gently push open the kitchen door and look around for its evening feed.

Would Trish ever move in here with him? Was it she who was afraid of commitment or Lincoln?

The break in Tenby, curtailed as it was, had been a chance to talk about the future, but she'd kept on about how unsettled her daughter would feel if they moved in with him now.

'Kate's nearly fifteen, Jeff, and it's a difficult age. If you were a parent, you'd understand. I've got to put her first.'

Would he ever be a parent? He was willing to be a stand-in for Kate's father, Vic Amos – happily remarried with a new baby imminent – but was that enough? It would have to be. Trish wouldn't want to interrupt her career now and did he really want to become a father when he was only a few years off fifty?

Before he made himself thoroughly miserable, he put the kettle on and reached for the Jamesons. He imagined being in Chris Darbyshire's place: a man his own age, starting out with a new partner, a baby on the way and yet almost certainly pursuing someone else. There was still so much they didn't know about him.

How would Jessica react to the news that he hadn't booked a stay at the Black Swan or caught the train to Bristol yesterday morning? Why had Chris told her he was on the train back to Barbury last night, when he evidently wasn't? What game had he been playing?

Trish rang. 'I thought you'd want to know how Dad is.'

'Sorry, I should've called you. How is he?'

'He's finding it so awkward, having his arm in plaster.'

'Lucky he's got you and Suki looking after him.'

'I'm sorry about Tenby. I know how much you were looking forward to it.'

'You were too, weren't you?'

'Well, yes, but you were the one who needed the break after that case in the summer.'

He didn't know what to say: hadn't they both needed a break, taking advantage of Kate being away, staying with her father for half-term?

'Listen,' he said. 'I've had a long day and I've got to be out early so… I'm glad Ted's okay.'

'So am I. Tripping over a rake, of all things.'

'Easily done. Night, Trish. Speak to you tomorrow.'

He could have told her how much he wished she was there with him, how much he longed to spend the night with her, but he rang off too quickly. He needed food, drink, sleep.

Tomorrow was going to be another long day.

THURSDAY 26TH OCTOBER

CHAPTER 8

Annie stood at the kitchen sink, staring out into the rainy, windswept garden. Her first morning in a world without Chris in it. They'd had so many plans when they'd started out together, but now what? Even though they'd been living separate lives, he'd still been a part of hers, there at the end of a phone, a WhatsApp message away if she'd needed him.

'Will you stay on here?'

She spun round at the sound of Molly's voice. 'Will I what?'

'Sorry. That was a stupid thing to say.'

'No, it wasn't, love.' Annie filled the kettle and switched it on. She was glad Molly had offered to stay the night, glad that Molly's father – her Uncle Martin – had let her. 'It's too soon to say what I'll do, but right now, I'll make some coffee.'

'I wish this was still a farm.' Molly gazed out of the window.

'I do too, but Grandad sold off most of the land even before I was born.'

Annie remembered the tumbledown old outbuildings where, despite her mother's dire warnings, she'd played hide and seek with her cousin Sherilyn. But then the developers had moved in and their childhood playground was lost.

Four generations of Bancrofts had owned Dobbins Farm and its sense of history had always been a comfort to her. Whatever had happened to all the photos her father used to show her? Snapshots of her grandparents, her father with his brother Martin and sister Lydia and their various horses, dogs and cats. Had her mother thrown the photos away after he died?

Molly picked up two mugs from the draining rack. 'Sherilyn says there used to be wild parties here with people from the theatre.'

Annie remembered those days with mixed feelings – exciting to be around such colourful characters but unsettling too. The combination of drink and good food, high spirits and mercurial temperaments – and drugs – had been a heady mix. Had her parents indulged in anything harder than the occasional spliff? They'd been young in the Sixties, after all.

'Theatrical digs could be pretty awful in those days, Moll. My mum and dad offered a sort of home-from-home to some of the actors in rep here. One of them told Mum he only looked forward to playing Barbury Theatre because he could stay at Dobbins Farm during the run.'

'Did you meet anyone famous?'

Annie shook her head. 'Not many of those actors became big names. It's an overcrowded profession, as my dad used to say.'

'Sherilyn's done okay.'

'Well, yes, she's been lucky.' Annie didn't care much for her cousin, Molly's half-sister. Even though Sherilyn was only three years younger than Annie, they'd been close only when they were small. As soon as they were teenagers, they'd been rivals, both longing to go on the stage and achieve fame – although only Sherilyn had succeeded.

Annie tried to focus on making the coffee, if only to keep at bay the thoughts that had churned in her head all night: the phone call telling her Chris was dead; the sight of his poor bruised face; the drive back here after she'd left the mortuary, knowing she'd never again see him or hear his voice. What was he doing in Coronation Gardens? It didn't make sense.

She put the mugs on the table and fetched milk from the fridge, moving on autopilot.

Molly picked her phone up and began to scroll through the screens while Annie poured coffee, trying to prepare herself for what the rest of the day might bring.

'Oh no!' Molly cried. 'Our Sherilyn's gone missing.'

CHAPTER 9

'Got something you'll be interested in. Front page news.'

Karen Bolitho was wrapping up for the day when the call came through to the newsroom. She dropped her coat onto her chair, sat down and turned her laptop on again.

'Oh yeah? Why will I be interested in it? Who am I speaking to?' She started the voice recorder on her mobile.

'Call me Jack. First names only.'

'So, Jack, it's Karen here. What have you got for me?'

'Sherilyn Croft.'

Oh God, not another so-called sighting. Who cares about that bloody woman? She's a has-been, yesterday's news. And she's turned up, hasn't she, papped trolling round Tesco's in full slap.

'What about her?' Karen tried to convey her lack of enthusiasm so Jack would give up and she could go home.

'Nate Newton. Nude photos et cetera.'

'Who?' Vague memories of some kids' TV thing years ago. She Googled his name, saw an actor with a grin as mischievous and wicked as the Artful Dodger's, his thick dark hair styled with a distinctive, lop-sided fringe. Oh Christ, *him*! 'What about him?'

'Mitchell Burnett.'

Her pulse quickened. '*The* Mitchell Burnett?'

'Yeah, *the* Mitchell Burnett.' Jack was grinning, she could tell. 'You interested now?'

CHAPTER 10

Lincoln didn't relish the sight of Christian Darbyshire's body being cut open. It was too much like seeing his own body on a mortuary slab.

He waited until Antonia Yardley had completed her initial examination – first impressions of the body in front of her, apparent cause of death, location of the knife wounds – and then he told her he'd have to leave.

'I need to go to Bradford-on-Avon, talk to someone he worked with,' he said. He'd decided to take Dilke with him, leaving the rest of the team to follow up other leads. 'I'll be out for the rest of the morning.'

'I'll let you know what I find as soon as I'm done. His partner was here earlier. She didn't seem to want to leave him. I had to get someone to take her back to the main building, give her a cup of tea.'

'She came on her own?'

'Her brother brought her, she said, but he was waiting in the car.'

'Not very supportive.'

Antonia laughed. 'Not everyone is as comfortable around dead bodies as you and I are.'

'I've got an office in Bristol, yes.' Fred August set mugs of coffee in front of Lincoln and Dilke. 'I prefer living here in Bradford and it's an easy enough commute – hop on the train, hop on a bus the other end. Parking round here's an absolute bastard so I sold the car. Terrible about Chris, just terrible.'

Lincoln and Dilke were calling on Darbyshire's writing partner in his apartment in one of Bradford-on-Avon's converted textile mills. With big semi-circular windows overlooking the river, the flat should have been full of character, but Lincoln was dismayed to find the interior bland and minimal, more like an office than a home.

August was a short, stocky man, and his high forehead and snub nose gave him the look of a bespectacled baby. He was dressed in a cream-coloured linen tunic over matching wide-legged trousers, like a martial arts outfit.

'Were you and Chris meant to be working together on Tuesday?' Lincoln asked.

'Tuesday?' August looked mystified. 'Which Tuesday?'

'The day before yesterday.'

'I haven't seen Chris for weeks. We haven't worked together since…' He shut his eyes, trying to remember. 'July. It was the fourteenth of July, Bastille Day. We went to the wine bar next to the office. They'd decorated it with French flags and bunting and they were playing that awful accordion music and…'

'Not since the fourteenth of July?' Lincoln glanced across at Dilke. Now it was *their* turn to be mystified. 'We understood you were regularly working together in Bristol.'

'No, no, no. We haven't collaborated on anything since March. We only got together in July because some one-horse TV channel approached us about writing a daytime soap. We met up to go over it together. We turned it down. If you're offering peanuts, hire a pair of monkeys to write it for you!' He picked up his coffee and took a sip. 'No, Chris and I haven't worked together since March.'

'But he was still travelling up to Bristol to work at your office?'

August shook his head, hugging his mug against his stomach. 'When Chris said he was going his own way, I terminated the rental on that office and found somewhere cheaper for myself, big enough for one, short let. He was working from home, wasn't he?'

'Some of the time,' said Dilke. 'Is it possible he rented somewhere else in Bristol without telling you?'

'I doubt if he could afford it. Times are hard and he'd got two women to support. I gather his wife's self-sufficient enough, but with a baby on the way with his new lady, he needed to save his pennies.'

'You've had some very successful series, though, haven't you?' Lincoln said. 'Are you saying he was hard up?'

August laughed. 'We're *all* hard up in this business. You can spend months developing ideas for a programme or a series, only to get the thumbs-down from everyone you take it to. Even when you get a commission, there's no guarantee your show will get made and you can't take it anywhere else. This industry's very small, very parochial. Yes, we did well out of two or three series five years ago, but we've been trying to strike gold again ever since – without success. Chris got sick of trying.'

'What's he been living on, then?' Dilke asked a question that wasn't really August's to answer, but his erstwhile writing partner answered anyway.

'His aunt's been paying him to ghost-write her autobiography, hasn't she? He started on it sometime last year when things started to go a bit slow. *That's* not gonna get finished now, is it? Listen, I won't speak ill of the dead and Chris was a lovely man in many ways, but he thought he could play away and Annie wouldn't find out. But she always did – well, most of the time. It sounds as if he was still playing away behind his new lady's back. He should've known he'd get caught out.'

Lincoln led the way back to where he'd parked the car. Bradford-on-Avon seemed to be such a higgledy-piggledy town, all flights of steps and sloping pathways, with pale stone buildings at odd angles to the road or the river, as if it had grown without any kind of plan.

He liked it, though, might even come back to explore it at his leisure one day. Maybe with Trish, though time together seemed increasingly hard to find. He kept taunting himself with the thought that her father's accident had been an opportune excuse for her to cut their holiday short, as if she'd found even a week in Tenby too long to be alone with him.

'How do you think you become a ghost writer?' Dilke asked as they made their way back to Barbury.

'God knows! It can't be easy telling someone else's story as if it's them writing it.'

'Do you know anything about the flat Chris had in London?' Dilke had asked August as they were leaving. 'A *pied à terre*, we were told.'

'*Pied à terre*? He stays in a bloody great apartment in Islington, courtesy of this old aunt of his. She used to be an actress. It's *her* life story he's been writing for the past year or so.'

'The aunt's story is probably on his laptop,' said Dilke now as they headed back towards Barbury.

'Except we don't know where his laptop is. And it's not her life story that's got him killed, is it? From what Fred August told us, it's as if Darbyshire was living a double life.'

'It's hard enough living *one* life!'

'Not complaining, are you, Graham? You're young, your whole life ahead of you, no responsibilities...'

'I'm living at home with my mum and I need to move

out. When they said Barley Lane was closing down, I was pleased, y'know? I had an excuse for putting in for a transfer.'

'It's *still* closing down. We've had a stay of execution while Park Street's got the builders in, but it's only a temporary reprieve.'

'You think Annie Darbyshire knew what he was up to?'

'I don't know. We need to speak to her again. Jessica, his partner, certainly didn't seem to suspect anything. And Toby, the brother – let's have a word with him as soon as we can, make sure we're not looking at something closer to home.'

'But if it really was a mugging, the rest of it's irrelevant, isn't it?' Dilke dismissed Darbyshire's complex personal life with a wave of his hand. 'It's hard for his wife, for his girlfriend, to find out he's been sleeping around and not going where he's said he's going. But that's not a police matter, is it? That's just...fallout.'

Lincoln pulled into the yard behind Barley Lane and they got out.

'Assuming it really was a mugging. Why leave his wallet behind? Why stab him, twice, and then walk away without his phone or his cash?'

'His phone should've dried out by now, shouldn't it?' said Dilke. 'The tech team can get something out of it soon.'

Back at his desk, Lincoln waited impatiently for a call from Antonia Yardley, though he wasn't sure what more the autopsy would reveal except, with any luck, a better idea of the type of weapon used. Restless, he crossed to the whiteboard and studied it, resenting its refusal to help him out.

Where was Darbyshire going when he was supposed to be getting on a train to Bristol yesterday morning? Was he meeting someone, heading somewhere in town to work on his aunt's "autobiography"? With any luck, Breeze would have found some CCTV cameras farther along Station Road and they could begin to track his movements in the hours before his death.

The phone rang.

'Christian Darbyshire's autopsy,' said Antonia. 'Cause of death, loss of blood from two knife wounds. Bruising to the face suggests he was punched several times before being stabbed. He was also kicked or stamped on while he was on the ground, resulting in a traumatic pneumothorax. A broken rib punctured his lung.'

'A sustained attack, then, not just two swift jabs with a knife.'

'Knives.'

'Knives?'

'Yes,' she said. 'A long-bladed kitchen knife and a filleting knife.'

'Christ. So there was more than one attacker?'

'The filleting knife went pretty much straight in, suggesting the assailant was a similar height to the victim. The wound from the kitchen knife has an upward angle, suggesting that the other attacker was much shorter.'

'Anything else?'

'Traces of vaginal fluid. He'd recently had penetrative sex.'

'How recently?'

'Since he'd last showered, so sometime on the day he was killed, presumably. I can't be any more definite than that without more tests.'

Sex with Jessica before he left home that morning? Or had Darbyshire had sex with someone else during Tuesday?

'And he'd eaten about an hour before he died. Mushroom pizza, hardly digested. And red wine.'

He thanked her. Where had Darbyshire eaten that last meal and with whom?

His desk phone rang as he hung up on Antonia. It was DCI Claire Connors.

'What's the latest, Jeff? It's chaos here.'

He could hear sawing in the background and the whine of a cordless drill. He visualised his boss standing in the middle of a building site, but he guessed she simply needed to shut her office door.

'Chris Darbyshire's turning out not to be the man we thought he was, ma'am.' He told her what they'd found out.

'Why the lies?'

'Good question.'

'I don't want the press finding any of this out, not yet anyway. If Darbyshire loses the public's sympathy, we'll lose their support, precisely when we need them to be looking out for his killer.'

'*Killers*. Looks like he was stabbed by *two* people.'

'That's not just a mugging, is it?'

'It doesn't feel like it, ma'am, no. Any news on Ritchie Payne or the Croft woman?'

'No sightings of Ritchie, and I'm thinking Sherilyn Croft has gone off grid by choice. She turned up at her parents' house on Tuesday. There was a row and she walked out. Her stepmother got into a bit of a state, tried to report her missing yesterday but was told to give it another twenty-four hours. Somehow, though, it got onto social media and the next thing you know, it's this big celebrity mystery. She's a grown woman of forty, for fuck's sake, behaving like a teenager. If that's what fame and fortune do for you…' She sighed, exasperated.

'I'm going to talk to Darbyshire's wife again, find out what more she can tell us. She was still in shock when we spoke to her yesterday.'

'Let's hope she can help. You'll be pleased to hear I'm getting reinforcements.'

'Ma'am?'

'An acting DI from Trowbridge is joining us while Nevin's off sick. Tim Anderson. I'm told he's ambitious and keen.'

That's what they'd said about DCI Dale Jacobs, Connors's predecessor, and look what happened there! Lincoln would take 'hardworking and steady' over 'ambitious and keen' every time.

'When does he start?'

'Later today, with any luck. Media briefing tomorrow?' And she rang off.

Who was Tim Anderson? The name wasn't familiar, but since Trowbridge and Barbury were separated by most of Wiltshire, it was unlikely that Lincoln's path and Anderson's had ever crossed.

'Annie Darbyshire,' he said as Pam appeared in the doorway. 'Coming with me to the Old Farmhouse to talk to her again? Woody can hold the fort while we're out.'

CHAPTER 11

'It doesn't seem real.' Annie led Lincoln and Pam into the large kitchen, its big windows overlooking a wild-looking back garden. 'I keep thinking I'll wake up and find that Chris is still alive and that I've dreamt it all.'

She put the kettle on, then lifted a large tabby cat off one of the chairs drawn up to the table. The cat took its time stretching before sauntering off into another room.

'Have a seat.' Annie waved at the now-vacant chair. Lincoln noticed that her auburn hair was the same colour as his wife Cathy's. He guessed she was about the age Cathy would be now if she'd lived.

'We've talked to Fred August,' he said, dragging his thoughts back to the present. 'He told us he and Chris hadn't worked together for several months. Did you know about that?'

'Chris and I separated before Christmas. I've no idea what he's been working on. He and Fred used to be in the office all hours when they'd got a commission, but for the last two or three years, things have slowed down. That's why he and Fred had other projects on the side.'

'Other writing jobs?' asked Pam.

'Yes, like editing other people's scripts. He did some voice work from time to time – audio books for a company in London – but I expect even that's been drying up. Too many people chasing too few projects.' The kettle boiled and she turned away to make the drinks. 'He had a lovely speaking voice. Chris may not have been on the stage any more, but he hadn't forgotten what he learnt at drama school.'

'Did you know he was a ghost writer?' Lincoln asked.

'A ghost writer? No, but I'm not surprised. I've heard the money's good.'

'According to Fred, he was writing his aunt's autobiography for her.'

Annie froze in the act of setting the mugs down on the table. 'His *aunt*? He hasn't got an aunt.'

'In London,' said Pam. 'She was an actress.'

'That's *my* aunt! Lydia Bancroft. She always had a soft spot for Chris. In fact, she brought us together. He had a tiny part in a Terence Rattigan revival and Lydia was the big name, the one that brings the punters in.'

Pam was impressed. 'My mum's always been a fan of hers. So she's your aunt?'

'My father's sister, yes.' Annie swept her hand through her hair. 'I had no idea Chris was still in touch with her.' She sat down across from them. 'Lydia and I haven't always seen eye to eye, so he must've thought it best not to tell me in case I thought he was being disloyal. Oh God, I'll have to tell her what's happened. She'll be devastated. What with that and Sherilyn going off...'

'What's your connection to Sherilyn Croft?' Lincoln asked.

'We're cousins. She's really Sherilyn Bancroft. Croft's her stage name. Lydia's *her* aunt too. I bet Sheri's thrown one of her famous tantrums and gone off somewhere just to wind everybody up, get herself talked about on social media.'

No love lost between those two! 'You don't believe she's really missing?' Lincoln stirred some sugar into his coffee.

'No, and now Molly's upset and...' Annie picked up her mug, took a sip. 'Sherilyn's her big sister. Half-sister. Molly's naturally over-anxious and she needs stability, not more drama. She was going to stay here with me until the weekend, but she's gone back home because she's worried about Sheri.'

'You're on your own here?'

'Yes, and before you ask, I'm fine. But why all these questions? Chris was mugged, wasn't he?'

'The attack could've been personal, not random,' Lincoln said carefully. 'His wallet was still in his jacket, full of cash and cards. They didn't take his phone. The violence that they used…'

She cut across him. 'They? You said *they.*'

'There were possibly two attackers.'

'And we know he didn't take the train to Bristol that morning,' Pam added, though Lincoln hadn't wanted to reveal that much yet. 'Despite what he'd told Jessica.'

Annie laughed bitterly. 'Ha! He tells the girlfriend one thing and does something else entirely. Par for the course. Look, there's no point pretending, Chris could be a bastard sometimes.' She stood up and carried her mug to the sink, tipping her coffee away and slamming the mug down on the drainer. 'A stupid, thoughtless bastard.'

'Do you know if anything was troubling him, problems between him and…'

She turned back. 'I told you, we've lived apart for nearly a year and I haven't seen him for weeks.'

'But you've kept in touch?'

'He'd email every other week, silly things he'd spotted in the paper or on the news, mutual friends he'd heard from. Probably just a feeble excuse to contact me. To be honest, I didn't always respond. His new partner was pregnant and I didn't think it was fair on her or me to try to prolong our marriage, but he didn't want to let go.'

Lincoln could hear the resentment in her voice,

the grudging resignation that she and Darbyshire both needed to move on, even if he'd continually sabotaged her attempts to do so. Had he, perhaps, held out hopes of Annie taking him back? Would she have let him come back to her if he'd suggested it? Her tone now might be bitter, but deep sadness lay beneath the surface, he could tell.

'Any money worries?' Pam asked. 'You said he had to take on lots of projects on the side after the steady work dried up.'

'He must've been managing,' Annie said, 'or he'd have been pressing me to put this place on the market.'

'It's a lovely old house,' said Pam.

'It's been in the Bancroft family for generations.'

'You said he sometimes dropped in on you. Did he still have any belongings here?'

'He left a few things in his study – papers, books, old files. You don't want to look at it, do you?' She sounded as if she hoped they'd say no, but Lincoln was afraid this might be the only opportunity they'd get.

'Yes please.' He stood up before she could change her mind and, after a short hesitation, she led them upstairs and along a narrow landing to the older part of the house. She climbed a few more steps and then opened a door onto an airy room overlooking the back garden and the woodland beyond it. Lincoln could imagine a time when this house was at the centre of a sprawling farm, with not another house in sight, only trees and fields.

'Here.' Annie waved at a utilitarian computer desk, a few folders stacked to one side, a blank space where Darbyshire's laptop must once have sat. 'I'll leave you to it.' She seemed uncomfortable here in a room her husband would never occupy again, so she retreated, leaving the door ajar.

Pam crossed to the window and gazed out. 'Nice view, but what are we looking for here? This isn't his current office.'

'No, but if he came back here from time to time, maybe he kept things here he didn't want Jessica to see.' He looked around the room, his attention snagged by a framed photo on the window sill: a wedding photo so like his own and Cathy's, he couldn't suppress a gasp.

'Boss?' Pam turned to see what had startled him.

'Nothing.' He looked away from the photo on the sill, the bride with her auburn hair, the groom looking as if his suit should have been a size larger. Yes, the couple could have been him and Cathy, best man Nick Chance hovering out of shot. Whatever had become of Nick?

Pam flipped through the folders on the desk. 'A few receipts, old bank statements, income tax stuff. Nothing more recent than December last year.'

'That's when they split up. Anything current is probably at Jessica's.'

'This is more interesting.' Pam pulled a folder from the bottom of the pile. 'Lydia Bancroft.' She extracted a black-and-white photo and held it up to him. It was a studio shot of Bancroft in her youthful heyday: long blonde hair, prominent cheekbones, glossy lips pouting at the camera. He recognised her now, though he wasn't sure what he'd ever seen her in. She must be eighty-something now.

'Only that one photo?'

'A few more.' She spread them out on the desk, snapshots taken in the garden of the Old Farmhouse, he guessed, when Lydia was a girl of twelve or thirteen; studio portraits of the ingénue drama student; and stark monochrome images of her on stage in rep wearing exaggerated theatrical make-up and the costume of a

Victorian heroine. 'And some sort of list.' She pushed it across to him.

'Intro. Bancroft family history. Childhood. Drama school. First roles. Agent trouble. Television break. Death of Hamilton Vaughn. Old Vic. BBC 70th birthday tribute.' He pushed it back to her. 'It reads like the outline of the life story he was writing for her. Is that all there is?'

'Lots of old theatre programmes from the 1960s.' She plucked one out. 'Barbury Theatre, June 1964. *The Playboy of the Western World.* She played Pegeen Mike. And look at all these reviews: "Lydia Bancroft is exquisite as the tempestuous young peasant girl"; "Bancroft shines in a production that fails to do justice to her considerable talents"; "Miss Lydia Bancroft..."'

Lincoln interrupted her. 'Is any of this relevant? We need something that tells us what Darbyshire was doing *now*. Sorry, Pam, but we haven't got time for this. Okay, so Annie Darbyshire's aunt was a famous actress, but this is getting us nowhere. Come on.'

'Should we take any of this with us?'

'No, leave it.'

He led the way downstairs, unsettled by the sight of the wedding photo that had stirred up uncomfortable memories. He hadn't heard from Nick Chance in years, rarely thought about him these days. They'd been best mates at school, but within a year or two of Lincoln's wedding, Nick had moved to the States to practise law. He'd met his wife, Nell, at the wedding – she'd been Cathy's chief bridesmaid – and the couple had settled in Boston, rarely returning to England. Not even for Cathy's funeral. A bitter taste flooded his mouth.

'Can you think of anyone who might have had a grudge against Chris?' Pam asked Annie when they got back to the kitchen.

Annie turned her gaze to the window as gusty rain suddenly slammed against it. 'Unless there was someone else in Jessica's life before she met Chris… But they've been together over a year now. If she had a jealous ex-boyfriend, he'd have taken it out on Chris sooner than this, wouldn't he?'

'Probably. How did Chris meet her?'

'Through one of his television jobs. She worked at the studio, something menial. Told him she wanted to be a writer. He offered to read some of her work and the next thing you know, he's sleeping with her.' Annie lifted her chin in a defiant gesture. 'And then he moved out.'

'Did he ever mention Jessica's brother, Toby?' Lincoln asked.

'Not long before we separated, he said he'd started to help Toby with his writing. It'll be a real blow to him, losing Chris.'

'The Darbyshires had a daughter, Gracie,' Woody told Lincoln when he got back. He'd found an Instagram post from 2014 of the family enjoying a holiday in Malaga. The girl looked about sixteen, pretty and smiling, standing between her parents in the sunshine.

'*Had* a daughter?'

'Killed in a car crash two years ago, coming back from a party at Upavon. Her friend Tara was driving, hadn't long passed her test. Both girls died at the scene.'

That's why, really, I don't want kids, Lincoln thought. Too much to lose. Gone in a moment.

'Maybe that's why they split up,' Pam said. 'Something like that, it would put a strain on any marriage.'

'Any joy tracking Darbyshire from the station on Tuesday morning?' Lincoln asked.

Woody shook his head. 'I'm waiting for Breezy to report back.'

Lincoln checked his watch and picked up his keys. 'Come on, Pam, let's get back to Standish's Farm, talk to Jessica Hale again.'

CHAPTER 12

Jessica Hale responded with wry amusement when Pam asked her if she and Darbyshire had made love before he left home on Tuesday.

'In this state?' She pointed to her bump. 'You're joking, aren't you?' But then she realised the reason for the question and amusement became dismay. 'You mean he was screwing someone?'

'It looks that way.' Pam gave her a sympathetic smile, but Jessica looked away.

'Did Toby get on okay with Chris?' Lincoln asked.

Jessica nodded. 'Chris was sort of mentoring him, helping him make the right contacts. Toby doesn't put himself forward, doesn't socialise hardly at all. Like me, really.' She stroked her bump protectively. 'Without Chris, I'm not sure he can get anywhere with his writing.'

Unlikely that Toby had wanted Darbyshire out of the way, then.

Lincoln stood up. 'We need to see where Chris worked when he was here.'

'I'll take you up to his office.'

'No, that's okay. We'll find it.'

They left her sitting unhappily at the kitchen table while they climbed the winding stairs to the low-ceilinged first floor, where Darbyshire's cramped office overlooked the barren concrete yard.

Post-it notes and memos fluttered on the corkboard behind his desk, but Lincoln found nothing there of obvious interest. He searched the desk drawers while Pam took a look at some box files on the shelf.

'There's a load more stuff about Lydia Bancroft here,' she said. 'He must've written about a hundred pages of her life story already.' She lifted a stack of typescript out of the box. 'And there are photos from her starlet days, letters, notes, newspaper cuttings, all sorts. Should we take it back with us?'

'Hardly relevant, is it?'

She shut the box file with a snap and shoved it back on the shelf. 'You think he was going up to London to talk to Lydia when he said he was going to Bristol?'

'Perhaps, but why lie about it? Did he think Jessica would be jealous of a washed-up actress old enough to be his mother? There are some memory sticks here and a backup drive. Let's bag them up and take them back.'

Breeze had found CCTV footage that showed Darbyshire walking along Station Road on Tuesday morning as far as Barbury Theatre. He'd paused outside, then climbed the steps to the building's ornate front entrance.

'But his meeting about the arts centre wasn't till the following day,' Lincoln said. 'Had he got the day wrong?'

'The bar's open there from quite early,' said Breeze. 'I checked. They do teas and coffees in the morning.'

'Maybe he was meeting someone there,' Dilke suggested. 'Or it was somewhere quiet for him to write. We know he had his laptop with him.'

'If he wanted somewhere quiet, he could've gone to the library.'

Dilke grinned. 'Yes, boss, but the library doesn't do proper coffee.'

'The theatre must have CCTV,' Breeze said. 'We can see if he was meeting someone.'

Lincoln added the new information to the timeline on the whiteboard.

'Right, so we've got a gap of twelve hours between him going into the theatre about quarter to ten – possibly for a coffee – and a dinner of mushroom pizza and a glass or two of wine. After which, presumably, he got out of a car in Cranbrook Road, went into Coronation Gardens without his coat and, between ten and ten-thirty got stabbed.'

He tried to shut out the memory of Darbyshire lying on the riverbank yesterday morning, his clothes sodden, his face streaked with mud.

'Card transactions?' Pam asked.

'We should have a report tomorrow.'

'Wouldn't you think the driver would come forward? They must know something bad happened to him after he got out of the car. Did they just drive off and go home?'

'With his overcoat and bag,' Dilke put in. 'And his laptop.'

Lincoln didn't have an answer. 'Why did he get out of the car and go into the Gardens? To take a leak? To have sex?'

Breeze gave a dirty laugh. 'He'd have to be desperate. It was pissing down!'

'Was he lured out of the car?' Lincoln wondered. 'Did he see someone in distress and go to their rescue?'

'What's happening about his phone?' asked Dilke.

'Still waiting for the tech team to get back to me. I've sent them the drives we brought back from Tisbury but everything takes so bloody long.' He chucked the marker pen onto his desk. 'We can't do much more tonight. First thing tomorrow, check Barbury Theatre, see if he met anyone there on Tuesday morning.'

His phone rang: the DCI calling.

'There's been a development, Jeff.' Her tone didn't

bode well. 'A white van's been found abandoned up at Lookout Hill. Someone tried to torch it, but they didn't make a very good job of it and a lot of it's survived. Could be the van that Ritchie Payne got into on Spicer Street.'

Lincoln's spirits plummeted. 'Any sign of him?'

'No, but there was a trainer in the back. We need to get it identified, see if the Paynes recognise it.'

Was she expecting him to volunteer? Didn't she have a new DI starting? Couldn't the keen and ambitious Tim Anderson from Trowbridge call on Bert Payne and his wife? Be shown the bedroom with the mice in a cage, the left-behind blister pack of meds.

'I can send someone from here,' she began, but he cut across her.

'We'll go,' he said. 'Send me some shots of the trainer.'

When the photos came through, he took Pam with him to call on the Paynes, reminding her, as they pulled up outside the maisonette, that they needed to stay positive. No news is good news.

But as soon as Bert saw the photos of the smoke-blackened trainer, he waved them towards his wife. She took one look and started to cry.

CHAPTER 13

Lincoln stopped at Trish's house on his way home that evening. As he climbed the steps to her front door, two at a time, he wondered if she'd be there or at her father's. The house seemed to be in darkness and there was no answer to his knock, so he guessed the latter.

But then, as he was making his way back to the car, light flooded the pavement as the front bedroom curtains were swept back and the window was flung open.

'I was tidying Kate's room while I had the chance,' Trish called down to him. 'You want to come in?'

They sat in the kitchen over coffee and some of the cherry buns she'd baked for Ted. She looked tired, her ash-blonde hair tied up in a messy topknot.

'How's the case going?'

'Which one?' He steered his thoughts away from the trainer that almost certainly belonged to Ritchie Payne, trying instead to concentrate on Darbyshire's murder. 'Remind me to put my affairs in order before I go out walking late at night.'

'You're talking about Chris Darbyshire? What skeletons have you unearthed from his closet?' Then, holding a hand up, 'No, I know you can't tell me and I don't really want to know. I knew him slightly.'

'You did?'

'He came into the library at the start of the campaign to replace Barbury Theatre. He wanted to know more about its history, get some background. And of course, he came to me, since I'm the local history expert.' She tucked her thumbs behind imaginary braces and puffed her chest out. 'But that was two or three years ago, of course.'

'A new theatre was going to be part of the Paragon, wasn't it?'

The construction of a brand-new arts centre had been a flagship project for the local council last year, but when one of the principal backers was put behind bars – largely thanks to Lincoln and his team – the council pulled out and the Paragon arts centre never got beyond the planning stage.

'That's right.'

'What did you think of him?' Lincoln helped himself to more coffee.

'I liked him. He was easy to talk to, passionate about a new theatre, keen to do some research. He made his name writing drama series, but you have to get your background right, even if you're making stuff up.'

'He was ghost writing Lydia Bancroft's life story. He'd been working on it for the last year or so.'

'Oh gosh, Lydia was one of Dad's pin-ups when he was a lad. Her and Julie Christie. I didn't realise Lydia was still alive.'

'Alive and well and living in London.'

'Fancy that! I must tell him.'

'Do you know Annie, Chris's wife?'

Trish shook her head. 'She's a teacher, isn't she, at Barbury Fields? Her dad was a writer, Gordon Bancroft. Lydia is Gordon's sister. And then there's Martin, their younger brother, who's Sherilyn Croft's dad. The Bancrofts owned Dobbins Farm but sold most of it off to the developers who built Hyperion Avenue.'

'I should've come to you first, saved my team a lot of research time.'

'I'm a librarian,' she said with a grin. 'If *I* don't know

the answer, I usually know someone who does.' Then she became serious. 'The Darbyshires lost their daughter in a car crash, didn't they? Somewhere on the Plain? She was coming back from a party.'

'Yes, near Upavon.'

'God, if anything like that happened to Kate…' She broke off and he laid his hand over hers.

'Don't even go there.'

'Was Chris really mugged or was there more to it? There's lots of speculation on Twitter.'

'Such as?'

'People asking why he was in Coronation Gardens, was he gay, was he attacked by queer bashers, can't decent folk take a walk in a park at night, et cetera et cetera? Nothing helpful.'

'We're trying to fill in the blanks. Find out where he went on Tuesday, who he was with.'

'If nobody's come forward yet, they probably won't, will they? Unless they're forced to.'

He finished his coffee and stood up. 'I'd better be going.'

'You want to stay the night?' Trish looked up at him expectantly.

Exhausted, all he wanted to do was sleep. 'I won't be good company.'

'I wasn't asking you to entertain me! Kate will be home at the weekend. We won't have the house to ourselves again for a while. Stay over,' she urged gently. 'Keep me warm tonight.'

FRIDAY 27TH OCTOBER

CHAPTER 14

'The van up at Lookout Hill belongs to Harry Priest,' said Woody next morning, before Lincoln had even hung his coat up. 'He reckons it was nicked from his junk yard in Finisterre Street some time on Tuesday.'

Lincoln was familiar with Harry Priest, a market stallholder who'd been caught selling substandard electrical goods and handed a hefty fine. He'd bounced back, though, flogging cheap knock-off designer handbags and luggage instead, with a line in imported cigarettes on the side, according to rumours.

'Park Street are handling this one, Woody. Connors has got an acting DI transferred from Trowbridge. Name's Tim Anderson. You ever come across him?' He picked his mug up and headed for the kettle, pleased with himself that he'd managed to get up in time to have breakfast with Trish.

'I don't recognise the name. We'll be collaborating, will we?'

'If we must.' Lincoln's coffee was strong and sweet, the best fuel for his brain at this time in the morning. 'Had Harry reported the van stolen?'

'Hadn't got round to it. Reckon he was hoping it would be a write-off when it was found and he could screw a bit more out of his insurance company.'

'Knowing Harry, he hadn't even got round to insuring it.' Lincoln turned his laptop on, to be greeted by an email he'd been waiting for: Darbyshire's mobile phone had at last dried out and the tech team was examining it for anything relevant to the investigation.

'Let Park Street follow up on the van, Woody.' Not our problem, he told himself. Let Trowbridge Tim deal with it.

'Darbyshire met a woman at the theatre on Tuesday morning.' Dilke shoved a memory stick into his laptop. 'They're talking like they're *really* good friends.'

He and Pam had called at Barbury Theatre first thing and checked the CCTV footage of the bar to see if Darbyshire had been meeting anyone there.

'He seems a naturally touchy-feely guy,' Pam said. 'But the way he and this woman are talking…'

'See for yourself, boss.' Dilke sat back from his screen so Lincoln could lean in.

The camera, suspended above the door into the bar, captured Darbyshire breezing in, overnight bag over his shoulder. The bar was cramped, with barely enough room for the café tables and chairs set out there. When he strode over to a table where a woman sat alone, she stood up and they hugged – more warmly and for longer, Lincoln felt, than casual friends would hug. After parking his bag and overcoat on the seat beside him, Darbyshire sat down across from her and they began a close, heads-together, conversation.

'See the way she puts her hand on his arm.' Pam nodded at the screen. 'And then he starts stroking her shoulder.'

'Shame we can't see his face,' said Lincoln. 'But you can tell from her expression that they know each other well.'

The woman was thirty-something and petite, her heart-shaped face framed by a mass of dark, wavy hair. After a few minutes, Darbyshire went up to the bar, returning with two coffees.

'I'll fast forward,' said Dilke, 'until this bit here.' The frames whizzed by until he pressed play. The coffee cups were empty and the couple were deep in conversation – and then Darbyshire suddenly sat back. The woman reached out to him, but he fended her off, clearly upset about something she'd said. He shoved his cup away and got to his feet, gathering up his bag and coat and heading for the door. A moment later, the woman stood up and went after him. They disappeared from view.

Lincoln leaned back. 'Bit of a lovers' tiff? I wonder what that was all about. And the meeting he was supposed to be going to on Wednesday morning? Had he made that up?'

'No, that was real enough,' said Pam. 'A breakfast meeting, eight o'clock, booked in the name of Barbury Arts Centre Campaign. The guy behind the bar said the woman is Leanne Milner, the council's arts officer.'

'You'd better go and talk to her. Could be our first positive lead.'

Pam and Dilke had been gone only a few minutes when Lincoln's desk phone rang.

'How exactly am I meant to get in?' the caller grumbled. 'I'm outside your front door and there's not even a doorbell.'

On the doorstep, he found a lanky young man, frustrated by trying to get in, Acting DI Tim Anderson.

'Barley Lane isn't public access anymore,' Lincoln explained as he ushered Anderson inside. 'There's a notice on the front door but…' He leaned round to point it out, only to see that the print had faded to nothing and snails had reduced the notice to little more than a paper doily. He led the new arrival through to the incident room and showed him where to hang the smart gaberdine he was wearing over a smart suit. 'So, you're from Trowbridge?'

'That's right. Temporary transfer. DCI Connors said you'd bring me up to speed on the Ritchie Payne case.' Anderson produced a tablet in a rugged rubber cover and tapped in a passcode that brought the screen to life. He unbuttoned his jacket and smoothed his tie down.

Lincoln told him what little they knew about Ritchie Payne's movements on Tuesday evening. 'And now the white van's been found, partially burnt out. They didn't tip enough petrol over it. It doesn't take a genius to torch a van.'

'I understand the vehicle owner is a Mr Priest who says it was stolen from his yard. What makes you think Garvin Steele's got anything to do with this?'

'Have a seat.' Lincoln waved him across to Pam's vacant chair and parked himself on the corner of his own desk. 'Steele was implicated in a similar incident back in the summer. A lad called Alfie Corrigan was drinking in a pub in town, had a bit of a set-to with Steele and ended up dead in the river. He'd drowned, but he'd been beaten up first.'

'Like Christian Darbyshire.'

Lincoln shook his head. 'Darbyshire didn't drown. He was knifed in Coronation Gardens, a public park with a river running through it. He was left on the riverbank, but it was the stabbing that killed him.'

Anderson nodded. His hair didn't move, held in place by a surfeit, in Lincoln's opinion, of gel or pomade. Not that there was a lot of hair to hold in place, since the back and sides of his head were closely shaved, leaving a broad ridge on the top, a subtle version of a Mohican. The suit and tie, the button-down collar, all suggested he took pride in his appearance. Too much pride?

'The trainer they found in the van – do we know that it's Payne's?'

'Yes,' said Lincoln. 'I showed photos of it to his grandparents and they identified it.'

'It's a popular style, though, isn't it? Loads of guys his age, his income bracket, will have trainers like that. We shouldn't assume, should we?'

That was usually Lincoln's line. 'No, you're right, Tim, we shouldn't assume. Has it been sent for forensic testing?'

'DCI Connors didn't feel it would be a good use of resources. Unlikely to yield DNA.'

Disappointing but understandable. The trainer had been lying in the wrecked van for at least two nights, exposed to the elements and damaged by smoke.

Anderson stood up and crossed to the whiteboard, appraising it critically. 'So where was Darbyshire in the hours before he was found dead?'

Bristling slightly at this encroachment on his own case, Lincoln told Anderson what little they knew so far.

'You think he was having an affair with this woman he met for coffee?'

Lincoln grinned. 'The body language suggested he and Leanne Milner were pretty good friends. They left the theatre together around eleven, but we don't know what he was doing until he had pizza and wine within an hour of his murder. I've sent someone to talk to her.'

'And no CCTV coverage near the riverbank where he was found?' Anderson jabbed the sketch map of Coronation Gardens and the street that ran past it, Cranbrook Road.

Lincoln felt as if he was having to account for himself to a senior colleague rather than sharing his findings with an acting DI, twenty years his junior.

'Because I was thinking,' Anderson went on without waiting for a reply, 'if we have a window for the attack, then we can look for cars passing cameras farther back along this street, nearer the centre. Even if there's no camera right there by these Gardens, any vehicle driving past would've been picked up a few seconds earlier by cameras elsewhere along that route.'

Lincoln knew he was right, but trawling through CCTV footage for the one- or two-hour window before Darbyshire was attacked, not knowing what vehicle to look for, not even being sure a camera would have picked it up… To echo the DCI's sentiments, it hadn't seemed like the best use of resources.

'It's the next thing we need to do,' he conceded. 'Unless Leanne can shed some light on who he was meeting.'

'And a motive?' Anderson glanced over his shoulder at Lincoln who, once more, felt he was being examined and found wanting.

'He'd been lying to Jessica, his partner, about where he was going, where he was working, and I'm guessing he was cheating on her. He'd had sex sometime on Tuesday – and it wasn't with her.'

'Jealous lover? Jessica getting her own back?'

Lincoln shook his head. 'I don't think she suspected any of it. We've ruled her brother out. He hardly seems to leave home and was relying on Darbyshire to help him get some writing work.'

'No other motive? Did Darbyshire owe money?'

'Not that we know of. We're still trying to find out more about him.'

Anderson cast his gaze round the incident room. 'How do you all fit in here?'

'We manage. And it won't be for much longer. This station's scheduled for closure sometime soon.' Hell, was Anderson expecting a desk to be found for him? A chair and laptop?

'Don't worry, I won't be working from here, but obviously we'll need to liaise closely. Do we look for those CCTV cameras first, see if we can pick up a car with Darbyshire in it?'

We?

'I'll get my team onto that while you carry on looking for Ritchie Payne. I'm not sure…' He broke off as Anderson's mobile rang.

'It's the DCI.' Anderson turned away to take the call. 'Yes, ma'am. He's here with me now. I'll tell him. Yes, fine.' He rang off and turned back. 'They've found a SIM card in the wreckage of Mr Priest's van.'

'Ritchie Payne's?'

'Possibly. Or it could belong to one of the guys who stole the van. The numpty must've taken the SIM card out so his phone couldn't be tracked.'

'And then left the SIM card behind.' Lincoln hoped this was the breakthrough they needed. 'I'm surprised it survived the fire.'

'I've seen the photos. The left side of the van escaped most of the damage. The SIM was in a crevice under the seat. We should have the guy's ID by the end of the day.'

'Unless it's a burner phone – no pun intended.'

Anderson grinned, then went over to the wall map and studied it intently. 'Where was the van found?'

'Lookout Hill.' Lincoln jabbed the map to indicate the stretch of downland beside the Southampton road, an old brick signalling tower on top. 'Popular picnic spot by day, risky wilderness after dark.'

'Any chance Payne's body could've been dumped there?'

Lincoln thought of the untamed hillside, where thorny bushes and a few wind-warped trees partly shielded an old chalk pit. A thorough search of the area would take days, a week, even if they used a drone.

'The immediate vicinity will have been searched,' he said. 'But if his body's been dumped, it's more likely to be somewhere more wooded, like Greywood Forest.'

He pointed out to Anderson the dense woodland that snaked across the downs above the Wylye Valley on the western side of Barbury. They were both talking as if Ritchie Payne was dead. Was there a chance, even a slim one, that the vulnerable young man was being held somewhere or was lying low, afraid – for some reason – to go home?

Anderson peered at the map. 'Once they'd torched the van, how did they get away? They must've had a second vehicle to take them away again.'

Lincoln agreed, but CCTV coverage there was minimal, only some speed cameras on the main road. 'Let's hope the SIM leads us to a name.'

Anderson picked his tablet up, preparing to depart. 'Is Harry Priest above board? Any chance he's implicated in this?'

'He's a tricky one, admittedly, but I can't see how he's involved – apart from having his van stolen, of course.' Belatedly, Lincoln remembered his manners. 'Sorry, Tim, I should've offered you a tea or a coffee.'

'No, it's fine. Need to get back to Park Street.'

'Welcome aboard. You'll find Connors is a good DCI. What you see is what you get.'

When Pam phoned the council's Leisure Department ahead of dropping in on Leanne Milner at work, she was told the arts officer had called in sick.

'Then we'll drop in on her at home,' said Dilke.

They were soon drawing up outside her Victorian semi-detached villa on the western side of the town. A bright red Toyota Yaris was outside, a pass for the council staff car park inside the windscreen.

'Nice here,' said Pam, realising this road was only about five minutes' drive from the scene of Chris Darbyshire's murder. 'It must have been a separate village years ago. You feel as if you're away from the town, even though it's only a few minutes' drive. Best of both worlds.'

'You missed your vocation, Pammy. You should've been an estate agent.' Dilke locked the car and started up the front path. 'Breezy keeps on about buying a house for him and Rosie.'

'Where's he going to get the money? He's always broke.'

He rang the doorbell several times, but it was a good minute before Leanne came to the door. Pam recognised her from the theatre's surveillance footage, but in the flesh she looked younger and softer – and today, quite vulnerable. Beneath a baggy cardigan, she was still in her pyjamas, her eyes smudgy with yesterday's make-up, her dark curls uncombed.

'It's about Chris Darbyshire,' said Pam. 'Can we come in?'

'What do you need to know?' She led them into the glass-roofed extension at the back of the house.

Family photos hung in the hallway and in the kitchen diner: happily smiling children – two boys and a girl – pictured from babyhood to their teenage years. Their father looked clean-cut and professional, like the ideal dad in adverts. A picture-perfect family.

'We understand you met with Chris on Tuesday morning,' said Pam, as she and Dilke perched themselves on stools either side of the shiny kitchen island. 'Can we ask you a couple of quick questions about that?'

'Of course. It's terrible, what happened to him. He

was such a lovely guy.'

'Those are your kids?' Dilke nodded at the photographs on the wall.

'Yes. Russ has taken them to Glastonbury for half-term, to his mum's, but I was too busy at work to take the whole week off. I was going to join them at the weekend, but I've felt so rough the last couple of days, I haven't left the house.' She offered them tea and put the kettle on. 'So, what did you want to ask me?'

'You met him in the bar at Barbury Theatre on Tuesday morning,' said Dilke. 'Is that right?'

'How did you know about that?' she demanded, affronted.

'The staff there identified you from the CCTV.'

'Christ, can't you even have a cup of coffee in private these days? You're spied on everywhere.'

'We're just trying to piece it all together,' he said. 'Find out who Chris was with on Tuesday, what his plans were.'

She took her time making the tea, clattering around irritably, not saying anything until she was sitting down again. 'What do you want to know?'

'Did he say what he was doing for the rest of the day?' asked Pam.

'He was going to the library to look something up and then he was meeting Orlando Snell.'

'Orlando Snell?'

'He's an actor – or used to be. He does voice coaching these days. Chris was working on something to do with the theatre and he was hoping Orlando could lend him a scrap album or something he'd got.'

'A scrap album?' Dilke made a note.

'Orlando collects anything to do with the theatre, never throws anything out…' Leanne looked away towards the glass doors into the garden. There were tears in her eyes.

'What was Chris working on?' Pam asked. 'Did he tell you?'

'He's been writing Lydia Bancroft's life story – you've heard of her? She was kind of close to an actor who killed himself during the run of a pantomime they were in together. Chris got excited because there was a bit of a scandal…'

Dilke looked up. 'A scandal? To do with his suicide?'

'Yes, something to do with some kids who were in the panto. Chris didn't tell me much except it was ages ago – 1990 or something. Lydia made him think there was some sort of *mystery* behind it and that got him interested.'

She got up to fetch the tea, surreptitiously wiping away her tears. Pam thought back to the images of the couple sitting together in the theatre bar, the way Leanne touched Chris's sleeve, the way he stroked her shoulder.

'Did you and Chris often meet for coffee?' she asked casually.

'Most Tuesdays. I have a late start at work on Tuesdays so we usually meet at the theatre.'

'To talk about work?' Another casual question, but Pam watched the woman's face carefully.

'And Barbury Arts Centre Campaign. We're both committed to making it happen.' She was biting her lip now, trying not to cry. Her eyes were brimming.

Pam took a chance. 'You were close, weren't you?'

'Oh God!' Leanne dumped the tray of cups down and sank onto her stool. She put her head in her hands, no longer bothering to hide her distress. 'We never meant it to get serious, but it ran away with itself.'

Pam leaned in closer. 'You were lovers?'

She nodded. 'We'd go to a hotel in Bristol, somewhere no one knew us. I'd tell Russ I had to be away overnight for work. I work such irregular hours he didn't query it. We'd meet for a meal some evenings before Chris caught his train home. Russ thought I was meeting a girlfriend or doing something for work. We were very discreet. We didn't want to hurt anyone.'

'Did his partner know?' Dilke asked.

'I don't think so. When he told me she was pregnant…' She paused to wipe her eyes and blow her nose. 'When I knew she was expecting, I said we should stop. And we didn't see each other for a while, but it was so difficult…'

'What made Chris leave the theatre bar so abruptly that morning?' asked Pam. 'He seemed upset about something.'

'Oh, that! He lost it when I told him I'd seen his wife at the theatre last week with Paddy Noble. He got up and stormed out. I wasn't expecting him to react like that, not after they'd been apart for so long. It's been nearly a year, but I suppose…' She paused to take a deep breath. 'I went after him. Told him I was sorry and he calmed down a bit.'

'You know Annie?'

'We met once or twice to talk about developing drama in schools, but that was a while ago. There wasn't the money for it then and there's even less money now.'

'And Paddy Noble is…'

'He teaches at her school. Taught both my boys. Nice man.' She gulped back another sob. 'I can't take it in. That I'll never see Chris again. And I wish I hadn't upset him, telling him about her and Paddy. I keep thinking how we walked down the steps of the theatre and Chris went one way up the street and I went the other and… And that was the last time I ever saw him.'

CHAPTER 15

Valerie Bancroft felt stupid now, reporting her stepdaughter missing on Wednesday, so soon after she'd stormed out of the house.

'Does she have vulnerabilities?' the call handler had asked. 'Do you believe she's at risk?'

'She's been drinking.'

'Was she drunk? Unfit to drive?'

'She wasn't drunk and she's not allowed to drive.' Not since she'd flipped her car at Stirling Corner on her way to the television studios at Borehamwood – the third car she'd wrecked in a matter of months. The tabloids loved it. And although Sherilyn was forty, she still behaved like a teenager or a ladette in her twenties.

'And what's her name?'

'Sherilyn Croft.'

'What, *the* Sherilyn Croft?'

And that's how it started. Someone somewhere must have said something and the socials had got hold of it in a matter of hours.

Valerie poured herself another large glass of red wine and carried it across to the sofa by the window. Was midday too early for wine? No, it was never too early for wine and she needed cheering up. It looked miserable outside. Typical October, grey and wet. She couldn't face leaving the house, even though she needed to shop.

There were journalists and photographers outside. Only one or two, but that was enough to bother her. Going to the door would just encourage them.

Sherilyn had stormed out of the house on Tuesday night after a row about money. Most rows with Sherilyn were about money – or her lack of it. Funny how she always found the money for yet another brow lift, new veneers on her teeth or having her tits hoisted up a few more inches. As if anyone noticed…

And she must've found the money for a cab, though where the cab took her, Christ knows!

Martin couldn't understand why she kept coming back home, but Valerie understood perfectly. Sherilyn knew her daddy would always bail his little girl out.

This time, though, what with Marty being retired now, *properly* retired, and so much needing doing to the house, they had to watch every penny. It was all right for Sherilyn, swanning in unannounced, pleading poverty and holding her hand out, but the cash simply wasn't there.

'No,' Valerie had said to her on Tuesday. 'Not this time, Sheri. Your dad can't afford it.'

'It's nothing to do with you. You're not my mum.'

'Thank God!'

And Sherilyn had stomped upstairs.

When, twenty minutes later, she'd come thundering down the stairs, she'd been clutching a Waitrose carrier as well as her overnight bag.

'I'm going,' she'd snapped. 'I know when I'm not wanted.'

But wrestling to unlock the front door, she'd dropped the carrier bag, spilling necklaces, rings and bracelets onto the hall carpet.

Valerie had stared in disbelief. 'What are you doing with my jewellery?' Furious, she'd turned to Martin, who'd come out to see what the fuss was about. 'Aren't you going to say anything, Marty?'

He'd shrugged. 'She needs the money and we don't have any. And really, Val, when do you wear any of that stuff?'

'And this was *my* mother's jewellery,' Sherilyn had yelled. 'By rights, it should be mine, not yours.'

And she'd rushed away, taking most of the jewellery with her. Yes, some of it had belonged to Martin's first wife, although he'd always said Valerie should have it, probably because he knew Sherilyn wouldn't look after it. But some of that jewellery was Valerie's own. Why wouldn't Martin stand up to her?

Valerie tried to report her missing, hoping she'd be picked up by the police, but they weren't interested. Too soon, they said. Give it a bit longer.

And then on Wednesday, Radio Presford FM started running a competition, Sherilyn Sightings. 'Just a bit of fun,' the presenter said, when Valerie phoned in to complain. She'd thought Marty might have stirred himself, but hell would freeze over before he got off his backside.

'She's *your* daughter, Marty,' she'd said. 'You're the one who should be doing something.'

Friday today and no one had seen Sherilyn, not for certain, since Tuesday night. And now Annie's husband was dead. Valerie had a mind to pick up the phone, call Annie, offer her condolences, but what could she say? Chris and Annie had been apart since before Christmas, hadn't they? Valerie had hardly known him, although Molly seemed to have stayed in touch with him since then. Had she had a bit of a crush on him when the Darbyshires were still together?

Chris was dead at, what, forty-six? Forty-seven? And with a baby on the way. That's what was so unfair, men being able to start a new family in their forties while women had to go for it while they were young. Too late for Sherilyn, probably.

Valerie had a sudden vision of her stepdaughter meeting the same fate as Chris, her personal life laid bare. The tabloids would love that.

No, she didn't feel like leaving the house, not just yet. She'd order the groceries online, get them delivered, stay indoors out of sight until there was news, one way or the other.

'Suppose Sheri doesn't come back?' Molly wandered into the room, cuddling one of her sister's stupid teddy bears. 'Mum? Suppose something terrible's happened to her?'

Valerie held her arms out to her daughter, hugging her to her, teddy bear and all. 'Let's not think like that, love,' she whispered into Molly's hair. 'Sheri will be all right, you'll see.'

CHAPTER 16

DCI Claire Connors phoned Lincoln soon after Tim Anderson had left Barley Lane.

'I've arranged a media briefing for twelve-thirty, Jeff. A general update, no family, just the basic facts as we know them.'

'You want me there or will you use Tim?' Anderson certainly looked more presentable for the cameras than Lincoln did.

Connors scoffed. 'Throw Tim to the likes of Karen Bolitho? It's his first day here, have a heart! Anyway, he's gone off to see Harry Priest, find out a bit more about how his van got stolen. The keys were in it when it was found. Who leaves their van unattended on Finisterre Street with the keys in the ignition? That's as good as putting a big sign on it saying TAKE ME.'

'Any luck with the SIM card?' Lincoln feared it would prove to be from a burner phone, no contract, nothing to identify its owner.

'We've got a name and the guys here are running it against the databases. I hear we've got into Darbyshire's mobile at last and those backup drives you brought back from his home office. Just need to go through it all now.' She paused. 'What did you think of Tim?'

'Seems very efficient.'

'I'm hoping he'll stay but he needs to find somewhere to live.'

'Plenty of flats to rent in town.'

'That's no good for his kids, is it, Jeff? He'll want a garden like he's got in Trowbridge.'

‘He’s got kids?’

‘One’s three, one’s a few months old. He didn’t tell you?’

Lincoln sniffed. ‘It didn’t come up.’ And he hadn’t thought to ask. Anderson hadn’t struck him as a family man. Just goes to show.

A list of Darbyshire’s recent bank transactions arrived, showing nothing out of the ordinary except that he’d paid £48.35 at Pizza Marino at nine-fifty on Tuesday night – an expensive meal for one, but about right for *two* people dining together with wine. Darbyshire and a companion, but male or female?

When Lincoln phoned the pizzeria, a recorded message told him it didn’t open till six so he’d have to try again later.

Then Pam and Dilke returned from talking to Leanne Milner.

‘Darbyshire was meeting a man called Orlando Snell on Tuesday,’ said Dilke. ‘An actor, a protégé of Lydia Bancroft’s.’

‘Orlando Snell? Never heard of him.’ Lincoln wrote Snell’s name on the whiteboard. ‘What was the meeting about?’

‘Snell had information about some scandal involving an actor who committed suicide, someone Lydia was close to. Darbyshire was intrigued by it, wanted to find out more. Snell was going to show him a scrapbook or something.’

‘And Leanne and Darbyshire were having an affair,’ said Pam. ‘She came out with it surprisingly quickly. They’d go away overnight. She told her husband it was to do with work.’

‘It would explain his trips to Bristol,’ Dilke put in.

Pam grinned. ‘But they were very discreet, unquote.’

‘Our Mr Darbyshire was quite the ladies’ man.’ Lincoln turned back to the board. ‘Could Orlando Snell be the other diner at Pizza Marino on Tuesday night? What do we know about him?’

Dilke checked his notes. ‘Lives in Bridgeford, does voice coaching. In his seventies. He could’ve been the one driving Darbyshire along Cranbrook Road that night.’

‘And now he’s scared to come forward. We need to speak to him. Got a photo?’

Dilke found a headshot of a distinguished-looking man with thinning grey curls he brushed forward so they sat on his forehead like a laurel wreath. He had a broad, open face and an unnaturally white smile.

‘Fancy a trip over there? I’ve got to be back by twelve thirty but Bridgeford isn’t far.’

‘And Annie’s got a boyfriend,’ said Pam. ‘Leanne saw her with him, told Darbyshire when they met at the theatre on Tuesday morning. She thought he knew, but he didn’t. That’s why he got up and stormed out the way he did.’

‘Got a name for him?’

‘Paddy Noble. He and Annie teach at the same school. He’s not a suspect, though, is he?’

‘Everyone’s a suspect until we know they’re not.’ Lincoln wrote Noble’s name on the whiteboard next to Annie’s, wondering why she hadn’t mentioned him herself. ‘We need to follow up on that. Can you do that, Woody? Graham and I will go and see Orlando Snell. Let’s hope he’s at home.’

Snell lived in a tall, rambling old house on the main road running through Bridgeford, and Lincoln and Dilke were admitted by the actor’s housekeeper, Janice Shepherd.

‘Though I don’t live here,’ she said. ‘I just “do” for him.’

Jammed between two other buildings, its narrow frontage was deceptive. The house went back and back until, at the end of the flagstone passage, it met a twisting staircase that wound up two further floors.

'This used to be a bakery,' she said, 'with the shop at the front and the bakehouse out the back here. When Orlando bought it, he turned the bakehouse into a studio and ran a little café in the front for tourists, but it never really took off. No parking, you see. People don't like walking anywhere these days, not even from the car park down the street.'

Up the staircase they went, heading for the first-floor living room where she expected to find her boss. She knocked on the door.

'That's strange,' she said, when she got no answer. 'I didn't hear him go out.'

'When did you see him last?' asked Lincoln.

'Tuesday morning. I've been away for a few days.' She opened the door on an empty room. Empty of Orlando Snell, at least, because it was certainly full of books, antique ornaments, paintings and furniture. 'Oh, I wonder where he's got to.'

'Any clue as to when he was last here?' Lincoln cast his gaze around the room, hoping for a discarded newspaper that might show Snell had been here since the night Chris Darbyshire was killed. The only newspaper he saw, though, was last weekend's *Sunday Telegraph*, its various sections scattered across the big desk under the window. 'Do you know what he was doing on Tuesday evening?'

'Tuesday? Oh!' Janice put a hand over her mouth. 'That was the night Mr Darbyshire was attacked, wasn't it?'

'You know him?'

'Not personally, but I know *of* him because of all he's done for the theatre – or tried to do. Orlando met him through their campaigning for the Paragon, but of course, that all fell through.' She crossed to his desk, locating his diary under the newspaper. 'I wouldn't normally do this but…' She thumbed through the pages to find the entry for Tuesday, 'Here we are. Auction rooms at eleven, manicure at two. Meet C Darbyshire – with three question marks. That's all.'

Lincoln guessed that the meeting with Darbyshire was over dinner, which meant Snell could have been one of the last people to see him alive and maybe the only witness to the incident in Coronation Gardens.

'What car does he drive?'

'He's got a big old Rover. Old-fashioned like him.' She smiled affectionately, but then her face fell. 'But where *is* he?'

Lincoln prowled round the room, absorbing what he could from Snell's books: Greek and Roman mythology, Robert Graves, Agatha Christie, Margery Allingham and Dorothy L Sayers. Books on elocution and acting techniques, guides to valuing antiques. 'Family?'

'No,' said Janice. 'He was cast out for being queer. That's what he always tells people anyway, although I think there's a brother in Frome.'

'And he knows Lydia Bancroft, doesn't he?' said Dilke. 'The actress.'

'Oh yes. She used to come here quite often years ago because she's got family in Barbury.' She ran her gaze anxiously round the room again. 'I suppose I'd better check upstairs, but he never has a lie-in, it's not his style.'

Lincoln and Dilke followed her up to the second floor. She rapped smartly on the bedroom door, paused, then rapped again. No response.

'Shall I?' Lincoln stepped forward to open the door,

wary of what he might find beyond it. Even more wary, Janice took a step back.

But the door opened on a huge, empty room, poorly lit by windows too small for it. Compared to the cluttered living room, it was furnished with almost spartan simplicity, its floorboards bare except for a rug beside the bed.

Rushing in behind him, Janice let out a little cry. 'Oh! He hasn't been here since I left. The bed hasn't been slept in while I've been away. He'd never be able to make it that neatly himself.'

Lincoln looked round the rather sad bedroom. Something institutional about its bare neatness, shades of a dormitory at a school or hostel – except Snell had the whole room to himself. It wasn't a bedroom to which you'd bring a lover.

'Maybe he went to stay with someone while you were away, rather than look after himself,' Dilke suggested.

'Yes, he might have. Why didn't he let me know, the silly man?' Cheered up, she ushered them out of the bedroom and back along the landing.

'What's in there?' Through a door that stood ajar, opposite the bedroom, Lincoln glimpsed a cramped study, with a desk and shelves, archive boxes, more books.

'Oh, that's his museum.' She laughed. 'He must've kept every programme and script from every performance he's ever been in, right back from when he was a juvenile in about 1960.' She dug into the capacious pocket of her overall and pulled out an iPhone, checked for messages and missed calls, shaking her head that there were none. 'I'll call him.' She turned away while she waited for him to answer.

She turned back. 'He must've switched it off.'

There was nothing more they could do so, with Snell's

phone number and car registration noted, Lincoln and Dilke headed back to Barbury.

'Confirm with Pizza Marino that Darbyshire's companion on Tuesday night was Snell,' Lincoln told Dilke on the way. 'Then we need to run through surveillance footage from any cameras between the restaurant and Coronation Gardens. Darbyshire paid the bill at nine-fifty, so we need to look out for the Rover driving past the Gardens any time after that.'

He imagined the scenario: Darbyshire and Snell finish their pizzas, push their plates aside, top up their glasses and talk about Lydia Bancroft. Snell can plug some of the gaps in her life story that Darbyshire can't fill – especially the scandal surrounding the death of an actor she was close to.

'You think this actor's suicide is significant?' asked Dilke. 'This mysterious scandal?'

'Not very likely, is it? We're talking about something that happened a long time ago.'

'1990, Leanne said.'

'Like I said, it's a long time ago.' It troubled Lincoln that Snell hadn't been home since the murder. If he'd been there when Darbyshire was attacked, he could be running scared, the only witness…

Or had the attack been aimed at *him*?

So many possibilities, so easy to bark up the wrong tree – or a whole forest of them. And he could do without the press conference Connors had called.

The media briefing was held in an over-heated, under-ventilated room on the ground floor at Park Street. Journalists and photographers crammed into it in their damp anoraks and rain-soaked hoodies, cameras beeping and mobiles pinging. The windows steamed up and the air in the room grew thick and moist.

Connors told the gathering that Chris Darbyshire had died as the result of a violent attack by more than one assailant. It may have been a mugging that ended tragically or he may have been targeted.

'Mr Darbyshire was fatally stabbed on Tuesday night around ten-thirty, a few metres inside the entrance to Coronation Gardens, close to the riverbank. We believe he got out of a car in which he was a passenger. We urgently need to trace the driver of that car.'

She paused while a stock photo of a Rover 75, along with Snell's registration number, appeared on the screen behind her, then said, 'We are not releasing the name of the driver at this stage, but if anyone knows where this car is now or has seen it since Tuesday night, they should get in touch with us now.'

'Do you know *why* Mr Darbyshire was going into the Gardens at that time of night? Was it for sex?'

Even though he couldn't yet see her face in the scrum of journalists, Lincoln recognised the voice of *The Messenger*'s Karen Bolitho. She'd blow everything up for the sake of a headline-grabbing story and worry about the consequences later – if at all. 'Was he meeting someone there?'

Connors was cautious in her answer. 'We cannot say as yet. He may have gone to help someone he believed was in distress.'

'Does his death have any connection with the disappearance of Sherilyn Croft?' asked someone else.

'I cannot comment at this stage.'

Connors's caution was commendable, Lincoln thought, but he was afraid it might prove counterproductive. If the press were given too little information, they'd speculate instead.

'We are aware that Mr Darbyshire's wife and Sherilyn Croft are cousins,' he said, 'but we don't believe that has any bearing on this case.'

'And the disappearance of Ritchie Payne?' Karen Bolitho's pencil was raised in the air like a baton.

He'd been wondering when someone would ask. 'We are investigating several lines of enquiry,' he said, as cautious as his boss had been. 'As yet, we…'

'You found one of his trainers, didn't you?' Bolitho again. 'His grandparents identified it as his.'

Connors slapped her hand down on the table. 'The focus of this media briefing is the fatal attack on Chris Darbyshire. I am *not* prepared to discuss anything else until we have more to tell you. As I've already said, we are anxious to speak to the driver of this Rover 75. If anyone sees this vehicle, possibly abandoned somewhere, please call us at once. That'll be all.'

And, gathering up her papers, she got to her feet, obliging Lincoln to do the same.

'What kind of shit show was that?' She strode ahead of him down the corridor to her office. 'Bloody Bolitho!'

'Maybe it was too soon to hold a press conference. They expected us to have something more solid and we don't even know for sure that Darbyshire was at the restaurant with Snell.'

'Now you tell me.' She flung open the door of her office and stormed inside, Lincoln trailing in her wake. 'Okay, Jeff, so what are we looking at?'

He really didn't know. 'A murder and two disappearances, unrelated to each other. Yes, Ritchie Payne was – *is* – a fan of Sherilyn Croft, and Sherilyn Croft is a cousin of our murder victim's wife. But thousands of lads fancied Sherilyn in her prime, or so I'm told. The fact that she's Annie Darbyshire's cousin is merely a coincidence.'

Connors dropped her paperwork onto her desk and picked up an open can of diet lemonade. She took a thirsty swig before flopping into one of the easy chairs by the window. 'This guy that Darbyshire had dinner with, the guy driving the Rover, were they lovers, d'you think?'

'Lovers?'

'Don't be obtuse, Jeff. Orlando Snell, actor, single guy, lives alone. Has dinner with Darbyshire, who's been an actor and is also, technically, single. Snell stops his car by Coronation Gardens. Are they heading in there for a bit of fun? Looking for sex with a stranger?'

'You've been reading the tweets.'

'Of course I've been reading the bloody tweets. And no, nobody's mentioned Snell yet, but it won't be long before someone identifies the Rover as his car, puts two and two together and…' She held her hands out, inviting Lincoln to imagine the consequences.

He lowered himself into the other easy chair. 'Apart from the fact that it was pissing down that evening, so not conducive to open air sex… Darbyshire was meeting Snell to get information for the book he's ghost writing for Lydia Bancroft, that's all. Trust Karen Bolitho to go for the salacious angle, the hook that'll catch her readers' attention.'

'Or does she know something we don't? What's this scandal all about? Something local?'

'An actor killed himself during the run of a pantomime, someone Lydia knew. She thought there was more to it. Darbyshire was intrigued, wanted to dig deeper. I suppose he needed information from Snell to corroborate what Lydia had told him. He was going to the library to do some research and later, we assume, he and Snell were meeting for dinner.'

'Can you ask your spies at the library what he was looking at?'

'My spies? Trish, you mean?'

'Or does it contravene some sacred librarians' code?'

'Trish and I were still in Wales or on our way back, but maybe one of her colleagues will know.'

Connors hauled herself to her feet, chucked her empty can in the bin and returned to the seat behind her desk. 'Find out what this scandal was all about, Jeff, before that bloody Bolitho woman beats us to it.'

'Are you busy?'

Trish was standing at a big display board in the entrance to the reference library, rearranging pictures of Barbury Abbey through the ages, but she turned round, smiling, at the sound of Lincoln's voice.

'Busy? Sort of.' She ran her hand down an engraving of the Abbey in the seventeenth century.

'I thought this exhibition was over.'

'It finishes tomorrow, but some little joker's been moving the pictures around when nobody's looking. I don't want Steve from the museum to drop in and find the abbey's been turned upside down and the captions switched around. I told him he should have put it somewhere the staff could keep an eye on it, but he wouldn't listen.'

'Can I borrow you for a few minutes?'

She checked her watch. 'Hang about by the newspapers and I'll come and get you when I've done this.'

Ten minutes later, they were standing on the landing with bad coffee from the drinks machine.

'Chris Darbyshire was planning to do some research here on Tuesday,' said Lincoln, keeping his voice low. 'It was something to do with Lydia Bancroft, some sort of scandal she'd told him about. Could be totally irrelevant, but I'd still like to know what he was investigating.'

'Ask Bryony. She was here then.'

Bryony, Trish's assistant, agreed to talk to Lincoln – as long as he left the office door open.

'It's not that I don't trust you,' she said in a tone that failed to convince him, 'but I'd feel more comfortable.'

Bryony remembered helping Mr Darbyshire on Tuesday, she said, late morning, early afternoon, but she hadn't known his name at the time. She would have contacted the police about him being in the library that day if she'd made the connection.

'He looked so much smarter on the news,' she said. 'The photo they used made him look younger, too. It didn't look like the same chap.'

'Do you know what he was working on?'

'He'd got various books piled by his laptop, but then he asked for my help with the microfilm reader. He wanted local newspapers for the first quarter of 1991. I loaded the microfilm onto the machine for him and left him to it.'

'He didn't say what he was looking for?'

'Something that happened in January, February or March 1991. Obviously.' She gave him an unfriendly smile.

'Can I look through the same microfilm?'

Bryony sniffed. 'I'll have to load it for you, assuming the machine's free.'

The early months of 1991 were dominated by bad weather and acts of terrorism that were only briefly covered in *The Messenger.* Twenty-seven people were killed by gale force winds in January and heavy snow brought parts of the country to a standstill. A mortar shell was fired at 10

Downing Street. The Birmingham Six were freed. The poll tax was scrapped. People were killed or injured when bombs went off at Paddington and Victoria stations in London.

And in a bedsitting room in Barbury, Wiltshire, on Sunday January 6th, actor Hamilton Vaughn, sixty-three, was found dead after taking his own life.

Lincoln thought back to the book outline Darbyshire had left in his study at the Old Farmhouse. One of the chapters was to be devoted to the death of Hamilton Vaughn. Was this the scandal that had so excited him? Was it even a scandal?

A grainy photo accompanied the report of Vaughn's death in Inkerman Terrace, a single row of Victorian redbrick houses backing onto the railway line. The actor's photograph – from his passport, perhaps – revealed a glum-looking man.

Hamilton Vaughn's body had been found by a friend concerned about his welfare, said the report, under an eye-catching headline: *PANTO DAME FOUND DEAD IN FLAT*. An inquest had been opened and adjourned. Police were investigating, but it was understood that there were no suspicious circumstances. The manner of his death wasn't disclosed.

> The suicide of Mr Vaughn (real name Vaughn Hamilton) may be linked to a recent incident at Barbury Theatre where he was starring as Dame Spriggins in Jack and the Beanstalk. An understudy will take over his role for the remainder of the run.

What incident? Lincoln hoped he'd be able to find out more from the internet back at Barley Lane, rather than having to trawl through more back issues of *The Messenger*.

Trish was nowhere to be seen and Bryony was now sitting at the enquiry desk.

'Can I print some pages off?' he asked her.

'It's twenty pence a sheet,' said Bryony. 'The printer's in Ms Whittington's office, so I'll have to fetch them for you when they're done.'

He went back to the microfilm reader and selected the pages he wanted. By the time he'd sent them to the printer, Bryony had disappeared and he couldn't wait any longer.

He pushed open the door of Trish's office, only to find her in a clinch with the man from the museum – Steve Quilter.

CHAPTER 17

The baby wouldn't stop crying. Iris sat on the stairs, her hands over her ears, trying to shut out the noise for a minute, two minutes, five minutes. Her stomach ached, her head throbbed and her back hurt. Her boobs were sore and the skin all over her body was on fire.

And Tyger wouldn't stop crying.

She stared down into the hall. Shoes were piled inside the front door – Garvin's mostly, his stinky trainers, his work boots. Dried mud from the boots lay against the skirting board. It would only take a minute to sweep it up and chuck it out the front door, but she didn't even have the energy to fetch the dustpan and brush from the kitchen.

There was a smell, a fucking disgusting smell, and it was coming from Tyger because he needed changing. But Iris was afraid to bend over his cot in case she threw up over him. That smell! He shouldn't smell that bad, should he? Was there something wrong with him? Maybe it was her milk that was bad, something wrong with *her* that made his shit smell so awful.

Garvin was working on a building site near Amesbury, going off every morning in a van first thing, back late. Then out to the pub, not even stopping for a meal.

She couldn't face food. She didn't bother to cook for herself or order anything in. He'd get a kebab on his way home, might bring her a packet of crisps if he remembered.

'You've got to keep your strength up,' he kept telling her. But she didn't know how, hadn't the energy to put the baby in the buggy, push him to the corner shop.

He'd stopped crying. Could she be arsed to go down and put a wash on, dump the nappies in the bin, make herself a drink? The fuck she could!

Her phone rang: Garvin calling, checking up on her. Were you asleep? You going back to bed when you should be watching the baby? You been out? You ironed my shirt? You been down the shop? She dreaded answering, but he'd be mad if she didn't.

'Gonna be late, babe,' he said. 'Don't wait up.'

She wanted to ask him where he was going but that would only make him angry and he still wouldn't tell her. He'd expect her to cover for him, though, like she did the night Ritchie Payne went missing. Garvin was gone all night, only she told the police he was home by ten-thirty like he told her to. She didn't like lying, but what else could she do?

'Okay,' she said now.

'Can't hear you.'

'I said, Okay.'

He rang off, no goodbye, no asking after the baby or her. If she walked out of here with Tyger tomorrow, he wouldn't miss either of them, but he'd hate how it would look. And where would she go, anyway? At least she had a roof over her head.

She'd go and make a cup of coffee. The moment she opened the living room door, she heard the sound that made her heart sink: the baby was crying again.

CHAPTER 18

Lincoln returned to Barley Lane in a daze. He'd backed out of Trish's office without either her or Steve Quilter seeing him and had hurried out of the library into the rain.

Was Trish really involved with that creep from the museum?

And he hadn't got his printouts. Bugger!

Maybe he'd misunderstood the situation. No, he hadn't. Quilter had his arms round her. No mistaking that!

He strode into the incident room, fuelled by anger. Why Quilter? How long had it been going on? If she was involved with Quilter, why had she asked Lincoln to spend last night with her?

Woody and Pam were back from questioning Annie Darbyshire about her relationship with Paddy Noble. They were friends, not lovers, she'd said, and he'd been away in Wales on a field trip all week.

'We'll need to confirm that,' Lincoln said.

'Of course. And the DCI called just now,' said Woody. 'Reckon there's a bit of a mystery about that SIM card, the one the CSIs found in Harry Priest's van.'

Lincoln pulled his chair out, turned his screen on. 'What's the mystery? The techs at Park Street identified the owner, didn't they?'

'Yes, but that's just it; it belongs to a young lad called Isaac Keats.'

'One of the lads who took the van?'

'Isaac went missing in September 2011.'

Lincoln sat back. 'Ah. Where's he been for the last six years? Living rough?'

Woody shook his head. 'He disappeared walking home from college in Trowbridge. He was seventeen.'

'Then how does his SIM card turn up in Harry Priest's van?' Lincoln couldn't think straight – his mind skidding back to Trish's office, Quilter's arms around her...

'The DCI's got Tim Anderson looking into it, but she said Isaac's phone hasn't been used since he disappeared.'

Lincoln thought about Priest's reputation for selling dodgy electrical goods. Was he selling second-hand mobiles too? Maybe Isaac had run away from home, flogged his phone for cash, bought himself another phone off-contract, then vanished off the grid. Or was there more to it than that?

'What did they think happened to him back in 2011?' He went over to the whiteboard, unsure where, in the grand scheme of things, he should put Isaac Keats's name. Was he a suspect in the theft of Priest's van? A suspect in the abduction of Ritchie Payne, assuming Ritche had, indeed, been abducted? Or was Isaac, too, a victim?

'No one knows. He was doing okay at school, no issues at home, Well, nothing bad enough to make him run away and disappear. He only had a few quid on him and his bank account hasn't been accessed since the night he went missing, when some cash was taken out of an ATM in Westbury. But he's never turned up, dead or alive.'

'Right, so instead of having a lead on the theft of the white van, we've got ourselves a further mystery. Is that what you're saying?'

Woody shrugged. 'Reckon it's not as straightforward as we thought.'

'Did we *ever* think it was straightforward?' Lincoln ran his hands through his hair. 'Let's leave Tim Anderson to get on with it. He knows where we are if he needs any help.'

He felt angry and sad. Breakfast with Trish this morning had been a bright spot in a difficult week, but it had all been an illusion. She was involved with someone else, had merely been humouring him last night, taking pity on him…

His desk phone rang, making him jump, and his heart raced. Christ, now what?

'I believe you're looking for me.' The voice of an older man, his words carefully enunciated. 'My name's Orlando Snell.'

Snell was staying with his brother in Frome, over the county border in Somerset.

'But I don't think my brother would appreciate the police turning up on his doorstep. Especially when I am most certainly *not* the person you should be looking for. I'll meet you in an hour at the Royal Oak in Corsley Heath.' He hung up without waiting to hear if this arrangement was acceptable.

Lincoln put the phone down. Was it really going to be that easy? Everyone was looking for Orlando Snell in his Rover 75, but he'd come forward of his own volition.

He took Woody with him, resisting the temptation to quiz him about Trish on the way – Did you know your sister-in-law's involved with Steve from the museum? Has she said she's dumping me? – and discussing Ted and his broken arm instead.

They parked outside the pub and went in. The bar was quiet at this time of day so Orlando Snell was easy to spot at a corner table facing the door. With introductions done and drinks in front of them, he began an urgent explanation.

‘I’m totally innocent,’ he insisted. ‘How d’you think I feel, seeing my car plastered all over the newspapers and the bloody internet? I wasn’t with Chris on Tuesday night. I want to make that clear from the start.’

Lincoln exchanged a look with Woody. It wasn’t going to be that easy after all. ‘You did meet him that evening, though, didn’t you?’

‘No, we met in the afternoon in Costa Coffee. Not my favourite coffee shop, but he wanted the free Wi-Fi. We talked for an hour or so and I left him there, working on his laptop.’

‘What did you talk about?’ asked Woody.

‘His book. Lydia Bancroft’s book. He’s writing her life story.’

‘We know,’ said Lincoln. ‘He was her ghost writer.’

‘She would’ve written it herself, but it’s her hands – arthritis.’ Snell held his own hands up, large and square with evenly trimmed nails. ‘She can’t hold a pen, can’t use a keyboard. Chris was talking to her, writing it all down.’ He paused to sip his drink – gin and tonic with a slice of lime. ‘She’s still very lucid, a brilliant memory. Took me under her wing when I first went on the stage. Over the years I’ve become one of her closest friends. Chris wanted to run a few things past me, make sure he’d got his facts straight.’

‘About anything in particular?’

He hesitated. ‘I don’t even know that it’s relevant. It happened so long ago.’

Lincoln leaned closer to the table. ‘Tell us and we’ll decide for ourselves.’

‘He wanted to know about Hamilton Vaughn.’

‘Who’s Hamilton Vaughn?’ Woody looked puzzled.

Lincoln knew only what he’d gleaned from the brief newspaper report of Vaughn’s death. ‘Real name,

Vaughn Hamilton,' he said. 'An actor who killed himself in January 1991 during a run of *Jack and the Beanstalk* at Barbury Theatre. Playing Jack's mother, wasn't he, Mr Snell?'

'Yes, Dame Spriggins. And he was a *wonderful* pantomime dame. But sadly, he got very low and took his own life.'

Lincoln wanted to probe a bit. 'Wasn't there more to it than that? The newspaper report mentioned an incident that might have led to his death.'

Snell tutted. 'There was an *accident*. The theatre has a youth group, the Board Treaders, and the best of them get a chance to be in the panto every year. Four of them were in *Jack and the Beanstalk* that year, three lads and a girl, but one of the lads had a bad fall. Vaughn let it prey on his mind as if it was *his* fault. I suppose he felt responsible, as one of the older members of the cast and part of the management. The accident cast a bit of a shadow over the start of rehearsals and so the atmosphere was a bit...tense. And Christ, the way those kids behaved towards him because he was gay. They were old enough to know better. Sherilyn Croft was one of them – and look how she's turned out!'

Woody's eyebrows went up. 'Sherilyn Croft? Really?'

'And Nate Newton was another one,' Snell went on. 'He only got a part in the panto because the other lad fell off the stage. Looked pretty, but he couldn't hold a note.'

'Nate was in that TV serial, wasn't he,' Woody remembered. 'The one about the kids who run away from boarding school? Used to look forward to that every week. Reckon we all wanted the same hairstyle as him at the time.'

Snell sneered at the idea. 'I can think of more admirable role models. Cocky little sod. The other two

Board Treaders in the panto were the Burnett brothers, Mitchell and Cody. Their father, Bill, was theatre manager at the time and, of course, wouldn't hear a word said against either of his precious sons.'

'Mitchell Burnett was in the panto here in Barbury?' Woody sounded impressed. He turned to Lincoln. 'Did you realise he was on the stage here, boss?'

Lincoln shrugged. 'I don't even know who he is. Okay, I know the name but beyond that…'

'He's doing that history programme at the moment,' Woody told him. 'And he presented the television awards this year.'

Lincoln nodded vaguely. 'D'you remember the name of the boy who fell off the stage, Mr Snell?'

'Simon something. No, Simeon. Simeon Piper. Beautiful lad, very blond, good voice. He was messing about down stage, lost his footing and tumbled into the orchestra pit. Damaged his spine, ended up in a wheelchair.'

'And that's why Vaughn took his own life? Because of what happened to Simeon?'

Snell shifted in his seat. 'There was something else.' He looked quickly to left and right as if wary of eavesdroppers. 'One of the boys accused Vaughn of molesting him.'

Sexual assault. Lincoln sighed. *That* was what made for scandal, not an unfortunate accident. 'Was it reported to the police?'

'Not that I know of.'

'Which of the boys made the allegation?'

'I don't know, but if you ask me, those Board Treaders got together to fabricate a story, to get back at Vaughn for telling them off for messing around backstage. One of them led him on and then tried to blackmail him.'

'A honey trap?'

'Yes, and all because he ticked them off for misbehaving. Okay,' Snell conceded, 'they were kids, but they were old enough to know better than to play their putrid pop music at full volume in the dressing rooms and make fun of other actors when they fluffed their lines.'

Lincoln could imagine the friction, generations clashing in the fevered atmosphere behind the scenes. 'You're saying Vaughn took his own life because these lads – Mitchell, Cody and Nate – got together to accuse him of assaulting one of them?'

'And Sherilyn. The boys and Sherilyn. They set him up.'

'And that's what Chris Darbyshire was looking into?'

Snell nodded, clutching his glass tightly. 'And Lydia has never been convinced it was suicide. She told Chris she was sure Vaughn was murdered.'

'By the kids who set him up?'

'No, no! They could be little sods, but they weren't *that* bad! And, frankly, I've never gone along with her theory. But the idea of a murder mystery… I could tell that Chris was keen to investigate it and Lydia was pushing him to get some answers. Though how she thought he could prove anything after all this time…'

'Do *you* think he was murdered?' asked Woody.

'Frankly, no. Vaughn always dreaded the end of a run. Like so many of us theatre folk, he needed that adrenaline rush every night, and when the end of a run was in sight…' He picked up his glass and drained it. 'Lydia hates to think he didn't turn to her for help, so she wants to blame somebody else.'

'What did Chris believe?' asked Lincoln.

'He was still gathering information so he could put

it all together. I told him what I could remember and he typed it up as I was talking. I was counting on him to restore Vaughn's reputation so his memory wasn't tainted by those bloody Board Treaders.'

'Was Chris planning on talking to anyone else in the cast?'

'Eventually, I suppose. But he wanted to look at the evidence first.'

'Evidence?'

'When those kids set out to trap Vaughn, they sent him notes and photos, drawings, letters. He kept them all, put them in a sort of scrapbook he was going to show to Bill Burnett if he had to. When Lydia found Vaughn's body, she...' He cleared his throat, fidgeting with his empty glass. 'She knew he'd been putting this scrapbook together, knew where he kept it. She didn't want it falling into the wrong hands, strangers raking through it, so she took it away with her.'

'She could've been removing evidence from a crime scene,' Woody said severely, as if Snell was to blame. 'If she thought he'd been murdered, she should've left everything where it was for the police to investigate.'

Snell shrugged in resignation. 'She panicked. She could hardly put everything back where she found it afterwards, could she? Official verdict – suicide. Case closed.'

'And the scrapbook?'

'She kept it safe for years, but when she was down here on a visit a year or so ago, she asked me to look after it for her.'

'You showed it to Chris Darbyshire?'

'Yes. He was really excited by what was in it. He wanted to borrow it, but I didn't want to let it go. We agreed that I'd scan the most significant things and email them to him but then of course…'

There was a pause while they all thought about Darbyshire, a meeting over coffee, death.

'Did Chris say what his plans were for the rest of the day?'

'He was going to a friend's house, he said. He'd skipped lunch because he'd be eating out later and he'd spent ages in the library looking at old newspapers.'

'He didn't mention the friend's name? Male, female?'

Snell shook his head. 'Sorry. If he said, I didn't take it in.'

'Why didn't you go home that night?' asked Lincoln. 'You haven't been home at all since then, according to your housekeeper.'

'You've spoken to Janice?'

'We came to your house when we thought you might've been the last person to see Chris alive.'

'Actually,' Snell said awkwardly, 'I met up with someone that evening and we went back to his place. Then on Wednesday I saw the news about a murder in Coronation Gardens and there was something on Twitter about Chris Darbyshire RIP and…' He shuddered. 'I didn't fancy going back to an empty house, so I came over to Frome. Crashed at my brother's for a few days.'

He didn't look the sort of man who'd "crash" anywhere, but still.

'What were you afraid of?' Lincoln persisted. 'That someone was after you too?'

'Let's just say…' Snell broke off as a woman approached the bar, placed an order, glanced over at them. Once she'd paid for her drink and taken it across to a table beyond earshot, he carried on. 'There are people in the public eye today who wouldn't want the world to know how they'd teased and baited a much-loved actor and hounded him to his death.' He sat back. 'Now then, Inspector Lincoln, how do I stop the newspapers treating me like a wanted man?'

Dilke phoned while they were driving back to Barbury.

'I got hold of the manager of Pizza Marino,' he said. 'He says Darbyshire was there with a *woman* on Tuesday night, not Orlando Snell.'

'Yeah, we've just left Snell. He met Darbyshire in the afternoon, for coffee. Could the manager describe this woman?'

'Dark brown curls, petite, late thirties. Sounds like Leanne Milner. Except she told me and Pam she saw Chris for the last time that morning, when they parted company outside the theatre.'

'Sounds as if she's being a bit economical with the truth.' Lincoln sighed. 'You and Breezy, check for cameras along Cranbrook Road, see if there's any footage of her and Darbyshire driving along there. Me and Woody are on our way to check Snell's alibi for Tuesday night. See you back at Barley Lane.'

Snell's companion on Tuesday night was called Jackson Irving – 'though I go by Jackson on its own. You know, like Prince.' He lived in a flat above a greetings card shop in Abbey Street. Neat and clean, it was full of an eclectic mix of second-hand furniture, some of the items refurbished but most of them not. He said he'd arrived home only minutes before Lincoln and Woody rang his doorbell and he apologised unnecessarily for the flat being untidy.

'This about the old guy?' He plumped the cushions and twitched the curtains straight, switched on some of the table lamps that dotted the room. 'He in some kind of trouble? I seen his car on the news.'

'By the old guy, you mean…' Lincoln sat down on one of the two wooden settles that Jackson used instead of dining chairs.

'Ollie. First names only. Met at Carew's.'

Carew's was Barbury's pre-eminent gay bar.

'What time were you there?' Woody tried to get comfortable on the other uncushioned settle.

'Most of the evening. I seen him come in quite early, but we didn't pal up till a bit later. Look, I'll show you.' He dived for his mobile, thumbed through screens until he found a selfie he'd taken with Ollie. Jackson was sticking his tongue out, one arm round Snell's neck, pulling him in so their cheeks were touching, although Snell looked more embarrassed than enthralled. The time stamp was 21:08 on Tuesday night.

'Hit it off as soon as we met,' Jackson went on. 'We come back here after a few drinks at Carew's, made a night of it. Quite a mover for an oldie. And I recognised him after a bit. Used to be on telly in something years ago. Orlando Snell.'

Woody sniffed. 'You didn't think to get in touch with us after the public appeal?'

'Thought he'd see it himself and call you.'

'What time did he leave in the morning?' asked Lincoln.

'We was still in bed half-seven, when my alarm went off, but when I come out of the shower, he was gone. Thought that was a bit rude, not even stopping to say goodbye, but some old guys… they're ashamed, y'know? Cold light of day, consumed by guilt.'

'Where did he leave his car? There's no parking here, is there?'

'Left it outside the kebab shop a few doors down. You can park there overnight as long as you're gone by eight.

Hey, perhaps that's why he took off so early, so he didn't get a ticket. Hadn't thought of that.'

Back at Barley Lane, there was CCTV footage to look at, from the four cameras Dilke and Breeze had found along Cranbrook Road.

Tim Anderson had been right; they should have checked for cameras along that road as soon as Darbyshire's body was discovered, but they hadn't known the time frame then, Lincoln told himself, and nor had they known that the car they were looking for was Leanne's red Toyota Yaris.

But sure enough, at ten-eighteen on Tuesday night, in heavy rain, a Yaris went slowly past each camera, a woman at the wheel. At one point, she leaned forward to wipe the inside of her windscreen: Leanne Milner. And a moment later, her passenger leaned forward to clear away condensation with the palm of his hand: Chris Darbyshire.

Then the car drove on into the stretch of poorly lit road that bordered Coronation Gardens. No cameras. No clue about why Leanne stopped the car or why Darbyshire got out, without an overcoat, in the rain.

Lincoln stood between his team and the whiteboard, gathering his thoughts for a briefing. He uncapped his marker pen and turned to the board, the names dancing before his eyes. How to connect any of this?

Breeze noisily unwrapped a baguette he'd bought while he and Dilke were out.

'I was hungry,' he said when Pam glared at him.

Lincoln underlined Chris Darbyshire's name with a sweep of his pen. 'Come on, we've got a murder to solve.'

The team settled down and he pressed on.

'Darbyshire was attacked on the riverbank in

Coronation Gardens on Tuesday night. We have CCTV of him being driven along Cranbrook Road by Leanne Milner at twenty-two-eighteen but nothing to show us why she stopped the car by the entrance to the Gardens. All we know is that Darbyshire got out, went into the Gardens and got stabbed. Twice.'

A soft groan from Breeze. His baguette had leaked tomato pips onto his T-shirt. 'Oh fuck! This was clean on this morning. Rosie'll kill me.'

'Just as long as she waits until after we've solved this case, Dennis.' Impatient, Lincoln turned back to the board. 'Darbyshire and Leanne met in the theatre bar that morning. They left together, parted outside, and then Darbyshire went to the library to work on a book he's writing with Lydia Bancroft. At around three, he met Orlando Snell at Costa Coffee, more research for the book. He told Snell he was going to a friend's house and then eating out later. We now know it was Leanne that Darbyshire took to Pizza Marino.'

Pam tutted. 'Why didn't she tell us that when we talked to her?'

'People lie.' Breeze dabbed uselessly at his T-shirt. 'All the time.'

'At the library,' Lincoln went on, 'Darbyshire looked up newspaper back issues for 1991, researching an actor called Hamilton Vaughn who committed suicide here in Barbury. There was some sort of mystery surrounding his death, which got Darbyshire interested. Lydia Bancroft thought Vaughn was murdered.'

'Why?' asked Dilke.

'She was the one who found the body. Unfortunately, she took stuff away from the crime scene – if that's what it was – making it impossible to prove one way or the other. Not then and certainly not now.'

With quick sweeps of his marker pen, Lincoln drew lines between Lydia's name and Vaughn's, between her name and Darbyshire's, between Darbyshire's and Vaughn's. A triangle with a question mark at the heart of it.

'Orlando Snell told us one of the boys appearing in the pantomime accused Vaughn of molesting him,' Woody said.

Breeze looked up. 'Cuh, I can see where this is going – ageing luvvie comes on to innocent kiddie and gets snubbed. Can't handle the shame and rejection. Tops himself.'

Lincoln snorted. 'A pretty cynical assessment, Dennis.'

'Guess who was in the pantomime,' Woody said, beaming. 'Apart from Lydia and Vaughn? Nate Newton, Sherilyn Croft and Mitchell Burnett.'

'What, *the* Mitchell Burnett? The presenter?' Breeze was impressed.

'Yes. His dad, Bill Burnett, was the theatre manager.'

'Do we think Sherilyn's disappearance and Darbyshire's murder are linked?' Pam asked.

Lincoln stared at the whiteboard. He kept seeing an image of Trish and Steve Quilter in her office, embracing. 'I don't know. I really don't know.'

'Then who did Darbyshire have sex with on Tuesday?' Breeze wanted to know.

'Must've been Leanne,' Pam guessed. 'Her husband and the kids were away for half term so she and Chris would've had the house to themselves. After he left Costa, he could've gone back to her house, waited for her to get back from work.'

'Then they have a quickie before going out for pizza,' Breeze chipped in. 'And he was probably planning on spending the night there after they'd eaten. So much for staying at the Black Swan.'

Lincoln popped the top off his marker pen, popped it on again. 'Any suspects?'

'Her husband? Russ Milner?' Dilke offered. 'She may think he doesn't know, but…'

Pam shook her head. 'He's been in Somerset with the children all week, at his mum's.'

Breeze leaned back in his chair, peering at the stain on his T-shirt. 'He could've put somebody up to it. Good alibi, being at his mum's with the kids.'

Lincoln added Russ Milner's name to the whiteboard. 'Now we've got the CCTV along Cranbrook Road we need to scour it for any other individuals or vehicles that could've been tailing Leanne's car. I don't believe her Yaris was stopped at random, do you?'

'We need to speak to her again, don't we?' Pam was already getting to her feet.

CHAPTER 19

There was no red Toyota Yaris parked outside the Milners' house when Lincoln and Pam arrived there. The house was in darkness.

No one came to the door. 'She must've gone to join Russ and the kids for the rest of half-term,' said Pam. She called Leanne's mobile and left a message when voicemail kicked in. She put her phone away. 'What are you thinking, boss?'

He started back down the path towards the road. 'I'm thinking she's the only witness to a murder and now she's gone AWOL.'

'But why didn't she call for help that night or report it?' Pam wondered. 'She'd have had to admit she and Chris were having an affair, but don't you think her husband already knew about that?'

Lincoln didn't reply. To his shame, it had taken him months to realise his wife had fallen for somebody else. Cathy's erratic hours at the hospital, his own crazy schedule. By the time he'd found out that something was going on, she and Andy Nightingale were planning on moving in together and it was too late to put things right.

'Where did you say the husband's taken the kids?'

'Glastonbury. To his mum's.'

'Let's see if there's anyone in next door. Perhaps they can help.'

But Leanne's neighbour knew only that you could see Glastonbury Tor from the mother-in-law's kitchen window.

'Sorry, that doesn't narrow it down much, does it?' the woman said. 'Is it an emergency? There hasn't been an accident, has there? I saw Leanne driving away this morning around lunchtime. She's alright, is she?'

'As far as we know,' Lincoln assured her. 'But we need to speak to her or Russ as a matter of urgency.'

'Oh, hang about…' The woman – sixty-something, her grey hair in pigtails – ducked back into her house, then reappeared with a hopeful smile. 'Russ gave me this when I said I fancied doing the Glastonbury Festival this year.' She thrust a business card at them. 'I didn't get there in the end, but I kept the card. Juniper Farm. That's where his mum lives. She lets it as an Airbnb when the Festival's on.'

By the time his team had reassembled at Barley Lane, Lincoln had contacted Avon and Somerset police. Could someone call at Juniper Farm to see if Leanne Milner was there? He wondered how long it would take them to send someone. Did Glastonbury even have its own police station these days?

'We need to catch a break.' Breeze leaned back in his chair, arms folded across his chest. 'If we knew *why* Darbyshire was killed, we'd be halfway to knowing who killed him – or had him killed.'

Lincoln agreed. 'We need Leanne Milner to tell us why she stopped the car where she did. That's the break we need.' He checked his watch, silently urging Avon and Somerset police to get back to him. He glanced up at the whiteboard and something flashed in front of his eyes: Trish with Steve Quilter. He shook his head to rid it of the image and turned back to his team.

'Listen, it's after half seven, we're all tired, we've been at this all day. Get yourselves home, rest, sleep. Come back refreshed as early as possible. We've got a lot done already so, as Dennis says, we just need to catch a break.'

As the team packed up and slowly dispersed, his phone rang: DS Jenny Reedy from Avon and Somerset police. But the news wasn't good.

'We've called at Juniper Farm and spoken to Russ Milner,' she said. 'But he doesn't know where Leanne is. He was expecting her sometime this afternoon, but she hasn't shown up and isn't answering her phone. It's only, what, an hour's drive from Barbury? Ninety minutes?'

'Something like that. She was seen driving away from home around lunchtime. Did he have any idea where she could be?'

'He's calling her friends to see if they've heard from her and we'll be looking out for her too. A traffic camera should pick her up sometime soon, wherever she is.'

'Thanks. Has he got my number?'

'I left it with him. Is this to do with that writer that was murdered? Is this woman a suspect?'

'She's probably our only witness.'

'You think she's in danger herself?'

That thought had crossed his mind. He guessed Leanne had driven away from the scene because she wanted to hide her illicit love affair with Darbyshire. But she could also have feared being identified and tracked down by his killers.

'Yes, it's possible,' he said. 'We're pursuing various leads, but they've ended in dead ends so far.'

'We'll let you know as soon as we hear anything.'

By the time he put the phone down, he was the last one left in the incident room. The last one left at Barley Lane. It was late but not too late to do a bit more research, follow up another lead. He made a note to himself to liaise with Tim Anderson in the morning, see if he'd got anywhere in the search for Ritchie Payne.

He was tempted to call Trish, decided against it. Called her anyway.

'You okay?'

'Of course I'm okay,' she said, sounding surprised to hear from him. 'Where did you go this morning? Bryony said you left your printouts behind.'

He shut his eyes, imagined her at home. Wished he could be there with her. 'Sorry, I got a call to come back here. Forgot all about them.'

'It's okay, I picked them up for you. You were researching Hamilton Vaughn? What is this, a cold case review?' He could hear her smiling.

'You know about Hamilton Vaughn?'

'Of course. He always played the dame in the panto at Barbury Theatre. Probably acted in lots of other plays, too, but that's the only role I remember him in. I was ten or eleven when he died and it was such a shock. He hanged himself, didn't he? I knew all about hanging from my history lessons, but I'd never thought about how you could hang *yourself.* And it really upset me. Someone I'd seen in the flesh, dying like that. That age, you don't think about death, do you?'

'Don't you?' Lincoln certainly had.

'And then, years later, there were rumours that he'd assaulted one of the boys in the cast. I suppose that's why he killed himself, before the police were onto him. Just a dirty old man.'

'They were *allegations*, Trish. They were never investigated. He could've been innocent.'

'No smoke without fire. You want to pick up these printouts? I'm working tomorrow. You could pop in.'

'I'm working tomorrow too. I won't have time to "pop in", no.'

His sarcasm was wasted on her. 'Okay then,' she said brightly, 'I'll hang onto them for now.'

A welcome warmth greeted him when he opened the front door of the Old Vicarage. He'd reset the central heating timer so it came on before he got home. No point being cold for the sake of being frugal.

That had been his parents' weakness, worrying about every last penny even though they were comfortably off – although 'comfortably' wasn't really the right word. They made their furniture last long past its sell-by date, kept the thermostats low, ate sparingly, eked out their pensions as if they didn't deserve a few treats in their old age.

He was determined not to get like that, although their marriage had been solid, blessed with a daughter and son, Ruth and Paul, close together and then himself, a late and unexpected addition, when his father wasn't far off retirement. Maybe he was hard on them, but he simply wished they'd spent a bit more on themselves instead of worrying about having enough to leave to their children.

He made himself coffee and rooted around for something quick to eat, a meal to distract him from wanting several glasses of whiskey. He found a packet of curry-flavoured rice, laid it on a plate and put it in the microwave.

Why hadn't he asked Trish about Steve Quilter? Because he knew there was no innocent reason for them to have their arms around each other. But *Steve Quilte*r, of all people!

He needed to look at the Hamilton Vaughn case in more detail. If there had been a police investigation of any kind, into the allegations against him or the nature of his death, there should be records somewhere. He'd look tomorrow if…

Bang! He'd forgotten to snip the rice packet and it had exploded as it heated up, peppering the inside of the microwave with grains of bright yellow rice.

He slammed the door on it, his appetite lost. But he was still thirsty and a glass of whiskey would help that, for sure. As he was about to pour himself a second glass, his phone rang.

'It's Annie Darbyshire.' He visualised her, auburn hair the same shade as Cathy's, pale skin. 'I phoned my Aunt Lydia to tell her about Chris. She told me something you might want to know.'

'Yes?' He put the bottle down, glass still empty. 'Go on.'

'For a long time, she was friends with an actor called Hamilton Vaughn. He was found dead during the run of the panto they were both in, but she always thought his death was suspicious. The verdict was suicide, but she wanted Chris to look into it.'

Nothing Lincoln didn't already know. 'We'd heard he was researching Vaughn, yes. What does your aunt think really happened?'

'She's convinced Vaughn was murdered, but how could she know? He hanged himself. It would take a forensic pathologist to prove someone else was involved.' She laughed softly. 'Listen to me, telling you something you know far better than I do.'

'You wouldn't be the first. Did she say anything else about Vaughn?'

'There were rumours that he was grooming one of the boys, but she didn't believe them. She was sure he was set up by those kids. That they'd made the whole thing up for a bit of fun. How did she think Chris could find anything out after all this time? He was a scriptwriter and he'd done a few documentaries, but he wasn't an investigative journalist, for God's sake!' Her tone was indulgent rather than scornful. 'He was going to do a podcast about it, he told Lydia, a sort of true crime thing, *The Death of a Pantomime Dame.* Can you imagine? All those armchair detectives. I'm surprised Lydia even knows what a podcast is.'

A podcast would certainly have reached a far wider audience than Lydia's life story. Orlando Snell had shown Darbyshire the scrapbook containing letters and photos that Vaughn's 'victim' had used to taunt and threaten him. Such material would certainly have added evidence to a true-crime investigation, evidence of a honey trap laid by one or more of the young Board Treaders.

'Annie, who else knew Chris was planning this podcast?'

'I have no idea. He'd told Lydia not to tell anyone and she hadn't even told *me* until today, but it's hard to keep these things secret once you start asking around.'

'Why do you think he wanted to keep it secret?'

'If Chris accused those kids of being responsible for Vaughn's death by faking allegations against him, he'd be accusing Nate Newton and the Burnett brothers and my cousin Sherilyn. They were teenagers then but they're all grown up now and kind of famous. I don't suppose any of them would be proud of hounding a gay man to death when they were kids. But would someone *kill* to keep that secret?'

SATURDAY 28TH OCTOBER

CHAPTER 20

'Isaac Keats.' Tim Anderson chucked a black and white photo onto Lincoln's desk. It showed a teenage boy with a mass of tight corkscrew curls not far short of an Afro, freckles dotting his nose and cheeks, a toothy grin. He wore a pale hoodie over a dark T-shirt. 'Date of birth, August 5th, 1994. Disappeared in Trowbridge, September 23rd, 2011, a Friday.'

Lincoln shook his head slowly. 'Not sure I remember this case. I assume Trowbridge dealt with it initially?'

'Yep. His mum thought he'd gone off with his mates for the weekend without telling her. Didn't raise the alarm until the Sunday night. His phone was turned off on the Friday, never been used since and, as you know, the SIM card turned up in the wreck of Harry Priest's van. Isaac's cash card was used to take money out of an ATM in Westbury the night he disappeared – another reason everyone thought he'd gone off with his mates for a fun weekend.'

'But his mates knew nothing about it?'

'Didn't seem to have many mates, from what I've read in the files. Mixed race in a mostly white school. Black mum. White dad who didn't stick around for long. Thinking was, Isaac's run off to London, Bristol, Cardiff, wherever. And that's how kids disappear.'

Lincoln stared at the boy's photo, wondering what had become of him, wishing there were ways to stop lads like this slipping through the cracks. Would his disappearance have been dismissed as readily if he'd had *two* white parents?

'Any clues at all?'

Anderson shook his head. 'The usual sightings that came to nothing. Talk of some older guy hanging around near the college, chatting to the lads. Always the lads. Never tried to chat up the girls. But I found this, too.'

He slipped a folder onto the desk, *Greenaway, Bob* printed on the cover. Lincoln opened it to see a photo of another boy, white, his hair shorn close. His left eye had a droopy lid as if he was half-closing it as the camera shutter clicked. He was in school uniform, the knot of his tie tight and small.

'Born July 1974,' said Anderson sombrely. 'Disappeared in Swindon on September 21st, 1990.

Lincoln looked up expectantly. 'And what was the theory?'

'That he'd run away from home, gone to London. He was adopted as a baby, started playing up as he hit his teens, wanting to find his real parents. No chance of that. Dumped as a newborn outside a chapel in Chippenham. Got in with a bad crowd at secondary school. Bunked off school the day he disappeared, seen talking to an older guy at a burger van. That was the last confirmed sighting.'

'And no mobile phone?'

'Not many kids had them then.'

'You're thinking the two cases are linked?'

Anderson shrugged. 'It's possible.'

Lincoln looked again at the boys' photos, twenty-one years between them, almost to the day. 'How did you come up with this Greenaway kid? There must be dozens of other missing boys in the files.'

'It's one of the cases my dad used to talk about.' Anderson pulled up a chair and sat across Lincoln's desk from him.

'Your dad was CID?'

'Yep. Thirty years. Always said it was a case that stayed with him, the way the kid vanished into thin air.'

'Happens too often.' Lincoln let the photos drop back onto his desk. 'But that SIM card the CSIs found in Harry Priest's van – it could've been dropped by whoever owned the van before him or he could've bought Isaac's phone without knowing where it came from.'

'Or Priest could've had something to do with Isaac's disappearance and, potentially, with Bob's.'

'Your dad ever mention Priest? Was he a person of interest when Bob went missing?'

'No mention of Priest in the file,' Anderson said. 'So if he was ever in the frame, it wasn't official. Wish I could ask my dad, but he died last year.'

'Sorry to hear that. What about the rest of his team? Any of them still around?'

'Nearly thirty years after Bob was last seen? Either retired or dead.' Anderson shunted his chair back where it came from. 'Ritchie Payne was last seen getting into that white van.'

'Which Priest said was stolen from outside his yard. But Ritchie's in his mid-twenties, a young man walking home from the pub. He's not a lad in his teens.'

Anderson nodded across to the whiteboard where Ritchie's photo gazed back. 'Does he look twenty-five?'

Lincoln had to agree that Ritchie, skinny and vulnerable, looked no more than a teenager – last seen striding across town to catch the bus home to his grandparents and his pet mice. 'You've run your theory past the DCI?'

'Not yet. Wanted to see what you thought first.'

Flattered, Lincoln told him he thought he was onto something. 'But right now, Tim, Chris Darbyshire's murder takes priority here. Keep looking for Ritchie. Dig into Harry Priest's background, see how long he's had that van, any previous owners. If you find out he bought it two years ago, say, you'll have to assume Isaac Keats's SIM got there before Priest became the owner.'

'So where are we with the Darbyshire case?'

Lincoln brought him up to speed. 'And now we're waiting for Leanne Milner to turn up.'

'Think she's implicated in some way?' Anderson crossed to the whiteboard, studying the photo of the dark-haired arts officer.

'She lied to us about being with Darbyshire on Tuesday afternoon and evening, and now she's disappeared. She may have nothing to do with the attack on him, but she's making things worse by running away, not telling us what she knows. Even if she didn't see the attack on him, she could tell us why she stopped the car by Coronation Gardens, why Darbyshire got out.'

'You think his attackers were waiting for him in the Gardens?'

'Must've been. Although it was a filthy night and there's only a flimsy sort of shelter, so they probably weren't there long before Leanne drove past.'

'Could they have come across the river from the other side?' Anderson shifted his attention to the wall map. 'There's this whole network of footpaths and bridges, isn't there, crossing the water meadows?'

'Yes, but the path's been blocked off that end since last weekend for dredging. The only access to the crime scene is the path from Cranbrook Road.'

'You've gotta hope the Milner woman turns up soon. Okay then. I'll leave you to it. Better go and brief the DCI.'

On his own once more, Lincoln wondered again why Leanne had stopped the car. Did someone jump out in front of it? If they'd seemed threatening, surely her instinct – Darbyshire's too – would have been to drive on, to get away.

'Was that the DI from Trowbridge?' Pam swept in, shedding her cycling gear on the way to her desk. 'I passed him in the car park.'

'Tim Anderson.' He told her about the SIM card from Isaac's phone, Anderson's desire to connect Isaac's disappearance with Bob Greenaway's, to connect both of them with Harry Priest.

'Bit of a stretch, isn't it?'

'I've told him to concentrate on finding Ritchie. You look glum. What's up?'

'I read Leanne wrong, didn't I? She gave us that sob story about seeing Chris for the last time on the theatre steps that morning and I believed her.'

'Don't beat yourself up about it. Let's find her. Find out what happened Tuesday night.'

When Russ Milner phoned a few minutes later, Lincoln braced himself for having to tell him his wife was having an affair. Before he could say it, though, Milner told him he knew she was sleeping with Chris Darbyshire. No need to break it to him gently.

Lincoln felt a rush of relief. 'You understand why we need to speak to her?'

'She was with Chris the night he died?'

'Yes. But we don't know why she stopped the car by Coronation Gardens.'

'She wouldn't have stopped there unless it was an emergency,' Milner said. 'She's never liked driving along that stretch of road after dark, but I suppose she felt safe because Chris was with her.'

'You sound very accepting of the affair, Russ.'

'Think I should get angry? No point. I've known

about it for months, but I knew it wouldn't last. Nothing did with Chris.'

'You knew him?'

'I worked with him on the Paragon project until the council canned it. We spent many a happy hour in one pub or another. He was having a midlife crisis, sleeping with a girl half his age but wanting to stay with his wife. He asked my advice and I told him he had to make up his own mind. He left Annie and, a few months later, he's sleeping with *my* wife even though his girlfriend's pregnant. I'm not like him, Inspector. I want to keep my family together, not break it up. Whatever Leanne's done, we'll get through it.'

'When did you last speak to her?'

'Yesterday morning. She said she was leaving home around midday. She should've been here by two-thirty, or three at the latest. I'm worried sick about where she is, but for the kids' sake I'm trying not to show it.'

'Where might she go if she was in trouble? Her own family?'

'She hasn't really got anyone, apart from a few friends in Barbury. I can't believe she'd turn to them rather than me.'

Lincoln stared at his heaped-up in tray without seeing it, thought about Milner standing at his mother's kitchen window and seeing Glastonbury Tor.

'If she contacts you, Russ, please, *please* get her to call us. It's vital that we speak to her, find out what happened that night.'

As soon as he put the phone down, he realised that by admitting he knew about his wife's affair, Milner had confirmed himself as a suspect. Might he have arranged to have Darbyshire killed? He couldn't be ruled out, despite his solid alibi. Had he been a little over-eager to talk or was he simply trying to be helpful, to make it clear he'd already forgiven Leanne and only wanted her back, safe, with him?

'Woody, check out Russ Milner's background. Find out what he does for a living. He says he worked with Darbyshire on the Paragon project, seemed to know him quite well.'

'Will do.' Woody turned back to his screen, where news headlines had popped up. 'Sherilyn Croft's been spotted in London. Reckon that means she's no longer missing. Do we need to speak to her?'

Lincoln was finding it hard to believe that Darbyshire had been targeted because of a prank some teenagers had played on a pantomime dame nearly thirty years ago. 'According to Orlando Snell, it was one of the boys that Vaughn took a shine to, not her.'

'But didn't he say all four of the Board Treaders were in on it?'

'The DCI won't want us traipsing up to London if we can find out more by staying here. I'll call Snell, see if there's anything else he can tell us. I'm curious about this scrapbook he showed to Darbyshire.'

Snell's housekeeper, Janice Shepherd, answered his phone and went to fetch him. A few minutes later, Lincoln heard him call out to her.

'I'll take it in the living room, Shep.' A click, a pause, another click, and then he came on the line.

'Was Sherilyn Croft involved with what happened to Vaughn,' Lincoln asked. 'This honey trap thing?'

'She wasn't as bad as the boys, but she was a cheeky little madam.'

'You said one of the boys accused Vaughn of assaulting him. Do you know which boy?'

The line went quiet. Lincoln visualised Snell in

his living room, weak autumn sun lighting upon the decorative bowls and pitchers clogging every flat surface, the oil paintings on his walls, the shelves of books on antiques and the theatre.

'Vaughn had a soft spot for Cody, the younger Burnett boy. Frankly, I can't see Vaughn being foolish enough to make an overture unless he'd been given a come-on and even then… Cody was only fifteen.'

Lincoln guessed that Snell knew only too well the dangers of misinterpreting 'come-ons', especially in a fevered backstage atmosphere, in cramped dressing rooms and dark corridors. And in 1990, the boy would have been three years below the legal age of consent.

'They baited Vaughn,' Snell went on, his voice unsteady with emotion. 'They baited him and led him into a trap. But what could anyone say? The Burnett boys' father ran the theatre and Bill was *not* a man you fell out with. And the *kids* are always the victims, aren't they? Because kids are always *innocent*, aren't they?'

'Mr Snell…'

'Those kids tried to catch Vaughn out. His scrapbook's proof of that.'

'We'd like to take a look at this scrapbook, if you don't mind.'

'What, take it away with you?' Snell sounded anxious, protective.

'We'd take good care of it.'

'I'm sure you would, but…' He broke off, turning away from the phone to call out to his housekeeper. 'Yes, cheerio Shep. Have fun. See you in the morning.' He turned back. 'My housekeeper's off to see her daughter. Have I got to bring this scrapbook to the police station?'

'We could come to you if that's easier.' Lincoln was desperate not to put obstacles in the way of seeing the scrapbook. 'I'll get one of my team to come to your house.'

'Who will you send? I need to know who you'll send.'

'I'll come myself. About two o'clock suit you?'

'That's good, that's good.' Snell broke off again. 'Sorry, there's someone at the door. Trust them to turn up when Janice isn't here to let them in! I have to go.' Abruptly, he hung up.

CHAPTER 21

Valerie Bancroft turned the television off with an impatient jab at the remote control.

'Look at that,' she said as Molly wandered in, still in her pyjamas. 'Sherilyn can push a trolley round Tesco's, but she can't be arsed to let her family know she's okay.'

'She phoned me,' Molly said, yawning. 'She's staying at Nate's in Borehamwood.'

That did nothing to reassure Valerie. Nate Newton was from a criminal family, wasn't he? His dad was in jail off and on, his uncle was a dodgy car salesman with a wheeler-dealer son.

But Sherilyn wanted a good time, to drink, spend money, do drugs. You could tell just by looking at her that she had a coke habit. She was a second-division celebrity, a personality to invite to openings and launches and first nights of third-rate shows, to the birthday parties of other second-division celebrities. Just you wait, Sheri! You'll be back on the cover of those cheapo magazines before you know it, caught by someone's camera with your hair unwashed and no make-up. Before and after photos, *with* a septum and *without*.

'What's so special about Borehamwood?'

'It's near Elstree Studios,' Molly went on, still intent on her phone.

'He's acting again? I thought he'd chucked it in.'

'He did, but his little girl's in some kids' TV thing.'

'I wish Sheri wasn't still in touch with him. We all know what happened last time she hung out with him.'

A driving ban, photos of her wrecked car all over the

tabloids, Nate's wrecked face ditto – at least his injuries had healed, most of them. Sherilyn had been well over the limit, should never've got behind the wheel. Nate should've taken the keys off her when they were both off their tits on drink and coke.

'That was aeons ago.' Molly flumped down at the breakfast table. 'They met up at a *Harbinger Hollow* convention in London last month.'

God, that ridiculous series they were in when they were kids. It should've sunk without trace, but it attracted a cult following among students and other devotees of afternoon television.

Molly reached for the Shreddies, tipped a load into her bowl, drowned them in milk. 'Mitch Burnett was there too. She said it was like old times. I wonder when she's coming home?'

CHAPTER 22

After Orlando Snell had so abruptly ended their call, Lincoln turned to Chris Darbyshire's phone records. They revealed no clandestine meetings, no late-night calls to yet another girlfriend. But on the day he died, he'd texted Leanne within minutes of his pregnant partner dropping him off at Tisbury station on Tuesday morning.

Still OK for coffee? Theatre bar?

She'd responded with a row of hearts. At twelve-thirty, he'd texted her again.

Sorry about earlier. Touched a nerve.

My bad. Stay the night? Pick u up on corner 5-ish after work.

He'd responded with a row of upward-pointing thumbs, adding:

Table booked for 8.30. Plenty of time for…

Lincoln could guess what the ellipses signified. And there was the text he'd later sent Jessica, saying he was on the train and leaving Bristol – except he'd sent it during dinner at Pizza Marino. His last text. Ever.

As expected, the memory sticks and backup drive brought back from Standish's Farm contained only scripts Darbyshire had been working on for other writers and an early draft of the opening chapters of Lydia Bancroft's life story. No mention of Hamilton Vaughn. Anything he'd written about the pantomime dame must be on his missing laptop.

How suddenly a life can end. On Tuesday, Darbyshire had gone to the library, then met Orlando Snell. Leanne had picked him up on her way home from work and they'd made love while they had the house to themselves. They'd gone out to eat at Pizza Marino, leaving around ten. And then, within half an hour, he was dead.

'Russ and Leanne Milner.'

Lincoln looked up to see Woody standing in front of him, notebook in hand. 'What about them?'

'Not much of a presence on social media. Reckon they both use it for work rather than personal stuff. Russ runs a PR company near Andover. Leanne posts about arts projects she's been involved in.'

'Friends she might have gone to?'

'Nobody listed,' said Woody. 'But Russ must know who her friends are. You think she's got Darbyshire's laptop with her?'

'Or it could still be at her house. I spoke to Orlando Snell. He's willing to hand over the scrapbook he showed to Darbyshire. I said I'd go over to Bridgeford to pick it up.'

'This pantomime dame thing couldn't have any bearing on the murder, though, could it, boss? We're talking twenty-six, twenty-seven years ago.'

'Yes, but Darbyshire clearly thought it was worthy of a podcast and Snell seems very protective of that scrapbook. I'm thinking we should speak to Lydia Bancroft.'

'And then the Board Treaders? Not that I can believe someone like Mitchell Burnett would have anything to do with Darbyshire's murder – he's a top-notch television presenter.'

'So people keep telling me.'

Woody chuckled. 'If anyone's got dodgy connections, it's Sherilyn Croft. All her partying, the drink and the drugs. She kept some bad company back along. According to the newspapers, anyway,' he added, in case

Lincoln thought he still followed her career. ‘She was all over the headlines at one time.’

‘Then let’s check out all four Board Treaders, just to be sure.’

CHAPTER 23

'I told you, I don't have it. I've left it with someone.'

Orlando Snell squirmed in his seat, pulling against the cable ties that bound his wrists to the chair arms. He could feel blood and snot running down his upper lip and longed to be able to wipe them away.

The tall one stood over him, poised to strike him again. 'The fuck you have! Where's the fucking scrapbook?'

Behind him, Snell heard the other one ransacking his shelves, wrenching drawers from the bureau, emptying shopping bags and his old satchel onto the carpet. His new books hit the floor, his new sweaters. Everything was spoiled.

'I can't tell you. I don't know where he lives. I don't even know his proper name. Please...'

The blow shut him up. That's all they wanted, to hurt him, to humiliate him. Thugs, the pair of them. Why the hell had he let them in? Had they waited until they saw Shep leaving, knowing he'd be on his own once she'd gone?

Bloody thugs, not much more than kids but vicious as buggery. How did they even know about Vaughn's scrapbook? Had they been *following* him? Had they seen him show it to Chris Darbyshire on Tuesday? Oh fuck! How could he get out of this? And how the hell had he managed to leave the bloody thing at Jackson's?

'All right,' he said, 'if you'll just untie me, I'll show you where it is.'

The tall one straightened up. 'Sure?'

'Promise.'

'He's bluffing,' the other one said, a softer voice, higher pitched. A girl?

The tall one stooped down, hooking his blade under the cable tie and ripping it in two. The pain was intense, but his hand was free.

'And the other one,' Snell said, but the instant the knife slid under the cable tie, he made a grab for it. If he could only –

Dark. Everything was dark. Quiet. He was on the floor. Couldn't move. Couldn't feel anything. Thoughts slipping out of reach. Gone.

CHAPTER 24

Where was that number for Lydia Bancroft? Lincoln picked through the accumulation of paperwork on his desk, consigning much of it to the shredding pile as he searched. At last he found the number scribbled on the flap of an envelope and dialled it.

It took a minute or two for the ageing actress to comprehend who he was and why he was phoning.

'I'm devastated,' she said. 'When Annie phoned to tell me Chris had been *murdered*... I'd already seen about it on the news, of course, but they made it sound like a mugging. And I feel so *responsible.* I shouldn't have asked him to find out what happened to poor Vaughn all those years ago, because, of course, I could have got it wrong. About him being murdered. Maybe Vaughn *did* take his own life. No one likes to think a friend didn't feel able to reach out to them when they needed them.'

More or less what Orlando Snell had said.

'You think that's why Chris was killed?' Lincoln persisted. 'Because he was looking into Vaughn's death?'

She sighed hopelessly. 'Darling, I'm just a stupid old woman. What would I know?' She turned away from the phone to take a sip of something. 'It's my fault for laying it on a bit thick to keep Chris interested. I'm putting it to rest now. I've learnt my lesson.'

Lincoln caught sight of the clock, realised he was running out of time to get to Orlando Snell's by two.

'What about the scandal Chris was looking into?' he asked. 'Vaughn being accused of grooming one of the youngsters in the cast?'

'I really can't remember what happened. I know one of the children fell off the stage and Vaughn blamed himself for not catching him in time, but as for the rest of it…' Another sip. 'I was silly to stir things up, but Chris seemed *so* thrilled… I loved him and I can't *bear* to think all his work will be wasted, but there it is. That's life.' And she hung up.

Why had she suddenly changed her mind about the nature of Vaughn's death? She'd rescued his scrapbook when he died. She must know about the allegations the Board Treaders made against him, the very reason for the scrapbook's compilation.

Or had Orlando Snell got it wrong?

'We need to get over to Bridgeford, Woody.' He grabbed his car keys and coat. 'Come on.'

As he drove, Lincoln relayed his conversation with Lydia Bancroft.

'Long time since anyone's called me darling,' he said. 'But she sounds as if she's still on the ball. So why do I get the feeling she was trying to back off, play it down?'

'Reckon Darbyshire's death has shaken her up. Especially if she thinks it's to do with Hamilton Vaughn. But it can't be, can it, not after all this time?'

'Depends what Darbyshire thought he was on to. If he'd told her he was going to expose a few famous names, she might be getting cold feet now he's wound up dead.'

Even as he said it, Lincoln realised how far-fetched that sounded.

'More likely it's to do with his complicated love life,' Woody said.

'Which reminds me. Someone needs to have a word with Jessica Hale. She knows Darbyshire was playing away, but Leanne's name is going to hit the media any minute now. She needs to be warned.'

'I'll send Pam over. What about warning his wife?'

'I'll speak to Annie later.'

The street door of Orlando Snell's house was slightly ajar when Lincoln and Woody arrived a few minutes after two. No one answered their knock, so Lincoln pushed the door wide open and they stepped inside.

'No Janice?' They went down the long narrow passageway to the back of the house, checking the downstairs rooms for Snell's housekeeper. Then Lincoln remembered. 'She was going out while he was on the phone to me. Off to her daughter's, he said.'

Up the stairs they went, Lincoln feeling more and more apprehensive as they climbed. And then he saw it, as he drew level with the landing floor – a body lying full length along it. Smelt it, the rusty-metal stench of blood.

Scrambling up the last few stairs, he rushed to the man's side and sank to his knees next to him. But it was too late. Orlando Snell was beyond help, his eyes swollen shut, his face battered, a pool of blood beginning to congeal beneath his head.

While Woody rang for help, Lincoln checked for a pulse and wasn't surprised when he couldn't find one. He made a rapid assessment of the scene before standing up and stepping away from the body. No sign of a weapon. The man's skin was still faintly warm. He'd been dead only a short time. But why were his shirt cuffs bloody?

Was his attacker still here? Giving the body a wide berth, Lincoln checked the other rooms. The study had been ransacked, the shelves emptied, papers and books strewn on the floor. The living room was in a similar state of chaos, with desk drawers gaping and furniture overturned, ornaments sent flying onto the floor, a porcelain dish smashed, a brass figurine lying on the carpet among the shards. A heap of brand-new books had been tipped out of their Waterstone's carrier, some winter jerseys raked from a Debenham's bag – Snell's last shopping spree heartlessly emptied onto the floor.

Whatever his attacker was looking for, they'd had a hard time finding it. Were they after the scrapbook that Lincoln and Woody had come to collect? But how did they know about it?

He slowly went down to the first-floor landing to wait. Eventually, he heard sirens and saw the sweep of blue lights. Woody stepped back as first a paramedic and then a police constable charged up the stairs.

A quick exchange of IDs, the briefest explanation of why two detectives from Barley Lane were in the house.

Lincoln turned to Woody. 'Get hold of Janice Shepherd and tell her what's happened. I'd better update the DCI.'

'Okay.'

'Snell is dead,' he told Connors when she answered. 'His place has been turned over.' Turned over by somebody who wasn't interested in his antiques, his books or his silverware.

'That's all we need.' She exhaled. 'You seriously think this is to do with Darbyshire nosing around into some old guy's suicide?'

'Bit of a coincidence if it isn't.'

'Any idea who's behind it? I've got to tell Youngman something.'

DCS Youngman would indeed need mollifying, Lincoln guessed, especially when news of Snell's death hit social media. He might not have been a high-profile actor, even in his heyday, but that wouldn't stop the likes of Karen Bolitho at *The Messenger* making the most of it.

'Snell told us the kids in the panto set a honey trap for Vaughn, trying to make out he was grooming one of them. If Darbyshire had exposed that, some famous names would've been tarnished. Those kids were teenagers then, but at least one of them is rather more famous now.'

'And who's that?'

'Mitchell Burnett.'

'The guy who does that history thing? The guy off *Celebrity Mastermind?*'

'Yes.' He'd have to take her word for it. 'Snell had a scrapbook of material that Vaughn had kept as proof of what they'd got up to. Showing that he'd been set up and was innocent.'

'That's something a man like Burnett would want to keep quiet about. But as for having someone killed! And where's the proof?' She paused. 'I'm going to keep a lid on this as far as possible,' she said at last. 'Snell disturbed a burglar; that's what we'll say until we know a bit more, okay?'

Out on the pavement, as they looked for CCTV cameras, Woody told Lincoln he'd got hold of the housekeeper, and she was making her way back from her daughter's.

'Though what she can do while it's a crime scene…'

'Someone rang his doorbell around eleven while I was on the phone to him. He cut our call short to go down and answer it.'

'I've spotted three cameras already. Reckon at least one of them will have picked up whoever came to his front door.' Woody took his phone out. 'I've got a number for Snell's brother in Frome. You want me to go over there, see if he knows anything more?'

Lincoln nodded, realising as he looked round for more cameras that he was shaking. 'I'll stay here, at least until Antonia Yardley arrives.' Assuming she was the doctor on duty.

He tried to order his thoughts as he watched Woody depart. Half an hour ago they'd arrived to collect a scrapbook that might reveal a motive for Chris Darbyshire's murder. Lincoln had been sceptical about its significance, so many years after the incidents it recorded, but now the man guarding it was dead and the scrapbook itself had vanished.

When Antonia arrived, he followed her up to the first-floor landing, hanging back to avoid contaminating the scene while she went about her business.

'Blunt force trauma,' she announced eventually, standing up. 'A heavy blow to the back of the head. But there's more. There are lacerations on his wrists from something like cable ties used to restrain him and he's been hit about the face. I'd say he's been tortured.'

CHAPTER 25

A chill wind chased Pam across the concrete yard of Standish's Farm as she crossed to Jessica Hale's cottage.

'Chris was with Leanne Milner on Tuesday evening,' she said once she was settled in the cosy kitchen.

'The woman from the council?' The young woman sounded more disgusted than upset. 'He was always on about her, how gutted she was when the Paragon project was scrapped last year. And that's who he had sex with on Tuesday?'

Pam nodded. 'They were on their way back to her house when Chris went into the Gardens.'

'Why, though? Why did he get out of the car there? Did she stop the car and *make* him get out?' Jessica rocked herself gently, massaging her bump. 'Was she part of this? Did she set him up? You don't drive off if you've nothing to hide. You don't run away. And where's his laptop? Has she still got it? It's got all his Lydia Bancroft stuff on it, all that work he's been doing…' Her eyes filled with tears. Pam reached out to her, but she shrugged her off. 'No, don't!'

Pam sat back, letting her shed a few angry tears. No sign of her brother today. How would she manage when she had a new baby to look after? The house itself was comfortable enough, but the wide yard outside with its industrial units – most of them apparently vacant – seemed isolated and bleak, and the farm was miles from Tisbury itself.

'When's the baby due?'

'Fourteenth of December, but the first one's often

late, isn't it?' Jessica gazed round her wildly. 'How am I going to cope on my own?'

Pam phoned Lincoln from the car before she left Standish's Farm.

'I've told Jessica about Leanne,' she said. 'You can imagine her reaction. Did you pick up the stuff from Orlando Snell?'

'No, but someone else did. He was dead when we got there – tortured, probably – and the house had been ransacked.'

'Oh God!' She visualised the photos on the whiteboard of Chris Darbyshire and Snell, the crime scene photos of the riverbank. What had Chris stumbled on that someone wanted to keep hidden?

She started the car and reversed a little way before turning. As she glanced in her rearview mirror, she saw Toby Hale watching her from the metal staircase leading down from his first-floor flat. She lifted her hand to acknowledge him, but he didn't respond. As she drove out of the yard, he was opening the front door of his sister's house and going inside.

While Pam was calling on Jessica Hale, DI Tim Anderson was heading to Harry Priest's.

Priest operated out of a former timber merchant's off Finisterre Street. Wooden doors across the entrance to the cobbled yard were pegged open now but were most likely closed after dark, so his white van must have been nicked in daylight. Anderson could see stacks of cardboard boxes and crates on the far side of the yard beneath an overhang, with a bicycle pushed in among them.

To the left, a narrow passageway led to a cabin marked 'OFFICE PRIVATE'. The cabin door opened and a sturdily built man in his late sixties stepped out. He wasn't tall, but he looked as if he lifted weights to keep himself fit – although shifting wooden crates around must have been good exercise.

'Mr Priest? I'm Detective Inspector Tim Anderson. I'm here about your van. Just checking a few details.'

'Sending an *inspector* to "check a few details"?' Priest's tone was scathing. 'Run out of coppers, have they? No little WPCs to send?'

Anderson made a show of looking at his tablet, although he already knew all he needed to know about Harold Peter Priest, born in Brislington in October 1950. 'You bought the van in 2009, correct?'

'If you say so. Had it a long time, yeah. Until those little bastards nicked it.'

'You've got cameras here?' Anderson had spotted them when he came in off the street.

'Yeah, but they've been fucked for a while. They're more for deterrent purposes.'

'Not working, though, are they, in either sense.' Anderson grinned at him, although Priest didn't seem the sort of guy you could share a joke with, not if you were police.

'There's only so much I can do to stop these thieving little bastards from taking advantage.'

'Any idea who took your van?'

'Joy riders, of course.'

'And your van's top speed is…'

'You don't have to drive fast to get your kicks. Sometimes it's enough to nick someone else's property and then destroy it. That's what they wanted, something they could set fire to.'

'Didn't make too good job of it, though, did they? You've seen the photos?'

Priest turned away with a sneer when Anderson scrolled to images of the white van, badly damaged, a write-off, even if parts of it were still intact.

'Can't look at it,' he said. 'That's my livelihood, that van. I'm gonna have to hire one to shift my goods until the insurance company comes good.'

Anderson scrolled through to the photo of a charred trainer. He positioned himself so Priest couldn't easily look away.

'This trainer was in the back,' he said. 'Belongs to Ritchie Payne. He's still missing.'

'Yeah, well, he must've been one of the little tossers who took my van. He's not missing, he's lying low.'

'Doesn't seem the sort of thing he'd get involved in.'

'Who knows what he'd get involved in? I know his grandad and that family's a bunch of losers.'

Anderson scrolled to another image and held his tablet up for Priest to see: Isaac Keats.

The man's first reaction was shock, but then he narrowed his eyes as if he had trouble seeing the screen. 'Who the fuck's that?'

'A boy called Isaac. We found his SIM card in your van.'

'SIM card?'

'Out of his mobile phone. Of course, you buy and sell mobiles, don't you? Maybe that's how it got there.' Anderson went on holding the tablet up, moving it slowly nearer to Priest's face. 'See him better now, Harry? Ring any bells? He went missing, September 2011.'

'You think I'd remember that?'

'You might if you'd bought a mobile phone off him around the time he disappeared. Or if you'd given him a lift in your van, say. Unless you can think how else his SIM card got there.'

Priest pinched his lower lip, shook his head. 'You accusing me of something? Because I don't like what you're suggesting. You got something you want to charge me with, go ahead. Otherwise, fuck off out of it.'

He began to turn away, but then Anderson held up his tablet again, this time with the face of young Bob Greenaway filling the screen – close-shaven head, droopy eyelid, school tie with its small, tight knot. Priest's reaction told Anderson he recognised the boy, twenty-seven years after he'd disappeared.

'Ever been to Swindon, Harry?'

Priest wiped his mouth. 'I go all over – when I've got a fucking van.'

'Remember Bob?' With both hands, Anderson thrust his tablet into Priest's face so he couldn't dodge it. 'Remember him, Harry?'

'This is harassment, this is. I'm a victim of crime. You should be ashamed of yourself, harassing me like this.'

'Where were you Tuesday night, Harry?'

'Home, where d'you think?'

'Anyone to vouch for you?'

'No. I live on my own.'

Anderson tucked his tablet under his arm. He might have provoked a revealing reaction from Priest, but he still hadn't got any hard evidence he could use.

'Wish I could tell you something about who nicked your van,' he said, trying to sound as if he meant it. 'Insurance company playing ball?'

'Not so's you'd notice, but I'll manage. Now, if there's nothing else you want to ask me, kindly leave my yard.'

Anderson leaned towards him and pressed his card against Priest's chest. 'You never know when you'll need to call me, Harry. Anything you can remember, any little thing, I'll be pleased to hear from you.'

And he strode back onto Finisterre Street, more certain than ever that Harry Priest knew more than he was saying.

But now what?

Back at Park Street, he replayed the conversation in his head, certain that Priest's reaction to the photos of Isaac and Bob had given him away. He went in search of someone who might know more about Priest and his business. He tracked down a PCSO called Hayley, whose regular patrol included Finisterre Street.

'He's okay,' she said, clearly relishing a chance to share her local knowledge with this new detective inspector. 'There's always been rumours about where he gets his stuff from but there's no point asking him cos he'll never tell you straight. I tried asking one of the boys once, but he didn't know either.'

'Boys?'

'He's always got a few lads hanging around. They help with the loading and stacking. You often see him in the yard having a brew with two or three of them, like a little tea party, all sitting round on old chairs. Keeps them off the streets.'

'How old are these lads? School age?'

She shrugged. 'Sixteen, seventeen? Excluded, probably, nothing else to do. Expect he slips them some cash for helping him out.'

Anderson tapped a few notes into his tablet. 'Nothing that's ever seemed a bit off to you? Old guy, young lads?'

Another shrug. 'You can read bad things into any relationship like that, but the lads seem happy enough to be round him. There's no coercion, if that's what you mean. And they're sixteen plus – all legal.'

Legal, yes, he thought as he thanked Hayley and went back to his desk, but is it a sign of something more sinister, a man in his sixties hanging out with teenage boys?

He'd requested CCTV footage that might show the van being taken from outside the yard, but he had yet to receive it. If the van had been driven away in daylight, where had it been for those few hours before it picked up Ritchie Payne in Spicer Street that night?

The tech team had tried tracking Ritchie's phone but without success. By now, the battery would be flat. Most likely – if his suspicions were correct – the mobile had been chucked into the dense scrub at Lookout Hill, where the van was found smouldering. From what Lincoln had told him about the terrain, there'd be little chance of finding it.

But if Ritchie had been killed, where was his body? Anderson needed to see Garvin Steele. Judge for himself if he was capable of murder.

Steele was slumped in front of the television when his partner, Iris, let Anderson in.

'I've talked to you lot already,' he grumbled, when Anderson introduced himself.

Anderson nodded at the screen. 'Watched the game, did you?'

'Went to extra time and they still didn't fucking score.' Steele banged his empty lager can down on the coffee table, in among cigarette papers and tobacco. The room wasn't smoky, though. He must smoke outside for the sake of the baby, whose cries came from upstairs.

'Wondering if you'd had any thoughts about where Ritchie Payne might be.'

'Why do you lot think I know where that fucker is?' Steele pitched forward on the sofa and started to roll a cigarette. His fingers were chunky, nails bitten to the quick, yet he made his cigarette with surprising deftness. Lots of practice, probably.

'I'm new here, but I've heard there was some trouble back in the summer between you and a lad who ended up in the river.'

'He drowned.' Steele slid his tongue along the gummed edge of his Rizla, ran his fingers along the finished roll-up to smooth it out before tucking it behind his ear. 'That's what happens when you get drunk and fall into the river. Black people aren't good swimmers, are they? How many d'you see swimming at the Olympics, eh?'

Anderson breathed hard, resisting the temptation to rise to the bait. 'Ritchie Payne got into a white van after he left the pub. Know anyone with a white van?'

'You're fucking kidding me, right? Most of the guys I know, the ones with jobs, they drive white vans. *I* used to drive a white van when I was doing delivering. The van what collects me for work every day? *That's* a white van.'

'This van was nicked from Finisterre Street earlier in the day.' Anderson sat down, transferring a bundle of blue baby clothes from the seat to the arm of the chair. 'Belonged to a guy called Harry Priest. You know Harry?'

'Everyone knows Harry. Hope he gets it back.'

'Someone set fire to it. Covering their tracks, whoever they were.'

'Not surprised.' Steele reached forward to tidy up his stash of Rizlas, fold up his tobacco pouch, pocket his box of matches.

'Wonder how far Ritchie could walk with only one trainer on.' He showed Steele the photo of the blackened trainer left behind in the van.

'The fuck's it got to do with me how far he can walk? Try and pin this on me and you'll look fucking stupid.'

The baby started to wail even louder and Steele shut his eyes, cursing.

'How old is he?' asked Anderson.

'Seven weeks.'

'What's his name?'

'Tyger.'

'Another week or two, he'll be crying a bit less. No wonder you go out most nights. My wife thinks I only took this transfer to get away from our little one.'

'How old's yours?'

'Nearly four months. Dilly.' He heard Tyger's screaming reach a pitch, then cease. 'It gets easier,' he said. 'Trust me.'

'Fuck that.' But Steele said it with a grin.

'Garvin, if you know anything about what happened to Ritchie…'

'You got my statement. I got nothing to add.'

'Okay. Well, thanks for your time.' He left his card on the table next to the Rizlas and stood up. 'Where do you work?'

'Amesbury. Big new development, two hundred-odd houses.'

'You're a brickie?'

'Chippy.' Steele got to his feet, keen to show him out.

At the front door, Anderson turned to see Iris, so much smaller than her partner, sitting on the top stair. Although it was growing dark, she hadn't put the light on, but even in the dark he could see she looked tired. And scared.

CHAPTER 26

Two young men dressed in jeans and hooded anoraks had arrived at Orlando Snell's soon after eleven that morning. The taller of the two had rung the bell and, when Snell had opened the door, had led the way inside. One of them carried some sort of tool bag, big enough to take a hammer or mallet – whatever had dealt Orlando Snell a fatal blow – or to carry away the precious scrapbook of incriminating evidence.

Over an hour later, the security camera over the shop next door picked them up as they made a hurried exit and disappeared out of shot.

'One tall, one short,' said Lincoln as he and Woody reviewed the footage on Woody's screen. 'Just like Darbyshire's attackers. But who are they and who's put them up to it? These two probably weren't even born when Hamilton Vaughn was on the stage.'

'What's in that scrapbook that's so important? Who does it implicate?'

'Vaughn put it together to show that the Board Treaders were making stuff up about him grooming one of them. I suppose he wanted to cover himself if Bill Burnett found out what was going on.'

'It could have backfired,' said Woody. 'Suppose Burnett had refused to believe his sons could be guilty of something like that? He might've involved the police, painted Vaughn as the culprit.'

Lincoln shook his head, at a loss. 'How can we know what was going on nearly thirty years ago – especially now we've lost our key witness, Orlando Snell? We need to talk to these former Board Treaders. What do we know about them?'

Woody checked his notes. 'Cody Burnett's been working in a theatre in Massachusetts since 2010 and, presumably, he's still there, so I reckon we can rule him out.'

'That narrows our suspect pool down a bit. That leaves us with Mitchell Burnett, Nate Newton and Sherilyn Croft.'

'Mitchell's a hot-shot TV personality, as you know…'

'As I've been told.'

'He presents documentaries, does a bit of writing. He's mostly London-based, I reckon, although he's got a house the other side of Barbury, in the Chalke Valley.'

'And Nate Newton?'

'He was in loads of things when he was a teenager, but after a while you only saw him on celebrity things like *Big Brother*. Sherilyn's the same – known more for what she gets up to than for her acting skills.' Woody chuckled. 'I reckon her biggest audience these days is on Instagram.'

'We need to talk to those three as soon as we can.' Lincoln nodded at the screen. 'Have you got a photo of Vaughn there?'

Woody found a photo of Bill Burnett and Vaughn together. Joint managers, toasting Barbury Theatre's golden jubilee in 1987, according to the caption. Until then, Lincoln had only seen newspaper photos of Vaughn in his padded pantomime costume, theatrical make-up and towering wig, but here was a neatly built man with a pleasant, handsome face, curly grey hair and lively eyes – a striking contrast to the unflattering passport photo used in the media reports of his death.

Bill Burnett looked altogether bulkier, with a rugged

face and thick dark hair. Between the two men stood a young woman, identified as Eloise Burnett.

Lincoln read out the rest of the caption. '"Mr Vaughn has put much of his own money into keeping the theatre afloat in these difficult times, but his investment is certainly paying off as profits rise and audiences come back for more." His own money? Don't theatres get grants?'

'Yeah, but grants get cut from year to year, don't they? A theatre can't rely on external funding. Reckon you need to run it like a business. That's why Barbury Theatre does a panto every year – it's a guaranteed money-spinner. Stage a panto for eight weeks and it pays for the riskier plays you produce the rest of the year.'

'So, if Vaughn had enough money to bankroll Barbury Theatre, why was he living in a scruffy bedsit in Inkerman Terrace?'

'Maybe some of the plays didn't perform so well.' Woody beamed at his unintended pun. 'And he'd only be living in the bedsit during the run of the panto.'

Lincoln remembered where he'd seen the photos of Vaughn's bedsit: the newspaper archives he'd consulted at the library. He still hadn't collected the printouts he'd left behind in Trish's office – which made him think of her in a clinch with Steve the Museum Man.

Woody sat back from his keyboard. 'You still think Darbyshire was killed because of what happened to Hamilton Vaughn?'

'I was beginning to doubt it until Orlando Snell was killed, but that scrapbook's obviously central to all of this. Whatever's in it, someone wants to stop anyone else seeing it.'

'You think Lydia Bancroft's in danger?'

'I doubt it. Those thugs probably don't even know

of her existence. I wish we could get more out of her, though.'

Lincoln recalled the frustrating conversation he'd had with her. She'd become very vague about the allegations against Vaughn and had said she'd exaggerated her suspicions about his death simply to get Darbyshire hooked. Had she changed her tune because she was scared? Would the DCI let him go up to London to talk her in person?

'Islington?' The DCI sounded more shocked than angry when he said he'd like to call on Lydia Bancroft in person. 'I need you *here*, Jeff, not zipping off to bloody Barnsbury.'

'It's more like Holloway Road.'

'Speak to the Met, get them to call on her and do a welfare check, if you think the old girl's in danger.'

It had been a difficult week and he could understand her frustration. He felt it too: several leads but very little hard evidence; witnesses who disappeared or got themselves killed.

'I'll get onto the Met,' he said, not surprised that she'd refused his request. 'We need to make sure she's extra cautious about callers.'

'*Who* was Darbyshire going to implicate with this podcast of his? Who cares what these minor celebrities got up to when they were teenagers!'

'*They* might care.'

'Enough to have two men murdered? Sorry, Jeff, I don't buy it. You're saying that one of the Board Treaders paid these bastards to kill Darbyshire and Snell?'

'If you don't want to get your own hands dirty, you find someone who'll do it for you.'

'Stop and think for a moment. If Mitch Burnett paid

some hoodlum to kill a writer working on a podcast about him prick-teasing some old comedian who should've kept his hands to himself, *that* becomes the story. Don't you see how ridiculous your theory is?'

Feeling bruised, he ended the call. He needed to contact the Met, but how would Lydia react if a couple of burly police officers banged on her front door or buzzed her entry phone?

He'd speak to Annie Darbyshire first. She could prepare her aunt before a patrol car rolled to a stop outside her door.

He phoned her a little later and told her, briefly, that Orlando Snell had been found dead, probably killed by whoever killed her husband.

'Oh God! Is it because of what Chris was working on?'

'It looks that way. Orlando showed him a scrapbook that Vaughn put together before he died, but now Orlando's dead and the scrapbook's missing.'

'You think they'll come here?'

He couldn't lie to her. 'It's possible but unlikely. They've got the scrapbook and that may be all they were after. Still, be careful about answering the door without checking who's outside.'

'You've warned Jessica?'

'I will do. There's something else. We've released the name of the woman he was with on Tuesday night. It's Leanne Milner. She works for the council as…'

'Leanne? He was with *Leanne*?' Annie sounded incredulous.

'You know her?'

'Sort of. We talked about getting more students involved in drama, but it didn't come to anything. No funding.' She went quiet, but he could still hear her ragged breathing. 'Where is she now?'

'I can't say at this stage.' And he really couldn't, even if he'd wanted to. 'I just wanted to let you know before it's all over the media.'

"Thank you, I appreciate that. But Leanne! And when Jessica's baby's due in a few weeks. I'm finding it hard to forgive him.'

'Annie, I spoke to your aunt, but she tried to play down the seriousness of what's happened. She may not be in any danger, but I can't take any risks. She's going to get a visit from the Met police, making sure she's okay. Can you phone her, let her know a police car might turn up?'

'She'll love that. No, really, she will. All that attention,' she said, with a soft laugh.

He had visions of Lydia Bancroft reacting like that over-the-hill actress in *Sunset Boulevard*, enjoying the publicity, the flashbulbs exploding around her, even though she was being arrested for murder: Norma Desmond, ready for her close-up.

'Seriously, Annie,' he said. 'Until we catch whoever's doing this, she needs to be careful. You both do.'

CHAPTER 27

A speed camera caught Leanne Milner's Toyota Yaris at eleven fifty-nine on Friday morning as she headed through Bridgeford, ten miles over the limit, but her number plate hadn't been picked up since.

'She must've taken the back road towards Warminster,' said Pam, studying the map on her screen. 'But then what? No way she could've dodged every camera between there and Glastonbury.'

'So where is she?'

Woody was getting ready to go home. 'She could've changed cars.'

Lincoln stared at the whiteboard, his eye caught by the bright white smile of Russ Milner. When Leanne's husband had called him yesterday, he'd imagined him in his mother's house in Glastonbury, but he could've been phoning from anywhere.

'You're right.' He sidestepped to the wall map. 'Supposing Milner drove to meet her near Warminster? She parks her car somewhere out of the way, transfers her stuff into his car and he drives her – where? Back to Glastonbury? Or is she lying low somewhere in between?'

'We need to track his car,' Pam said. 'We've been thinking he's at his mum's, waiting for Leanne, but he'd be doing something, wouldn't he? Going to look for her before we got to her.'

Lincoln rang DS Jenny Reedy to tell her what he thought was going on. 'I'm guessing Russ has picked her up from somewhere, taken her back to his mum's.'

'We'll call on him,' Reedy promised. 'Are you wanting to arrest her?'

'She's done nothing wrong, legally, but we do need to speak to her urgently. I can understand if she's too scared to come forward.'

'Look,' said Pam when he'd come off the phone. 'The Instagram page for his company. Russ Milner showing off his new car.'

Lincoln looked at her screen: Milner leaning against the bonnet of his brand-new Hyundai, arms folded, ankles crossed, smiling, the 67 number plate visible behind his legs. He looked as perfectly groomed as a male model, a handsome man who knew exactly how handsome he was. 'Well spotted! I'll pass the details on to Jenny. Our colleagues in Warminster can look out for the Yaris.'

'Could she have caught a train from there?' Pam wondered. 'Not to Glastonbury, obviously, but to London, maybe? Bath? Bristol? If she's trying to disappear…'

'But she'd have been in greater danger in the days straight after Chris's murder. Why didn't she run away then?'

'She was scared, couldn't think straight.'

At the whiteboard, he stood face to face with Leanne. How much had she known about Darbyshire's podcast? Did she really think he'd been killed by a couple of violent thieves. Or did she know there was more to it?

And would they ever get to ask her what really happened that night?

CHAPTER 28

When he got home, Lincoln fed Tux before flopping into the rocking chair to which he'd treated himself in the summer: vintage Parker Knoll, re-upholstered in corduroy the colour of dark chocolate.

He should feed himself – and not just with Jamesons. But the events of the day had exhausted him. Before he knew it, ringtones roused him from sleep – landline and mobile shrilling simultaneously. Not sure where he'd left his mobile, he reached for the cordless phone, answered groggily, clearing his throat, wiping drool from his chin. How long had he been asleep?

'Bloody hell, Jeff, you sound rough.'

Who the…? He knew the voice, couldn't place it, his head woolly with sleep. And his mobile was still ringing somewhere. He lurched into the hall to track it down.

'I'm sorry, I…' Just as he located his mobile, still in the pocket of the jacket he'd left on the newel post, it stopped ringing.

He turned his attention instead to the caller on the landline. Who was it? And then a memory shook down and fell into place. This was a voice he hadn't heard for nearly twenty years.

Nick. His old friend, Nick Chance.

'He didn't trip over a rake.'

Lincoln struggled out of sleep, roused once more by his mobile ringing. 'Who didn't trip over a what?'

'Dad. Dad didn't trip over a rake. He fell.' Trish sounded angry rather than anxious. 'He had a fall. It's not the first fall he's had, but he's never told anyone until now.'

'I suppose at his age…' He couldn't work out what time it was or even what day. His head throbbed.

'But Jeff, he's not *that* old. And he's always been so fit.'

'Does he black out?'

'He won't talk about it. Suki's going to make him an appointment with the doctor. He probably needs tests. It could be anything.'

'Exactly. It could be anything – a virus, he could need new glasses, maybe his knee gives out.'

'But it's serious.'

'It *could* be serious, Trish, yes. But don't blow it up out of all proportion until you know a bit more. And he won't talk about it if you alarm him with all the awful things it *could* be.' He rubbed his eyes, trying to read the clock on his radio: not far off midnight. Why wasn't she phoning Steve Quilter in the middle of the night to ask advice about Ted?

'I tried you earlier, but you didn't answer.'

'I had a call from an old friend. Must've been the same time you were trying to get hold of me. Bit of a surprise.'

'What old friend?' She sounded suspicious.

'Nick. He was our best man.'

'How d'you mean?'

'At our wedding. Nick was best man when Cathy and me got married. I haven't seen him in, well, in decades. He moved to the States, but he's come over here for a bit. He's in Southampton. Wanted me to meet him while he's here.'

'But you're working. You can't drop everything and rush off to Southampton.'

'He's coming here. To Barbury.'

'Oh.' She went quiet.

'Listen. Trish. Don't worry about your dad until you know a bit more. If *you* worry, *he'll* worry. Wait until he's seen the doctor.' *And then phone Steve*…

'I'm frightened, that's all.'

His turn to go quiet, wishing he could say the right thing, wishing he could be with her. 'When's Kate home?'

'Tomorrow.'

'Trish, the other day, at the library…'

'Yes?'

But he lost his nerve. He couldn't ask about Steve Quilter. It could wait. 'Never mind. Listen, get some rest. Things'll seem better in the morning. There's nothing more you can do for your dad until you know for certain what the problem is. Call me tomorrow.'

She hung up with a half-hearted 'Goodnight'. He was tempted to phone her back but stopped himself in time. No, let her phone Steve. Let Steve Quilter the Miraculous Museum Curator sort out her worries over Ted.

He went downstairs to make himself some coffee, have something to eat.

Sitting in his dimly lit kitchen with two rounds of toast and an over-ripe banana, Lincoln replayed Nick Chance's phone call in his head.

'It'd be great to meet up while I'm in England, Jeff,' Nick had said warmly. 'I don't get over very often so I want to make the most of it.'

'You're still based in Boston?'

'Sure, but we have offices in the UK too, in Southampton. I've been asked to work on a case in your neck of the woods.'

'What sort of case?'

'I'll tell you when I see you. You free tomorrow?'

'Nick, I'm in the middle of a murder investigation.'

Two murder investigations – or was it three? 'But maybe we can meet later in the day?'

'Sure. In a bar someplace? Give me the name and I'll find it.'

Even when they were best friends at the grammar school in Worcestershire, Nick had been a high flyer – university and law school, the pick of jobs in legal firms. When Lincoln and Cathy got married, Nick was about to take up a position in his firm's Boston office. Next time he returned to England, he too was married – to Cathy's friend and bridesmaid Nell. They'd met at the Lincolns' wedding, fallen in love and moved to the States together.

'How's Nell?'

'She's fine. Still over there, looking after the boys, Nick Junior and Sam. They're both in high school.'

Lincoln could hear the transatlantic twang of an Englishman who'd spent a good many years in Massachusetts. He thought of his own big sister, Ruth, long settled in the suburbs of Chicago with husband Reg. When had he last spoken to her? He couldn't remember. A fist-sized lump of clay weighed heavy in his chest.

'Sorry we couldn't get to Cathy's funeral. You got our card?'

Had he? Another life… Lincoln could hardly remember who'd sent their condolences.

'Yes, thanks. So how long will you be over here?'

'As long as this case takes. I'll tell you more when I see you.'

They arranged to meet in the bar of the Black Swan on Sunday evening and then Nick rang off, leaving Lincoln to wonder how he'd got his landline number.

Nick must have done well for himself, even if he'd had to leave England to do so. Did Lincoln envy him?

Of course he did, but he wasn't going to let it get to him. He'd got enough on his plate without comparing himself to the man who'd been his friend longer than anyone else he knew – albeit with a hiatus of nearly twenty years.

Before the past caved in on him, he'd poured himself a consoling glass of Jamesons and taken himself upstairs. He'd put his drink aside, lain down on the bed to shut his eyes for a few minutes and fallen asleep with Tux curled up at his feet – until Trish's phone call woke him at nearly midnight.

Useless dwelling on this kind of stuff now. He locked up and went to bed, only to lie awake into the small hours, wondering where he'd gone wrong, how Nick seemed to have everything while Lincoln had somehow let it all slip away.

SUNDAY 29TH OCTOBER

CHAPTER 29

'Next week in your Messenger: the dead actor and the child star; the sordid story of Hamilton Vaughn's suicide; and the role played in his downfall by one of TV's top-earning personalities.'

Woody looked up from his laptop, aghast. 'Have you seen this? It's on *The Messenger*'s webpage.'

Lincoln read Woody's screen. *The Messenger* claimed to have an album of intimate love letters, secret notes and explicit photos revealing a torrid sex scandal behind the scenes at Barbury Theatre in 1990. The only name it gave was 'the much-loved' Hamilton Vaughn.

'What the hell? How could *The Messenger* have put this story together so quickly? The scrapbook was only stolen yesterday.'

Had those young thugs tortured and killed Orlando Snell so they could sell this material to the newspapers?

'I thought killing Darbyshire and stealing Snell's scrapbook was about *suppressing* this story, not making money out of it.' Disgusted, Lincoln picked up his mug and headed for the kettle. He needed coffee, badly. His brain felt like a wad of wet cottonwool wrapped in barbed wire and he wanted to bang his head against something, anything, to make the pain stop. But what he'd seen on screen had made him feel queasy.

'Is it Karen Bolitho, d'you think?'

'Who else?' Lincoln switched on the kettle and spooned extra coffee and an extra spoonful of sugar into his mug. 'But has she any idea where that album came from? She's handling stolen goods. I'd better go and see her, find out what she's playing at.'

'There won't be anyone at the newspaper offices today, will there? It's Sunday. And don't go by the clock in here. The clocks went back overnight, so it's not ten past ten, it's ten past *nine*. You could've had another hour in bed.'

'Not sure my cat understands the end of daylight saving.'

When he arrived at *The Messenger* offices an hour later, bearing coffee and two Danish pastries, Bolitho bounded down the stairs to let him in, clad in a red tracksuit and trainers. When they reached the untidy open plan office on the first floor, he saw she was completely on her own.

He dumped the coffees down, chucked the bag of pastries onto her desk and pulled out a chair. 'So, how did you get hold of this scrapbook of Vaughn's?'

She peeked inside the bag and pulled out an apple Danish before answering. 'Someone approached me with it.' She chomped hungrily on the pastry, sweeping crumbs off her zipped-up chest as they fell. 'Missed breakfast. Ravenous.'

But he couldn't wait for her to finish eating. 'You know that scrapbook was stolen from Orlando Snell?'

She stopped mid-chomp. 'The guy who was murdered?' Flakes of pastry flew towards him.

'The very same. Whoever took it, killed him.' Not what the DCI had wanted the press to find out, but he was desperate to know how Bolitho had acquired it.

'But that can't be right – I've had that scrapbook since Thursday.'

'Since *Thursday*?' That didn't make sense. Snell was robbed and killed on Saturday. Or did those murdering thugs go away empty-handed? 'Who passed it on to you?'

'I can't disclose my sources.'

'Bollocks!' He glared at her as he took an angry swig of his coffee. She was welcome to the other pastry. He had no stomach for it and his headache was still pounding away inside his skull. 'You're still going to write a story about Hamilton Vaughn, even though that scrapbook was stolen from Orlando Snell? Anything for the sake of a sexy story, eh, Karen?'

She had the grace to look chastened, but not for long. 'Isn't that what Chris Darbyshire was doing? Delving into shenanigans backstage at Barbury Theatre? That was *his* sexy story. Why's that so different from what I'm doing?'

'And see what good it did him. Come on, where did you get the scrapbook? Just tell me who passed it to you.'

'I told you, I…'

'You can't disclose your sources. I get that, but you are obstructing an investigation. Suppose someone else gets killed because of this? Happy to have that on your conscience? Suppose someone comes after *you*?'

Her pastry finished, her coffee cooling, she looked momentarily stunned. She reached out for her drink and took a sip before lifting her gaze to meet his.

'A friend of Orlando Snell's,' she said at last. 'Orlando left it with him. And if he left it with him on Wednesday, then Orlando was still very much alive.'

'Are you going to hand that scrapbook over to me?'

'My editor's got the *Mail on Sunday* interested. He scanned some of the photos and emailed them to someone he knows there.'

'Too bad. Hand it over.'

She reached for the second pastry but then changed her mind about eating it. She patted the bag closed and sat on her desk. 'I can't. It's locked in the safe and only my boss has access.'

'Call him. Get him to come in here. Karen, I need that scrapbook. Call your boss. Get him to open the safe.'

'But I…'

'Can you show me the scans, at least?'

She slid down off her desk and went to her laptop. 'We scanned a selection. Enough to give the *Mail* a flavour, but we kept the best bits.'

'Show me.'

He stood behind her as she brought up scan after scan on her screen: letters written in a childish hand, "I've always thought you were a very nice man…"; a Polaroid photo of a boy of fourteen or fifteen, stripped to the waist and with his hands on the buckle of his belt as if he was about to slip it undone; a typed letter asking for a hundred pounds, "or I'll tell everyone what you've done."

Another photo was of the four young Board Treaders, arms linked, smiles wide, as rehearsals started for *Jack and the Beanstalk*. Someone had written their names above their heads: Mitch, Cody, Simeon, Sherilyn. This photo must have been taken – perhaps by Nate Newton? – before Simeon took that fateful tumble into the orchestra pit.

Yet another shot was of two boys in bed together. It didn't take much imagination to guess what they were doing to each other – or were pretending to be doing. Whatever it was, they were having fun. Two dark-haired boys: Mitchell and Nate.

And there were two very different versions of Hamilton Vaughn, one in his dame costume, the other in his rehearsal gear of V-neck sweater, jeans and baseball boots.

'Put these on a memory stick, please.'

'But what about my story?'

'What about it?' He watched her raking through her drawer for a spare USB drive. 'Ask your legal department where you'll stand if you share this material online or distribute it in print. This is crucial evidence in a murder investigation and you won't even tell me its provenance.'

Bolitho copied the images and documents for him. 'I can't tell you how my contact got hold of it, but he assured me Orlando left it with him.'

Jackson, thought Lincoln. The young man Snell had gone home with the night Darbyshire was killed. Snell had the scrapbook with him when he met Darbyshire in the afternoon. He'd gone on to Carew's, where he'd clicked with Jackson, who told them Ollie had left in a hurry next morning, anxious to avoid a parking ticket. Had Snell left the scrapbook behind in Jackson's flat in his haste?

She ejected the memory stick, held it out to him. 'Here.'

'Kill the story, Karen, before you get yourself and *The Messenger* into trouble. *The Mail on Sunday* can look after itself. I need that scrapbook ASAP. If it can't be today, make it tomorrow. Okay?'

When Lincoln got back to Barley Lane, Woody was studying the wall map.

'Leanne's Yaris has been found abandoned near Boyton.' He jabbed at a narrow road that roughly shadowed the A36 going west. 'Warminster phoned while you were out. Some riders called it in because it was blocking a bridleway.'

'Any sign of Darbyshire's laptop?'

'The car was locked, but they got it open. Nothing inside, nothing in the boot. I called Jenny Reedy to tell her she can stop looking for it.'

'What's the betting Russ Milner drove from Glastonbury on Friday afternoon and picked Leanne up before she reached the main road?'

'Or else she's become another victim.'

Lincoln called Milner, wondering how he'd react to the news that his wife's car had been found abandoned halfway between Barbury and his mother's house.

'She's probably lying low for a day or two,' he said, sounding surprisingly calm. 'She must be worried that Chris's killers are after her too.'

'You can't think where she might have gone to lie low?'

'No, I can't, but I'm sure she'll be in touch as soon as she feels it's safe. I'll let you know as soon as she contacts me.'

Frustrated, Lincoln made himself a coffee and took it back to his desk, knocking back a couple of aspirin to tackle the headache that had settled behind his eyes.

'You saw Karen Bolitho?' Pam was hovering. 'She hasn't been dealing with the killers, has she?'

'No, she got the scrapbook from Jackson, the young bloke Snell spent Tuesday night with. He must've left it behind in Jackson's flat because he was in a hurry to move his car next morning.'

Lincoln thought of the beating Snell suffered, the torture, the shopping bags of new books and clothes emptied onto his floor. If he'd had those bags with him when he went to Jackson's, he probably hadn't even noticed he'd left the most important bag behind – the one containing the scrapbook.

But did he tell his attackers where that bag might be?

'You think they'll go after this Jackson guy?' Dilke asked.

'If they've seen *The Messenger*, they'll know they're too late to get hold of it. Now, let's see what Bolitho's given me.' He transferred the images from the memory stick to his laptop and sat back.

The first scan was of an unsigned note on lined paper: "Dear V, thank you for helping me with my lines last night."

'Sounds innocent enough,' said Woody.

'But then there are these photos.' Lincoln ran through scans of several Polaroids that showed a youth undoing the buttons of his shirt, slipping it off, undoing the belt of his jeans, slipping the jeans down over his narrow hips. He wore a silver identity bracelet, its chunky links catching the light. In one photo, his head was bent, his straight blond hair falling forward over his face: Cody Burnett, fairer-haired than either his brother or Nate.

One scan was of a photo torn from a soft porn magazine: two young men engaged in horseplay on a rumpled bed. Horseplay or foreplay?

Woody groaned. 'Can you imagine the effect on an innocent fifteen-year-old?'

Lincoln was more cynical. 'Assuming we're talking about innocent fifteen-year-olds. These kids allegedly tried to trap Vaughn into making a pass at one of them so they could blackmail him.' He pointed to the scan of a clumsily typed note: "£100 or I'll tell everyone what you've done". 'These scans seem a bit tame, but there must be something in that scrapbook that's a threat to *somebody*. Why else go to such lengths to get their hands on it?'

'Are we sure the guys who turned over Orlando's place and killed him are the same guys who killed Darbyshire?'

'We can't be a hundred percent sure, Pam,' Lincoln said. 'But one of Darbyshire's attackers was tall, the other much shorter. Just like the men in hooded anoraks seen entering and leaving Snell's house. But as to *who* they are…' He shrugged.

'We went over the CCTV from Cranbrook Road,' said Dilke. 'The only possible suspect was a cyclist who got a bit close to Darbyshire's side of the car at the traffic lights. No way of identifying him, though – hood up, head down – and he could be perfectly innocent.'

'What about the other end of Cranbrook Road?' Pam asked. 'Did we look for CCTV along there, or doorbell cameras?'

'Of course we looked.' Dilke was defensive. 'There were no houses near enough to the road.'

'What about those flats – Ebbesbourne House? They back right onto Cranbrook Road.'

'Yes, Pam, they do, but they're still some distance away,' Lincoln said. 'No one in those flats is likely to have spotted something going on down in the street, especially that late at night.'

'Shouldn't we check, though?' she persisted. 'We didn't include them in the house-to-house, did we?'

Lincoln had to concede it might be worth doing, but would the DCI agree? It would mean deploying more uniforms than she'd want to spare, especially with so many officers committed to the search for Ritchie Payne.

'Reckon we can rule out the ground and first floors,' said Woody. 'The boundary wall must block the view of the street and Coronation Gardens.'

'Start on the top floor and work down, then,' said Dilke. 'People with top floor flats must have the best view. Some of them might even have binoculars. You could watch birds on the water meadows from those flats.'

The phone interrupted them. Jenny Reedy from Avon and Somerset told them Russ Milner's car hadn't triggered any ANPR cameras since Thursday. If he'd picked Leanne up on Friday, he must have been driving a different car – or someone else picked her up.

CHAPTER 30

'It's great to see you, Jeff.' Nick Chance was studying Lincoln's face as if assessing how the years had treated him.

When he'd arrived at the Abbey Bar of the Black Swan a few minutes after six, Lincoln had been afraid he wouldn't recognise his old friend and best man, but the moment he caught sight of him, with his coarse dark hair and strong jaw, arching eyebrows and long nose, he knew it was Nick.

After the requisite exchange of small talk, Nick leaned in, looking earnest.

'I guess I should tell you why I'm over here.'

'A case in this neck of the woods, you said on the phone.'

'More a kinda damage limitation exercise.' Nick put both hands round his glass and stared at them. 'I've been engaged by Cody Burnett.'

'Cody Burnett? But isn't he in the States?'

'He's been over here since August, spending a few months working with the new guy at Barbury Theatre. But then he heard someone was writing about some actor he knew from way back, asking questions, digging up dirt, and he kinda got alarmed.'

'Hamilton Vaughn?'

'You've heard of him? Cody's a buddy of mine so he asked me for my professional help. And here I am. I can tell you now, he had nothing to do with what happened to that guy, nothing at all. But some screenwriter's got hold of the story and…' He stopped when Lincoln tutted and sighed. 'What?'

'That screenwriter was Christian Darbyshire – and he's dead. Murdered on Tuesday night.'

'You're kidding me,' Nick sank back, deflated. 'This writer guy was *murdered*?'

'Possibly because of what he'd found out about Vaughn's death.'

'No way.'

'What's Cody afraid of, if he had nothing to do with what happened to Vaughn all those years ago?'

'Cody's got a solid reputation in theatre on both sides of the Atlantic. He wants his name kept out of it. He can't have armchair detectives creating mischief for the sake of a TV show.'

'It was a podcast, Nick. Chris was working on a podcast.'

'TV show, podcast, whatever. It's defamation.'

'Defamation? It's gone way beyond that. I'm the senior investigating officer on the case. Unfortunately for you and Cody, he and his brother and Nate Newton and Sherilyn Croft are all suspects. Darbyshire was silenced to protect someone's reputation, to stop this story coming out about them setting Vaughn up, trying to implicate him as a paedophile.'

'You don't know that's why Darbyshire was killed.'

'Not for sure, no. But those kids pulled a stupid stunt that probably made Vaughn take his own life. Darbyshire was investigating that, which makes it the most likely motive for his murder, so I have to investigate it too.'

'So you've set your sights on Cody and his brother? And then you'll make the facts fit your theory?'

'Come on, Nick, that's not how I work.'

'That's how it sounds to me. You're saying the only suspects are four people who were kids at the time all this was going down?'

'I can't talk about an ongoing investigation.'

'Come on, Jeff, I'm your oldest friend.'

'And you're representing one of the suspects in a murder case. Friendship doesn't come into it. It can't.' Lincoln hated the way this was going. Here he was, meeting Nick for the first time in years and they were arguing. About work, for God's sake. 'It's too late, anyway.'

'Too late for what?'

'Too late to keep this quiet. The local press has got hold of the story, and possibly a national tabloid, so if your fight is with anybody, Nick, it's with them, not me.' Lincoln banged his glass down and stood up. 'This meeting's over, okay?'

And he strode out of the Abbey Bar.

Lincoln raced back through rainy streets to his car. He shouldn't have told Nick that the four Board Treaders were all suspects. Too late now.

He'd go back to Barley Lane and put in a few more hours. On his way, he stopped at a petrol station to buy a sandwich – the last one in the chiller, half-price, yesterday's sell-by date – and a packet of peanuts. Trish would despair of him, but at least the sandwich had tomatoes in it, or a half of one.

Pam was still at her desk, though she looked as if she was about to knock off. 'The DCI rang a few minutes ago, boss. She's been trying to get hold of you, but you weren't answering.'

Lincoln sat at his desk and prised open the sandwich packet. A rancid smell rose from it and, with a muttered 'Bugger!', he chucked it in the bin.

At least he still had the peanuts.

He checked his phone: airplane mode. He'd switched it over while he was talking to Nick. He switched it back and phoned Connors as he watched his inedible sandwich slowly slide deeper into the rubbish.

'At last,' Connors said. 'DCS Youngman wants an update, Jeff, and I'm damned if I know what to tell him after this garbage appeared on *The Messenger* website. It's Karen Bolitho, isn't it? Christ, that woman's a fucking liability.'

'Someone got hold of Snell's scrapbook days ago and offered it to her. She put that teaser on the website before she found out Snell was dead.'

'You've got it back?'

'Not yet, but I should be able to get hold of it tomorrow morning.'

'I want you *here* tomorrow morning, Jeff. Send DS Woods to pick up the scrapbook. I'm sure you're not the only one who can charm Karen Bolitho into doing the right thing. I need an update in person from you and Tim Anderson so I can tell the DCS we're making progress. *Please* tell me you're making progress.'

'We're making progress.'

Could she tell he was lying through his teeth?

Trish rang as Lincoln was getting out of the car. He locked it and started towards his house. He really must get round to installing better outside lights.

'Jeff, are you avoiding me?'

'Of course not.' He patted his pocket for his door keys. Lying through his teeth again. Steve Quilter with his arms around her in her office.

'You said to phone you.'

'I did?'

'Yes, when I called you last night. I've still got those printouts. You said you'd be in for them.'

'Sorry, Trish, things are manic at the moment. Juggling

two cases, three cases… Christ, I've even lost count of how many bloody cases we're working here. Hang on.' He tripped on the edge of the step, thudding into his front door shoulder first. He let himself in, switched on some lights and headed for the kitchen, glad to be home at last. Happy to see that his bottle of Jamesons wasn't quite empty. 'You okay?'

'Suki thinks Dad's got Parkinson's, but we can't get him an appointment till the week after next.'

'She may be jumping the gun a bit. There are other things it could be.'

'I'm so scared of losing him. Kate's staying an extra night at her dad's. You want to come over?'

Of course he did, but what about Steve the Museum Man?

'I would, Trish, but I've had one hell of a day. I'll give you a ring tomorrow. And whatever's the matter with your dad, there'll be things they can do.'

'You think so?'

'Yeah, of course.' He didn't have a clue what he was talking about. 'I'm sure.'

MONDAY 30TH OCTOBER

CHAPTER 31

Monday morning in the conference room at Park Street nick.

'So what's the latest?' said DCI Claire Connors at the head of the table, with Lincoln and Tim Anderson on either side. The polished surface of the table reflected the can of diet Coke that she had placed close to her notepad and phone. 'You first, Tim.'

Ritchie's phone had been found, turned off, in his bedroom, forgotten when he went out to the Brewery Tap.

'We've got two guys on CCTV jumping into Priest's van outside his yard that morning,' Tim said triumphantly. 'They drive away as if it was sitting there ready for them.'

He played the footage: two young men of average height, athletic build, in tracksuit bottoms and hooded sweatshirts with sleeveless puffa jackets on top. Neither resembled Orlando Snell's attackers.

'But where was the van until it picked Ritchie up at nearly ten that night?' Lincoln asked. 'Do we know?'

Anderson shrugged. 'Somewhere without camera coverage. Priest doesn't have an alibi for Tuesday night. Says he was home alone, no one to vouch for him.'

'He lives over the shop?'

Anderson glanced at his notes. 'No, ma'am, Barbury Hill Avenue.'

'Nice address,' said Lincoln. 'Big, detached houses.'

Anderson grinned. 'Not white-van-man territory, then.'

Lincoln grinned back. 'Only for deliveries. A bloke like Harry must lower the tone.'

'He's owned that van since 2009, so if anyone knows how Isaac Keats's SIM card got dropped in his van, it's him.'

Connors rapped her Coke can on the table top. 'Are we taking our eye off the ball here, guys? Nothing points to Harry Priest being involved in Ritchie's disappearance. His van was nicked by a couple of lads who persuaded Ritchie to let them give him a ride and then they tried to torch it. Unless Ritchie's hobbling around with only one trainer on, I think we can assume something bad has happened to him.'

Anderson sucked his cheeks in. 'Your point being, ma'am?'

'My point being that you're concentrating on Priest because of this possible – *possible* – connection to an abduction six years ago and an even earlier one in 1990. Screw Harry Priest! We need to focus on these lads who picked Ritchie up on Tuesday night and drove off with him. Who are they? Does anyone recognise them? Yes, we've only got piss-poor CCTV images but that could be enough to get someone phoning in. You need to get those images out there now.'

Chastened, Anderson closed his tablet. 'I'll get that sorted.' He ran his hand over his hair, stood up and strode out of the conference room, leaving Lincoln and Connors staring at the table top.

'Got some better news, Jeff?' The Coke can was empty and she pushed it aside impatiently.

'We're checking into the background of the four kids from the theatre, the Board Treaders. Chris Darbyshire got Cody Burnett rattled enough to seek legal advice and I'm guessing the other three have been getting nervous too.'

'Nervous enough to take out a contract on Darbyshire? Nervous enough to have Orlando Snell tortured and killed?' She sounded sceptical, but it was the only lead he had.

'Maybe there's more to it than we realise.' He described some of the images Karen Bolitho had copied for him. 'There's probably stuff in that scrapbook that spells out what those kids were up to. They knew Vaughn was gay, that he'd given Cody a lot of attention. They tried to trap him into making a pass at him. Maybe they took compromising photos of them together, who knows? And then they blackmailed him.'

'This is the honey trap you told me about? I find it hard to believe a guy like Mitchell Burnett would get involved in a plot to kill Darbyshire, no matter what the motive.'

'He may not be involved, but at this stage we can't rule him out. Someone wanted to silence Darbyshire. Someone was desperate to get their hands on that scrapbook. And until his laptop turns up, we won't know what else Darbyshire had found out.'

'And you think the Milner woman's got the laptop?'

He nodded. 'Or she could've left it at her house.'

'Then let's get a search warrant. You said Cody Burnett had sought legal advice. How did you find out about that?'

'I know the man he turned to.'

She cocked her head, quizzical. 'A conflict of interest?'

'None at all, ma'am.'

She shoved her chair back, got to her feet, grabbed the empty Coke can, her notepad and phone. 'Keep me posted, Jeff. I'll tell DCS Youngman something positive, but you know I don't like having to lie.'

As he was leaving via the incident room, Lincoln

paused by Anderson's desk as power tools screamed in the background. The young DI was staring fixedly at his screen.

'How do you work with all this going on around you?'

Anderson sat back and looked up at him. 'With difficulty.'

'The DCI's got Youngman breathing down her neck, Tim. That's why she's so prickly. Personally, I think you're onto something with these older cases, but you can see why she wants us to focus on what's in front of us now.'

'You know what's top priority here? Granite worktops.'

'Granite…?'

'Some guy in Folly Hill, name of Fogarty, is having his house gutted and refitted. Went to check on the building work yesterday, found the whole kitchen missing.'

'The whole kitchen? What, you mean ripped out?' Lincoln wanted to laugh, but Anderson's pained expression stopped him.

'No, he'd done that with his *old* kitchen. This was all the new stuff – units, worktops, electrics, appliances, floor tiles, all boxed up ready for installation.'

'Ready for someone to nick them, you mean? An inside job? A contractor tipping someone off?'

'Fuck knows! But some of the guys here are working on *that* instead of looking for Ritchie Payne.'

Lincoln clapped him on the shoulder. 'Stick to what you're doing. Never mind the rest of it. And you'll send out the CCTV of the white van crew? The blokes Ritchie went with?'

Anderson grinned. 'Don't *you* start!'

'Russ Milner called,' Pam told him when he got back.

He headed for the kettle and switched it on. 'Leanne's turned up?'

'She sent him a text.'

'She *texted* him?' The kettle switched itself off again. He glared at it, switched it back on. It switched itself off.

'There's no water in it,' Pam said. 'The kettle. It's turning itself off because there's no water in it. It's a safety feature.' She leaned round him to lift it off its base. 'I'll fill it up.'

'He got a text last night around nine,' she said, returning. She hovered close as if she didn't trust him to make himself coffee without supervision. He had a pleasant, if fleeting, sense of being looked after, of being taken care of. 'She said she's fine, she's sorry, she's got to go away for a bit and not to worry.'

'No clue as to where she's gone?'

'He sounded as mystified as the rest of us. He's heading back to Barbury so the kids can be at home while everything's so uncertain. He was leaving after he'd rung here.'

'We should be able to catch him when he gets back.'

'Why wait till Sunday night to text him?' she wondered. 'Leanne must've known he'd be worried sick when she didn't turn up at Glastonbury on Friday afternoon.'

'Woody not back from *The Messenger*?'

'He only left a few minutes ago,' Breeze said.

'He'd better get there in time.' Lincoln had visions of Karen Bolitho's editor refusing to surrender the stolen scrapbook and sending it off to *The Mail On Sunday*.

'I've started looking into Nate Newton,' Breeze went on. 'His dad was done for armed robbery thirty years ago and did ten years. Nearest thing Nate had to a father figure when he was a kid was his uncle, Dave Newton.'

'*The* Dave Newton? Presford Motors?' Lincoln's interest was piqued. Dave Newton was a career criminal of some distinction locally. He'd rarely got caught, a man cut from the same cloth as Pete Doubleday, with whom Lincoln had had several run-ins over the last few years but who now resided out of reach, in Spain.

Dave's car dealership had made him rich, but for every twenty sound vehicles he sold, there'd be a dodgy one – cut-and-shut or stolen or both. Lincoln had never understood how he got away with it.

'Yep,' said Breeze. '*That* Dave Newton. He'd certainly have the means to do over Darbyshire and Snell if Nate asked him to.'

'And Nate's motive?' Lincoln was drawn to the whiteboard and the photo of a young Nate. With his cheeky grin and lopsided fringe, he looked like a fugitive from a boy band.

'He's done okay for himself in the last few years. Married, settled down. His little girl's starring in some kids' show that's coming out soon. Wouldn't want to jeopardise all that, would he? Which would give him a motive for getting Darbyshire silenced.'

'Good work, Dennis.' Lincoln could hardly wait to slap a mugshot of Dave Newton on the whiteboard. 'See what you can come up with on Uncle Dave, then. It's a start.'

He caught sight of the clock. Russ Milner would be well on his way home to Barbury by now.

He turned to Pam. 'Coming with me to the Milners'? We need to find that laptop.'

They arrived just as Milner's Hyundai drew up, three leggy teenagers spilling from it as soon as the handbrake went on – two boys and a girl, dark-haired like their mother.

Milner regarded Lincoln and Pam warily as he

climbed out of the car. Slim, brown-haired, not quite as tall as Lincoln and a few years younger, he gave them a curt nod as Lincoln did the introductions.

'Have you found her?'

Lincoln shook his head. 'Not yet, I'm afraid. We're here to look for Chris's laptop. It wasn't in your wife's car, so there's a chance it's still here.'

He looked put out. 'Didn't you trust me to look after it if I found it?'

'It's routine, Russ, nothing to do with whether or not we trust you.'

'We'll be discreet,' Pam promised.

'Sorry. This is a living nightmare. I'm trying to stay upbeat for the kids' sake, but it's getting harder to pretend everything's going to be okay.' Without another word, Milner strode down the path to let his sons and daughter into the house.

Lincoln and Pam worked quickly, leaving the family in the small front room while they searched, starting with the main bedroom. Leanne had clearly left in a hurry, frantically grabbing anything she needed, not bothering to shut drawers or cupboards as she went.

Nothing turned up in the boys' bedroom, but Pam found Darbyshire's khaki holdall in a linen cupboard in their sister's room. Lincoln hoped the laptop was inside, but the ease with which she lifted the bag up told him it probably contained only some unused overnight essentials: toothbrush and deodorant, a change of underwear and a clean shirt, a phone charger.

'Look.' Pam nodded towards a row of framed photos on a low shelf: the Milner children with an older woman and two sheepdogs, Glastonbury Tor in the background. 'A Land Rover.'

'His mother's?'

'Must be. I'll make a note of the reg.'

'I'll get back to Jenny Reedy, see if she can find out where it's been the last few days.' He could already hazard a guess: the Land Rover had driven to Boyton, picked Leanne up and taken her somewhere in or near Glastonbury.

'You haven't heard anything more from Leanne, Russ?'

They'd finished their search and were standing beyond the teenagers' earshot.

Milner shook his head. 'I hope and pray she hasn't done anything stupid.'

'Can you access her card transactions?' asked Pam. 'That would tell us where she's taken money out or paid for things.'

'We've got separate accounts. I can't get at them without her passcodes and they'll all be on her phone.'

'Any idea who picked her up from Boyton? A friend or relative she might have trusted?'

A shrug. 'I'm sure she'll be in touch when she's ready.'

Lincoln's patience ran out. 'We can't wait until Leanne feels she's *ready*, Russ. She witnessed a murder, or at least the events leading up to it. Until we've spoken to her, we have no idea what made her stop her car by Coronation Gardens. This whole case is hanging on what she can tell us.'

Russ backed away from Lincoln's anger. 'I'll keep texting her, try to get her to come home.'

'If she's afraid to come back, Russ, tell her we can protect her. But unless she agrees to talk to us, she's on her own.'

'Got the laptop?' Breeze looked up from his keyboard, a bacon bap resting on a paper bag next to his mouse pad.

'No,' said Pam, pulling her chair out and dropping into it, despondent. 'But we've got Chris's holdall. From the state of her bedroom, Leanne must've left in a hurry on Friday. Everything was in a mess.'

'But not like it had been turned over,' Lincoln added, thinking back to the state of Orlando Snell's house.

'Cuh,' said Breeze. 'My fiancée rang 999 one night when she heard someone trying the door of her flat. Uniform comes in, looks around. "Oh, and you've been burgled too," he says, and Rosie goes, "No, it's always like this."' He chuckled. 'Messy cow, my Rosie. There was that time she...'

'Woody still not back?' Lincoln cut in. He tried not to look at the accusatory whiteboard as he made his way to his desk, but it lured him back. Thanks to Breeze, Dave Newton's mugshot now adorned it.

'He phoned a few minutes ago to say he was starting back.'

'Who *actually* killed Darbyshire?' Lincoln asked, without expecting an answer. 'And how do we find out without Leanne bloody Milner?'

'I've been looking into the Burnett brothers' background,' said Pam. 'Their mother was American so they've got joint British and American citizenship. Cody's been living abroad for the last few years, working at a theatre in Boston, so I haven't been able to find out much about him. Mitchell, on the other hand...'

'The famous TV presenter,' said Lincoln. 'So famous I'd never heard of him.'

'Well, if you bought yourself a television, boss.' She grinned. 'He's into history too, not just a pretty face. Plenty of interviews saying much the same: loves history, enjoys being in front of the camera, wanted to make his mum proud. His dad, Bill, wanted him to follow him into theatre management, but Mitchell didn't fancy all the admin. Was married to a writer, Roz Ryan, but they divorced two years ago. He's got a flat in London and a place in the Chalke Valley.'

'We'll need to speak to him,' Lincoln started to say, but then Woody barged in with a padded envelope the size of a sofa cushion. Inside was the famous scrapbook.

Woody dumped it on his desk and shrugged his way out of his parka before opening the envelope with care. 'It's not really a scrapbook,' he said, easing it out. 'It's a big ring-binder with photos and papers in plastic sleeves so you can take them out. I was expecting everything to be stuck down like a *proper* scrapbook, but it's not.'

They all looked at the glossy ring-binder lying tantalisingly on the desk.

Lincoln rolled his sleeves up. 'So, let's see what we've got.'

CHAPTER 32

PC Darren Buckle trudged up the stairs to the top floor of Ebbesbourne House – the old hospital transformed into flats. He'd have used the lift, but he'd had a bit of a thing about lifts ever since his mum took him to House of Fraser to get some new pyjamas when he was five or six and the lift got stuck between floors. Twenty-odd years on, he still preferred the stairs if he had the choice.

He'd lost count of how many flights he'd gone up and down doing this house-to-house today, but it made a change from his usual routine and he'd been invited in for a cup of tea twice, once with biscuits.

Not one of the residents had seen anything on the night of the murder. Well, you wouldn't, would you? It was a filthy night, chucking it down. He remembered the rain because he'd been out in it, picking up a couple of druggies in Jubilee Park with Jezza, waiting for paramedics to turn up because the girl had obviously overdosed or taken something she wasn't used to. The fella was fine. Off his head, but you'd expect that. He was shit scared about the girl and had begged a passer-by to call someone. The old lady – no mobile, of course, out in the rain walking her three sausage dogs – had flagged down their patrol car.

Neat timing, that, him and Jezza driving by at just the right moment. And the paramedics had got there in time to save the girl. Of course, she'd probably go and do the same thing again. That's the trouble with addiction. No matter what the risks, you'll always do it again because *not* doing it is even worse than nearly killing yourself.

He knocked on the door at the end of the landing. No answer, although he could hear movement inside, he was sure. Knocked again. Waited. A rustling, like someone trying to be really, really quiet until he went away.

He moved on to the next door. The woman who lived there invited him in, offering him tea or coffee, but he declined. He'd rather get on and finish this landing.

'I bet *he* hasn't opened his door, has he?' She tilted her greying head towards her neighbour's flat. 'He never lets anyone in. No visitors. I sometimes hear the phone ringing, but he never answers it, lets the answerphone take it. I haven't exchanged two words with him in all the months he's been here.'

Darren casually cast his gaze around the flat as he asked his set of questions and waited for the woman – Teresa, her name was – to reply. He wandered over to the window that overlooked Cranbrook Road, Coronation Gardens and the water meadows beyond, with Barbury Abbey in the distance. Quite a view!

'I like to watch the seasons change,' she was saying. 'All the different birds in the water meadows. And look at the colour of those trees, reds and yellows, so pretty. *Him,* though, him next door, he's out on his balcony at *night*, would you believe? What does he think he can see at *night*? He's got binoculars, but you can't see anything in the dark, can you? Binoculars or not.'

'You can get night-vision binoculars. What d'you think he's looking at, then, at night?'

Teresa made a disapproving face. 'There's always talk of goings-on in the Gardens after dark, but you'd have to be a pervert if you wanted to stand and watch all that going on, wouldn't you?' She held Darren's gaze as she seemed to realise what she'd said. She shuddered. 'Oh, I'm not living next door to a *pervert*, am I?'

CHAPTER 33

The only surface big enough to lay out the contents of Vaughn's ring-binder was a trestle table used for Christmas buffets in the days when Barley Lane had a full complement, including uniformed constables, a desk sergeant and three clerical assistants.

Those days were long gone, but the table remained, folded up and stored behind the door in the walk-in stationery cupboard. Now erected for the first time in years, it was ideal for spreading the contents of the scrapbook Orlando Snell had left in Jackson's flat and that Jackson had sold to *The Messenger.*

Letters, notes, photographs, press cuttings, everything was in chronological order, starting with a rehearsal timetable dated October 16th,1990. Rehearsals began on Saturday October 20th. The Board Treaders rehearsed only at the weekends, until a week before the panto opened, when they were expected to be at rehearsals every afternoon after school.

Lincoln recognised some of the items from the scans Karen Bolitho had shown him, but he hadn't realised how much material there was.

'The Polaroids are dated,' Woody pointed out. 'It's printed on the edge: November 13th, 1990.'

He tipped them out of the plastic sleeve. About twenty faded photos, once bundled together with a rubber band, which had since perished and given way. They formed a sequence, a slow, provocative striptease by a fair-haired teenage boy whose face remained obscured in all but two photos. In the background, costumes hung from a clothes rail beside a big mirror surrounded by bare lightbulbs.

'Reckon that's a dressing room at Barbury Theatre,' Woody said.

'And that must be Cody.' Lincoln noted the boy's androgynous good looks, his floppy fair hair and dark eyelashes. His body was lightly muscled, his skin clear and smooth. A chunky silver identity bracelet hung from his bony wrist. 'Snell said Vaughn had taken a particular interest in him.'

Pam read out two of the scribbled notes slipped into another sleeve: '"Dear Mr V, Thank you for going over my lines with me yesterday. How can I pay you back?"; "Dear Mr V, What can I do to make up for the time you spent helping me yesterday? I'll do anything." Underlined.'

'If Bill Burnett had found one of these little notes and thought Vaughn was trying to seduce his son,' Lincoln said, 'he'd have fired him on the spot, might even have involved the police. It's as if Cody – or whoever it is – is inviting Vaughn to make a move.'

'Entrapment.'

'Yes.' Lincoln picked up the Polaroids. 'Look at these photos. No one had camera phones in those days, so these aren't selfies, are they? If Cody didn't take these, who did? Vaughn? Mitchell? They'd have needed a Polaroid camera.'

Woody frowned at the pictures. 'Karen Bolitho seems to have taken it all at face value. She thinks Vaughn was a sexual predator putting pressure on Cody and the other boys to pose for him.'

'Does that look like a kid who's having pressure put on him?' Lincoln chucked the photos down. 'That's a kid who knows *exactly* what he's doing. And what about these two?' He nodded towards half a dozen pictures of Mitchell and Nate apparently pleasuring each other under carefully arranged bedsheets. 'I don't detect much coercion in those shots.' He sighed, impatient. 'We could spend from now until Christmas trying to guess what went on behind the scenes at that pantomime, but why waste time doing that? We need to talk to all these former Board Treaders.'

'But Cody's in the States, isn't he?' said Pam.

'He's back in England, keen to stop whatever spin Chris Darbyshire was going to put on this. If we could only…'

He was interrupted by the phone ringing: DCI Claire Connors.

'We've got a witness to Chris Darbyshire's murder,' she said. 'You'd better get over here ASAP.'

'Could be the break we need,' Connors said as she met Lincoln in the corridor at Park Street. 'He didn't see the actual attack, but he saw the car being ambushed. The house-to-house threw him up.'

'What's he been charged with?'

'Threatening behaviour. Tried to break down the door of his neighbour's flat after she told Daz Buckle, the constable going door-to-door, that he stood on his balcony at night with binoculars. Luckily, Daz heard the commotion from the landing below and went back upstairs. Name's Ian Wilkinson and he's got a history.' She thrust a folder at him. 'He's all yours.'

'Hello, Ian.' Lincoln took his seat in the hot and airless interview room. Ian Wilkinson was fifty-seven, unmarried and unemployed. Two pairs of night-vision binoculars lay in separate evidence bags on the table in front of him. 'Now then, what do you use these binoculars for?'

'Seeing things in the dark.'

'What sort of things?'

'Wild animals. Foxes. Badgers.' He didn't look overweight, but he had the soft pudginess of someone who ate badly and rarely took exercise. His hair was greasy and reached his shoulders. He kept tucking it behind his ears. 'Squirrels.'

'Squirrels?'

'Yeah, squirrels. Is there a law against it?'

Lincoln skimmed Wilkinson's history. 'You've done this kind of thing before, I see. Bit of a voyeur, aren't you? You've been cautioned in the past for looking in car windows at courting couples. What was that all about?'

'That was tarts, that was, and I wasn't doing any harm. They like to be watched. But I don't do that anymore. Don't go out much now.'

'What can you see from your balcony? Cranbrook Road? Coronation Gardens? *That's* why a police officer was banging on your door, Ian, not because your neighbour complained about you. He was banging on *everyone's* door because we want to know if anyone saw what happened on Tuesday night. You know a man was murdered in the Gardens? You heard about that?'

Wilkinson nodded. 'Didn't see what happened though. Well, not exactly.' He picked at a grubby thumbnail. 'I saw a car stop and somebody get out, but it was pissing down.'

'Did you see *why* the car stopped?' Lincoln didn't dare hope this unprepossessing man might have the answers they needed.

'Someone ran out in front of it. Small fella, skinny little fucker. Ran out in the road and banged on the bonnet, yelling something. I couldn't hear, of course, too far away, but he's shouting and pointing towards the river and the car pulls into the kerb and the passenger, biggish bloke, gets out and goes after him into the Gardens.'

'And then what?'

Wilkinson shrugged indifferently. 'Lost interest. The Gardens are all dark, aren't they? There's lamps all along the path, but they don't fucking turn them on. Money-saving? Penny-pinching, more like. Nothing to see, so I went back inside.'

'Did anyone else get out of the car?'

He shook his head.

'And how long were you watching for? Five minutes? Ten?'

'Five minutes. I waited for someone to come back out of the Gardens, only no one did. And then I thought, if they've had to call an ambulance, if it's someone gone into the water, I could be stood here half an hour. If I'd seen blue lights, I'd have gone back out and watched what happened, but I wasn't going to stand there on the balcony freezing my bollocks off.'

'No, of course not.'

'I filmed it.'

'What?'

'I film what I'm watching if I want. I filmed that.'

'You've got a camera too?'

Wilkinson scoffed at Lincoln's ignorance. 'The *binoculars* film it. There's a card inside.' He studied the two pairs of binoculars in front of him, jabbed the pair on the right. 'That's the ones I was using that night. The WULF ones.'

Before he returned to Barley Lane, Lincoln stopped by Tim Anderson's desk.

'How's it going?'

‘Still no trace of Ritchie Payne and it’s been nearly a week since he disappeared. But I found something interesting.’ Anderson reached for a folder on his desk, the old case of his father’s. ‘Bob Greenaway disappeared in Swindon in 1990, but from 1987 to 1989, he was living in Barbury. His adoptive parents were having marital problems, so he was put into foster care until they got their shit together.’

‘What are you getting at?’

‘Bob was living in Barbury from age thirteen to age fifteen. He could’ve met Harry Priest.’

‘I thought the DCI…’ Lincoln waved at the Greenaway file. ‘Not relevant, she said. Tim, if she thinks you’re working on this instead of looking for Ritchie Payne…’

‘I can do both,’ Anderson said calmly. ‘I can do both.’

CHAPTER 34

Lincoln handed Graham Dilke the memory card from Ian Wilkinson's binoculars.

'Pam was right – it was worth checking Ebbesbourne House after all. A bloke on the top floor saw a lot of what happened on Tuesday night. It's all on there.'

Dilke took the card from him and, a minute later, a sequence of three video files popped up on his screen. The first two were too grainy and dark to make anything out, but the third showed traffic passing slowly along a rainswept Cranbrook Road. From time to time, Wilkinson had tried to focus on Coronation Gardens but without success, so he'd returned his binocular gaze to the road.

And then a slightly built man in a hoodie rushed out in front of a car – Leanne's Yaris – slapping the bonnet and forcing her to stop. He was waving his arms wildly, pointing towards the Gardens, appealing for help. Darbyshire jumped out of the car and jogged after him as he disappeared into the darkness. Leanne pulled her car over so traffic could pass her. After a further two minutes filming the stationary Yaris, the video stopped.

'That's it?' said Breeze.

'Wilkinson got bored waiting for something to happen and went back indoors.'

'At least we know why Leanne stopped the car,' said Dilke. 'That guy didn't leave her much choice, the way he ran out. Darbyshire must've thought someone had fallen in the river.'

'See what happens when you play the Good

Samaritan.' Breeze stared glumly at the screen.

Pam was staring too. 'The one running out in front of the car – it couldn't be a woman, could it? A girl? Something about the way they move…'

'It's so grainy,' said Dilke, 'and happens so fast, but yeah, it could be.'

'Damsel in distress,' Breeze muttered. 'Works every time.'

'If we assume this was all a set-up,' Lincoln said. 'A stunt to get Darbyshire out of the car and into the Gardens, how did they know when Leanne would be driving past? It's as if they knew exactly where the car would be.'

'Comes back to her being in on it, doesn't it?' Breeze glanced at Pam as if expecting her to defend Leanne, but she didn't even try.

'Or…' Woody stroked his moustache thoughtfully. 'Or there was a third person involved.'

'A third person?' Lincoln groaned. Wasn't it complicated enough?

'Someone follows Darbyshire and Leanne from her house, sees where she parks before they go to Pizza Marino. Waits around, follows them back to the car and then tails them along Cranbrook Road. He tips the attackers off so they're ready to stop the car and get Darbyshire into the Gardens.'

'Then we're looking for *three* suspects.' Lincoln turned to the whiteboard. It was getting so crowded there'd soon be standing room only. 'Graham, go back over the CCTV you and Dennis got from Cranbrook Road. Look out for a car that's tailing the Yaris. And yes, I know it was a filthy night with crap visibility but look again.'

Breeze nodded, then reached for a plastic sleeve containing pages cut from a glossy porn magazine,

Advocate Men. He slid them out, handling them gingerly as if they might be soiled.

'You'd have been popular, Sarge,' he told Woody. 'Moustaches were all the rage back then.'

Woody scowled at him and stroked his moustache protectively. He nodded at Breeze's jacket. 'Leather's never gone out of fashion in some circles either, has it?'

Breeze grimaced. 'Cuh, look at the state of this lot. Posing like – oh, what's this?' A piece of paper had slipped out from between the pages and fluttered to the floor. Huffing and puffing, he bent down to pick it up. 'A clipping from the *Swindon Advertiser,* September 26th, 1990. *Search for missing schoolboy enters fourth day.*'

'Is that about Bob Greenaway?'

Breeze handed it over. 'Where does he fit into all this?'

'He doesn't.' Lincoln skimmed through the news item. 'But Tim Anderson's father was one of the team investigating his disappearance. Tim has a theory that it's linked to Isaac Keats, the lad who disappeared in 2011. And where did Isaac's SIM card turn up? In Harry Priest's van.'

Pam gasped. 'Tim thinks Harry Priest abducted Isaac *and* the Greenaway kid?'

'And Ritchie Payne.'

Woody looked doubtful. 'But there's twenty-seven years between Bob's disappearance and Ritchie's.'

'With Isaac's disappearance in between.' Lincoln laid the newspaper cutting at one end of the table, out of the way. 'But that's for Tim to investigate. *We* need to find out who killed Chris Darbyshire.'

'We could have a stab at what happened backstage,' Breeze suggested. 'No pun intended. We've got to start somewhere.'

'So let's look at what we know.' Lincoln uncapped his

marker pen and advanced on the whiteboard. 'Rehearsals begin in October 1990. Simeon Piper falls off the stage and Nate Newton replaces him. There's tension between the kids and Vaughn. He takes a shine to Cody Burnett so the kids set out to get him into trouble. They make it look as if he and Cody have got a thing going on, that he's taking pictures of the kid or asking Cody for sexy photos of himself. They write notes that sound as if Vaughn's been accepting sexual favours in return for helping the boy with his lines.'

'And if Vaughn fell for it, they'd get some kind of evidence and blackmail him,' Pam said. 'Was that the plan?'

Lincoln nodded. 'According to Orlando Snell.'

'Why the pages from gay magazines?' Once more, Breeze regarded *Advocate Men* with suspicion and disdain. 'To give the kid some ideas?'

'It all adds to the image of an older man trying to corrupt a teenager.'

'Reckon the only kid involved was Cody,' Woody argued. 'Nothing implicates the other kids. Bolitho could be right, it's exactly what it looks like. Vaughn took those Polaroids, trying to seduce the kid. It was their little secret.'

Nick Chance had been vehement in his denial of Cody's involvement, but had he protested too much?

'Yeah, but did they actually have sex?'

Pam groaned. 'Trust you to focus on that, Breezy!'

'It's a valid point,' Lincoln said. 'All the Board Treaders were under the age of consent at the time. Any kind of sexual activity with any of them would have been illegal, even if they'd consented. Vaughn would've been in big trouble if the police had got involved. He saved this stuff to cover himself if any of this came out.'

'So if he was innocent, why kill himself?' Pam gazed up at the whiteboard, arms folded.

'Assuming he really did kill himself.' Breeze grinned. 'Old Auntie Lydia could be right. Someone did murder him.'

Dilke had picked up the newspaper clipping about Bob Greenaway. 'This boy that went missing… He's about the same age as Mitchell Burnett, born in 1974. You think they knew each other? Maybe they were both in the Board Treaders.'

'Bob didn't sound the sort of lad who'd get involved in the theatre,' said Lincoln.

'Maybe they were both at Barbury Fields.'

'The comprehensive? Pam, you were looking into the Burnetts, weren't you?'

'Mitchell and Cody went to a private school, St Luke's, but they could've met the Greenaway kid at Scouts or football or something.'

'Or just hanging about,' Breeze put in. 'That age, we're all good at hanging about.'

Lincoln was drawn away by the sound of an email alert on his laptop. At the end of a messy day, it was good news at last.

'The forensics have come back on Chris Darbyshire.' He didn't bother to hide his excitement. 'One of the attackers must've cut themselves during the attack and left some of their blood on his clothes. And we've got a DNA match.'

CHAPTER 35

'Don't forget you've got a phone interview with that woman from *The Guardian* first thing tomorrow, Mitch.'

Mitchell Burnett looked up from his laptop as his PA got ready to leave for the day. 'No, I won't forget.'

Bloody *Guardian*. He could do without that kind of distraction right now, but with sales of his latest book getting sluggish…

'See you in the morning.' Fenella departed and the cottage went quiet, except for Horatio slurping water from his bowl inside the back door.

Mitchell poured himself a brandy, took it to the window and stared out into the rain. Did it ever fucking stop? Yes, it rained in London but somehow, up there… Thank God Fenella had taken the dog out before she left.

He tipped his head back, trying to loosen the muscles in his neck and shoulders, solid with tension. How could a silly incident from twenty-odd years ago disrupt his life so badly? Surely he could handle it?

His ex-wife phoned, but he let her call go to voicemail. Too tired to talk to Roz now. Too tired to eat, even though Fenella had put something out for him by the microwave.

'Just sling it and ping it,' she'd said, but he couldn't be arsed.

This would go away, this Darbyshire affair. What could the bloody man have found out after all these years? It would be fine. Nate and Sheri didn't seem bothered. He wasn't sure about Cody. They hadn't spoken for months. For years.

He knocked back his drink, poured himself another and stood by the fire to drink it. Horatio padded in and slumped down beside him, stretching his skinny lurcher legs out and grunting once or twice before falling asleep. Mitchell stepped carefully over him and returned to his desk. He still had work to do.

TUESDAY OCTOBER 31ST

CHAPTER 36

She looked about fourteen, but the girl sitting across from Lincoln and Pam was nineteen years old, nearly twenty. Small and skinny, with baby-fine hair hanging limply either side of her face, she gnawed her thumbnail, edgy and sullen.

'Alana Terry.' Lincoln lifted his gaze from her file to her face. Her eyes were dull, with dark shadows beneath them, as if she hadn't slept for a long time. 'How did you get mixed up in this, Alana?' He showed her a still from Ian Wilkinson's video of a slightly built figure bringing Leanne Milner's car to a halt in Cranbrook Road.

'Is that me? You don't know that's me.' She leaned forward, close to the table top.

'We know you were in Coronation Gardens that night, Alana. And we know you stabbed Chris Darbyshire.' Lincoln leaned closer too. 'They make it look so easy on the television, don't they, stabbing someone? Push the knife in, pull it out again. But it's harder than it looks. Especially if you're not used to doing it and you're not very strong, a bit nervous. You push the knife, only it doesn't go in as smoothly as you think it will. It suddenly stops with a jolt, but your hand keeps going. Your hand slides along the handle and onto the blade and that's when you cut yourself. Like you did on Tuesday night.'

He held his hands out, palms up, inviting her to do the same. To his surprise, she accepted his invitation and laid her hands, palms up, on the table. A grubby Elastoplast was peeling away from the skin between the thumb and forefinger of her right hand, exposing a ragged tear.

It had taken only three drops of her blood on the waistband of Darbyshire's trousers to identify her as one of his killers.

He pulled his hands back. 'You haven't done anything like this before, have you?' He was perusing her file again, taking in the several arrests for possession, one of soliciting and one for affray after she and another young woman got into a fight in a nightclub. He wondered how she'd got caught up in premeditated murder.

She pulled her hands back into her lap. 'I ant done nothing.'

Lincoln laid on the table a photo of Darbyshire taken from Fred August's website. Beside it, he laid a photo of Darbyshire's body on the riverbank, his face collapsed, his clothing drenched, blood soaking his shirt.

'Makes you feel good, does it, Alana, reducing this man to this one?' He tapped the photos in turn. He wanted to show her photos of Snell's body, but at this stage he had too little evidence to prove she'd been involved in that death, even though he was sure she was one of the two hooded figures who'd called on him on Saturday afternoon.

She stared at the photos. On the rainy riverbank, in the dark, she probably hadn't waited long enough to see what damage she'd done, but surely she'd visualised it since? Revisited the scene in her mind. Gone over those few terrible seconds when she and her accomplice drove two knives into Darbyshire and left him for dead.

'You'll have to carry this all on your own, Alana.' Pam was gentle but firm. 'But why should you be the only one to go to prison for this? Because you didn't act alone, did you? Perhaps it wasn't even your idea to hurt Chris – you just went along with it.'

This seemed to hit home and the girl looked to Wilf Evans, the duty solicitor, for advice. He raised his eyebrows encouragingly and she blurted out, 'It were Tawny as got me into this! You should be looking for Tawny!'

'And who's Tawny?' The name meant nothing to Lincoln. 'Is that a nickname?'

'It's a joke,' she said, although she wasn't smiling. 'His surname's Howell. Don't know what his first name is. He's just Tawny.'

'Where can we find him? Same place we found you?'

She shook her head. No, Tawny wasn't to be found in a bivouac in the underpass. He had somewhere better to go than she did.

'Lives on a farm, but I never been there. I got on the back of his bike after we… after we left the guy in the Gardens. He dropped me back at my bivvy. Ant seen him since. He owes me.'

'What's Tawny got against Chris Darbyshire?' Lincoln shut her file and folded his hands on top of it. 'Why did he want him dead?'

'Money.'

'Chris's money?'

'Money for killing him.'

'Whose money was it, then? Who paid Tawny to kill him?'

Her thin curtains of hair shifted slightly as she shook her head. 'He said best I don't know.'

'How did you know Chris would be there that evening?' Pam asked.

'We bin tailing him all day, from the theatre to the library and then he went for a coffee. He were ages in Costa because he met that Snell fella. Then he hangs about for his girlfriend and Tawny takes over from me so

I can get a takeaway, warm up indoors somewhere.' She wiped her nose with the cuff of her thin jersey. 'Tawny follows them back to the pizza place, tells me to wait in the Gardens until I gets a call from him to say he's on his way. Fucking freezing in them Gardens, that shelter thing. Roof's full of holes, all the rain coming in. I probably got pewnomia.'

'How did you know Chris was at the theatre that morning?' Lincoln asked.

'Tawny got a call. Some fella at the theatre tipped him off. Don't ask me who.' She put her head down on her folded arms. 'All I wanna do is sleep.'

'You can sleep all you want once you've told us what we need to know. Where can we find Tawny Howell?'

CHAPTER 37

As soon as CCTV images of the white van's crew hit the media, Tim Anderson got a response. Numerous names were put forward to Crimestoppers, but it was a detective constable on his own team who clinched it.

'That's Milo Dodds and Luke Costello,' DC Jay Vallis told him. 'They've been in and out of trouble most of their lives, usually for petty theft or fighting. Abduction doesn't seem like their style. They often work for Harry Priest, lifting and carrying. Hanging out at the gym makes for strong muscles.'

'Which gym's that?'

'Lindy's. Used to be a furniture showroom. Open all hours. Well, not quite, but almost. You work out?'

'I run,' said Anderson. 'I do a bit of work with weights at home.'

'I used to do yoga, but I kept falling asleep before the end of the class. You want to check it out? Maybe catch them training?'

At Lindy's, they spotted Dodds and Costello heading for the fire door and crashing through it.

'They saw me coming,' Vallis said.

Anderson had to admit that the tall, broad-shouldered detective, with her blonde updo and green leather jacket, was easy to spot.

'We'll pick them up at home,' he said. 'Taking off like that is kind of an admission of guilt.'

A trumpet blast from her mobile announced an incoming text and she smiled as she read it.

'You know that kitchen that went walkies from Mr

Fogarty's house in Folly Hill? Call just came in as a result of the appeal. Those two were seen shifting stuff into a white van in Fogarty's driveway. They saw his neighbour watching, told her the wrong things had been delivered and they were taking them back to the warehouse.'

'And she believed them?'

'Why wouldn't she?'

It was all falling into place. Harry Priest's van left his yard – stolen, according to him – on Tuesday morning. Dodds and Costello drove it to Folly Hill, where there were no traffic cameras to pick it up. Once they'd loaded it up with Mr Fogarty's brand new, yet-to-be-installed kitchen, they headed off to deliver it. But where? Priest's yard? A lock-up somewhere? A new customer?

That evening, they'd driven back into town, stopped in Spicer Street to invite Ritchie Payne on board – and then what?

Anderson opened his car door. 'Let's have another chat with Harry Priest.'

CHAPTER 38

Trevor Howell, nickname Tawny, lived with his farm-worker father in a tied cottage on the edge of Barbury, deep in the Woodford Valley. When a patrol car pulled up outside, a few seconds ahead of Lincoln and Dilke, Howell Senior came out onto the front step, eyes narrowed.

'He's not here,' he said, before anyone asked him where his son was. He was in slippers and shirt sleeves, his mud-caked gumboots standing beside the door.

'When did you last see him?' Lincoln's gaze took in the scatter of outhouses across the puddle-filled yard and a collection of vehicles in various states of repair or decay. A mountain bike was propped against the nearest shed, the mud on its tyres and chassis still glistening.

'Couldn't tell you for sure. He comes and goes.'

'Been out on your bike?' Lincoln nodded at it. 'Not easy to pedal in Wellingtons, eh?'

Howell scowled but didn't argue.

Dilke stepped forward. 'We've got an arrest warrant for Trevor, Mr Howell. If you obstruct us…'

'Arrest him for what?'

'On suspicion of murder.' Lincoln watched the man's face fall. Tawny had been in trouble through most of his teenage years, involved in petty crime off and on ever since. Now, at twenty-four, he was implicated in murder.

To his credit, his father didn't try to defend him or to stop the police entering the cottage to search for him. He just stood aside while uniforms and Dilke went indoors.

'Murdered who?' he asked Lincoln, fumbling a cigarette out of a battered packet and lighting it.

'Chris Darbyshire.' Lincoln looked away across the soggy fields that surrounded the cottage. 'Trevor works with you here?'

'Nah. He's a mechanic. Works for Presford Motors.'

'A mechanic must come in handy round the farm.' Not that any of the vehicles on display looked as if they'd been worked on for a while.

'Never see him. Does lots of overtime for Dave.'

'Dave Newton, is that?'

'Yeah, but it's his son Craig that runs the garage. Dave operates at arm's length these days.'

Nate Newton's uncle, the untouchable Dave, who'd made his money flogging cars that weren't all they were cracked up to be.

'Arm's length, eh? And why not, if you can afford to sit back? Does Trevor run any errands for Craig?'

He should've known he was pushing his luck. Howell Senior drew on his cigarette, clamping his lips shut around it. A slight shake of his head told Lincoln he wasn't going to say another word about his son.

Lincoln went inside. The front door opened straight into the living room, no hallway, stairs to the upper floor hidden behind a door in the corner. Dilke came clattering down these stairs to greet him with the news that Tawny was nowhere to be found.

'Got this though.' He held up a wad of used banknotes in a plastic zip lock bag.

'Searched the wardrobe?' Tawny's clothes would have been heavily bloodstained after he knifed Darbyshire.

'Nothing much in there and there's nothing in the laundry basket.'

Lincoln looked out of the window at the yard between

the cottage and its shabby outbuildings. 'There's a fire bin down there. Check he hasn't tried to burn anything.'

A minute later, he saw Dilke in the yard, raking through the contents of the fire bin, and went down to join him.

'Some bits of cloth, boss. Too charred to identify.'

'Worth fishing out, though. Bag it all up. Forensics may be able to salvage something. Never say never.'

As Dilke retrieved brittle scraps of scorched material and slid them carefully into a big evidence bag, Lincoln spotted something through the metal grille in the bottom of the bin: a filleting knife, its handle melted into a knobbly lump of fluorescent plastic, its blade sooty but intact.

He reached in and pulled it out. 'I think we've found our other weapon, Graham. Alana had the kitchen knife and Tawny had this one.'

Dilke grinned as the knife was lowered into another evidence bag. 'All we've got to do now is find him.'

'I don't think he's far away.' Lincoln nodded towards the mountain bike. 'The mud's still wet. He's here somewhere.'

They crossed the yard to the outbuildings that were already being searched by uniform. Lincoln turned back to see Howell Senior watching them keenly.

A door banged open at the far end and a stack of buckets toppled over as a figure sprang from the last shed.

Trevor 'Tawny' Howell.

He tore off towards the fields with Dilke and one of the uniforms after him. He was well ahead until the ground began to get boggy. His sprint became a comedy routine as he tried to pull first one foot and then the other out of the mud. He fell to his knees, trapped by his own feet. Dilke and the constable had to grab him under the armpits to haul him out, covering themselves in mud and muck in the process.

Lincoln watched as the three tramped back to the cottage.

'You shouldn't have tried to make a run for it, Tawny,' he said. 'You must've known you wouldn't get far. And now your clothes are wet and you stink of shit.'

'Fuck you!'

Lincoln shrugged. 'Suit yourself. Let's get you back to Park Street.'

'Lord Almighty, Jeff, did you have to bring him back here?' DCI Claire Connors clamped a hand over her nose and mouth as she watched Trevor Howell being led downstairs to be charged.

'I didn't fancy travelling with him all the way to Melksham or Swindon, ma'am, and the sooner we get him into clean clothes, the better for everyone.'

She looked down at Lincoln's shoes and trouser bottoms. 'You'll need to change when you get home too. Those shoes are a write-off.'

He looked down. Yes, she was right. He'd sent Dilke home already, hoping that his mum wouldn't go overboard at the sight – and smell – of her precious son. Seeing the state of his own shoes made him resolve to keep a spare pair at Barley Lane in future. At least most of what was on him was mud, not cow shit.

By the time he was sitting across from Howell in the interview room it was nearly two. His feet were clammy with cold and his stomach was growling with hunger, but there was no time to waste.

'Okay, Tawny, tell us where you were on Tuesday night.'

'Can't remember. That's a week ago.' Cleaned up but with a rash of livid spots around his mouth and chin,

Howell looked younger than his twenty-four years. He was cocky, though, as if he knew there was precious little forensic evidence linking him to Darbyshire's murder and even less connecting him to Orlando Snell's. They'd got Alana's blood on Darbyshire's clothes and might yet find a match for her fingerprints in Snell's house, but Howell had clearly been more careful about leaving traces of himself at either scene.

'I'll give you a few facts to remind you.' Lincoln glanced across at the duty solicitor, who was doing a good job of keeping out of it. 'On Tuesday night, Chris Darbyshire was being driven along Cranbrook Road when your friend Alana jumped out in front of the car, forcing it to stop. She begged him to help her because someone in Coronation Gardens was in trouble. Chris, being the kind-hearted man he was, didn't think twice about going to her aid. And then you jumped him, the pair of you, and stabbed him. Coming back to you now, Tawny?'

'Her word against mine, innit?' The young man retained his defiant expression, with no hint of remorse.

'It is indeed, yes.' Lincoln opened his folder, took out a photo and laid it in front of Howell. 'We retrieved this knife from under the incinerator in your dad's back yard. True, the handle's got out of shape in the heat of the fire, but you must recognise it. Why try to burn it?'

A frown creased Howell's forehead. Had he really expected his knife to be completely consumed by the flames?

'And we've got your clothes – or what's left of them. Should give us some good evidence linking you to the murder.'

Lincoln wasn't sure that was true, but he could see Howell was worried.

'You're bluffing.'

'Am I?' Lincoln tapped the photo of the knife, its handle grotesquely deformed. 'What was your beef with Chris Darbyshire?'

'Didn't have one.'

'And yet you knifed him. You and Alana. Stabbed him to death and left him lying on the riverbank in the rain where no one was likely to find him until it was too late. Sounds a bit irrational to me, inflicting that sort of damage on someone you'd never even met. Or was it Alana who wanted to kill him? Did you kill him because Alana told you to?'

'Nothing to do with her.'

'Say that again.' Lincoln glanced at the tape machine as if keen to capture Howell's exoneration of his accomplice.

'I said it weren't nothing to do with Alana.'

'But you've really landed her in it, haven't you? The two of you stabbed Darbyshire to death, then she hopped on the back of your bike and you cycled away like you were just having a bit of fun in the rain. Why kill him, Tawny? If you wanted his money, his phone, you could've knocked him about a bit, shoved him on the ground, gone through his pockets. You didn't have to kill him. In fact, you didn't even seem to want his money. His wallet was still full of cash when he was found. You missed that?'

'No comment.'

'So, if you didn't have a beef with him and you weren't trying to rob him, why kill him? Why were you tailing him all day?' Lincoln saw alarm in Howell's face. 'Yes, we know all about that. I'm guessing someone paid you to tail him, someone who *did* have a beef with him. They paid you so much you didn't need to rob him. Tell us who paid you to murder him, Tawny.'

'No comment.'

'Are you going to carry the can for them? They pay you enough to go to prison for them?'

'No comment.' Howell hung his head. The spots around his mouth grew redder.

'Did you know he was going to be a dad?' Lincoln laid down the same photos he'd laid before Alana. 'Course you didn't. How could you? You knew nothing about him. Someone told you to kill him and you didn't ask any questions. Just went ahead and obeyed them. Let them dictate what you did that night. Which, of course, means *they've* decided what happens to the rest of your life. The rest of your life could be spent in jail, Tawny. That doesn't seem fair to me. Does it to you?'

Howell fixed his gaze on his hands, clasped on the table.

'Who hired you, Tawny?' Lincoln took a chance. 'Was it Craig Newton?'

Howell's head shot up at the sound of his boss's name and alarm filled his eyes.

'No comment,' he said, but Lincoln had got his answer.

CHAPTER 39

Harry Priest wasn't playing ball.

'Don't know what you're talking about.' He went on shifting boxes of assorted junk across his yard while Tim Anderson and Jay Vallis asked their questions. 'What would I want with a new kitchen, eh? You can see what I buy and sell – used goods, second-hand, stuff to upcycle. I told you, my van was nicked. Obviously, that's why those tossers nicked it – so they could use it to steal a kitchen and flog it on.' He turned to face them after he'd dumped a box of tarnished candelabra at their feet. 'Not guilty,' he snapped. 'I'm the injured party here.'

His self-pity was wasted on Anderson. 'You know these lads, though, don't you? Luke and Milo?'

'Wankers, the pair of 'em. Coming round here to "help out"? Help theirselves, more like.'

'When were they here last?' asked Jay, her hands thrust into the back pockets of her jeans.

'Haven't worked for me for weeks, but I expect they remembered I load the van up first thing, knew I'd be in and out of the office while I was loading up. Waited till my back was turned and then jumped in.'

'Should know better than to leave the keys in it,' Anderson said. 'Surprised it hadn't been nicked before.'

'Most people are trustworthy and I rely on that.' Priest's smile was sarcastic, but it showed his teeth, yellow and uneven. 'You're in my way.' He tried to push past with a box of musty-smelling books. 'I'm already out of pocket because I can't do my market stall today, not having a fucking van. Now you're hindering me in the pursuit of my occupation.'

Tim stepped back to let him pass. 'And we're in pursuit of *our* occupation, Harry. We'll be back with a warrant to search these premises. Okay?'

Back at Barley Lane, Dilke – in a change of clothes and seemingly recovered from his adventure at the Howells' cottage – was studying his screen intently.

'Been going over that CCTV of Cranbrook Road, boss,' he said as Lincoln strode in. 'Looking for anyone who might have been this third suspect the Sarge was talking about.'

'A *possible* third suspect. We don't know for sure that's how Howell and Alana knew exactly when Leanne would be driving past.'

'Apart from this bike that got really close to the car at the lights – that must be Howell, yeah? – I noticed this Mini. It's behind them all the way from the traffic lights, tail-gating the Yaris.' Dilke sat back to let Lincoln see his screen.

A 2009 Mini, metallic grey or some other pale colour, was close behind Leanne's car as she entered Cranbook Road and proceeded towards the poorly lit stretch alongside Coronation Gardens.

'I enhanced the image as much as I could to read the number plate. It ends in either 09ESW or 09ESV. I checked and it's 09ESW that matches the Mini. And guess who it's registered to? Craig Newton.'

'Tawny Howell's boss? Nate Newton's cousin?' Suddenly more optimistic, Lincoln crossed to the whiteboard, where the names of the four Board Treaders were writ large. 'I think Nate just became our prime suspect.' He drew a ring round the name in thick marker pen. 'At last, we're getting somewhere.'

He rang the DCI. 'I want to bring Craig Newton in for questioning first thing in the morning.'

'Because his cousin was one of the Board Treaders?'

'Because Trevor Howell, one of Darbyshire's attackers, works for him. He hasn't named him outright, but we know he runs errands for him – and I think we know what that means.'

'Don't make it mean more than it should, Jeff.'

'The Newtons are a dodgy lot – Nate's dad, his uncle, Craig...'

'You've got more compelling evidence?'

'CCTV footage of Craig tailing Leanne's car as she drove along Cranbrook Road.'

'That's more like it. Okay, but be careful. We don't want this blowing up in our faces. The DCS is already unhappy about how long it's taken to get anyone in custody. Is the Howell lad talking?'

'Not yet, but he can't hold out for ever.'

While Lincoln was on the phone, Woody had been checking Craig Newton's background. 'Forty-three, married, one of the directors of Presford Motors. He's come close to losing his licence, the number of times he's been caught speeding. And uniform have called on him several times after neighbours complained about loud parties. Oh, and a report of a domestic, but Zelda, the wife, called it a misunderstanding so it didn't come to anything. He lives in Hyperion Avenue,' he added. 'Must be one of those executive homes down the road from the Old Farmhouse.'

'You think he and Chris knew each other?' Pam wondered, but Lincoln shook his head.

'I doubt it. A road like that, neighbours never get close.'

'And you really think Nate's put him up to this?'

'It seems too much of a coincidence that Tawny Howell, one of Darbyshire's killers, works for Nate's cousin. We'll bring Craig in tomorrow morning, see what he's got to say for himself. At the same time, we'll talk to Nate. Where do we find him? Who was looking into Nate Newton?' Lincoln looked round expectantly.

'Me,' said Breeze, interrupted on the way to put the kettle on. 'He's in Borehamwood, near the studios. Anyone else want a cuppa? Hang on, someone's rattling the front door.' Empty mug in hand, he lumbered out to the entrance hall, returning with a dark-haired man in an expensive overcoat and bright red cashmere scarf. 'Someone to see you, boss.'

It was Nick. Lincoln felt instantly ashamed of the way he'd stormed out of the Black Swan on Sunday evening.

'You want a cuppa?' Breeze raised his mug towards the newcomer.

'I'm good, thanks.' Nick undid his coat and slid his scarf off. 'Hey, it's actually warm in here. Most everywhere I've been today, it's freezing.'

Lincoln was about to lead him to his desk when he realised Nick would be able to see the whiteboard from there, so he steered him instead towards the stationery cupboard – the walk-in store room just big enough to accommodate a desk and chair. Pushing the door half-closed, he waved Nick towards the chair while he leaned against the wall.

'Sorry about the other night, Nick. I wasn't expecting our meeting to stray so quickly onto the topic of Cody Burnett.'

Nick held his hands up, as if the fault were all his. 'If I'd known then that Darbyshire was dead… But I'll say again what I said when we met: Cody had nothing to do with Vaughn's death. Chris Darbyshire was trying to implicate him, digging up dirt that would fit the story he'd concocted. That was why Cody was keen to shut him up – to shut him up with a cease-and-desist letter, I should say, not by stabbing him to death.' He smoothed his hair back. 'Just so we're clear.'

'Darbyshire wasn't accusing Cody of *murder*, was he?' Christ, wasn't this case complicated enough?

'No, no, but that stupid stunt with the photos and the letters – that's most likely what drove Vaughn to kill himself.'

'How did Cody know that Darbyshire was looking into Vaughn's death?'

'From a friend, I guess. Someone else who'd been approached.'

'I need the name of that friend. Anyone who knew about Darbyshire's project is potentially a suspect.'

'Come on, Jeff. You really think one of the Board Treaders has grown up to be a *killer*?'

'One of them may have grown up to be someone who'd pay *someone else* to be a killer, yes. I can't rule anyone out. Why did you come here, Nick? You know I can't tell you anything that isn't already in the public domain.'

'Okay, okay. For the record, I'm sorry our meeting ended on a kinda sour note. Guess we shouldn't have tried to mix business with pleasure. Maybe when all this is over…'

'I'll buy you a beer.'

'I'll hold you to that, my friend.' He rose, reaching out to shake Lincoln's hand, gripping his elbow at the same time. A politician's handshake.

'I'll show you out.'

Back at his desk, Lincoln tried to order his thoughts.

Even though his money was on Nate Newton as the Board Treader behind Darbyshire's murder, he couldn't rule out any of the others. The photos in the scrapbook, the evidence that the kids were trying to set Vaughn up – that could damage any one of them. Whose reputation might suffer the most? Mitchell Burnett's.

According to his website, he'd be presenting a BBC series next year on England's declining rural industries and had already signed a contract for the accompanying book.

Curious about him, Lincoln found a YouTube clip of one of his programmes, a documentary on Stonehenge from earlier in the year.

'Can you imagine a time,' Burnett intoned as he advanced towards the camera, coat collar turned up, 'when these hills were covered with dense woodland?' He spread his arms to the landscape, the massive grey stones of the monument looming over the bleak downs behind him.

Tall and well-built, with dark bushy hair, the broadcaster had an air of amiable authority, like a sympathetic history teacher. His dark eyes were bright with enthusiasm for his subject matter and he had a voice both firm and friendly. Lincoln could see why he'd attracted so many fans.

Silencing Darbyshire would certainly be in his interests, but it would destroy his reputation completely should anyone find out about his involvement.

Tomorrow, Craig Newton would be brought in for questioning and Lincoln would travel up to Hertfordshire to interview his cousin Nate. If his suspicions were correct, he wouldn't need to look any further.

CHAPTER 40

When Lincoln got home, he heated some soup and drank it at his laptop while he found out all he could about Nathaniel 'Nate' Newton. Now forty-four, Newton was married, with a daughter who was already a rising star of children's television. In interviews, he seemed proud of his father's criminal past, as if it gave him a credibility he'd otherwise lack. His own television career had nose-dived in his twenties, but voice work and commercials had kept him afloat since then. He still accepted the occasional acting role but claimed his job nowadays was 'managing the kid'.

But was he guilty of procuring Chris Darbyshire's murder?

Someone knocked on the front door. Since it was Hallowe'en, his first thought was trick-or-treaters. The shops had been full of cheap decorations for weeks and he was tired of seeing pumpkins for sale everywhere.

Yet, when he opened the door, there was no crocodile of Hallowe'en-costumed children, their parents holding torches.

It was Trish.

They stared at each other for a moment.

'Can I come in?' She set one foot on the threshold, waiting for his invitation.

'Yes. Yes. Sorry.' He stood back to let her in.

'I can't stay long. I've left Kate on her own, although when I left she was on the phone to Paloma, grumbling about homework. I've got those printouts.' She held out the sheaf of pages he'd left at the library after he found her in Steve Quilter's arms in her office.

'Thanks,' he said, taking them. 'I should've come in for them sooner.'

'Well, you've got them now.' She slipped her coat off, dropped it over the banister and went ahead of him into the kitchen where his messy soup mug sat beside his laptop. 'Are you eating properly? Soup's very salty, you know. And you need your vegetables. Shall I make some coffee?'

He stood back and let her fill the kettle, seek out cups and coffee jar, sugar and spoons. Since he'd seen her last, she'd changed her hairstyle, doing away with the scrawny ponytail from which strands were always escaping. Now her ash blonde hair was cut in a boyish bob.

'I thought you were growing it.' He gestured at her hair.

'Got tired of it.' She teased the shorter style almost shyly as if unsure of it. 'Suki's hairdresser was able to squeeze me in. You like it?'

'Looks great. How's your dad?'

'Fed up with having his arm in plaster and having to rely on me and Suki all the time. And he's worried about losing his balance.'

'See what the doctor says. It may be nothing more than an age thing.'

'Maybe. Anyway… I did a bit of research into Hamilton Vaughn for you, since there wasn't much in those printouts of yours.' She read from her phone screen. 'Born Vaughn Hamilton, South Wales, 1927. Left school at fifteen, got a job on a local newspaper. One of his first tasks was reviewing plays at his local theatre and he caught the acting bug. An actor I've never heard of took him under his wing, pushed him to go to drama school and supported him until he got work. Vaughn was a proper actor before he went into panto.'

'Isn't panto "proper acting"?'

'You know what I mean.' She dumped her phone on the table.

'Not sure I do.' He picked up his soup mug and carried it across to the sink. Their paths crossed as she went to make the coffee. 'You still think he was a dirty old man, don't you?'

'I told you, Jeff, there were rumours flying around years ago. I suppose I was too young and naïve to think there could be two sides to the story. Are you saying he was innocent?'

He sat down at the table once more. 'I'm saying that you shouldn't rush to judgement. Nobody should.'

She sniffed, stung by his rebuke. 'You want to hear what else I found out or are you going to leave me on the naughty step?'

'Of course I want to hear what you found out. Go on.'

She made the coffee and carried on. 'He was in various theatre companies over the years and was part of a group that went into schools to introduce teenagers to drama.'

'Working with teenagers?' Alarm bells rang. Had there ever been a time when older men working with youngsters had *not* set alarm bells ringing?

'Before the days of DBS checks, of course,' she said.

'Not that DBS checks are much use if the bloke in question hasn't come to the attention of the police.'

'I'm sure the schools would've made sure there was a teacher on hand if a lot of strange actors were on the loose.' Trish returned to her notes. 'The last school session he did was in Swindon, summer 1990. Not long after that, he came to Barbury to start rehearsals for the panto.'

'Swindon?' Why did that ring a different sort of bell? 'What else did you find out?'

'He had a house in Marlborough. Not very big but quirky. I found some publicity photos of him in the garden. And yet, according to the probate records, he only left a few thousand.'

'He'd been putting a lot of his own money into Barbury Theatre for a while before he died.'

'That might explain it.'

Why was Trish here and not with the museum's Wonder Boy? Was her new hairstyle for *his* benefit?

'What happened to the house in Marlborough?'

She shrugged. 'He must've sold it and put the money into the theatre. Or maybe it was sold after he died and the proceeds used to settle any debts. The estate would be what was left after that.'

Lincoln frowned at the coffee she'd made for him, although it wasn't the coffee that was causing him consternation but the mystery of what had happened to Vaughn's money.

'And he was married, briefly,' she said. 'To Lydia Bancroft.'

'Are you sure?

'I've done my research, Jeff. Of course I'm sure.'

'When was this?'

'1954. He was twenty-seven, she was nineteen. Marriage annulled 1956. Maybe it was never consummated. If Vaughn wasn't really into women… Oh, sorry, am I rushing to judgement?'

He cast her a filthy look. 'He had to put up with plenty of innuendo from those kids during the pantomime. Give the bloke the benefit of the doubt, at least.' He picked up his coffee and inhaled its comforting aroma. He hated arguing with her, especially now that Museum

Man was in the picture. 'Anything in your researches about a significant other, male or female?'

She shook her head. 'But back then, people kept quiet about same sex relationships, didn't they, even as recently as 1990?'

'It was Lydia who found his body.'

'God, that must've been awful, especially after they'd been so close.' Sitting down across from him, she took a few sips of her coffee before pushing it aside. 'You think someone else will write her life story now?'

'I doubt it. Chris probably got drawn towards the mystery of Vaughn's death because it was more interesting than anything Lydia got up to.'

'You still don't know who killed Chris?'

'We've got someone in custody and we think we know who put them up to it. I'm hoping they'll be in custody too before long.'

'And if you're wrong?'

He didn't want to think about it, let alone talk about it. 'Let's hope I'm not. Changing the subject… Did Kate have a good time at her dad's last week?'

'So-so. She's always a bit down when she comes back from Vic's. Seeing him with a new family makes her feel like she's the poor relation. Gail's baby is due around Christmas, so everything revolved around her, Kate said. Gail mustn't do too much, mustn't get stressed.' She laughed coldly. 'I can't remember Vic being that solicitous when *I* was pregnant!'

'Chris's girlfriend is expecting their baby mid-December.'

'I don't envy her. It's bad enough when you've got a partner to share the burden, but when you're on your own…' She pushed her mug aside. 'Is something wrong? With you, I mean, with us? It's just that you've been sort of distant these last few days.'

'This case is a bugger, that's all.' He avoided her gaze, studying his coffee as he stirred in another spoonful of sugar. 'Doesn't leave much time or energy for anything else.' He checked the time. 'You don't want to leave Kate on her own too long, do you?'

'Trying to get rid of me?' She stood up and he thought how tired she looked. Was worrying about her father keeping her awake at night? 'Listen,' she said. 'I'm sorry if I misjudged Hamilton Vaughn. I'll see if I can find out anything else about him, okay?'

WEDNESDAY 1ST NOVEMBER

CHAPTER 41

Woody and Pam, backed by a team of uniforms, arrived at Craig Newton's house early next morning, waking his wife and her teenage son but failing to find the man himself. Trying to restrain a boisterous and noisy Staffie, Zelda complained loudly at being barged aside in her own hallway.

'You could've let me get properly dressed,' she snapped, as the uniforms searched the house. 'Given me time to run a comb through my hair.'

Woody paid little attention to her concerns. 'Where's Craig?'

'He isn't here, hasn't been here for a day or two.' She wrenched the dog's collar. 'Shut up, Pirate.'

'So where is he? You must know where he is.'

'If I knew, I wouldn't tell you.' She dragged the dog across the room, heading for the door, but her son, a gawky lad of sixteen or seventeen, eyes huge behind thick lenses, loped over and took the dog from her, making a fuss of him, calming him down.

'What car's he driving?'

Zelda shrugged theatrically. 'How should I know? He can take his pick from the showroom.'

'Mrs Newton,' Pam tried to sound sympathetic, but this woman's husband was probably responsible for the murder of two innocent men and she had little time for her. 'Zelda. He must have been in touch with you. Where is he?'

'With his dad in Spain for all I know.'

'We can arrest you for obstruction,' Woody warned

her. 'You want that?'

The boy spoke up. 'Don't arrest Mum just because my stupid stepdad isn't here. Whatever he's done, it's not *her* fault.'

'Rocco, I'm warning you…'

'Try his showroom,' Rocco went on, undeterred. 'He sometimes sleeps in his office there.'

'Thank you, Rocco,' said Pam, and she and Woody headed off to Presford Motors.

The forecourt of Presford Motors was a sea of second-hand cars sparkling in the morning sunshine. A young man in overalls was cleaning the windscreen of a small Daewoo, but when Woody asked him if his boss was around, he shoved his cloth into his overall pocket and led them into the showroom. 'You'll want to talk to Brian.'

A much older man, slowly typing at an untidy desk, looked up as they approached.

'They're here for Craig, Yorkie,' the lad said before he went back to his windscreens.

Brian York stood up stiffly and came round his desk. 'Who shall I say?' But when Woody and Pam showed their IDs, he grimaced and shook his head. 'You'd better go through.' He led them down a short corridor to a windowless office.

Rocco hadn't been wrong. Craig slept in his office sometimes. A sofa bed was shoved against one wall and the air smelt ripe with seldom-changed bedlinen. But where was Craig?

A lavatory flushed nearby and then a bulky man in his forties loomed in the doorway, yesterday's *Sun* in his fist.

'Police here to talk to you, Craig,' said Yorkie, quickly leaving them to it and returning to the showroom. 'I'll put the kettle on.'

'Your employee Trevor Howell is in custody,' Woody began, taking the only spare chair while Pam sat on the very edge of the sofa bed. 'He's been charged with the murder of Christian Darbyshire in Coronation Gardens on October 24th. Did you put him up to it?'

Craig frowned in apparent consternation. 'Did I *what?*'

'We think you paid him to follow Darbyshire on Tuesday and then kill him.'

'This is that little scrote getting back at me for sacking him. Christ, that little…' He shook his head, lost for words.

'When did you sack him?' Pam asked, trying not to notice the musty smell emanating from the pile of discarded clothing beside her.

'It'd be the twentieth.' He unzipped his tracksuit top a little way and scratched his bare but hairy chest. He watched Pam carefully, but she made a point of not letting her gaze leave his face. Prat!

'Where were you on the night of October 24th?' Woody asked.

'What was that, a Tuesday?'

'The Tuesday Chris Darbyshire was murdered, yes.'

'Home, I expect. You've talked to my old lady? Although she might've been out herself that night…'

'Is this you, Craig?' Woody pushed a photo towards him. The CCTV image of him in his Mini, close behind Leanne's Yaris.

'Could be. Looks a bit like me. Not flattering, are they, these speed cameras?'

'This was CCTV in Cranbrook Road,' Pam said. 'You appear to be following the car in which Chris was a passenger.'

'So? I expect I was following a lot of cars that night,

crawling along, all that rain. Nothing to say I was tailing that little Yaris on purpose, is there?'

'Bit of a coincidence, though, isn't it?'

He tossed the photo back at Woody. 'Think we're done here.' He pushed his chair back and lumbered to his feet. 'You take the word of that skinny-arsed kid over mine, and me a respected businessman? I sacked him, he's getting back at me. Fuck knows who paid him to off Darbyshire – if someone did. But it certainly wasn't me.'

Taking his time, Woody picked up the photo and restored it to his folder. 'Spoken to your cousin Nate recently?'

'Nate? Don't tell me that fucker's trying to land me in the shit as well!'

'Reckon that's a no, then.'

'Yes, it's a big fucking no. And if you want to question me again, you can do it with my solicitor present.' Craig held the door open. 'Yorkie! Show these people out.'

CHAPTER 42

'Is this a formal interview or are we just chatting?' Nate Newton flopped down on the sofa opposite Lincoln and Dilke. His spacious living room overlooked an unremarkable back garden – an oblong of artificial grass, cluttered with patio furniture and a tarpaulin-covered barbecue.

It was nearly midday by the time they'd reached Borehamwood, a Hertfordshire town beyond the north-western boroughs of London. Nate's boxy seventies house stood within walking distance of the railway station and was handy for Elstree Studios, where his daughter Chelsea was starring in a children's adventure serial.

Lincoln couldn't help thinking that, had he stayed on in the Met instead of moving down to Wiltshire with Cathy, he might have ended up somewhere like this, between the M25 and the North Circular, a place of retail parks and commuter traffic, between the city and the countryside, without the benefits of either.

And here was Nate Newton, Wiltshire born and bred, who'd been lucky enough to land a career-defining role while he was still at secondary school.

'You can't think I had anything to do with Chris Darbyshire's death,' he protested when Lincoln explained why he and Dilke had come calling. 'I never even met the guy.'

He was alone in the house, he said, otherwise he'd offer them a cup of tea or coffee or even something stronger, but if it was all the same to them, he'd rather get on with answering whatever questions they had and then they could fuck off back to Barbury. He smiled as he said it.

'We're fine,' said Lincoln, even though he was dying for a coffee. 'Isn't Sherilyn staying with you?'

'Not anymore. She went home. Is this gonna take long?'

'Tell us what we need to know and we'll be out of here.'

Nate's teenage good looks had aged into a gauntness that suggested hard times along the way – hard times reputedly made easier by drink and drugs. He was scrawny now rather than slim, his shaggy dark hair had thinned and turned grey, and his trademark lopsided fringe was no more than a few untidy wisps.

'Fire away.' He lounged back on the sofa, right leg crossed over left, right foot tapping the air to music only he could hear.

'Did you know Chris was writing about Hamilton Vaughn?'

'Yeah, I heard about it from Sheri. We met up at a *Harbinger Hollow* convention, first time in years.'

'*Harbinger Hollow*?' It rang bells but Lincoln looked to Dilke for clarification. Dilke shrugged. He didn't know either.

'It was a TV series me and Sheri were in. They run a convention every year for the fans – HarCon. This year it was in Camden Town and my agent got me a spot signing autographs, selfies with the fans, you name it. Good money for a weekend's work. Sheri was there too and we met up. Just like old times. We go way back, her and me. Mates, that's all.' He grinned again.

Lincoln noticed two or three gaps where teeth were missing. Expensive house but no money to spend on a dentist?

'What can you tell us about the events leading up to Mr Vaughn's death, Nate? We heard there was tension behind the scenes.'

'Tension? The guy was a fucking nonce. You ask any of them and they'll tell you the same.'

Dilke had his notebook at the ready. 'Can you give us a bit more detail?'

Nate uncrossed his legs, recrossed them the other way. His left foot jiggled to a faster beat. 'Only what I heard, okay? But he fancied Cody Burnett, always whispering to him in dark corners and – fuck – there were plenty of *those* backstage. And how did Simeon Piper end up in the orchestra pit? Vaughn fucking shoved him over the edge.'

'And you saw him do that?' Dilke leaned in. 'You saw Vaughn push him off the stage?'

'Yeah.' Nate looked from Lincoln to Dilke as if checking they believed him. 'I was there. Not near enough to save him from falling, but... Yeah, I was there.'

'What was *your* part in the panto?' asked Lincoln.

'Christ, now you're asking.' A bark of laughter as he pushed a few wild strands of hair back from his forehead. 'Oh yeah, one of the kids the giant snatches off the street and takes up to his castle. Jack climbs the beanstalk to rescue us.' Another quick look from Lincoln to Dilke and back again. 'Why're you asking?'

'There were parts for only *four* children. Look.' Lincoln held out a photocopy of the theatre programme in Vaughn's scrapbook, and the photo of the Board Treaders, arms linked, at the start of rehearsals: Mitch and Cody, Sherilyn and Simeon. 'See? Only four children. I assume you took over Simeon's role after he had his accident. You weren't going to be in the panto originally, were you?'

'Er…no, no. Five of us were up for four parts. And then Sim hurt his back. It's an ill wind, eh?'

'But we're really here to talk about the allegations of sexual assault.' Lincoln left hanging his insinuation that Nate might have had something to do with Simeon's fall. 'Who made those allegations at the time? Was it Cody? He was the alleged victim, so it's logical that…'

'Look, it's a long time ago. I can't remember the ins and outs – if you'll pardon the expression.' Big grin. Nate uncrossed his legs, leaned his elbows on his knees. 'We all complained about Vaughn.'

'To the police?' Knowing they hadn't.

'No. We would've done, eventually, but I suppose we just wanted him to quit.'

'Quit the panto? He was playing the dame, wasn't he? There'd be no panto without the dame.'

'Orlando was his understudy, Orlando Snell. He'd have been fine. The show must go on.' Nate's smile was tentative now, as if he wasn't sure where this was going.

'Didn't anyone report him to Mr Burnett?' Dilke asked. 'Wouldn't that have been the sensible thing to do?'

'Teenagers don't do sensible. We thought we could handle it ourselves. Sorry, another *double entendre*. That's what happens when you spend your formative years doing pantomime.'

Lincoln grinned, as if sharing the joke. 'Been in touch with your cousin Craig?'

'Craig?' Nate looked genuinely puzzled. 'Not for a long time. Bit of a falling-out a while back. Why're you asking?'

'We think he was involved in Chris's murder.' Lincoln watched Nate's face intently, noticing the way his eyes narrowed and his cheeks lost what little colour they'd had.

'Craig? Are you sure?'

'We're sure,' said Dilke. 'But since we can't think why he'd have an issue with Chris, we're assuming he was put up to it by someone who *did* have an issue with Chris.'

'And you think that someone is me.' A statement, not a question. 'Look, I've made some mistakes in the past, okay? I slept around, I drank too much, I got into drugs. But that's all behind me now. I met an amazing woman, cleaned up, settled down. Got two kids. Got some voice work lined up. My little girl Chelsea's about to hit the big time on kiddies' telly. I'd be a fucking idiot to throw all that away, wouldn't I?'

'You might've been afraid stuff was going to come out in Chris's podcast,' Lincoln suggested. 'Stuff you'd rather keep hidden.'

'Stuff like what? Winding Vaughn up, you mean?'

'Setting him up, more like. The explicit photos, the suggestive little notes…'

'We were *kids,'* he said, cutting across Dilke. 'No excuse, okay, but we didn't know the old fella would go home and top himself. And what were we guilty of? We wrote a few silly notes, took some naughty photos. Oh, and I think we left some gay porn mags lying around for him to find.' The memory amused him. 'Mitch nicked those from the paper shop while Sheri went up to the counter and kept the guy talking. We were just having a laugh, y'know? Look, the whole thing started out as a joke to get back at him for telling us off all the time. And then it got boring, so we stopped.'

'You stopped,' said Lincoln,' because the object of your campaign of harassment was dead.'

'No, you're wrong! We'd given the whole thing up *way* before Christmas. Mitch came over all goody-goody, scared of what his old man would say if Vaughn walked out so late in the day. Look, it was *Vaughn* the punters came to see. We realised that as soon as the run started.' He leaned forward over his knees, hands clasped, no attempt to hide his tension. 'You really thought this was down to me, this murder? Because of my old man?'

'Two murders,' said Dilke. 'Chris and Orlando.'

'And it's not because of your father,' Lincoln put in. 'It's because we believe your cousin Craig set up the attack on Chris and, presumably, the attack on Orlando Snell.'

'He did?' This clearly came as a shock. 'Then I'm an easy target, aren't I? An ex-con for a father, a chancer for an uncle, a fuckwit for a cousin. Obvious suspect. Mud sticks. If people get the idea this had anything to do with me, I can kiss my career goodbye. And Chelsea's.'

'What about the other Board Treaders?' said Dilke. 'The Burnett brothers, Sherilyn. Any of them anxious to keep Chris quiet?'

Nate shrugged. 'You'd have to ask them.'

'Who else knew you had – let's say – criminal connections?' Lincoln didn't see the need to dress it up.

'Never made a secret of it. They all knew about my dad and my Uncle Dave – Mitch and Cody and Eloise, Sherilyn.'

'Eloise?'

'Eloise Burnett. The big sister. Whoa, she was a looker back in the day, but she was twenty-three, twenty-four at the time, and I didn't fancy ending up with an older woman.'

Lincoln made a mental note to follow up on this Eloise. He recalled the newspaper photo Woody had found, Vaughn with Bill Burnett and his daughter toasting the theatre's golden jubilee in 1987, when she'd have been about twenty.

He'd travelled here expecting to confirm Nate Newton as the most likely suspect. But his confession to the harassment of Vaughn had come all too easily. He didn't seem ashamed of what he and the other Board Treaders had done, so why would he want to silence Darbyshire?

Were the other three Board Treaders going to react similarly? Was this pool of suspects about to drain away?

Should Eloise Burnett's name be in that pool?

Lincoln stood up. 'How often do you see Craig?'

'I haven't seen him for years and if he turned up here, I'd slam the door in his face and he fucking knows it.'

'Cops were here. Not local. From Barbury. They've just left.'

'Fuck it, Nate! What did you tell them?'

'Didn't tell them anything. They were asking about that nonce Vaughn and the pantomime. They were asking about Craig.'

'Craig? How did they get on to Craig?'

'Fuck knows! *I* don't know what he's been up to and he's my bloody cousin! Care to fill me in, Sheri?'

Nate heard her sigh as if he was asking her to do him an enormous favour. 'He's been taking care of business. The podcaster business.'

'That was *Craig*?' So the cops weren't joking when they said Craig was wanted for murder. 'You've got to go to the police, Sheri. You've got to get ahead of this.'

'Ahead of it? I'm part of it, Nate. We're both part of it.'

'Me? It's nothing to do with *me*. Think what this'll do to Chelsea! They're already talking to her about a second series and...'

'What'll it do to your little girl when people find out

you pushed Simeon Piper off the stage so you could take his place in the panto? How's that gonna look, eh?'

'What?'

'You know he died, don't you?'

'Who died?'

'Simeon. Because of what happened. Not right away, but being in a wheelchair, having trouble breathing… He was only twenty when he died, and that's, ultimately, down to you.'

'It was an accident. He was arsing around.'

'No, Nate, you pushed him. I saw you do it. Like I said, we've all got something to hide.'

CHAPTER 43

Annie Darbyshire put her head in her hands and groaned. All this admin to deal with in the aftermath of Chris's murder! She hadn't even got the death certificate yet.

Who told you these things when you got married, warned you about what you'd have to deal with when things went wrong?

Losing Gracie hadn't prepared her for this. Chris had taken care of the official stuff when their daughter was killed, leaving Annie to deal with contacting Gracie's friends and the rest of the family, directing her own grief to the organisation of the funeral and a celebration of the teenager's life.

She'd even reached out to the family of Tara, the girl who'd driven her car so fast and so erratically along country lanes that she'd sent it flying into the air when it clipped a verge. Flying into the air, with Gracie in the passenger seat without a seatbelt.

The night Gracie died was the last time Annie and Chris had made love.

He'd thought she blamed him for letting Gracie go out that night, but she didn't. He'd blamed himself even more. He'd given their daughter his blessing when she'd begged to go with Tara to a party in Pewsey, even though Annie had felt unsure.

'Tara's only just passed her test, Chris. I don't think it's a good idea.'

'It's only twenty miles and Tara's a sensible kid.'

'But she'll be driving at night. She won't know the road.'

'Then she'll go slowly. You know how much Gracie's looked forward to this party.'

But Tara hadn't gone slowly and Annie would never know whether the party lived up to Gracie's expectations. In the space of an evening, a night, her daughter was gone.

She was roused from her thoughts by someone knocking on the side door. Strangers always came to the front, but regular visitors knew the side door was the one to hammer on. It opened straight into the farmhouse kitchen that, years ago, had boasted a range and flagstones, a drying rack suspended from the ceiling with sheets and towels draped across it. How homely it had felt then. Now, modernised and streamlined, the kitchen felt cold and sterile. Empty.

She opened the door. Sherilyn stood there in an ankle-length puffa coat, pushing her hood back as she barged in.

'Christ, Annie, it's bloody awful out there. This drizzle's turned my hair into a rat's nest.'

She slipped her coat off, pulled a chair out and plonked herself down at the kitchen table with as much familiarity as Molly did, even though she hadn't set foot in this house in over a year. Indeed, she and Annie hadn't met since Chris left.

'I thought you were in Borehamwood or somewhere.' Annie had seen a photo of Sherilyn letting shoppers take selfies with her while she pushed a trolley round a supermarket.

'Got back last night. Much to Valerie's displeasure, the grumpy cow.'

'Coffee?' Annie had made herself a pot when she'd begun to tackle her heap of forms and it should still be warm.

'Wine. You got wine? I don't care if it's red or white as long as it takes the edge off.'

With two glasses and a bottle of red in front of them, they sat at the table, Annie wary of her cousin, Sherilyn breezily friendly as if there'd never been the slightest discord between them. But at last, after she'd poured herself a third glass of Pinot Noir, the reason for her visit became clear.

'Did you read what Chris was writing about Auntie Lydia?'

Annie shook her head. 'I didn't even know he was working with her until after… I've only just found out. I thought he was still writing a series with Fred August, but they hadn't worked together for months.'

'Oh, I knew he wasn't working with Fred any more,' Sherilyn said. 'Lydia told me all about that. That's why she offered him the ghost-writing gig last year. She knew he needed the money.'

'I know his work had slowed down but…'

'The work had *disappeared,* love. The last couple of shows he and Fred wrote together were absolute crap. No one was interested in anything else they were doing.'

'That bad?' Annie felt the wine relaxing her. She wanted to let everything go, to let her responsibilities slip away like a costume she could step out of. She wanted the pain to stop. She didn't want to think about who'd killed Chris. That it could be someone she knew.

Someone like Sherilyn.

'The police been here?' Sherilyn drained her glass, poured herself more wine.

'Yes, but I couldn't tell them much. Chris hasn't lived here for months.'

'They've just left Nate's. He called me, all wound up.

You know what they think, don't you? That it's all to do with that Hamilton Vaughn. They think one of us paid someone to kill Chris because of this podcast he was doing. You knew about that?'

'A true crime thing, yes.' She didn't want to admit she'd been in the dark about that, too, until Lydia had enlightened her.

'*You* don't think I'm involved, do you?' Sherilyn leaned close, peering into her face.

'I wouldn't have let you through the door if I thought that.' Annie picked up her own glass and emptied it quickly, avoiding her cousin's gaze.

'See, we've all got something to hide, Annie. Could be any one of us.'

'Who are you talking about?'

'The Board Treaders. Me and Nate, Cody and Mitch. We all did it, winding Vaughn up, trying to get him into trouble.'

'By accusing him of sexual assault? That's a bit more than "winding him up", Sheri. It ruined his life. He killed himself because of those allegations.'

'You don't know that. He was a miserable old sod at the best of times.'

'Don't you feel even a tiny bit responsible?' Annie glanced at Sherilyn's face, seeing how her obsession with plastic surgery had ruined it. She'd had brow lifts, cheek fillers and a procedure that narrowed her nose so much, it didn't look real. Her lips were like two shiny bolsters, their natural definition lost.

'It was the boys that set Vaughn up, Annie. Okay, I joined in, but it was just a bit of fun. Rehearsals were so bloody boring. But it was the boys that set him up.'

'You think one of "the boys" is behind this? You think Nate or Cody or Mitch had my husband killed?'

Sherilyn sat back in her chair, oblivious to Annie's mounting indignation. 'I don't know, but like I said, we've all got things to hide.'

'And what have *you* got to hide, Sheri?'

'Me? I saw Nate push that boy off the stage.'

'What boy?'

'Simeon Piper. You must remember him from when you were in the Board Treaders. His dad had that farm off the Bridgeford road.'

Annie recalled a fresh-faced lad a few years younger than her. He had curly hair so blond it was almost white. He had a sweet singing voice and was a natural dancer. 'Nate pushed him off the stage?'

'Nate got passed over for the panto. The only way he'd get a part was if another Board Treader had to pull out, so he got into a play fight with Simeon and shoved him into the orchestra pit.'

'But that's a six-foot drop.'

'Yeah. He broke his back. They had to carry him out to the ambulance on a board.' Tipsy now, Sherilyn giggled at the memory. 'Vaughn appeared from nowhere, but he wasn't quick enough to catch him. Poor old Simeon! But at least Nate got the part he wanted.'

'But didn't Simeon tell them Nate pushed him?'

'How could he? He was in a coma for three months and when he came round, he couldn't remember what happened.'

'And by then,' Annie said, bitterly, 'Vaughn was dead and you were keeping your mouth shut. Was that why you and the boys all ganged up on Vaughn with those stupid stories about him molesting one of them? Was Nate afraid he'd seen him push Simeon?'

Sherilyn shrugged. 'Maybe. And they weren't "stupid stories", not entirely. Vaughn was forever taking Cody aside, arm round his shoulders, whispering in his ear.'

Annie had heard enough. Chris was dead because of the scheming of four silly teenagers. And what about Orlando Snell? Both men – and Vaughn – dead because one talentless boy was desperate to cover up a selfish attack on another boy.

'But Sheri, you knew it was Nate's fault. You saw what happened.'

'Yeah, but I wasn't going to say anything, was I? Me and Nate were buddies. Still are.' She smiled slyly. 'Knowledge is power. If Nate ever crosses me, he'll find out he can't mess with Sherilyn Croft and get away with it.'

'You've kept it secret all this time? And now you expect me to keep your secret too?'

'Who you gonna tell?'

Indeed, who *could* she tell? Vaughn and Simeon Piper were long gone. If she got Sherilyn into trouble, Molly would be devastated and her Uncle Martin would never forgive her.

'But why did Mitch and Cody want to shut Chris up? What have *they* got to hide?'

Sherilyn lifted her glass in a toast. 'Mitch is a big name now, isn't he? Not gonna look good, is it, that he persecuted some old guy because he was gay. An old gay guy.' Another childish giggle. 'And it was Mitch who planned it all, the letters and the photos and the dirty magazines. He was the one who kept on about Vaughn being a paedo.'

'And Cody?'

'He wasn't very happy, but he went along with it.' She reached for the bottle again. 'Always under Mitch's thumb. He'd never stand up to him, like Mitch would never stand up to their dad.' She staggered to her feet and went in search of more wine.

Annie watched her, grateful that she'd never let herself get drawn into her circle.

'Vaughn fancied Cody and Mitch took advantage of it.' Sherilyn found a bottle of Pinot Grigio in the fridge and opened it. 'Actually, it was pretty mean, when you look back on it.'

'It was cruel.' Annie watched as her cousin sloshed Pinot into both glasses, spilling much of it. 'Mitch would lose a lot of fans if the truth came out.' She reached for her glass but didn't pick it up. She'd had enough to drink. She needed to stay alert. 'Is that why Chris was killed? To cover up an idiotic game you all played to get back at Vaughn?'

'Is Chris's laptop here?'

'Why would it be? He moved out last year.'

'I know, but after he died, the cops must've given you his personal stuff.'

'No, they kept everything.'

His clothes, wallet, watch, phone – all retained as evidence. But his laptop? Probably left at Leanne's before he took her out to dinner. A wave of nausea hit her and she shut her eyes until it had passed. What was on the laptop that Sherilyn wanted to see, or didn't want anyone else to see?

'The police must still have it,' she said, looking away. 'They've got everything else.'

Sherilyn didn't speak for a few minutes, sipping her wine thoughtfully. 'Mitch won't be happy to hear that. He'll want to know what Chris wrote about him.'

'What makes you think Chris had already written anything about Mitch? He'd have gathered information first, background stuff. That's how he worked. He may not have got as far as writing about any of you.'

That seemed to placate Sherilyn and she was quiet

again. Her gaze roamed the room. 'I can see why our Moll likes coming here.'

'I like having her around.'

'Valerie's always nagging her about what she eats, what she wears, why doesn't she go out more… The kid's naturally shy. Not like me.' She grinned. 'Remember the parties your mum and dad used to have here? Remember, Annie? The actors from the theatre? That guy who played Scott Joplin rags all night? You still got that piano?'

The baby grand had been sold after Annie's mother died. Chris used to say he'd buy it back, but Annie told him to save his money for when Gracie went to university.

Another wave of nausea. She could taste the sickly sweetness of the wine at the back of her throat. She pushed her glass away. 'No. The piano went.'

'Tell them you've got to have the laptop back. The police. Tell them you need it.'

Annie tensed. She didn't know where Chris's laptop was. Why was Sherilyn so concerned about it? 'What if they say no?'

'Tell them you *need* it. Make something up.'

'Okay, I'll try.'

Sherilyn's cheeks were flushed, her eyes glassy. 'Don't just *try*, Annie. Tell them. Insist!'

CHAPTER 44

It was dark by the time Lincoln and Dilke returned to Barley Lane. The days were getting shorter and Christmas was under eight weeks away. This year's panto at Barbury Theatre would already be in rehearsal, with a pantomime dame who'd probably never even heard of Hamilton Vaughn, let alone worked with him.

'We got nowhere with Craig Newton,' Woody said as Lincoln settled down at his desk. 'He said him driving along behind Leanne that night was just chance.'

'We tried to make him think Tawny Howell had put the finger on him,' Pam added. 'But he wasn't taken in.'

'Probably knows Howell's too scared to cross him. Even if he's in custody, he could be got at.' Lincoln's spirits sank even more. 'Did he give you *anything* useful?'

'Not really,' said Pam. 'He's been sleeping at the office, which suggests his marriage isn't too healthy. How did you get on in Borehamwood?'

Dilke told her what they'd learnt from Nate Newton.

'I didn't like him much,' Lincoln added. 'But I think he was telling the truth.'

The DCI phoned as Lincoln was making himself a coffee. No peace for the wicked. He had at least hoped for a few minutes to unwind after the journey back and the disappointment of having to dismiss Nate Newton as his prime suspect.

'We've arrested the two guys driving Harry Priest's van last Tuesday,' Connors said. 'Tim Anderson and Jay Vallis tracked them down: Milo Dodds and Luke Costello. They're being interviewed as we speak.'

'What have they been charged with?'

'Taking without the owner's consent in the first instance, although Tim's got a hunch they took the van with Priest's knowledge so they could load it up with Mr Fogarty's kitchen. He and Jay are going back to Priest's yard tomorrow with a search warrant. Let's hope they find something that leads us to Ritchie Payne.'

'And maybe Isaac Keats?'

'Not you, too, Jeff. If Tim mentions those old cases one more time…'

'How else can you explain Isaac's SIM card turning up in Priest's van?'

'He buys and sells mobile phones. And as for linking him to the Greenaway boy in 1990. That's nearly thirty years ago, and those boys didn't go missing in Barbury, did they? Isaac was in Trowbridge and Bob Greenaway was in Swindon.'

'Priest drives all over the place in his line of work, picking up junk, selling at local markets. And Bob lived in Barbury for a couple of years.'

'It's not enough, Jeff, not nearly enough. And even if it was, you'd need to let Swindon or Trowbridge handle it. It's their case, even if Harry Priest's on our patch.'

As soon as he put the phone down, Lincoln recalled what Trish had told him last night: before returning to Barbury to start rehearsals for *Jack and the Beanstalk*, Vaughn had worked with teenagers at a school in Swindon.

Bob Greenaway disappears in Swindon after being seen talking to an older man. Vaughn is in Swindon at the same time, summer 1990. Had they been wrong about him? Was it possible that he really was a man who preyed on teenage boys, as the Board Treaders had alleged at the time?

But then, Vaughn couldn't have abducted Isaac Keats eleven years later.

Lincoln sipped his coffee, staring at the whiteboard. He needed to re-arrange it to reflect Nate Newton's relegation from prime suspect.

In his own mind, Mitchell Burnett was the most likely candidate now, even if Connors didn't agree. He wanted to talk to him anyway, get his take on the Hamilton Vaughn affair, and so he asked Pam for his details.

Burnett wasn't answering his mobile but a woman answered the landline, explaining that she was Fenella Brooks, Mitchell's PA, and he wasn't there.

'He's had a series of meetings in London,' she said pleasantly. 'But I'm expecting him back on Friday. Can I ask what it's about, Inspector?'

'It's a private matter,' Lincoln said. 'I'd rather wait till I can speak to him in person.'

Pam was glowering at the whiteboard, hands on hips. 'Supposing it isn't *any* of the Board Treaders behind all this? Supposing it's somebody else entirely?'

'Who else has motive? Who else was Darbyshire writing about?' He grabbed his jacket and keys. 'In the absence of the great Mitchell Burnett, let's see what Sherilyn Croft's got to say for herself.'

'You've come to arrest me?' Sherilyn held her wrists out to Lincoln as if begging him to slap handcuffs on them. 'I'll come quietly. Although that's not my usual style.'

She was much smaller than her photos had led him to expect, petite beneath her Sweaty Betty top and leggings, but he wasn't about to underestimate her. Her face was heavily made-up, her brows two bold slashes above eyes that were thickly rimmed with kohl. The puffiness of her lips did nothing to soften the overall impression of hardness, and her breath smelled of alcohol.

'Have you been drinking, Ms Croft?' he asked, as he and Pam stood in the hallway of the Bancrofts' house on Folly Hill.

'Is the Pope Catholic?' She turned her back on them and waltzed down the hall.

Martin Bancroft emerged from the living room, interrupted in his perusal of *The Times,* his glasses pushed up on top of his head. 'What's going on?'

'We've come to speak to Sherilyn, Mr Bancroft,' said Pam. 'But we'll have to come back tomorrow, when she's sober.'

Bancroft regarded his daughter with disapproval bordering on disgust. 'Thought you'd given that up, Sheri. It's not us you're letting down, you know, it's yourself.' He looked up into Lincoln's face. 'What's this about?'

'That's between ourselves and Ms Croft.'

'Huh!' And he returned to the living room, slamming the door behind him.

'It's all Annie's fault,' Sherilyn said cheerfully. 'I went round to see her this afternoon and she brought the wine out.'

Lincoln wasn't about to let her off. 'We need to take a statement from you about your whereabouts last Tuesday. You'll have to come to Barley Lane tomorrow morning.'

'When do you want me?' She took a step nearer to him – near enough that he was hit by the stale sweetness of wine on her breath and the cloying musk of her perfume. 'Not too early, I hope. I'm not an early riser. Are you an early riser, Detective?'

'I have to be,' he told her, ignoring the innuendo. 'And it's Inspector Lincoln. I'll leave you my card.'

'Well, that was a waste of time.' Pam clearly hadn't been impressed. 'Really fancies herself, doesn't she, behaving like a woman half her age.'

'And is she going to turn up tomorrow morning or will she do a runner again?' Lincoln pulled the handbrake on. They'd hit the usual rush hour traffic, although they were going against the flow, driving into town. 'We need to look into the Burnetts' sister, too. Eloise. She'd be about fifty now. We shouldn't rule her out.'

'I didn't come across her when I was researching Mitchell and Cody, but I wasn't really looking for her. She may have a different surname now, of course. I'll see what I can find out.'

When they got back, Woody greeted them with the news that the Land Rover belonging to Russ Milner's mother had been off the road for at least two weeks, so couldn't have been driven to pick Leanne up.

'Back to square one?' Lincoln's gaze drifted towards the whiteboard. 'Did Milner borrow a car from someone else or did someone else pick her up?'

The whiteboard didn't respond.

'I just wish Leanne would text him again,' said Pam. 'Give us an idea of where she is and when she's coming home. She can't stay away for ever.'

'Wherever she is, she's got Darbyshire's laptop with her.' Lincoln didn't like to admit that he cared more about the laptop's welfare than Leanne's.

'Any luck with Sherilyn Croft?' Woody asked.

'Too pissed to be interviewed. I've told her to come in tomorrow morning. We may get something out of her then.'

'You think she's capable of organising Darbyshire's murder?' Woody sounded sceptical.

Pam reached for her cycle helmet, ready to leave for the day. 'I'd say she's too chaotic but maybe that's all just a smokescreen. She *is* an actress, after all.'

As the end of the day approached, Lincoln found himself alone in the incident room. When his desk phone rang, he ignored it. Then his mobile rang, so he thought he'd better answer it.

'I'm outside,' said Nick Chance. 'I've tried waving my hands at the door and shouting *Open Sesame*, but it's not working.'

Lincoln let him in, wondering what was so urgent that Nick couldn't wait till the morning. He led him away from the whiteboard once more, seating him at Breeze's desk. He offered him a black coffee and kept an eye on him while he made it.

'I met with Cody today,' said Nick, as Lincoln dumped his coffee down in front of him. 'We talked about Chris Darbyshire's murder and he was kinda shocked when I told him he was a suspect.'

'I need to interview him in the next day or two. And that's not an interview under caution, Nick, simply asking him a few questions.' Lincoln pulled up a chair and sat the wrong side of Breeze's desk, trying not to be distracted by the litter of unsorted paperwork, takeaway menus and crumpled food wrappers on it.

'I've got a favour to ask, Jeff. On Cody's behalf.'

Uh-oh. 'Yes?'

'You have some photos and letters he'd like back.'

'He's got no right to anything he sent Vaughn.'

Nick pursed his lips and tried again. 'It's the photos he'd particularly like back.'

'He *can't* have them back. Those photos are part of our investigation. Unfortunately, someone got hold of them before we did and sent them to the press, so even if I gave you the originals – and you know I can't – there's no guarantee they won't turn up somewhere in the future. If it's any consolation, Nick, the pictures are suggestive rather than explicit.'

Lincoln had to trust that Karen Bolitho had handed everything over to Woody and, indeed, that Jackson had handed everything over to *her*.

'Who else knows you've got them? I mean,' said Nick eagerly, as if he'd spotted a let-out, 'if you gave those photos back to Cody, who'd know you ever had them? Is your case going to stand or fall because of them? Don't you have enough other evidence?'

'You're asking me to interfere with the investigation? Seriously?'

'Can you imagine Cody's embarrassment, his humiliation, if those photos are brought up in court?'

'Can you imagine the even greater embarrassment and humiliation for *me* if I was found to have removed evidence and altered the log to save a suspect some awkward press coverage? Christ, Nick, I'm surprised you even asked me.' Lincoln finished his coffee and got up from his chair.

'Vaughn was infatuated with him.' Nick stood up too and followed him to the filing cabinet on which sat the mucky tray where the kettle and mugs were kept. 'Obsessed, even. You know that movie *Death in Venice?'*

Lincoln recalled Cathy making him watch some slow, maundering film starring Dirk Bogarde, with Mahler booming on the soundtrack while the Bogarde character yearned for the androgynous lad who was staying at the same Venice hotel. As he, at last, dared to approach the youth, Bogarde's character collapsed and died.

'You're likening Vaughn and Cody to the man and boy in that film?'

'Cody did nothing more than let Vaughn fall for him. It was the other kids who tried to take advantage of the situation and...'

'Don't make excuses for him, Nick. I'll make up my own mind when I've spoken to him.'

'If he could have just one or two photos back...' Nick was pleading now. 'He wants to protect his family. He doesn't want his wife and kids to think he's gay.'

Lincoln rounded on him. 'He was a fifteen-year-old boy under the influence of a man old enough to be his grandfather. If he *had* had feelings for Vaughn, would that be so very shameful in this day and age?'

'It could finish his marriage.'

'And being a suspect in a double murder case couldn't?'

Nick turned to go. 'I thought you'd be more understanding.'

'And I thought *you* would know better than to expect me to betray my principles.' Lincoln strode ahead of him towards the door. 'I'll show you out.'

'Jeff.' Nick lingered on the doorstep. 'It's two fucking photographs I'm asking for. Two fucking photos.'

'Like I said, those photos have been entered into evidence. And what's the big deal? They're Polaroids of a teenage boy taking his clothes off.'

'Jeff, please...'

'And you thought I'd casually remove something that crucial from evidence and hand it over to your client? Christ, Nick, even after all these years of not seeing each other, I thought you knew me better than that. The answer's no. That's the end of the matter.'

And with that, he eased the door shut, obliging Nick to step out onto the pavement and walk away.

THURSDAY 2ND NOVEMBER

CHAPTER 45

On Thursday morning, early, before it was light, a train driver reported a pile of builders' waste fly-tipped in a farm gateway next to the railway line: rotten timbers, empty paint tubs, parti-board, torn rubble sacks. Some heavy-duty polythene sheeting gave him most concern because it looked liable to venture onto the railway track if the wind got up.

Within a few hours, a maintenance crew turned up to take a look. A paint-spattered tarpaulin had already begun to dance towards the rails, so work had to be done. One of the men went behind some bushes to take a leak. As he was zipping himself up again, he caught sight of a rain-soaked bundle of fabric. More builders' waste, he thought, until he realised he was looking at the lifeless body of a woman.

Clearing up the fly-tipping would have to wait.

CHAPTER 46

The big double doors into Harry Priest's yard in Finisterre Street were already open when Tim Anderson and Jay Vallis arrived that morning with a search warrant.

'You've got a fucking nerve.' Priest emerged from his office, mug of tea in hand. '*I'm* the victim here. *I'm* the poor bugger who's lost his van and his livelihood.' He banged the mug down on top of a stack of boxes, slopping most of the tea onto the ground.

'Stay back and let us get on with it, Harry,' said Jay. 'If there's nothing here, you've nothing to worry about.'

Anderson scanned the cobbled yard, the crates, the boxes. There was a hell of a lot to search and the various elements of Mr Fogarty's stolen kitchen were unlikely to be here. The white van that had carried them away last Tuesday morning hadn't been filmed coming back into town until it drove into Spicer Street that night and gave Ritchie Payne a lift.

'Let's get cracking then,' he said, and watched while two uniforms made a start.

Within a few minutes, they'd turned up some unexpected gems: cartons of illicit cigarettes; crates of whisky of dubious origin; rolls of ten- and twenty-pound notes tucked behind the till in the office; a further six thousand in notes in the safe. They searched diligently for another hour or so until, just when they thought they'd find nothing more worthwhile, Jay discovered a wooden box, its lid scuffed and scratched, in the loft above Priest's office.

Anderson climbed the rickety stairs to see. 'What

have you got there?'

The box was full of pornographic photographs and magazines, hardcore stuff, foreign imports, some featuring adults, others featuring youngsters who looked some years below the age of consent. The oldest magazines were dated 1987, the newest 2010. Under the magazines were a dozen or so VHS tapes, home-made, labelled with the date but nothing else.

Jay and Anderson looked at each other. Jay was the first to speak. 'What the fuck have we found?'

While Anderson and Vallis were working their way through Harry Priest's yard, Lincoln was waiting in vain for Sherilyn Croft to arrive at Barley Lane.

'Either she's stood us up,' Pam supposed, 'or she's too hungover to get out of bed.'

Lincoln sighed in frustration. 'How do we pin anything on Craig Newton at this rate? So far, it's Tawny Howell's word against his that he hired him and Alana.'

'We'll have to work our way through the other Board Treaders until we find a connection. You're sure Nate's not involved?'

'I've been wrong before but no, I'm pretty sure Nate's in the clear.' Although it pained him to admit it. After his awkward meeting with Nick yesterday, and Cody's apparent anxiety to recover photos from the scrapbook, Lincoln was beginning to think Cody wasn't as blameless as Nick made out.

His desk phone rang. The DCI. He tutted. Now what?

'Thought you'd like an update,' said Connors. 'According to Tim Anderson, Dodds and Costello, our kitchen thieves, were tipped off by a guy who'd done some woodwork in Fogarty's house last month. He knew the Fogartys would be away for a few days so he gave Dodds and Costello the details, in exchange for a share of what they made when they sold it on. He even had copies of the house keys.'

'Don't tell me – Garvin Steele.'

He could hear Connors smiling. 'It was indeed. Maybe we're going to put him away after all.'

No sooner had Connors ended the call than another one came in: Warminster nick.

'A body's been found,' the detective sergeant told him sombrely. 'Could be your missing arts officer.'

Rain clouds were piling up on the horizon as Lincoln and Woody passed through the gate to where Leanne Milner's body lay beside the railway line, a few miles from Warminster. The wind was getting up, stirring the discarded polythene on the opposite embankment. Lincoln introduced himself to the uniformed officer guarding the scene, thinking he looked familiar.

'PC Dylan Wilcox, sir,' Wilcox said, clipboard at the ready. 'The suspicious death at Willow Cottage, remember? That lady shot in the kitchen? You attended with your DS.'

'Yes, of course. That was DS Cook from Park Street. She's moved on. This is DS Mike Woods from Barley Lane.'

With their coveralls on, they followed the route to where Leanne lay in a natural dip between the fence and some blackthorn bushes that would have screened her from passing trains. Doctor Viv Caddick – someone else Lincoln had encountered at Willow Cottage in July – was crouched over the body. Recognising him, she regarded him with a familiar disdain.

How pathetic Leanne's body looked. One arm flung

over her face, the other arm trapped beneath her, her legs crossed at the ankles as if she'd been hurriedly tipped out of a sheet or tarpaulin, with no attempt to arrange her limbs, to afford her some dignity. It was as if she'd been thrown away.

'Anything you can tell us about how she died or when?'

'You're joking, aren't you?' Viv stood up, pushing her hood back and revealing a bright blue fringe, a change from the magenta she'd sported in July. 'She certainly hasn't been struck by a train. I've seen plenty of train deaths and this isn't that. As to when…' A big shrug. 'You'll know more after the autopsy. Now, please bugger off so I can get on with my job.'

Lincoln and Woody withdrew, looking around the immediate area for any cameras – in vain. There wasn't a building in sight and whoever dumped Leanne's body had probably waited until it was dark, using their car headlights for illumination while they disposed of her, rolling her body out of a tarpaulin, perhaps, letting her fall any old how.

Woody stroked his moustache thoughtfully. 'Reckon she was killed soon after she dumped her car.'

'If it wasn't Milner who picked her up, who was it? Jenny Reedy says his car didn't leave Glastonbury during that time and his mother's is off the road.'

'He could have access to another vehicle. Could've got someone to help him.'

'Or it wasn't him. Forensics should tell us more. If she tried to fight someone off, there could be skin under her fingernails.'

'Where's all her stuff?' Woody wondered. 'She wasn't even wearing a coat.'

'If she thought she was going all the way to

Glastonbury, she'd have taken her coat off when she got in the car. Which makes me think it was Milner who picked her up.'

'In someone else's car.' Woody took a last look around the scene before they walked back to the car. 'So how did she manage to send him a text on Sunday night?'

'She didn't. But if he had her phone, he could send himself a text from it, make us think it was from her. Or someone else could've done. Let's not make assumptions.'

They peeled their coveralls off and got back in the car.

'We need to let Milner know she's been found,' said Lincoln, executing an inelegant three-point turn in the narrow lane. 'And we're going to tell him to his face, see his reaction. Come on, let's get it over with.'

When he heard that his wife's body had been found, Russ Milner sagged as if he'd been jabbed in the gut with a sharp stick. He leaned weakly against the door jamb and covered his mouth with his hand.

'You mean, she threw herself in front of a train?'

'That's not how it looks,' said Lincoln, thinking how much harder it would have been to establish how she'd died if her killer had left her body across the tracks. If Milner was the culprit, had he been unable to bring himself to desecrate his wife's body in that way?

'Oh God, the kids will be home from school any minute.' He reeled backwards into the house, lurching down the hallway to the kitchen as if the whole house was pitching and rolling. 'What am I going to say to them?'

'Tell them the truth,' said Lincoln. 'Right now, we need you to identify her. Can a neighbour keep an eye on things while you're out?'

'I'd rather wait till the kids get back.' He checked his

watch. 'They'll be here any minute. Or maybe I shouldn't break it to them until I've seen her, just in case it isn't her. And I can't break it to them and shoot straight out the door. I'll text Ben, tell him I've had to go out. He's my eldest. He's sensible.'

They hung back while he sent his son a text and waited for a confirmation. There was no need to rush, Lincoln knew. Viv Caddick would have to finish her examination and then supervise the start of the body's transportation to the mortuary at Presford General.

'Let's go, then,' Milner said, taking his coat down from the rack in the hall. 'Oh God, I hope you've got it wrong.'

CHAPTER 47

'I didn't think you'd want to see me.' Jessica Hale sank awkwardly onto a dining chair and waited while Annie settled herself on the sofa. 'I was going to call you, but I didn't know what to say.'

'Saying sorry would've been a good start.' Annie listened to herself sounding as if she was admonishing one of her Year 10s. 'But it's too late now. Chris is gone and we're left to pick up the pieces. How are you coping?'

'My brother's been very supportive. And you?'

'Not sure it's properly hit me yet.' Annie took a deep breath. Any minute now, she kept thinking. Any minute now it'll seem real. Until then…

'I don't know what to do with his papers, the stuff he was working on. Toby was going to throw it all away but rightfully, it's yours.'

And what about his clothes, thought Annie, his shampoo, his aftershave, all the things I've missed since he moved out? The towel left damp on the side of the bath, still smelling of his shaving foam; the mouthwash so strong it would strip paint; the coal tar soap he favoured. Those things had been rightfully hers, too, but this woman, this *girl,* had stolen them away.

'I'll take his papers now,' she said. 'Has his laptop turned up?'

'Not yet, as far as I know. His girlfriend must have it.'

'Yes, probably.' In spite of everything, Annie felt sorry for Jessica, the betrayer betrayed. 'We can sort everything else out later. As to the funeral arrangements… Well, we won't have to worry about that until the police have released his body.'

So businesslike she sounded, so detached, while her heart was in agony. She wanted to hug this young woman, who must be hurting as much as she was. But she also wanted to make her suffer, to pay for the damage she'd done.

'I'll get them for you.' Jessica started to get up.

'No, that's okay. Tell me where they are and I'll fetch them myself.'

Everything in the little room upstairs was boxed up, even a framed photo of Chris and Jessica together in the summer, before her baby bump showed. Box files, notebooks, pens and pencils, sticky notes, paperclips. A calendar like the one at home, and that wonky pottery mug he'd used as a pen pot. He was always knocking it over, so it had long ago lost its handle.

Tears stung Annie's eyes. She left the photo behind and, with the briefest of goodbyes, carried the cardboard box out to her car.

Annie took the box of Chris's things up to his study. She was bringing part of him home, where he belonged. She hadn't wanted to unpack the box, not yet, but Sherilyn's persistence about retrieving his laptop had unsettled her. Why was she so worried about that podcast?

She lifted some papers out of the box and leafed through them. Background notes on Barbury Theatre. A brief chronology of Vaughn's life, with gaps and question marks. Notes on a house in Marlborough – what did that have to do with anything? Notes on each of the Board Treaders, including poor Simeon Piper. Oh God, and a couple of nude photos of – Cody? Nate?

In spite of herself, Annie peered at them, wondering

who'd taken them and why Chris had them. In one photo, Cody was sitting back in a chair, clearly aroused, a look of ecstasy on his youthful face. In the other, he was wrestling with Nate, the teenagers' lithe bodies tangled together in a feat of acrobatics that was hardly erotic, although – presumably – it was meant to be.

She cast them aside and pulled more papers out of the box, finding a dozen photocopies of what looked like pages from an account book. Where did these pages come from and why had Chris got them?

She dropped them back into the box when she heard soft footsteps on the stairs. A moment later, Molly poked her head round the door.

'Can I come to you for a bit?' she asked. 'It's hell at home. Are those Chris's things?'

Annie checked that the nude photos were hidden deep down.

'Yes,' she said, 'but I'm going to put them away for now. Let's have some tea.'

CHAPTER 48

The discovery of a woman's body was all over social media even before Lincoln, Woody and Russ Milner arrived at Presford General. One of the railway clean-up crew had leaked it, Lincoln found out later, which explained why a convoy of three cars followed the van that was carrying the body back to the mortuary.

By the time Milner had identified Leanne and been given some time to compose himself, it was getting on for six o'clock.

'What happens now?' he asked as they drove him home.

'We'll need a DNA sample from you,' Lincoln said. 'For elimination purposes.'

'For elimination – what? You think *I* killed her?'

'It's so the pathologist can identify any DNA found on Leanne that *isn't* yours,' Woody explained. 'Your DNA is likely to be on her clothes from whenever you were last in close contact. The pathologist needs to eliminate that from any other DNA that's recovered.'

'What DNA will you find after all this time?'

'You'd be surprised.' Lincoln glanced in the rear-view mirror but couldn't see the man's face clearly.

'Who can have done this to her? Is it the same people that killed Chris?'

'Too soon to say. Someone will come to you tomorrow morning to take a swab,' said Lincoln. 'I'm sorry it's turned out this way, Russ. We were hoping to find Leanne alive, especially after you got that text.'

In the rear-view mirror, he saw Milner rest his head

against the car window and shut his eyes. He didn't say another word until they stopped outside his house. He opened the car door but took his time getting out. Was he about to confess? Lincoln held his breath.

'I don't know what I'm going to tell the kids,' Milner said. 'I was so sure it was a mistake.'

'Tell them the truth,' said Woody. 'That's always best.'

They drove back to Barley Lane.

'I don't envy him having to break it to his family.'

'Save your sympathy, Woody. Russ Milner's the killer.'

'What makes you so sure?'

'Gut instinct. And I know that's not enough, but…' Lincoln swung the car into the yard behind Barley Lane. 'She was driving towards Glastonbury, sticking to back roads, avoiding traffic cams because she didn't want us to stop her and bring her in for questioning. Who knew she was doing that? Russ. She probably called him as she was leaving home and he told her he'd meet her at Boyton.'

'You don't think Craig Newton sent Howell and Alana after her?' Woody was close on his heels as Lincoln hurried indoors.

'If Craig wanted to kill her, he'd have got to her the night Darbyshire died, or the day after. And he'd have got to her while she was at home, alone. No, I think Russ told her to dump her car and wait for him to pick her up so he could take her on to Glastonbury. Instead, he drove her somewhere secluded, killed her and dumped her body by the railway line as soon as it started to get dark.'

'And used her phone to send himself a text.'

'Exactly.'

Lincoln arrived at his desk and realised he'd been

doing the very thing he was always warning his team about: *never assume.*

Pam came over. 'Was it her?'

'Afraid so.'

'Suicide?'

He shook his head.

'You're thinking Russ killed her?'

He put his head in his hands, rubbed his face, suddenly so weary he couldn't think straight. 'Yes, but I've nothing to back it up beyond a natural distrust of him and that's not nearly enough. Let's wait for the autopsy.'

'There was a call from one of the CSIs while you were out,' she said. 'Something about some forensics reports getting mixed up. They didn't send us the whole report on Leanne's car, apparently, Some pages got picked up with another report by mistake. They're emailing you the whole thing again.'

Mystified, he turned his screen on. 'I hadn't noticed anything missing.' There was no forensics report waiting in his inbox. Maybe they'd send it first thing tomorrow morning. Why was nothing ever straightforward?

He got up from his chair and shoved it so hard against his desk that it rebounded, skating across the floor.

'Why does everything have to be so bloody complicated?' He grabbed his mug, slopping cold coffee onto his paperwork. Before he could finish mopping it up, his phone started ringing.

'Trevor Howell,' said the DCI. 'He wants a word.'

Lincoln had been gone only a few minutes when a call came through on Pam's phone. It was Jessica Hale.

'She's been found, then,' she said, before Pam had a chance to ask her how she was. 'Leanne.'

'I can't confirm anything, Jessica. I'm sorry.'

'It's all over Facebook.'

'It isn't official. We'll release a statement when we've got something definite to say.'

'Am I in danger? Will they come after me, too?'

'You're not in any danger,' Pam said, hoping against hope that she was right. 'But of course, if anything gives you cause for concern… You're quite isolated there at the farm. Is there anywhere you could stay for a bit, somewhere a bit nearer…' She nearly said "civilisation". 'Nearer other people?'

'Toby's here. Or I could go to my mum, I suppose, although we haven't spoken since Chris moved in here. Have you found his laptop? Did Leanne have it?'

'I can't tell you anything at this stage. I'm sorry.'

Jessica cut the call without a goodbye. Pam could understand her anger: she had a right to be kept informed, but discretion was vital. The less said…

Lincoln sat across the table from Tawny Howell, thinking how diminished the young man looked. Yesterday's bravado had gone.

'It were Craig, like you said.' He glanced sideways at his solicitor, Jean Vowles, who gave him the slightest of encouraging nods. 'Craig Newton. He paid us to kill Chris Darbyshire.'

'And did he tell you *why* he wanted Chris dead?'

'Weren't personal, he said. He were being paid by someone else.'

'Do you know who?'

'He never said. He come up to me at the garage two or three weeks back, said he wanted me to do some work for him, good money, cash in hand. Wanted me to keep tabs on this guy Darbyshire, find out where he went, who he were seeing, that sorta thing.'

'Keep tabs how?'

'We was to follow him, see if he had a routine. Only he didn't, not really. Except for shagging his girlfriend every couple of weeks. She works for the council. I seen the staff car park sticker on her car. Some mornings, he'd meet her at the theatre for a coffee and some nights I seen them go for a meal in town and she'd run him back to the train station, past Coronation Gardens.'

'Is that what gave you the idea of ambushing him there?'

A careless shrug. 'Dark there, innit? Easy to hide. Easy to get away.'

The murder hadn't been done on impulse, then.

Howell went on to describe how he'd got a call from Craig on the Tuesday morning that Darbyshire was in the theatre bar with his girlfriend. Follow him. Tonight could be the night.

Between them, he and Alana had watched Darbyshire all day. Howell had cycled to Leanne's house, waiting in the bus shelter across the road until she and Darbyshire drove back into town. He hung around until they left Pizza Marino, then cycled after them. As the car approached Coronation Gardens, he called Alana to warn her to look out for the red Yaris.

'It were kinda tight getting her to run out at the right moment. She left it a bit late and I thought she were gonna get run over, which weren't part of the plan.' He managed a cockeyed grin. 'She had to tell Darbyshire there were someone in the river.'

'What about Craig? Why was he there?'

Howell shook his head, puzzled. 'Craig weren't there.'

Hadn't he realised his boss was driving along behind the Yaris too? Or had Craig been there to make sure Howell and Alana didn't let him down?

'Has he paid you yet?'

'Only some of it.' Colour rose in his cheeks, the spots round his mouth rosy red.

'Promised me a car too. No way I could afford one otherwise.'

'Not going to get that car now, are you, Tawny?'

He frowned at his clasped hands. 'No.'

'Why did Craig want you to kill Orlando Snell?'

'He didn't. We went to get the bag of stuff he'd showed Darbyshire, only it weren't there. He said he left it somewhere. I were gonna let him go, but he went for my knife and Alana panicked. Hit him with, like, a gold statue off the shelf.'

'You're saying Alana struck Orlando Snell on the head?'

'Yeah, because she thought he were going for my knife. We got out of there fast. Waste of fucking time.'

'Sure you don't know who paid Craig to have Chris killed?'

Howell shook his head.

'You really want Craig to get away with this, Tawny? While you and Alana are locked up here, he's free to swan off to Spain with his dad. Does that seem right?'

'Spain? He don't like Spain. Says it's too hot.'

'But he's not going to hang around here, is he, once he knows we're after him?'

'He'll go to his lady friend.'

'And who's that?' Lincoln waited, holding his breath.

'He's never said. All I know is, she's older than him and she's got money.'

'You know where she lives?'

Jean Vowles looked pointedly at her watch. 'Do you intend to charge my client, Inspector?'

'Yes,' said Lincoln. 'But let him answer my question first.'

'Near Barbury somewhere,' said Howell. 'Couldn't tell you where.'

As he drove back to Barley Lane, Lincoln replayed the interview in his head. Someone had tipped Craig off that Darbyshire was at the theatre on Tuesday morning. From there, Howell and Alana had tailed him all day, right up until they lured him to his death in Coronation Gardens.

Cody Burnett was working at the theatre. Was he the one who'd contacted Craig?

Or was it Leanne, who'd arrived at the theatre bar before her lover and would have had ample time to contact him? Was Jessica Hale right? Had Leanne been in on it all along?

And who was this lady friend of Craig's?

FRIDAY 3RD NOVEMBER

CHAPTER 49

Lincoln waited while Antonia Yardley completed a preliminary examination. The mortuary was his least favourite place, especially this early on a dank autumn morning, but the solving of a suspicious death began here, with the victim. What clues would Leanne Milner's body reveal?

'First impressions?' Antonia talked into the dead woman's face as if she was addressing her. 'From the bruising round her throat and neck, death from manual strangulation. I should be able to confirm that when I've taken a closer look. It's likely she tried to fight off her attacker and I've taken scrapings from underneath her fingernails. Should be able to retrieve good DNA samples. You could get a match if her attacker's on the database, but of course, if they're not…'

'Here's hoping.' Lincoln was cautiously optimistic, although experience had taught him not to count his chickens too soon. 'She left Barbury around midday on Friday, heading for Glastonbury but never got there. Her car was found abandoned on Sunday morning.'

'She could've been killed as long ago as Friday but, given the exposure, the heavy rain and so on, it's hard to be sure. Her clothing may tell us something about where she's been since she left home.'

Lincoln recalled the text Russ Milner received from his wife on Sunday night, telling him not to worry while she went away to sort herself out.

'Got a suspect?' Antonia asked.

Did he? Leanne was fleeing the people who'd killed

her lover, but her husband knew what her plans were. She'd have trusted Russ when he told her how to avoid any possible pursuers: 'Stick to back roads, dump your car and I'll pick you up.'

Except, neither Russ Milner's car nor his mother's Land Rover had apparently left Glastonbury since the time Leanne abandoned her Yaris.

'She was having an affair with Chris Darbyshire. Her husband was aware and seemed very accepting of it and yet…' Lincoln shook his head.

'Husband or partner's always the first in the frame.' She turned away from the body. 'Any apple trees near where she was found?'

'Apple trees? There were a few bushes – hawthorn, maybe, blackthorn – but no apple trees. Why?'

'I noticed a strong whiff of fermented apples on her clothing, that's all. No rotting windfalls lying around near her?'

He shook his head. 'Could it be cider?'

'Could be, but it smelt more like, well, like rotting windfalls. We had a compost heap in our garden when I was a kid and Dad would chuck the windfalls onto it. It's a very distinctive smell. If it's apple pulp, there'll be residue on her clothes, in her hair if she was lying down in it or on her shoes if she's trodden in it.'

Leanne's ankle boots stood, bagged up, on the bench. The sight of her boots – what small feet she had – touched him.

'We're taking a swab from the husband this morning,' he said. 'We'll get that to you as soon as we can.'

'Thanks.' She returned to the body to continue her work. 'I'll let you know as soon as I find anything.' Without looking round, she added, 'You look like shit, by the way. Are you eating properly?'

'It'll be my New Year resolution. Keep me posted.'

With Tawny Howell's confession, they'd got enough to bring Craig Newton in for questioning, but when Woody and Pam went to Presford Motors to fetch him, they found his office empty, the sofa bed unmade.

'Said he was going home,' Yorkie the floor manager told them lugubriously. 'Said he needed a shower and a shag, not necessarily in that order.'

Pam and Woody exchanged glances and turned to go.

'He took a Honda SUV this time,' Yorkie said in disgust. 'It's me that gets my arse kicked by his dad when he takes them, not him. Dave'll kill me if that pillock wrecks another one.'

'I don't know where my husband is. I haven't seen him for days.'

In her smart house in Hyperion Avenue, Zelda Newton sat back in her capacious leather armchair. She had reluctantly let Woody and Pam in but insisted she didn't know where Craig was. At her feet, Pirate dozed on his front with his back legs sticking out.

'We've got a warrant for Craig's arrest,' said Woody. 'He's wanted for conspiracy to murder.'

'Murder? That's ridiculous.' She looked out at her garden, an arrangement of colourless shrubs around a big lawn. She was in her late thirties, Pam guessed, with a house full of streamlined furniture, uncluttered shelves, a home as neat as if it had been styled for a photoshoot in a glossy magazine.

But what use was any of that if her husband was heading for jail?

Last time Pam had seen her, Zelda had been roused rudely from sleep, a bathrobe over her pyjamas, but today she was dressed in expensive casuals: cream trousers, mint-green shirt, fawn ankle boots, long fawn jacket. What did Craig's lady friend look like? An older version of Zelda or the complete opposite?

'Do you know where his girlfriend lives?' she asked.

Zelda's gaze snapped back at once. Her eyes narrowed. 'Girlfriend? What girlfriend?'

'The girlfriend we've been told about,' said Woody. 'That's who he may have gone to now he knows we're on to him. He's wanted for questioning in connection with two murders, Zelda. If he doesn't give himself up, he's making things worse.'

'*Two* murders?' Her body language suggested calm, but her voice gave her away. Pirate pricked his ears up, alarmed, then staggered to his feet.

'The murders of Chris Darbyshire and Orlando Snell.'

'Orlando? That was *Craig*?'

The door opened wider and, hesitantly, Rocco came in. Pirate trotted over to him, butting against his legs. He fondled the dog's ears. 'Mum, you can't take the rap for what that creep's done.'

'Keep out of this, Rocco!'

'Zelda, if you hear from Craig, or if you can tell us anything that'll help us find him, call me.' Pam held out her business card, but Zelda wouldn't take it. She pointedly looked away – and didn't see her son reach out for it and slip it quickly into his pocket.

Meanwhile, Lincoln was skimming through the revised report on Leanne's Yaris. This version had an extra page which included a crucial detail: 'GPS tracker attached to car battery. Forwarded to DFT Devizes'.

'Leanne's car had a tracker installed. How do these things work? Any idea?'

'Don't look at me,' said Breeze.

'You attach it to your car battery,' Dilke explained, 'and it picks up signals from GPS satellites as you drive around. You link it to your phone or your laptop so you've got a record of where it's been and where it is at any given moment – depending on the signal. So there was one in Leanne's car?'

'Yes. It's been forwarded to Digital Forensics at HQ. Either she was scared her Yaris was going to get nicked or her husband was keeping tabs on her.'

'Cuh,' said Breeze, 'who'd nick a Yaris? Her old man didn't trust her, did he? Not after he found out she was shagging Chris Darbyshire.'

'Would we need Milner's phone or laptop to access the information?'

'No,' said Dilke. 'The tech team can download it. If Milner's been monitoring it on his phone, then he'll know exactly where she's been, even when he was in Glastonbury and she was here in Barbury.'

'And he'd know when she'd arrived at the meeting place they'd agreed near Boyton. Except his car didn't leave Glastonbury and neither did his mother's. If it *was* Milner who picked her up, he must've been driving someone else's car.'

'Seems a bit stupid leaving the tracker behind in the Yaris, though,' said Dilke. 'Makes him look guilty straightaway.'

Breeze chuckled. 'He couldn't very well pick Leanne up and say, "Leave your car here, darling, oh and hang on a sec while I take the tracker out." That would've been a dead giveaway.'

Lincoln made himself a coffee and stood drinking it while he stared at the whiteboard, willing it to give him a hint, a nudge in the right direction.

DCI Connors sounded doubtful when he rang her.

'Isn't it too soon to bring Milner in, Jeff? Where's your evidence? We've only just assigned a liaison officer to the family.'

He told her about the tracker. 'He was monitoring her movements.'

'So he's a jealous husband. Doesn't make him a killer.'

'But he must've used her phone to send himself that text.'

'You can't be sure that was him.'

What had happened to the rest of Leanne's belongings, he wondered? Handbag, overnight bag, coat and phone, along with Darbyshire's laptop. Had Milner taken them back to Glastonbury with him after he'd dumped her body?

Christ, had they been in the boot of the Hyundai when he brought the children home? Lincoln and Pam had searched the house, but they hadn't searched the car parked outside. A stupid mistake, he now realised.

'I could be wrong, ma'am, but I'm sure we'll find it's his DNA under Leanne's fingernails.'

'Wait till you get the results. If we jump the gun on this one, we'll end up looking like we don't know what we're doing. It's bad enough that we still haven't found Ritchie Payne.'

'Aren't Dodds and Costello talking?'

She groaned. 'Costello collapsed in his cell last night, possible panic attack, had to be rushed to hospital. We're waiting to hear how he is. In the meantime, Tim and Jay are having another go at Milo Dodds. They turned up a ton of porn at Harry Priest's yard, though. Priest swears it belonged to a mate of his, a Joseph Kelly, now deceased, who asked him to look after it for him.'

'He would say that, wouldn't he?'

'He could be telling the truth. The whole lot's pretty old. Tim's following it up, but I don't want him pursuing it at the expense of the search for Ritchie. And neither do I want to hear another word about those cold cases he's unearthed.'

'Bob Greenaway and Isaac Keats, you mean? But if Harry…'

'Too much of a distraction, Jeff. Tim needs to concentrate on finding Ritchie Payne.' She paused. 'We're unlikely to find him alive now, are we? We owe it to his parents – grandparents – to find out what happened and return him to them. There's nothing worse than not knowing.'

CHAPTER 50

Trish Whittington pushed open the door of the coffee shop and looked around. She was meeting someone for the first time and she wasn't sure what the other woman looked like.

She ordered a flat white and took a seat by the window so she wouldn't miss anyone arriving. Catching sight of her reflection, she was surprised yet again by her new cropped hairstyle. She no longer needed to keep tugging her skimpy ponytail through a scrunchie or tucking errant wisps of hair behind her ears. If it hadn't been for that embarrassing entanglement with Steve Quilter the other day…

The door opened and a tall, grey-haired woman stood there, eyes scanning the café from behind her scarlet-framed glasses. Her coat was bright red, long and belted, and under it she wore a black pencil skirt and knee-length red boots. She made a striking impression as she paused in the doorway before advancing towards Trish with her hand outstretched.

'I'm Kitty Hart-Taylor,' she said, grasping Trish's hand and dumping her capacious canvas bag on the opposite seat. 'I recognised you when I walked in because I've seen you at the library. I'll get myself a drink and then we can talk.'

Minutes later she was sitting across from Trish, sipping coffee and breaking open a packet of shortbread bites.

'So you want to know about Barbury Theatre.' She hauled her bag onto her lap and rooted through it, pulling out a sheaf of typewritten pages and plonking it on the table.

'It's Hamilton Vaughn I'm really interested in,' Trish said. 'You know, the pantomime dame who killed himself?'

'Dear Vaughn. That was terrible!' Kitty brushed shortbread crumbs aside. 'I started writing this little history years ago while I was working for the council. Revenue department. *Thunderingly* boring. Researching the history of Barbury Theatre was all that kept me sane. There's quite a bit about Vaughn in there, though I suppose it was Lydia Bancroft who knew him best. You've heard of Lydia?'

'My dad's always been a big fan.'

'Haven't we all?' She had a deep laugh and Trish found her easy company. 'So, how did you track me down?'

'I found your name on the theatre's Facebook page: Theatre Archivist, Kitty Hart-Taylor.'

'Huh! I *was* the archivist. Not any more. I was dumped. Their loss.'

Trish had arranged this meeting to see what more she could find out that might help Jeff. He'd been so cool towards her the last few days and she didn't know why. Of course, the holiday in Tenby had meant a lot to him – to her, too – but after her father broke his arm, she couldn't have enjoyed the rest of the week. There'd be other holidays, wouldn't there? Or were they heading for a break-up after all?

'I was devastated when I heard Orlando Snell was dead,' Kitty said, helping herself to another shortbread chunk. 'That man had a *huge* store of programmes, costumes, props. I mean, what's going to happen to it all? I'm telling you, if they auction it off, I'll be in there like a shot.'

'You're a big fan of the theatre?'

'Oh yes, always have been, ever since I was at Beedon House.'

'The school? But isn't that boys only?'

'I would've gone on the stage if I'd had my way,' Kitty went on, ignoring Trish's question. 'But my father didn't approve so it was out of the question. Now, what did you want to know about Vaughn? I had *such* a crush on him in my teens, went to every play he was in. I was fourteen, he was thirty-six, but I didn't see that as an obstacle.'

'You don't believe the rumours about him, then? About him pursuing one of the boys in the cast?'

'God, no! Some truly horrible things were said about him after he died – that he'd pushed some lad off the stage, that he was a kiddie-fiddler, an alcoholic. Dreadful things. Vile. But they didn't know him like I did.'

'I'd always assumed the rumours about him were true. I suppose I was too young to question it. I feel bad about it now.'

Kitty laid her hand gently on Trish's. 'Don't blame yourself, lovey. Be glad you're more open-minded now.' She picked up her cup again. 'Vaughn and I were close for a time, back in the late eighties. The summer before he died, he told me he'd put thousands into Barbury Theatre, but the debts were still mounting up.'

'Someone in the office not paying the bills on time?'

Kitty licked her finger to pick up crumbs from her plate. 'Or someone not paying them at all.'

Trish gasped. 'But surely…'

'Bill Burnett put on a string of plays that barely broke even. Things were dire. The audiences stayed away in droves and the theatre was going down the pan. As a last resort, Vaughn sold his house and used the proceeds to inject cash into the theatre to keep it afloat.'

Trish sipped her coffee, but it tasted bitter. She should've ordered tea instead. When had she last gone to Barbury Theatre? She'd been ten or eleven when she saw

Vaughn's last pantomime, *Jack and the Beanstalk*, with Lydia Bancroft as Ermintrude, the giant's mother. Her parents had been keen theatregoers, but apart from the panto, Trish rarely went with them. Was it because Suki had usually gone too? Or was it because Trish hated the scratchiness of the plush seats on the backs of her legs, having to sit still, hoping she didn't need the loo before the interval?

'How can you know which plays will bring the punters in?'

'You need good instinct combined with a flair for marketing,' Kitty declared. 'And Bill Burnett didn't have either. The theatre was losing money hand over fist. Vaughn poured thousands in to bail it out, hoping to get it back when things picked up, but the money didn't seem to make any difference. As fast as he was putting the money in, someone was taking it out again – or that's what he thought.'

'But who?'

'I often wonder why he took his own life. Was it because those mean little Board Treaders were hassling him? Or was he in despair about losing all that money? We'll never know.' Kitty stared glumly into the coffee cup cradled in her large hands.

Trish pushed her own coffee aside, unfinished. 'Was it someone in the accounts department?'

'The accounts department consisted of one young girl straight out of secretarial college. I doubt if she'd have had the nous to cook the books.'

'Then who?'

'My money's on Bill Burnett himself – no pun intended.'

'You think he was stealing from his own theatre company?'

'From the company he and Vaughn managed jointly. And I suppose he thought little Beryl Amos...'

'Who?' Trish sat up at the sound of her ex's surname. Of her daughter's surname.

'Beryl Amos, the accounts clerk. I tried to talk to her when I was writing my little book, but she wouldn't speak ill of 'Mr Burnett'. I still see her about. She works in that minicab office near the station.'

Trish made a mental note to track her down. Might she be a relative of Vic's? 'Did Chris Darbyshire come to see you?'

'God, that was awful, wasn't it?' Kitty set her cup down with a clatter. 'Poor Chris. He was going to be in town on Wednesday for a meeting at the theatre at some God-awful hour. Croissant and coffee at eight o'clock, way too early for me! And we were going to meet before he caught his train home. But then, of course, Tuesday night...'

Trish turned the pages of Kitty's typescript, pausing when she found a list of the theatre's managers over the years. Bill and Vaughn had been jointly in charge for a decade until Vaughn's death in January 1991. Later that year, Bill had been joined by Eloise Burnett, a partnership that lasted another ten years.

'Eloise? Is that Bill's wife?'

'No, his daughter, the apple of her father's eye.' Kitty's tone was sneering. 'She ran it with Bill until he died in 2001, and then she ran it on her own.'

'And she's still in charge?'

'No, she handed over to Jed Chamberlain earlier this year. Sorry, I haven't got round to updating the list. Jed's an incomer from Eastbourne, young, ambitious, full of bright ideas. As for Eloise – you probably know her as Eloise Gilbert.'

'The woman who owns that club?' Gilbert's was an exclusive country club just outside Barbury, in a beautifully restored house that had once been the Wiltshire seat of some aristocratic family. Frequently featured in the pages of upmarket magazines, it was *the* place for showy weddings and extravagant celebrations.

'She's certainly done well for herself,' Kitty conceded. 'Vaughn may have lost money on Barbury Theatre, but Bill Burnett certainly didn't. And Eloise has used her inheritance wisely. She and Jason Gilbert bought the house when it was still called Phoenix Place. Totally transformed it, relaunched it as Gilbert's – by which time she and Jason had married. But then, last year, Jason dropped dead on the squash court.'

'How dreadful!'

Kitty dabbed at her lips with a paper napkin. 'I've always thought the health benefits of sport are overrated. Eloise stepped back from the theatre after Jason died. She couldn't run Gilbert's *and* the theatre, so something had to give.'

Drinks and shortbread finished, they left the coffee shop and began to stroll back towards the library.

'Do you think Eloise would talk to me about Vaughn?'

'Don't count on it, lovey. I've never found her very approachable, but I can give you her contact details.' Kitty dug in her bag for her phone and passed Eloise's number on to Trish.

'And can I borrow your history of the theatre?'

'Of course. Forgive my terrible typing. One day, I'll pay someone to word process it for me. Oh, and you'll notice the author name's different.' Kitty handed the typescript over, jabbing the name on the front cover with an elegantly polished fingernail. 'That's who I used to be.'

Mystified, Trish hurried up the steps of the library and back to her desk, wondering how soon she could track down Beryl Amos. It was only when she looked again at the front cover of the typescript that she understood how Kitty could have attended Beedon House, an all-boys school.

A Short History of Barbury Theatre by Keith Hart-Taylor.

CHAPTER 51

Tyger was crying again. He hadn't wanted to feed, turning his head away from Iris's nipple when she tried to get him to latch on. Iris knew it was her fault. There was something wrong with her. She was bad for him, a danger to her baby. He was crying because he was unhappy. Too unhappy to feed, even though he must be hungry. He'd starve and it was all her fault.

It was Friday, so Garvin had gone out at the crack of dawn so he and his mates could finish early. He'd grumbled because Tyger had messed his nappy in the night.

'You must be feeding him wrong,' he told her. 'His shit shouldn't smell like that. What are you eating that's making it stink like that?'

When Iris had started to cry – she couldn't help herself, she was so, so tired – he'd hit her across the back of the head, knocking her against the headboard and giving her a big lump on her forehead.

'Please, Ty,' Iris begged now. 'Please don't cry. For Mummy. Please stop crying.'

The baby was red in the face, his eyes shut tight, his tiny hands balled into fists. He'd pause to take a breath and then he'd start yelling again, even louder. She laid him down on the bed, pulled her shirt closed, clamped her hands over her ears.

But still he went on wailing as if he'd never stop. If she went downstairs now, opened the front door and walked away, would he miss her? Wouldn't he be better off with someone who knew how to look after him?

He suddenly went quiet. She caught her breath, not daring to hope he'd stopped crying. He was looking in her direction, his gaze unfocused, but she couldn't bring herself to go to him, to pick him up. He whimpered, reaching up jerkily. And when he didn't find her close to him, he started to cry once more.

CHAPTER 52

Lincoln stood in front of the insolently taciturn whiteboard, hands on hips, his gaze sweeping across the photos and notes stuck on it. Of the four main suspects, he'd managed to interview only one: Nate Newton. Sherilyn Croft had failed to turn up yesterday and wasn't answering her phone today, but he was hopeful of tracking Cody down.

He also needed to set up a meeting with Mitchell Burnett, who should be back from London by now. He tried his mobile, but still no answer.

'Mitch has had to stay up in London another night,' his PA told him calmly when he got through on the landline. 'He should be back tomorrow.'

'Does he ever answer his mobile?'

'Not if he can help it.'

Impatient, Lincoln chucked his phone down on the desk.

'What about the sister?' Dilke was at the whiteboard now. 'Eloise. Her name isn't on the board.'

Lincoln remembered the thirty-year-old photo of her with Vaughn and her father, Bill. Nate Newton said he'd fancied her when he was a Board Treader, but she was too old for him. 'It should be, shouldn't it? And her motive?'

'Protecting the family's reputation? If either of her brothers was implicated in Vaughn's death, it wouldn't look good, would it? Especially if maybe her dad covered it up.'

Lincoln wrote her name on the board. Where was she now? Had she had a career outside the theatre?

Woody and Pam came in, looking dejected.

'Craig drove off from the showroom in an SUV this morning,' Woody said. 'No idea where. He hasn't gone home and his wife isn't co-operating.'

'Her son's a better bet,' said Pam. 'Rocco. I think if he knew where Craig was, he'd tell us. He doesn't think much of his stepdad.'

'As for the girlfriend,' Woody added, 'I don't reckon Zelda even suspected it. You think maybe Tawny Howell's got it wrong?'

Pam grinned. 'Or Craig's good at keeping secrets, like Chris Darbyshire was.'

'And look how *he* ended up.' Lincoln dragged himself away from the whiteboard. 'Who's coming with me to see Cody Burnett?'

The imposing frontage of Barbury Theatre would have looked more impressive if its stucco decoration of stylised harps and lutes was still intact. Over the years, bits had been knocked off like icing chipped from a Christmas cake. The once-pink render was flaking here and there, and where a drainpipe had broken away from the guttering, lurid green stains trailed down the wall, all the way to the pavement.

At the foot of the steep stone steps to the front doors, a sign directed wheelchair users along an alley to a door at the back of the building – although the alley was blocked by huge rubbish skips.

'Useless,' said Dilke, as he and Lincoln climbed the steps. 'You don't have to be in a wheelchair to need easier access. My mum would struggle to get up these steps.'

Inside the main entrance were more stairs, carpeted in a faded red. A door on the right led into the theatre bar, where Darbyshire had met Leanne for coffee on the day of his death. On the left was the box office, its shutter pulled down.

A well-built young man was half-heartedly polishing the brass handrails, but he broke off to ask if he could help them. He had gingery hair tied back in a ponytail, his fringe a frizz of curls.

Lincoln glanced at the man's badge: "Lenny, Caretaker". He showed Lenny his ID and told him who he'd come to see.

'Straight ahead,' said Lenny, and went on polishing.

They shouldered their way through swing doors to find themselves in the dim auditorium. Two men sat in the front row, one in the middle, one in the end seat. On stage stood a young actor, script in hand, a single spotlight shining down on him.

Lincoln gazed around at the rococo décor: opera boxes with velvet-covered balconies; swirly plasterwork; lots of chandeliers. But the seats were shiny with wear, the carpet threadbare, the blue velvet stage curtain patched and darned. This was a theatre down on its uppers.

The man on the end of the row turned round, spotted them and stood up. In a few nimble strides, Cody Burnett had climbed the auditorium steps to join Lincoln and Dilke at the back of the stalls. He was tall and skinny, with floppy fair hair and grey eyes, so different from his dark-haired and solidly built brother.

'Nick told me you'd be coming to talk to me,' he said quietly to Lincoln. 'I'm sitting in on some auditions, hoping to get back into the theatre here now there's a new guy in charge.'

'Hard to stay away, is it?'

'I've been doing this too many years to stay away for long. Shall we?' He led them through a door beside the stage and along a narrow corridor that smelt of drains.

He pushed open another door into a cramped dressing room, bright with bare light bulbs. 'Have a seat.'

Lincoln sat down on a chair that felt too flimsy to bear his weight, but Dilke stayed standing, leaning against the door frame. The dressing room looked very like the one in which Cody had been photographed as a fifteen-year-old schoolboy, with costumes hanging from a rail behind him.

Now, as a good-looking man of forty-one, Cody sat at the dressing table with his back to the mirror. His clothes were casual – jeans and a plain sweat shirt, trainers, a fitness watch on one wrist, a silver identity bracelet on the other – and he seemed relaxed in the presence of the two detectives who'd come to talk to him.

'What do you want to know?' He sat back, legs crossed. 'Should I have Nick here?'

'That's up to you,' said Lincoln. 'This isn't a formal interview, but if you feel you need him…'

Cody shook his head. 'So?'

'Did you know Chris Darbyshire?'

'Not really. I heard he was writing about Lydia Bancroft and was asking around about Vaughn. He should've been writing about *Vaughn,* not Lydia. He'd done a lot of serious acting before he became a pantomime dame – Shakespeare, Pinter, Wilde and the rest.'

'Sounds like you thought a lot of him.'

'Okay, let's not fool around.' Cody's tone was suddenly businesslike. 'You're here because of what happened backstage – or what everybody *thinks* happened.'

Lincoln spread his hands. 'Tell us your version of events, then.'

'Vaughn kinda fell for me, okay? The others joshed me around for being his favourite, but I could talk to that guy like I could never talk to my dad. Vaughn never treated me like a kid. He helped me with my voice, improved my projection like he thought I had a future on the stage, whereas my dad…' He shrugged.

'Did Vaughn ever get physical with you?' Dilke asked.

'No more than any drama teacher would, straightening my shoulders, tilting my head, correcting my stance. But I guess the others resented the attention I was getting. And then Mitch had this idea.' Cody stopped abruptly and lifted his gaze to the ceiling. 'Christ, when I think of it now… What the fuck did we think we were doing?'

The theatre dressing room had gone quiet while Cody Burnett marshalled his thoughts, his memories of all those years ago. The only sound was the rhythmic *shash-shash* of someone – presumably Lenny, the ponytailed, ginger-haired caretaker – sweeping the passage outside. His broom clunked against the skirting board and then *shash-shash, shash-shash…*

'Mitch knew this kid at Board Treaders,' Cody said, leaning forward on his chair, elbows on knees. He fidgeted with his ID bracelet, shifting it round on his sinewy wrist. 'Bob Greenaway, sixteen, about the same age as him. He didn't stick at Board Treaders long. He was kinda troubled, a tearaway. He and Mitch used to hang out together even after he quit, but then he moved back to Swindon. A few months later, he disappeared. Never turned up. It was a big news story at the time.'

'September 1990?' This was the disappearance that Tim Anderson's father had investigated.

Cody nodded. 'Mitch heard that Vaughn was working with teenagers in Swindon before he started rehearsals for the panto, doing drama workshops at Bob's school. Bob was seen talking to an older guy the afternoon he went missing and Mitch got it into his head that it was Vaughn he was seen with.'

Lincoln's pulse quickened. 'Why did he think *Vaughn* was involved?'

'Vaughn knew this guy, Harry something, supplied a lot of the props for the theatre. He had some sort of junk shop with lots of old furniture and stuff.'

'Harry Priest?'

'Yeah, that's the guy. Mitch heard that Harry fancied teenage boys, that a friend of his was put in jail for raping a boy and I guess Mitch thought, "birds of a feather".' Cody shrugged. 'Mitch was sure Vaughn had something to do with Bob disappearing.'

'So Mitch set a trap for him.'

'Yeah. And I was the bait.'

'But you and Vaughn…' Dilke began.

'Yeah, he was good to me and I felt real close to him, but Mitch was so sure he was right, he talked me into it. He wanted to expose Vaughn as the guy who took Bob.'

'What was the plan?' Dilke pulled a chair out and sat down.

'Mitch took photos of me taking my clothes off, got me to write these notes to Vaughn, little thank-you letters like I wanted to repay him for the way he'd helped me.'

'Expecting he'd ask for sexual favours in return?'

'I guess. I went along with it because I knew Vaughn *wasn't* like that. I was sure he'd prove Mitch wrong by *not* taking the bait.'

Lincoln sensed the plan hadn't worked out the way either boy had expected. 'What happened?'

Cody sat with his left ankle across his right knee, toying with the laces of his trainer as he talked. 'Vaughn wasn't stupid. He thanked me for the photos and thanked me for the letters. He was trying to be kind, like *I* was the one who'd misunderstood our relationship and he wanted to let me down gently. I told Mitch to stop before things got out of hand, but …'

'Mitch was convinced Vaughn had abducted the Greenaway boy?'

'Yeah. And Nate and Sherilyn – Christ, it was like we were the Kid Detectives or the Famous Five without the damn dog! Mitch had kept some photos back, one with me and Nate fooling around together, one of me…' He halted, shut his eyes. Trying to remember or trying to forget? 'I was sitting in a chair, no clothes on. I hated Mitch for making me do it, but he kept saying, "This is the money shot! This'll make him show his true colours!" But…'

'But Vaughn didn't react the way you thought he would?'

Cody shook his head. How long had he agonised over those photos? In the years since then, had his memory played him false, distorting the images, exaggerating their lewdness?

Although, Lincoln realised, neither of the nude photos Cody described had been among the Polaroids in Vaughn's album.

'Okay, we were stupid teenagers,' said Cody. 'But if those photos ever got out, if my wife ever saw them, my kids.'

'We don't have those photos. They weren't in Vaughn's scrapbook.'

He groaned. 'So I've got to wait till someone puts them on Instagram?'

'How did Vaughn react to the photos?' Dilke asked.

'Not the way Mitch expected.' Cody's tone was rueful. 'Not the way any of us expected. He called our bluff. When Mitch sent him those nude photos of me and Nate, he threatened to tell Dad everything. See, we thought – the *others* thought – Vaughn had something to hide, but he didn't. I guess he'd put up with it until then, but those photos were the last straw.'

'What happened?' Lincoln asked.

'Right before the performance that night, Vaughn shut the four of us in here with him, locked the door, read us the Riot Act. He said he'd been keeping track of everything we'd done and if we didn't stop harassing him, he'd tell Dad all about it. Scared the crap out of Mitch. We couldn't risk Vaughn walking out. Vaughn was the big draw. Dad would never forgive us if he quit in the middle of the run because of what we'd done.'

'And *did* Vaughn tell your dad?'

'No. We'd sure as hell have known about it if he had! Dad would've knocked the shit out of us.'

This version of events, though more graphic, echoed Nate's. Mitch *had* backed off when Vaughn stood up to him.

'But Vaughn thought I'd betrayed him,' said Cody, sadly. 'He'd taken me under his wing and I'd betrayed him. Dad thought Mitch had a great future, that I was an also-ran, but Vaughn had shown faith in me, told me I should try for drama school. But after that showdown…'

'Vaughn didn't feel he could trust you?'

'No. He never spoke more than a few words to me after that. I guess he thought I'd been playing him from the start. Mitch said he'd killed himself because of me, that I'd led him on. But I hadn't! Not like that.'

'Were you surprised that Vaughn took his own life?' asked Lincoln.

'I was fifteen. What did I know about depression or mental illness? But yeah, it surprised me that he'd killed himself before the end of the run. I can't get my head around that even now. That he'd let everyone down like that. He was always such a professional.' He sighed heavily, no doubt relieved to have told his version of the events leading up to Vaughn's death, although it didn't show his brother in a good light. 'My mother was really sick by then and she died a month after Vaughn. As soon as I could, I left home and went to drama school, rarely came back here.'

'How are things between you and Mitch now?' Lincoln asked gently.

'There's always gonna be tension between us. Guess I just have to live with it.'

'And your sister – are you close to her?'

Cody shook his head. 'We've never been close, not like her and Dad. Eloise is closer to Sherilyn than she's ever been to me. They've been best buddies since way before Sherilyn got famous. Who d'you think's been bailing Sheri out all these years? It's my sister who pays for her to go into rehab – for all the good it does. So, no, Eloise and I aren't close. I haven't seen her since I got back from the States. She was close to my dad and I never was. You can't overcome that sort of difference.'

'I can understand that,' said Lincoln. 'Me and my sister…' He didn't have the words. 'She lives in Chicago. I couldn't tell you when I last spoke to her.'

'You don't get on?'

'She was a teenager when I was born. Hard to relate to someone when the age gap's so big.' Never mind Ruth's tendency to criticise everything he did when he was growing up. Never mind her disgust that he'd wanted to join the police when he left school.

'You'll be talking to Mitch?'

'Yes,' said Lincoln. 'As soon as we can.' He paused. 'How would you have felt if Chris Darbyshire had gone ahead with his podcast? What would it have meant for you?'

'If it showed Vaughn in a good light, I'd have been all for it, but if he'd tried to sensationalise it, concentrated on the sex stuff…' He shrugged. 'Vaughn didn't deserve the reputation he got after he died. I guess I'd have wanted Chris to exonerate him somehow, to uncover the truth – whatever that is.'

CHAPTER 53

In interview room three at Park Street, Tim Anderson and Jay Vallis sat across the table from Milo Dodds. Anderson was short of sleep and short on patience. Baby Dilly had kept him and Aileen awake half the night and woken Arthur, who'd then begged to climb into bed with them. Aileen was trying to encourage the little boy to settle in his own room, but last night they'd caved in, both too bone-weary to resist his pleas. You can't reason with a three-year-old at two in the morning when you're too exhausted to argue coherently.

'Okay, Milo,' said Anderson. 'So you took Mr Priest's van from outside his yard when you saw he'd left the keys in it, yes? Garvin Steele had tipped you off about a house on Folly Hill that was being gutted, so…'

'He'd got keys to the house, Garvin had, from when he done some work there.' Dodds was twenty-four, with body-builder shoulders and biceps, tattoos on his neck and forearms, a silver bar through one eyebrow, the edge of one ear pierced with several silver rings. 'I thought it were for the insurance.'

Jay hooted with laughter. 'You thought Mr Fogarty had arranged to have his kitchen nicked so he could claim on his insurance? Really?'

'So you and Luke packed the kitchen bits into the van,' said Anderson, 'and took it where?'

'To his lock-up.'

'Whose lock-up?'

'Harry's. That's where we took it.'

'Thought Harry didn't know about you taking his

van?' Jay grinned as Dodds dropped himself into a deep hole. 'Whoops!'

He tried to dig himself out. '*At first* I thought Harry didn't know. But then Luke said we was going to Harry's lock-up, so he must've known. Yeah?'

'And where is this lock-up?'

'There's some garages up the Barbury Down estate, only most people park on the road and use the garages for storage. Harry uses his mum's. She's, like, ninety, but she's still living there with his sister and he uses her garage. She don't need it.'

'Why did you give Ritchie a lift that evening?' asked Anderson.

Dodds was caught out by this sudden change of direction. 'Ritchie?'

'You gave Ritchie Payne a lift in the van. Or was he helping you with the kitchen earlier in the day?'

'Luke seen him crossing Spicer Street when we was on our way to take the van back in the evening. He knew him from school. Thought it'd be a bit of a laugh having him along.'

'A bit of a laugh in what way?' asked Jay. 'Tells jokes, does he? A bit of a comedian, yeah?'

Dodds's cheeks flushed. 'No, he's… We was gonna wind him up. He's a bit thick. Special needs.'

She pitched forward. 'And that's funny?'

He couldn't look her in the eye. 'Luke thought so. We was a bit drunk,' he added, as if that excused them. 'Tough day, all that lifting and carrying, so we'd had a few cans. And then we fancied a bit of fun – only it got fucked up.' His head dipped.

Any hope of finding Ritchie alive evaporated in that moment.

'Just tell us what happened,' said Jay, her voice low.

Dodds glanced sidelong at duty solicitor Wilf Evans, but Evans continued to stare down at his papers, ignoring his client's unspoken appeal for help.

'Luke offered Ritchie a lift,' Dodds said at last. 'Told him we was going his way. Luke got a call from Garvin, wanting to know if we could give him a lift home. We picked him up too, outside the old hospital. He were laughing when he seen we'd got Ritchie on board, only Ritchie weren't happy.'

'Why was that?'

'Cos Garvin pissed him off in the Brewery Tap earlier, he said.'

'Did he say why?'

A shrug. 'Never said. Anyways, Gar had some weed, said let's stop the van somewhere for a smoke. Drove up the race course, parked up and had a few smokes. Only…' He broke off, studying his hands, the fingers thick and calloused, knuckles rough, the weathered hands of a much older man.

'Only what?' Anderson leaned in.

'Ritchie weren't interested in a smoke and Garvin were winding him up about it, shoving a spliff in his face. So Ritchie took a drag, no more'n a quick puff, really, that's all, but then he kinda groaned and next thing, he were on the floor, banging his head. His arms and legs were jerking all over the place. And he pissed himself and Garvin laughed. Then he went still.'

'He's epileptic,' Anderson said flatly. 'Smoking weed can induce a fit.'

'Really?' Dodds clasped his hands tighter as if bracing himself. 'A kid in my class at middle school, she had fits. Teacher tried to put a spoon between her teeth to stop her swallowing her tongue, but she bit him instead.'

'That's an old wives' tale,' said Jay in disgust. 'You

didn't try to put a spoon in Ritchie's mouth, did you?'

Dodds shook his head. 'Didn't have a spoon. Couldn't get near him anyway, he were thrashing around so much.'

'And what happened when he stopped convulsing?' asked Anderson.

'It were dark in the van. I couldn't see nothing. He went still and Garvin said, "Oh, he's sleeping it off now". And so we drove back towards town. We was feeling a bit shook up, y'know? And Ritchie's kinda quiet but…'

Anderson tried to imagine Dodds's reaction when he realised Ritchie wasn't just "sleeping it off". 'What time was this?'

'Eleven? Midnight? Garvin had to stop for a piss, so Luke pulled the van over onto the drove road. When Gar got back in, he checked on Ritchie and he says…' Dodds swallowed hard. 'He says there's something wrong, he must've choked or something. He weren't breathing and there were blood on his face. Garvin said there must've been something wrong with the weed. *I* wanted to take Ritchie to the hospital. We coulda dumped him outside and driven off, but he says, no, there's cameras, they'll get the number plates. So he says, drop him here, no one's gonna find him.'

'Which part of the drove road, Milo?' Jay asked. 'Can you remember where Luke stopped the van?'

Dodds hunched forward over the table. 'Up the hill from Bridgeford. There's some old barns there, kind of falling down. There.'

'Did Garvin dump him or did he bury him?' A question Anderson hadn't wanted to have to ask.

'Dumped him. There's ditches there, next to the field. Only took a minute or two.'

'And then what?'

'We dropped Garvin home. Luke dropped me home, said he'd get the van back to Harry in the morning.'

'You didn't think to tell anyone about Ritchie?' Anderson could barely contain his anger. 'You saw the appeals, you must've heard how his gran and grandad were desperate to know what had happened to him. But Ritchie was just a sad guy with special needs, wasn't he? "We've had our fun, we'll throw him away." Was that how it was?'

Jay's hand grazed his as she tried discreetly to take over. 'It was an accident, wasn't it, Milo? You didn't set out to kill Ritchie, did you?'

Dodds seemed to realise for the first time that this was about more than a stolen fitted kitchen. This was about murder, manslaughter at the very least. He was in real trouble. His face fell. He opened and shut his mouth without getting any words out. 'That were Garvin,' he managed to splutter at last. 'He said Ritchie were better off dead.'

Jay sat back. 'How did the van end up at Lookout Hill?'

'Luke phoned next day, said we gotta get rid of it, there's like blood and stuff and our prints, yeah? Says to drive over to his place soon as it's dark. I get there, there's the van with fucking Garvin in the back with a can of petrol. So we went up to Lookout Hill and I brung them back in my car after we'd torched the van. Stunk of petrol for days after.' He looked up expectantly, as if he deserved some sympathy for having to put up with a smelly car.

Jay laughed coldly. 'Except you didn't make a very good job of torching the van, did you?'

'How d'you mean?' Dodds glowered at her, clearly puzzled.

'Not enough petrol. You didn't destroy the evidence after all. No way you're going to wriggle out of this one, Milo.'

CHAPTER 54

Driving back from interviewing Cody, Lincoln took a call from DCI Connors.

'Ritchie's been found,' she said. 'His body was in a ditch a couple of miles out of Bridgeford.'

He'd known they wouldn't find the young man alive so long after his disappearance, but the news still came as a shock. He put his phone on speaker so Dilke could hear. 'How did he die?'

'He got in the van with Costello, Dodds and Garvin Steele. Steele forced a joint on him. He reacted badly, had a seizure. It could've been an accident but that doesn't let those bastards off the hook. If they'd had the balls to take him to hospital…'

'Who's telling his grandparents?'

'That's why I'm calling. Tim and Jay are on their way to arrest Steele. The Paynes already know you and Pam Smyth so…'

'We'll go.' Little as he wanted to return to that claustrophobic flat, he didn't want Ritchie's grandparents to hear the news from officers they didn't know – or worse, from reporters.

'I'll drop you off back at the station and pick Pam up,' he told Dilke. 'We've got to break the news to the Paynes.'

It was five-thirty and growing dark when Tim Anderson and Jay Vallis, with uniformed backup, took up position a few doors down from Garvin Steele's house on the Barbury Down estate. At five-forty, a works minibus drew up and dropped him off, driving away with a belch of exhaust fumes.

Anderson and Vallis approached the house first and banged on the door. A baby was crying inside and Jay raised her eyebrows.

'Tyger,' Anderson said.

'Tyger? What kind of name is…'

The door flew open and there was Steele, still wearing his donkey jacket. 'What the fuck?' He stepped back, trying to shut the door again, but Anderson pushed against it until he and Jay were both inside.

The baby's howl seemed to fill the house. Iris appeared at the top of the stairs, hands over her ears.

'He won't stop!' she cried. 'He won't stop!'

Garvin started up the stairs towards her. 'Shut the fuck up, you stupid bitch! Why don't you fucking…'

But he went quiet when two constables entered the house, their bulky presence overwhelming him.

'Let's go in here, Garvin.' Jay guided him back down and into the living room.

Anderson climbed the stairs as Iris disappeared into one of the bedrooms.

'I'm killing him,' she moaned. 'I'm poison. I'm toxic. My baby's dying because of me.'

He followed her into the small bedroom. A night-light cast huge shadows up the walls and over the ceiling.

Tyger was lying in a nest of blankets in a shallow plastic crate. A pungent smell hung in the room, so strong it was almost tangible.

'He needs changing, love. That's why he's crying.' He turned, expecting her to fetch a fresh nappy, wet wipes, whatever it took to clean the baby up, but she simply stood there motionless, glaring at her son as if she loathed him. Anderson had seen the same look on his wife's face when Dilly was a newborn: sheer exhaustion, horror that she'd brought another baby into the world when little Arthur was still so dependent on her.

But in Iris's face, there was something else. Something disturbing.

And then he saw the fresh cuts on her arm, as if a wild animal had dragged its claws across her skin. Saw the knife, plunging towards Tyger.

'No, Iris, no!' He flung himself forward to shield the baby and gasped in pain as the knife slashed his arm. 'Give it me, Iris. Give me the knife.' He reached for it, but she drew back and plunged the blade into him again, into his body, into his chest. His arm went numb and he felt a cold burning, searing yet icy.

Felt nothing.

Heard nothing except a woman shouting above him, 'Tim! Oh God! Tim!'

CHAPTER 55

The Paynes were surprisingly calm when Lincoln told them Ritchie's body had been found.

'But at least we know now.' Bert looked as if the stuffing had been knocked out of him. 'We'll have him back and do the right thing by him. I couldn't have lived with myself if we'd had to give up on him.'

'And you've got someone for it?' Mrs Payne asked Pam through her tears. 'You've found who did it?'

'They're in custody,' she said. 'They won't be hurting anyone else.'

A few minutes after getting back to Barley Lane, Lincoln took a call from the DCI.

'Tim Anderson's in hospital,' she said, her tone grim. 'He's been stabbed. He and Jay Vallis went to arrest Garvin Steele and the girlfriend went for him.'

He recalled the timid Iris obediently confirming Steele's alibi. His mouth went dry. 'Christ! How bad is it?'

'Touch and go. Jay's at the hospital. Someone's fetching his wife from Trowbridge. Her mum's looking after the children.' Connors sounded more upset than he'd ever heard her. 'He was trying to stop Iris hurting the baby. He and Jay went there expecting trouble from Steele, not from the girl.'

'There's nothing of her,' he said, inconsequentially.

'I'll let you know if there's any news.'

He put the phone down, trying to ignore the tremor in his hand: Anderson, cocksure but caring, driven to finding out what happened to Bob Greenaway, to finding Ritchie Payne when a stolen flatpack kitchen took priority with his colleagues.

He stood for a long time in front of the whiteboard, cursing it under his breath.

'You're meant to be helping,' he muttered at it, 'and you're not helping at all.' He drew a tentative line between Sherilyn Croft's name and the recently added name of Eloise Burnett.

'Boss?' Breeze was pushing a mug of coffee at him and he took it gratefully.

'Sherilyn is best buddies with Eloise, according to Cody. You think there's anything in that?'

Breeze waggled his eyebrows suggestively. 'You tell me, boss.'

'I mean, is she more involved with what's been going on than we realise?' Lincoln sipped his coffee and stared at the board.

'But she wasn't one of the Board Treaders, was she?'

'No, but she was close to her father. Helped him run the theatre at one time. If she thought Darbyshire's podcast was likely to damage Bill's reputation, she might have wanted to stop it.'

'Looks like we know bugger-all about her.' Breeze nodded at the blank space beneath Eloise's name.

'Then we'd better start finding something out.'

Two hours later, Lincoln was alone in the incident room, seeing what he could find on Eloise Burnett, when the phone rang.

Connors. His heart was thumping.

'Tim died,' she said. 'I've just come from the hospital.'

He didn't know what to say. He'd liked Anderson and couldn't imagine how the next few hours would unfold for his boss, for Anderson's family, for Jay Vallis.

'He was trying to save her baby,' Connors said into his silence. 'And she killed him.'

When Trish opened the door to him, she had a wooden spoon in her hand.

'I wasn't expecting you,' she said. 'I'm in the middle of making soup.'

Lincoln felt foolish turning up like this, but after hearing the news about Anderson, he'd wanted nothing more than to be with her, to be with someone who knew him better than anyone. Only as he'd started up her front steps had it occurred to him that Steve Quilter might be there with her, but he didn't care.

He followed her into the kitchen and slumped down at the table while she continued to stir a pan of something that smelt of onions.

'You okay?' She glanced back over her shoulder.

'The DI from Trowbridge, Tim Anderson, the bloke that Connors drafted in. He's dead.'

She spun round. 'What?' Soup dripped from the spoon onto the kitchen floor.

'Tim Anderson. He was stabbed.'

She dumped the pan on the worktop, turned the stove off. 'What happened?'

By the time he'd finished telling her what he knew, he was on the verge of tears. What was happening to him? He'd hardly known Anderson. Had never met his wife or his kids, didn't know what music he liked, what food, what places.

But his death had hit him hard. Nearly twenty years separated them, but Lincoln kept thinking how that could've been him twenty years ago, going about his job, doing his best to solve crimes, help people, make things right.

'Why the hell am I still doing this job?'

She sat next to him and put her arm around his

shoulders. 'Because you wouldn't be happy doing anything else.'

'I'm not happy doing this.' There, he'd said it. 'Not anymore.'

They sat in silence for a few minutes until she said, gently, 'Stay for supper. Kate's sleeping over at Paloma's tonight.'

He shrugged her arm away, stood up. 'I'm not hungry. What about Steve?'

'Steve?' Trish stood up too, a puzzled look on her face. 'What's this got to do with Steve?'

'I saw you with him. I know what's going on, Trish, but I wish you'd told me.'

'You *saw* me with him?' She took a step back. 'What are you talking about?'

'In your office the other day. You and Steve.'

She put a hand over her mouth. God, was she laughing at him? 'What did you think you saw?'

'You were… He had his arms round you. I thought…'

'Is this why you've been acting so weird the last few days? You really thought…'

'I haven't been "acting weird". I've been giving you space because…' He shook his head, unable to finish.

'Oh, Jeff.' She took a deep breath. 'It isn't what you think, it really isn't. We were talking in my office, Steve reached past me for a book that was on the shelf behind me and his arm brushed the top of my head. His cuff button got caught in my hair and the more he tried to untangle it, the more it got knotted up. Bryony was nowhere to be seen and I thought you were still over by the microfilm reader. He had to snip a chunk of my hair off to separate us.' She flicked her fingers through her bobbed hair. 'Hence my emergency visit to the hairdresser to get it tidied up.'

A weight lifted from his shoulders, from his heart. How stupid he'd been! 'Why didn't he cut his cuff button off?'

'What, and spoil his nice jacket?' She laughed softly, leaning her head against his. 'Did you *really* think I was having a fling with Steve Quilter? I thought you knew me better than that.'

The soup was beyond rescue, so she rustled up a mushroom omelette. As he watched her sliding it onto his plate, he realised he was ravenous. When had he last eaten? So much for trying to get into a routine of healthy meals, regular exercise, earlier nights, fresh air…

'Jeff, have you spoken to Eloise Burnett?'

Her question took him by surprise. 'Not yet. Why?'

'I was talking to Kitty Hart-Taylor, the theatre archivist – well, she *was* the theatre archivist – and… Remember we were wondering what happened to Hamilton Vaughn's money, why there was so little left in his estate?'

'He'd been ploughing it into the theatre.'

'Yes, but Kitty said he suspected someone had their hand in the till. In the months before he died, he kept putting money in but the bills weren't getting paid.'

'Someone dodgy in the accounts department?' Lincoln sat back, pleasantly full after the omelette.

'The accounts department was one inexperienced girl.'

'Then who?'

'He suspected Bill Burnett.' She whisked his empty plate away.

'But why would Burnett steal from his own theatre? It doesn't make sense.'

'He and Vaughn ran it together.'

The mishandling of the theatre's finances would

certainly be worthy of a cover-up, but where was the evidence? 'How does Eloise Burnett come into it?'

'She took over from Bill,' said Trish. 'If anyone knew what was going on with the theatre's finances, she'd be the one to ask.'

'Even if it meant implicating her father?'

'No harm in asking. She's Eloise Gilbert now. You know that country club out Amberstone way? Gilbert's? That's hers. Her husband was running it but he died. I've got a number for her if you want to speak to her.'

She picked her phone up. She was trying to help, he knew, and he felt a sudden surge of tenderness towards her.

'Okay, I'll try and get hold of her.' As he added the number to his contacts list, the evening's tragedy ambushed him again and he chucked his phone on the table. 'Tim Anderson's got two kids, a toddler and a baby. They won't remember him.'

'Stop it.' She sat down close to him. 'Stop it. Stay here tonight.'

But he knew nothing she could say or do would relieve his sense of futility, of the pointlessness of everything he did.

'I need to get back,' he said. 'I'm sorry about Steve. About doubting you, I mean. But when I saw you in your office with him…'

'Inextricably bound together.' She was grinning now, but still his mood didn't lighten. He needed to get home, shut himself away with a drink or two, some music, darkness.

'Call me when you get back,' she said as she let him go. 'Please.'

He hurried down the steps to his car, wondering why he was punishing himself this way. Wondering why he couldn't simply give in and let himself love and be loved.

Would it be such a hard thing to do?

SATURDAY 4TH NOVEMBER

CHAPTER 56

The atmosphere in the incident room next morning was sombre. Even though none of Lincoln's team had worked with Anderson, they were all shocked and saddened by his death and the manner of it.

Lincoln said, 'I know it's hard after what's happened but we've got to stay focused. We need to find Craig Newton and talk to Mitchell Burnett and his sister, Eloise.'

He'd found out that Eloise Gilbert, née Burnett, widow of Jason Gilbert, was fifty-one and the owner of Gilbert's, a country club and boutique hotel near Amberstone. Until Jason's death last year, she'd been running Barbury Theatre, but now Gilbert's took up all her time. In the interviews Lincoln had found yesterday evening she'd attributed her success to her father, who sounded little less than a saint.

Naturally suspicious of such high praise, Lincoln needed to find out more. But would Eloise be willing to talk about her father's possible mishandling of the theatre's finances in the month's leading up to Vaughn's death? He didn't think so. He'd need to tread carefully.

'I'm hoping to interview Mitchell today,' he said. 'And we need to find Sherilyn Croft.'

'She's on Instagram often enough,' Pam remarked. 'That's probably the quickest way to find out where she is. I'll try and track her down.'

Just then, Antonia Yardley phoned. 'Leanne Milner. As I suspected, manual strangulation. The skin cells under her fingernails match her husband's DNA.'

On any other day, he'd have punched the air in triumph, but today he simply felt the satisfaction of knowing his assumptions had proved correct.

'Remember I said I could smell rotting apples on her clothes?' Antonia went on. 'There was apple residue on her clothes and in her hair, though not on the soles of her boots, so I think her body was transported in a vehicle that had had apples in it.'

'Milner's car hasn't moved from Glastonbury since before Leanne left Barbury, and neither has his mother's.'

'That's cider territory, isn't it? Ever tried scrumpy? Lethal. Maybe he knows someone with an orchard?' She paused. 'One last thing, possibly not relevant. She was pregnant.'

Lincoln locked eyes with the late Leanne Milner's head shot, wondering how much sadder this case could become. 'Possibly not relevant how?'

'She may not have realised it herself – one missed period with few other physical changes. We could do tests to establish the paternity, but how useful is that for your case? If it was too soon for Leanne to know, her husband didn't know either, so it's unlikely to have been a motive. I can follow it up, see if I can determine who the father is, but it's so early in the pregnancy, I can't promise a definitive answer. It may come down to resources, how much your boss is willing to spend.'

'Put it in your report and I'll let her decide.' He already had a fair idea what the answer would be. 'Time of death?'

'Impossible to be precise because of the time she was lying out in the open, but I'd say between Friday afternoon and Sunday.'

Lincoln imagined the scenario: Leanne pulling up at the rendezvous she'd arranged with her husband, in a bridleway off that minor road near Warminster. Was she surprised that he'd turned up in an unfamiliar vehicle or had he forewarned her? She put her things in the back, took her coat off, ready for the drive to Glastonbury, got in. What had gone through her mind when she realised he wasn't taking her to join their children?

Had Milner killed her there, maybe a few yards off the road where trees and bushes would have shielded them from passing cars? Had he dumped her by the railway line in broad daylight? Or had he driven around with her body until darkness fell?

DCI Connors sounded relieved that at least one strand of this investigation was close to being wrapped up.

'Let's get Milner brought in,' she said. 'The sooner the better. And we'll be bringing Harry Priest in as soon as we can. He'll be charged with theft and perverting the course of justice – and that's just for starters. Garvin Steele's landed him in it.'

'No loyalty there, then.'

'And Steele's copped to Alfie Corrigan.'

Lincoln could imagine the DCI's satisfaction at solving that particular case of the black student Steele had picked on outside a pub in the summer, who'd later been found dead below the weir.

'Probably thought we'd go easy on him if he came clean.'

She laughed bitterly. 'Then he can think again.'

'And Iris?'

'She's sedated on a secure ward. The baby's in hospital too. Not a scratch on him, but he's got some sort of digestive problem. Nothing serious,' she added. 'Just needs medication, monitoring. And then foster care.'

Anderson would've been pleased to know little Tyger was going to be okay.

‘I’m going to call on Mitchell Burnett today, ma’am. For elimination purposes,’ he added before she could argue that a man of Burnett’s reputation wouldn’t involve himself in murder.

He hoped she was right.

CHAPTER 57

The Old Farmhouse was eerily quiet, but Annie didn't feel like putting on music or the radio. In front of her she'd got all Chris's papers, unpacked from the cardboard box she'd brought back from Standish's Farm. Reluctantly, she started to go through it again, a task that Molly had inadvertently interrupted the other day.

She skimmed the early chapters of Lydia's "autobiography", her heart catching at the sight of the careful marginal notes Chris had made in pencil to remind himself to do more research or cross-checking. She ran her finger over the indentations in the paper.

There were photocopies of pages from a ledger of some sort, presumably to do with the theatre. A handwritten record of payments to various firms, a printer, a costume hire company, a supplier of bar snacks. And what was this letter, still in its envelope, postmarked January 5th, 1991? Wasn't that around the time Vaughn died?

She slid the letter out and read the clumsily scrawled words: Dear V, Sorry I've got people worried. Alive and well and living in London (see above) Will be in touch again. Thanks for everything. Bob.

The address at the top of the letter was a flat in Oldfield Road, Stoke Newington, N16. Was this something else Lydia had taken from Vaughn's bedsit? She slid the letter back into its envelope and returned it to the box.

When, she wondered, had Chris decided to pursue the mystery of Vaughn's death rather than write about Lydia? Despondency overcame her. She couldn't do any more today.

Poor Chris! She put everything back into the box and carried it up to the room that, whatever happened, would always be his study, the way Gracie's bedroom was still Gracie's.

She dumped the box on his desk in the space where his laptop used to sit. As she went out again, she picked up the wedding photo from the window sill.

Oh, you silly, silly people, she thought, gazing at the two of them in their finery, Chris in a suit he'd borrowed from a slimmer friend, herself in a vintage sixties wedding gown.

Oh, you stupid, stupid people! If only you could have seen what was coming.

CHAPTER 58

Lincoln had expected Mitchell Burnett's home in the Chalke Valley, west of Barbury, to be a mansion or a minor stately home.

'It's just a cottage,' said Dilke, disappointed, as they parked in the village's main street and looked up at the Old Forge.

The single-storey house, with ivy-covered walls, a slate roof and a thatched porch, sat at the top of a grassy bank that rose up from the road and was accessed by half-a-dozen rough stone steps.

'Maybe this is his weekend bolt hole.' Lincoln used the dolphin-shaped knocker and they waited.

'Ah, the police,' said Burnett as he flung his front door wide open. 'Come in.'

The cottage interior had been modernised and enlarged by removing walls and incorporating what must once have been the blacksmith's shop. The whole of the original ground floor was now a large, low-ceilinged living room, with various rooms opening off it. French windows overlooked a walled yard full of terracotta pots of shrubs and ornamental grasses, where a fair-haired man in his thirties, in cargo pants, polo shirt and gardening gloves, was tending to them, pruning and shaping.

'The old blacksmith's yard,' Burnett said, following Lincoln's gaze. 'I wish I'd kept the original anvil.' He waved them towards the leather sofas either side of a low table. 'A local scrap merchant beat me to it, the bastard. Is this about Chris Darbyshire?'

'Yes,' said Lincoln. 'Did you know him?'

Burnett leaned back in his expensively upholstered armchair and ran both hands through his hair. It wasn't black, as Lincoln had thought, but iron-grey, a little silvery in front of his ears.

'Yes, through Barbury Theatre, but only slightly. He was already in the company as a juvenile when I joined the Board Treaders, but then he went off to Bristol Old Vic or somewhere. And after that, of course, he turned to writing.' He pitched forward as if eager to help. 'Latterly, he was writing Lydia Bancroft's life story, which must be why he was asking around about Vaughn.'

Dilke sat forward too, notebook at the ready. 'How did you know he was asking about Vaughn?'

'From one of the other Board Treaders. We met up a few weeks ago, a bit of a reunion in London.'

Into the room came a leggy, rough-coated, grey dog, a sort of hairy greyhound. A lurcher? Lincoln was never quite sure about dog breeds.

'This is Horatio,' Mitchell said, patting the dog on its flank as it came to stand next to him. 'Come on, old boy.' A moment later, it collapsed on the rug and stretched out to doze.

'We heard there was a bit of tension behind the scenes at the panto,' said Lincoln.

'Tension's in the nature of theatre.' A quick smile. 'We were kids in our first big production, larking around. The grown-ups were doing it for a living, taking it seriously – quite rightly, of course. But as teenagers do, we felt the need to rebel, to subvert. So yes, there was tension behind the scenes.'

'Were you concerned about what Chris might find out while he was doing his research? Any skeletons in your closet?' Lincoln tried to sound affable, but Burnett wasn't fooled.

'Of course not,' he said briskly. 'But Chris was desperate for a story and, as with ninety per cent of what he wrote, he resorted to invention. I hate to say it after what's happened to him, but he let himself be led down a rabbit hole when he got bored with Lydia's life story.'

'The rabbit hole being...'

'Did the Board Treaders drive Vaughn to take his own life? *That* rabbit hole.' Mitchell shifted in his seat, as if he couldn't quite get comfortable. 'How could we have known – how can any of us know now – what was going on in Vaughn's life? He was a gay man at a time when being gay was still something to be ashamed of. Every night after the show, he was going home on his own, probably knocking back a few drinks before he went to bed. The show was coming to an end, he was facing the rest of the winter alone, no more theatre for months.' He shook his head sadly. 'That would make any actor despair. The idea that it was all *our* fault...'

'In what way do you think Chris was going to blame you?'

Mitchell must have been wondering how much Lincoln knew. Pretending ignorance would have been disingenuous but saying too much would have been unwise.

'We teased him because we knew he had a soft spot for my little brother, Cody.'

'Teased him? Like how?' Dilke looked up from his notebook.

'We left some photos for him to find. Cody pretending to do a striptease. I think we may even have written him some silly letters. I really can't remember after all this time.'

'Did he try to take advantage of Cody?' Lincoln asked. 'Your brother was only fifteen. If Vaughn had tried to get physical...'

Mitchell shrugged. 'Does it matter now?' He looked from Lincoln to Dilke. 'It was years ago and Vaughn's long gone.'

Lincoln nodded, taking his time before asking the next question. 'Do you remember a boy called Bob Greenaway?'

A crease appeared between Mitchell's eyebrows and he scratched his forehead with his thumbnail. 'I don't think…'

'He'd been in foster care in Swindon, then lived in Barbury for a couple of years.'

'Oh, yes, that Bob. The one who went missing.'

'You were friends?'

'Briefly. He joined Board Treaders, but it wasn't really his thing. I'd forgotten about him until you said.'

'Did you ever think Vaughn might've had something to do with his disappearance? He'd been working with kids in Swindon, hadn't he, around the same time?

'Did my brother tell you I suspected Vaughn?'

Lincoln nodded. 'I can see why you might've done. Bob's never been found, so if you know anything that might help us find him…'

Mitchell spread his hands helplessly. 'It's so long ago. I barely remember what he looked like.'

'Would anyone like coffee?' A slim woman, thirty-something and blonde, emerged from the kitchen.

'This is Fenella Brooks,' said Mitchell. 'My PA.'

Lincoln smiled up at her. 'Yes, I believe we've spoken on the phone.' A PA working on a Saturday morning? Or was she more than simply a PA? She noted who wanted what and withdrew again.

He laid a photo of the Board Treaders on the table: Sherilyn, Mitchell, Cody, Simeon. He noticed that Mitchell wore a silver identity bracelet in those days. Did he still wear it, like his brother? He didn't think so.

'Did you know Vaughn kept all the photos and so on from that time, Mr Burnett? Did Nate Newton take this one? He's not in it, is he?'

Mitchell picked the photo up with almost tender gentleness.

'No,' he said. 'Dad took this one. Publicity for the start of rehearsals. *The Messenger* was always interested in which Board Treaders got into the panto each year. That's Simeon, with the blond curls. I used to call him Bubbles, you know, like the Millais painting. Sim took a tumble into the orchestra pit, a pretty nasty fall. Dad was scared the parents would sue the theatre, but they accepted it was his own fault. Still tragic, though.' He set the photo down. So much for not remembering anything about his time in the panto.

'And Nate replaced him – is that right?'

'Yes. I'm sorry, but where's this going?' A dark, impatient frown.

'We believe Chris Darbyshire was murdered to stop him investigating the circumstances leading up to Vaughn's death. You said yourself that you teased him because you thought he fancied your brother. But you also wanted to draw him out, didn't you? You suspected him of abducting Bob Greenaway and murdering him, so you used Cody as bait, hoping you'd catch Vaughn out.'

Lincoln produced the school photo of Bob that Tim Anderson had shown him. He watched Mitchell's face intently, saw the way his gaze fastened on the boy's face. Had he *really* forgotten all about him until just now? It didn't look that way.

Fenella came in with a tray of hot drinks, stooping gracefully to set it on the table.

'Don't forget you've got a call coming through from the States in a few minutes, Mitch.' She laid her hand briefly on his shoulder before she went back to the kitchen.

'My American publisher,' he said, glancing at his watch.

'We won't take up much more of your time.' Lincoln laid two more photos on the table: Mitchell and Nate in bed together, having – or simulating – sex.

He looked shocked for a moment but quickly recovered himself. 'Where did you get these?'

'Vaughn's scrapbook,' said Lincoln. 'How would you have felt if Chris had described these photos in his podcast or used them to publicise it? I can see why you'd want to stop him writing about Vaughn if he was planning to make use of photos like these.'

The room was quiet. Lincoln reached for his coffee, reached for the sugar, letting the photos lie, suggestive and insolent, on the table.

Mitchell cleared his throat. 'Okay, we were winding Vaughn up. Pushing him the way kids do, to see how far we could go. And we soon found out. There was a big row in the dressing room two or three weeks into the show. He tore into us, into *me* in particular, and we stopped. He was going to tell Dad what we'd been up to and there'd have been hell to pay.'

Lincoln nodded, put his coffee down, picked the photos up. 'When was this big row?'

Mitchell shut his eyes, took a deep breath, opened them again. 'The second week of December. We'd just broken up from school, in high spirits – and then he brought us down with a bump, threatening to go to Dad. I'm not proud of what we did, but neither am I ashamed. We felt justified. We thought we were going to catch a killer.' He laughed bitterly. 'You must know how that feels.'

Lincoln tucked the photos away in his folder. 'Yes indeed.' He paused a moment. 'So when Vaughn killed himself, not long after Christmas…'

'Hey, don't lay that at *my* door! The guy was a drinker, living alone in a seedy little bedsit with trains going by his window all hours of the day and night. His career was over. He was a has-been. What did he have to look forward to?'

'He was only sixty-three,' Lincoln pointed out. 'That's young for a pantomime dame. Did you ever go to his bedsit? You said it was seedy, so how did you…'

'I must've read about it. Am I being accused of something here?'

'No, Mr Burnett, we're just trying to piece things together. *Someone* paid to have Chris murdered because of the story he was working on, a story that could have shown the Board Treaders in an unflattering light. We need to find out who that person was.'

Fenella appeared at that moment and Mitchell got to his feet.

'I've told you all I can,' he said, obliging Lincoln and Dilke to stand too. 'If you have any further questions, I'll have to refer you to my lawyer.'

Disappointed by this sudden withdrawal of co-operation, Lincoln thanked him for his help and Fenella escorted them to the door.

The fair-haired gardener in the polo shirt was now working on the front of the cottage, pulling away dead leaves from the branches of a winding creeper. He paused as they stepped outside.

'My brother Philip,' said Fenella. 'Brooks and Brooks, Mitch's maintenance crew.' She gave a little laugh and, still smiling, watched them go down the steps to the car.

'That went well,' said Dilke as they drove away from the Old Forge.

'Getting on his high horse hasn't made me suspect him any the less,' Lincoln said, angry with himself for his handling of the interview. He should have taken longer to win Mitchell's trust instead of broaching the subject of Vaughn's death so soon. 'But we need more evidence one way or the other.'

'And there's nothing to connect him to Craig Newton, is there?'

'Not that we know of.'

'Three Board Treaders down, one to go.' Dilke grinned across at him as they sped back to Barbury. 'Maybe Sherilyn Croft will be more forthcoming.'

But Lincoln doubted it. They had to find her first.

CHAPTER 59

No sooner had he returned to Barley Lane than Lincoln had to head off to Park Street. He couldn't even stop for a coffee. Russ Milner was in custody and the clock was ticking.

'Don't let him get away, Jeff,' Connors begged before he went into the interview room. 'Whatever you do, don't let him talk his way out of it.'

'You think I killed my wife,' Milner said, even before Lincoln had sat down across from him. 'But I'm innocent.'

'We can get through this much more quickly if you tell me the truth, Russ. We *know* you killed Leanne. You've still got the scars from where she scratched you, fighting for her life.'

At Lincoln's request, Milner's arms and hands had been thoroughly photographed after his arrest. The marks had faded in the seven days since Leanne made them, but they were still visible.

'Those scars are from when I was helping my mother in the garden last week, clearing brambles.'

'Really? You want to tell us what happened last Friday, the twenty-seventh?'

'I told you. Leanne phoned to say she was leaving home, but she never arrived. On the Sunday, she texted me to say she had to get away for a bit. You'll have seen the text.'

'Why did you put a tracker on her car?'

Milner frowned at the sudden change of course. 'In case it got stolen. She'd have been lost without her car.'

'She's had the car for a while, but you only put the tracker on it this April, according to the app on your phone. Was that when you first suspected she was having an affair?'

'It was when she read something online about trackers and asked me to fit one. Nothing to do with her and Chris Darbyshire.'

'So what do *you* think happened to her? How did her body end up beside the railway line?'

'The people who killed Chris – they must've followed her.' Milner's eyes had a desperate look in them. 'They were afraid she could identify them. She was a threat to them.'

'They were the ones who sent you a text, pretending to be her?'

'Must've been. I should've realised it didn't sound like her, the way it was phrased.'

'You think they've still got her phone, Russ?'

'They'll have tossed it, won't they?'

Lincoln paused to read his notes. Dilke had found a small business, Noah's Press, not far from Juniper Farm, Milner's mother's house. Noah Dean sold apple juice locally, pressed from fruit from his own orchards. Jenny Reedy had spoken to him earlier and solved one part of the puzzle.

'You borrowed a van from Noah Dean the day Leanne left Barbury, didn't you, Russ? You told him you had garden waste to get rid of, but in fact you wanted the van for something else. You drove to where you'd told Leanne you'd meet her, on the back road near Boyton. Transferred her stuff into the van, locked her car. Did you kill her there, Russ, in that bridleway?'

Lincoln laid a photo of Dean's VW Caddy on the desk, the van's side panel emblazoned with the Noah's Press logo of a ripe apple oozing juice. Then he laid down a photo of the van's interior, the floor littered with stray apples that had been smashed and left to rot as Dean moved his crates around.

'It's a busy time for Noah Dean,' Lincoln went on. 'Picking apples, crating them up. A bit messy. Look at the floor of his van. We found apple pulp on Leanne's clothes and in her hair. Did you just chuck her body in the back of the van after you strangled her?'

Milner's gaze was fixed on the photos, his mouth clamped shut.

'Tell us what happened, Russ. What's the point of denying it when the evidence is stacking up all the time?'

The solicitor asked for some time alone with his client.

'Five minutes,' said Lincoln, and withdrew. His phone buzzed.

'Jenny Reedy called just now, boss,' Breeze told him. 'They've found Leanne's phone at his mum's house, her handbag and overnight bag too.'

'And the laptop?'

'Nope. Has he admitted it yet?'

'Tried to blame it on whoever killed Darbyshire. I've left him conferring with his solicitor.' He checked his watch. He'd give them a minute or two more. 'If the laptop isn't at his mother's house, where is it? They're not easy things to throw away.'

He kicked himself again for not checking the boot of Milner's car when he and the kids had returned to Barbury.

'I need to get back in there, Dennis. Thanks for the update.' And he returned to the claustrophobic interview room.

It didn't take long for Milner's defiant attitude to weaken and dissolve. He wasn't a hardened criminal. Lying didn't come easily to him.

'I didn't plan it,' he said. 'I would've let things carry on until Chris got bored and moved on to someone else, but when I found out she'd stayed at home so she could bring him into our house, into our *bed*...'

Two hours later, Lincoln walked into the incident room at Barley Lane, chucking his papers down on his desk with an air of resignation.

'The good news is Russ Milner's being charged with Leanne's murder. The bad news? Still no laptop. Says he never saw it.'

He made himself a coffee and unwrapped the cream cheese and cress sandwich he'd picked up from the coffee shop round the corner. He was ravenous. Did cress count as a vegetable?

'Any joy tracking Craig Newton down?'

Woody shook his head. 'Not so far. We tried his dad's place over in Amberstone but it's all shut up, no sign that anyone's been there for weeks. The SUV hasn't been clocked anywhere yet so I reckon he must be lying low somewhere.'

Breeze broke off from munching his way through a sausage bap. 'Cuh, he's probably in Spain by now. Plenty of ways he could've left the country without going through passport control.' He licked grease off his fingers and wiped them on his jeans. 'Find a little airfield and someone who'll fly you out, no questions asked, and you're on your way.'

'Thanks, Dennis, that's really cheered me up. Any sign of Sherilyn, Pam?'

'No, she's gone quiet on all her usual socials and Valerie Bancroft says she's not there now. I'll keep checking.'

'Listen,' said Lincoln. 'We've been pursuing the Board Treaders' honey trap as a motive for Darbyshire's murder, but there could be something else behind it.' He headed for the whiteboard. 'Vaughn thought Bill Burnett had his hand in the till.' He relayed what Trish had found out from Kitty Hart-Taylor.

'But where's the evidence?' Woody wanted to know. 'You'd be pretty stupid to steal from your own business.'

'But isn't that what embezzlers do, Sarge?' Pam said. 'They're the very people you trust, the ones you never suspect.'

'Vaughn had sold his house that summer,' Lincoln went on. 'He put the proceeds into the theatre's account, just to keep it afloat until business picked up. So if Bill was taking money out for himself, it was Vaughn's money he was stealing.'

'You think embezzlement is sexy enough for a true crime podcast?' Dilke sounded unsure. 'The sums of money involved would be peanuts. You're not talking millions in crypto currency.'

'I don't even know what that means,' Lincoln said with a sigh. 'Either way, it wouldn't look good, would it, that a respected manager was siphoning-off money from a theatre that was already struggling?'

'But if Bill Burnett *was* cooking the books,' Woody said, 'how could anyone prove it all these years later? You could bring a forensic accountant in, but the theatre's paperwork and Vaughn's bank records will be long gone.'

'But supposing the press got hold of it?' Lincoln could imagine what Karen Bolitho would make of that.

'The great Bill Burnett's reputation would be seriously damaged,' said Pam. 'Mitchell and Eloise wouldn't want to risk that.'

'But would either of them *kill* to protect their dad's name?' Dilke was still unconvinced. 'And where's the link to Craig Newton?'

Lincoln had to admit there didn't seem to be one. He looked for a recent photo of Eloise to put on the whiteboard and found one taken at Gilbert's for a feature in *Wiltshire Lifestyle.*

She was dark-haired, like Mitchell and their father. Shapely in a figure-skimming dress and high heels, she stood on the club's terrace, raising a glass, smiling brightly at a summer garden party. And beside her, his arm brushing hers, closer than a mere acquaintance would stand, was a heavily built man whose face was all too familiar.

Craig Newton.

Breeze leaned over his shoulder to see the photo. 'Shit!'

Lincoln felt goosebumps rise on his arms. Was this the connection they'd been looking for? 'An unlikely couple, wouldn't you say?'

Breeze chuckled. 'Some women like a bit of rough.'

'Reckon we need to go over to Gilbert's,' Woody said with a grin. 'That country club would be an ideal place for Newton to lie low.'

CHAPTER 60

The car park at Gilbert's was nearly full and there seemed to be plenty of customers coming and going from the stately Edwardian house that had once been Phoenix Place.

Lincoln paused in the foyer at the board listing all that Gilbert's had to offer. 'A spa? Since when has Barbury's water had health-giving properties?'

'Suki had a weekend break here as her birthday present from me,' Woody said. 'She went with one of her girlfriends. Said it did her the world of good.'

Lincoln was sceptical, especially when he saw the prices. Taking the waters or taking the piss?

A few minutes later, Lincoln and Woody were facing Eloise Gilbert across a glass-topped table in the conservatory of her private suite. She wore a sharply tailored grey suit over a scarlet polo neck, her diamond earrings and matching bracelet helping to convey an impression of elegant wealth. 'Yes, I know Craig Newton,' she said. 'But we're not friends.' She dismissed the *Wiltshire Lifestyle* piece with a wave of her hand. 'We were schmoozing, the way business people do when they get together.'

'He's wanted in connection with Chris Darbyshire's murder,' Lincoln said. 'If you know where he might be, Mrs Gilbert, it would be in your interests – and his – to tell us.'

'Why would *I* know where Craig is? As I said…'

'Yes, you said you're not friends, but that's not what we've heard.'

She sat back, affronted. 'Well, I don't know who *you've* been talking to.'

Was this interview going to run aground the way Mitchell's had? Anxious not to lose her, Lincoln changed tack.

'Did you know Chris was planning a podcast about Barbury Theatre? He'd been working on Lydia Bancroft's life story. Did he talk to you about that?'

'No, but then he probably knew better than to approach me. We fell out two or three years ago over the Paragon.'

'The arts centre project that got cancelled? What did you fall out over?'

'I was managing Barbury Theatre at the time and yet I seemed to be the last person to get a say in its replacement. Several of the people involved in the planning, Chris included, were hell bent on doing away with a traditional theatre altogether. I said I didn't want to get involved if my views were going to be ignored. Chris had the nerve to ask, in front of the whole committee, if I was opting out because I had something to hide.' She took a deep breath. 'I lost my temper,' she admitted, 'and walked out of the meeting. When Chris and some of his cronies launched the new campaign earlier this year, he didn't even bother to ask me if I wanted to be involved. Now, of course, I have nothing to do with the theatre and it's actually been a huge relief.'

'Vaughn had put a lot of his own money into the theatre in the months before he died,' Woody said. 'Did you know that?'

'I wasn't aware of that, no.'

Lincoln didn't believe her. 'Did you know Chris suspected your father of stealing some of that money?'

Spots of colour appeared in her cheeks. 'That's

ridiculous,' she said, her hands clasped firmly in her lap. 'If he'd *dared* to make such allegations in his *pathetic* podcast, I'd have sued him for slander. My father was the most honourable man…' She broke off and swallowed hard, as if fighting back tears.

'So there's no truth in that? Bills were getting paid on time? Cash flow wasn't a problem?'

'Cash flow's *always* a problem in a provincial theatre like ours. You take a gamble on every production you put on because there's no guarantee you've made the right choice. Luckily, Dad was very astute and the theatre thrived.'

'And the panto's always popular,' Woody put in.

Eloise regarded him coldly. 'Yes. We could always count on the panto.'

They left without finding either Craig Newton or Sherilyn Croft.

'If Sheri's not with Martin and Valerie,' Eloise had told them, 'she could be anywhere. She tends to sofa surf.'

But not, apparently, at Gilbert's.

'That would be the perfect place for someone to hide out,' Woody said as they drove away from the rambling old house. 'Craig could lie low there for days. But we'd never get a search warrant, would we, unless we had a better idea he was there?'

'No,' said Lincoln, not sure whether or not to believe Eloise. 'I still think he's probably heading for Spain.'

'She's very protective of her dad's reputation, isn't she?'

'They were very close by all accounts. Any slur on Bill Burnett is bound to reflect badly on her, too.'

'Yeah, but there's a big difference between suing Chris Darbyshire for slander and paying someone to kill him.'

They were nearly back at Barley Lane when the DCI phoned. 'Glad I caught you, Jeff. I want you to interview Harry Priest. Get here as soon as you can.'

CHAPTER 61

As the train pulled out of Waterloo Station, Lydia Bancroft rearranged her overnight case and bag on the seat next to her. No one had offered to put them in the overhead rack for her. Those days had gone.

She opened the little photo album she'd brought with her. Some of the snapshots were loose, drifting away from their captions. Where was the one that should have been above *V on Hungerford Bridge May 77*? Oh, there it was, sticking itself to another loose one, *Me and V – Embankment Gardens May 77*.

Who had taken that one of them together? They must have begged a passing tourist to use Vaughn's Instamatic.

Happy days! Now she was in her eighties, these were the memories she treasured. Not the theatrical performances or even the radio plays in which she and Vaughn had shared a microphone, but the simple days off together, quietly happy.

Chris had stirred it all up. She couldn't blame him. It was she who'd invited him to write her life story, record everything before she forgot, before she was forgotten. If he'd said no, would she have sought out someone else? Tried writing it herself? Well, that was out of the question, her hands the way they were, seizing up, aching all the time. And what did she know about computers?

Out of the blue, she'd fancied a return to Barbury. Not that she was afraid of being in the flat on her own, but after the police had turned up, assuring her there was nothing to worry about but… If there was nothing to fear, why were they warning her not to open her door to strangers?

This would be her first time back since Gracie's funeral. It would be Chris's funeral next, but when?

Her mind wandered back to her flat off the Holloway Road. She missed Chris being there. He'd been good company, grateful for somewhere to stay when he was in London. He'd recognised the names of most of the actors and actresses she'd known. Had soaked up all the gossip about them and typed it into his computer.

'You should bring Annie with you sometimes,' she'd said, but Chris had always had some excuse: she's teaching, she can't face London since we lost Gracie, she's got a cold, she's meeting friends.

He'd kept up the pretence for months, until Sherilyn told her the Darbyshires had separated before Christmas. He probably hadn't told Annie he was working with her Aunt Lydia in case it made him seem like a traitor. Lydia and Annie had never got on very well. Nothing as dramatic as a falling-out – she simply never felt as comfortable with Annie as she did with Sherilyn.

If only Chris had left his manuscript behind in her flat, or at least an early draft of it. But he'd kept his cards close to his chest, would never let her look at what he was writing.

'Sorry, Lydia, I'll jinx it if I talk about it too soon,' he'd said. He hadn't let her see so much as an opening chapter.

All he'd left behind in London were a change of clothes, a few toiletries and a little framed photo of him and Annie with Gracie that he kept on the bedside cabinet in the spare room.

What time did the train get in? She'd need to find a taxi. There'd probably be a porter to help, although she'd only got her bag and this small case on wheels. How surprised Annie would be to see her!

CHAPTER 62

Jay Vallis greeted Lincoln when he arrived at Park Street.

'I was all set to do the interview,' she said. 'But the DCI thinks Harry will respond better to a bloke.'

Lincoln shrugged. 'Not sure Harry responds well to *anyone* if he doesn't want to.'

'We're still working our way through the stuff in his mum's garage. It took ages to get the kitchen bits shifted out.'

'Let me know if you find anything else of interest.'

Interview room three was stuffy and reeked of hair oil and sweat – not a pleasant combination. Lincoln wished Priest had been put into room two, where he'd interviewed Russ Milner earlier – although that might have given him an even stronger sense of *déjà vu*.

'Dunno what this is all about,' Priest began. 'Those pikeys nicked my van and then they wrecked it and you've brought *me* in here as if…'

'Save it, Harry.' Lincoln dropped his folder on the desk. His fourth interview of the day, and the cream cheese and cress sandwich was repeating on him. He flipped the folder open. 'Luke and Milo took your van with your knowledge and consent, didn't they? So they could go to Mr Fogarty's house and load up with his new kitchen. Then they took it to your mum's garage where it was found, still in its shrink-wrap.'

Lincoln turned his phone to show Priest some photos of the garage interior. 'That *is* your mum's garage, isn't it, Harry?'

Priest nodded, running the tip of his tongue over dry lips. He glanced at the duty solicitor out of the corner of his eye, but she didn't look his way.

'It wasn't your idea to nick the kitchen, was it?' Lincoln went on. 'It was Garvin Steele's. He had keys to the house and he knew when the Fogartys would be away, but he didn't have transport. Which is where Milo and Luke come in. You'd got a nice big van and they knew you'd be up for it. "Just leave the keys in the ignition, Harry, and we'll do the rest." Was that how it was?'

'If you've got it all worked out, why're you asking me? Listen, I never said for them to pick that lad up and kill him, okay? That's nothing to do with me. That was Garvin's little bit of fun, that was, because that's the nasty piece of work he is.'

Lincoln didn't speak for a minute or two, re-reading Anderson's notes. Connors had decided against attempting to prosecute Priest over the porn found in his storeroom. There was no way to prove the dirty magazines and VHS tapes were his. The tapes had deteriorated too much to be viewable, so what they contained and who had made them would never be known. Joe Kelly had died in prison during a long sentence for raping a fourteen-year-old boy. If the magazines and tapes were Kelly's, as Priest claimed, then further investigation was pointless. "Not a good use of resources," the DCI would have said.

But there were still unanswered questions.

'What about Isaac Keats?' Lincoln pulled a photo of the boy from his folder, looked at it for a moment or two before putting it down on the table. 'Went missing in Trowbridge, 2011. Remember him, Harry?'

Priest didn't let his gaze linger on the boy's face. 'Like I told your colleague, the dead one, I don't know him.'

'How about Bob Greenaway from Swindon?' Another photo, another averted gaze.

Despite DCI Connors's discouragement, Anderson had done a fair bit of research into both missing persons cases. He'd discovered that, on Fridays, Priest routinely drove to a cash-and-carry warehouse north of Swindon to pick up stock for his market stalls. Bob and Isaac had both disappeared on a Friday from places on his likely route between Swindon and Barbury.

'Did you give Isaac a lift, Harry? Was that how his SIM ended up in your van?'

'I told you, I told the other one, I never…' A knock interrupted him.

Jay stuck her head round the door. 'Can I have a word?'

Lincoln got up and went out into the corridor. 'Make it a good one.'

'Evidence.' She held her phone up to show him photos sent over by the team searching the garage. 'They've found clothes folded up in a box in the roof space. Jeans, sweatshirt, boxers, sneakers, jacket.' She swiped to another photo. 'Library card in the jeans pocket, Wiltshire Libraries, Isaac Keats. There's blood on the boxers.'

'Send me the photos.'

A few minutes later, Lincoln returned to the interview room, his chest fiery with heartburn. He laid his phone on the table.

'What's going on?' Priest sounded worried.

'We've found something in your mum's garage, Harry.'

His eyes widened. Had he forgotten he'd hidden Isaac's clothes there six years ago?

Lincoln swiped through the photos, turning his phone to show Priest each one in turn. 'Why've you got this boy's clothes and library card, Harry?'

'I found them.' He licked his lips.

'You didn't think to report it to someone? You must've known he was missing. Why did you keep quiet about it?'

'Because of how it would look. Because of what my mate Joe Kelly was inside for.'

'Raping a teenage boy, you mean? Shall I tell you how it looks now, Harry?' Lincoln took his phone back and swiped to another shot taken in the garage: a black and white school photo captioned, in ballpoint, *Harry 1966.*

'This you, Harry?'

He frowned at it uncertainly, but Lincoln could tell he recognised it even if he hadn't seen it in a long time.

'This was in your mum's garage too. How old are you there? Fifteen? Sixteen? Suppose someone had tricked *you* into getting into their car, into their van and driven you away? Done things to you. Done away with you. How would your mum have felt, never knowing what had happened to you? Because that's what you did, isn't it, Harry? Made Isaac Keats disappear on his way home from college that Friday afternoon. Used his cash card to make it look as if he was going off for a fun weekend.' Lincoln stared into the teenage Priest's defiant face. 'You think your mum's proud of you, Harry, the way Isaac's mum was proud of *him*?'

There was a long pause, and then, 'I saw him miss his bus, offered him a lift.' Priest put his hands on the table, two fists, the knuckles white. 'He'd bought clothes off my stall a few times. Nice kid. I offered him a few quid for, you know…' He cast the solicitor a sidelong glance. 'Dunno why he got so upset.' He shook his head. 'I lost it. Grabbed him. He punched me and I punched him back. Tried to shut him up. Can't remember much else.'

He hung his head.

'And Bob Greenaway?'

A shrug, a shake of the head. 'I didn't kill him,' he said. 'I remember him, but I swear I didn't kill him.'

Claire Connors listened while Lincoln updated her.

'He buried the boy in Savernake Forest? Christ, that'll take some searching!'

'He thinks he can find the spot – it's where two tracks cross. But whether he'll be able to find it again after six years is anybody's guess.'

'I've already sent more CSIs over to Barbury Down. That garage is full of stuff that needs going through. He'd have got away with it, wouldn't he, if we hadn't had to clear that bloody kitchen out of there? Good work, Jeff.' She peeled the ring-pull off a tin of Fanta.

'It was Tim that cracked it,' he said. 'And Jay Vallis and the search team.'

'Okay, okay.' She swigged some of her drink. 'But he won't admit to killing the Greenaway boy?'

'No. Says he chatted to him but that's all.'

'You believe him?'

'He's in enough trouble already – I don't know why he'd deny it if he was guilty. There's no evidence connecting him to Bob, unless something turns up in the garage. What do we do now? Hand him over to Trowbridge?'

Connors reached for her phone. 'I'd better let them know what's happened. They'll have given up any hope of finding the Keats boy – dead or alive.' She put a call through to her opposite number in Trowbridge, tapping her pen on the desk as she waited to be connected. And then, 'Hey, yes, it's DCI Claire Connors here, Park Street. We've just solved a missing persons case for you. Remember Isaac Keats?'

SUNDAY 5TH NOVEMBER

CHAPTER 63

'Sorry, did I wake you?' Trish's cheery apology did little to soothe Lincoln's irritation at being roused so early on a Sunday morning.

'You did, yes.' He flung the covers back and slid out of bed, taking his phone across to the window. 'It's not even light!'

'I just thought you'd like to know what I found out yesterday.'

'Yesterday?'

'After work, I popped in to see Beryl Amos, the woman who did the accounts for the theatre when Vaughn was still there. She works in that minicab office near the station.'

'Beryl Amos?' He shut his eyes, trying to visualise the whiteboard, his notes, anything that might have had this woman's name on it. In vain.

'She's a cousin of Vic's. Vic, my ex. She was straight out of secretarial college when she went to work in the back office at the theatre, no more than a girl.'

'How did you know about her?'

'Kitty, the theatre archivist, spoke to her. When she was still Keith. And Chris Darbyshire spoke to her too.'

'When *who* was still Keith?' It was too early in the morning for this.

'Kitty. She used to be Keith. And she talked to Beryl about the accounts, and then Chris spoke to her. And then *I* spoke to her and she got very defensive.'

'Kitty?'

'No, Beryl. And she said something about Bill Burnett giving her the job because she was young and didn't really know what she was doing. Or maybe she meant she was too naïve to know what *he* was doing. Hands all over her, she said.'

'Who?' Lincoln needed coffee. Badly.

'Bill Burnett. Don't you think it's odd that Chris was looking into the theatre's finances for around the time that Vaughn died? What d'you think he suspected?'

'Trish, I have no idea. I'm hardly awake.'

'I thought it would help.'

'It will. It has. I need to clear my head a bit so I can take it all in.'

'I'll text you.'

He rang off, promising to call her later, and headed for the shower. Who was Beryl Amos? And what damage might Trish have done, trampling all over an active murder investigation?

An hour later, he was standing in front of the whiteboard, trying to fit Beryl into the jigsaw puzzle. Trish had texted him, explaining that Beryl had kept the theatre's accounts around the time that Vaughn was rehearsing *Jack and the Beanstalk*.

> **Got v defensive when I asked her about the accounts. Chris asked her that too. She was only doing what Bill Burnett told her to, she said.**

Woody arrived, looking unhappy.

'Ted's had another funny turn,' he said. 'He was too giddy to get out of bed this morning.'

'When's he seeing the doctor?'

'Not until Friday, unless there's a cancellation. Suki's on the phone first thing every morning, waiting to see if a slot's opened up.'

'At least he didn't fall over again. One broken arm's enough.'

'She was phoning Trish as I was leaving, telling her not to come over for lunch today.'

'Talking of Trish,' Lincoln told Woody about Beryl Amos. 'Darbyshire must've thought he was onto something with the theatre's finances. Maybe he'd found proof that Bill Burnett was fiddling the accounts.'

'Still can't see someone killing him to cover it up. Well done for getting Harry Priest to confess,' Woody added. 'Tim Anderson was right about him, wasn't he?'

'He was right about him killing Isaac Keats, but we've got nothing to connect him to the Greenaway boy.'

'Reckon they might turn up another dead body in Savernake when they go digging for Isaac.'

'Yes,' said Lincoln grimly. 'They might.' It had been enough to see photos of Isaac's library card, his bloodied pants, his sneakers. The search of the garage could yet turn up his college books and bank card, his watch. 'Let's get back to Chris Darbyshire.'

On the whiteboard, the triangle he'd drawn days ago connecting Darbyshire, Lydia and Vaughn seemed to be mocking him. Lydia had persuaded Darbyshire that Vaughn had been murdered, but what evidence was there? And why did she back off when Lincoln tried to talk to her? Had she realised she'd got it wrong? Or had someone got to her?

He went back to his desk and looked up reports of the inquest into Vaughn's death, recorded under his given name of Vaughn Emlyn Hamilton.

The inquest was held in April 1991, three months after his death. On the afternoon of Sunday January 6th his landlord, Cyril Carter, let himself into the flat to fix a leaking tap. Instead, he found Vaughn dead, hanging from a clothes rail, a long scarf used as a noose.

Wasn't it *Lydia* who'd found him? Had she frantically gathered up Vaughn's scrapbook and left his body for poor Cyril Carter to find?

No other witnesses were mentioned and the report concluded with the verdict that Mr Hamilton had taken his own life while the balance of his mind was disturbed.

Might Carter still be around?

It didn't take Lincoln long to find a phone number for a C W Carter living at Inkerman Terrace, a few doors away from number thirteen, the house where Vaughn had died. Would he be willing to talk? It was the middle of a damp Sunday morning. He'd probably still be getting up or having his breakfast, but it was worth a try.

'Dad's just come in from the allotment.' Cyril Carter's son led the way into the cosy living room. So much for the old chap still being in his pyjamas. 'He'll be with you when he's got his boots off.'

'Vaughn was a lovely chap,' Cyril said when Lincoln explained why he was there. He must have been about seventy, but he had a boyish face and lively eyes. 'We'd become friends despite the age gap, and it shattered me, finding him like that. I'd never seen a dead body before.'

'Did you ever doubt that it was suicide?'

'Not at the time, no, but I read up on it afterwards. When someone hangs themselves, the bruises are usually high up and at an angle, aren't they? I saw his bruises close up and they were lower down on his throat, horizontal. But the pathologist would've seen that, wouldn't he, if there was any doubt that it was suicide?'

'I'd have thought so.' But emergency services and medical personnel would have been overstretched at that time of year. The examination might have been hasty.

Mistakes could have been made. 'Can you tell me more about that day?'

They sat down in armchairs by the open fire. 'I'd gone round to mend a tap that wouldn't turn off properly. Thought he'd be at the theatre, so I let myself in. It was four o'clock, already dark.' Cyril's gaze drifted out of focus as he recalled that winter afternoon. 'Switched the light on and there he was. There was a clothes rail built into the alcove with a curtain across, you know, instead of a wardrobe. The curtain was drawn back and he was there, hanging by his scarf, like he was trying to kneel down. Horrible sight, it was. I thought he was having me on, making a face at me, sticking his tongue out, but then I realised…'

'It must have been a terrible shock.'

'It was. I sold the house later that year. I couldn't go in there without thinking…' He shook his head, full of regret. 'I blame myself, telling the police what he'd told me, that he'd always suffered from depression. Straight off, they thought suicide. What if they didn't look hard enough because of what I'd said?'

'If there was nothing to suggest anyone else was involved…' Lincoln knew how tempting it was to accept the easiest answer.

'Yeah, but you always wonder. I felt sorry for the young constable who turned up. It was his first dead body too.'

'Can you remember his name?'

Cyril thought for a minute. 'Bradman. PC Bradman. Can't tell you his first name.'

Lincoln made a note, relieved the surname wasn't Smith or Jones. If Bradman had been in his early twenties then or even younger, he might still be around.

'Anything else strike you at the time, Mr Carter?'

'I remember thinking, how's he done that with the lights off? He'd have been at the theatre the night before until well after ten, so whenever he killed himself, it would've been dark. How could he see to tie his scarf and hitch it over the curtain rail with the lights off? And that curtain rail must've been six foot off the floor and Vaughn wasn't a tall man.'

'You're sure there were no lights on?'

'Positive. I remember switching them on as I went in. Saw him there, making a face at me.'

Neither of them spoke for a few minutes, watching the coals shift in the grate. The lights must have been on when Lydia arrived at the bedsit sometime before Cyril, and, without thinking, she'd turned them off as she left. Lincoln didn't tell Cyril he *hadn't* been the first to find the body.

'Did you tell the police the lights were off when you got there?'

'Didn't think about it until later and then it didn't seem important. But it's nagged away at me all these years.' He leaned back in his chair and fixed Lincoln with a critical eye. 'Are you thinking he was murdered? You won't be able to prove anything now, will you?'

'We'll see.' Lincoln got to his feet. 'Did Chris Darbyshire contact you?'

'We had a quick chat on the phone, but I was on my way out, couldn't stop. We were going to meet up but then of course…' He shrugged. 'I told him the constable's name in case he could help. Shame, what happened to him when it did. It sounded as if he was onto something.'

After he'd left Cyril, Lincoln headed up Inkerman Terrace and stood outside number thirteen. It looked smarter than it had in the newspaper photos from 1991, but only a little. The apology for a front garden was taken up with wheelie bins, and the old sash windows had been replaced with varying styles of uPVC ones. A train cruised by, high up at the end of the back garden, slowing to enter Barbury Station.

Had Mitchell Burnett ever come here to this little cul-de-sac close to the railway? Lincoln recalled the disparaging way he'd dismissed Vaughn: a drinker, living alone in a seedy little bedsit, with trains going by his window all hours of the day and night.

'Did Vaughn have many visitors, as far as you know?' Lincoln had asked Cyril.

'Lydia Bancroft dropped in from time to time – used to see her little car go by, one of those Citroens with the soft top.'

'A 2CV?'

'Yeah. Terrible driver. Always went up on the pavement trying to turn round. Never saw anyone else visiting. I asked him once why he didn't want a bigger place. "Everything I need is at the theatre, Cyril and that's where my friends are, too." He liked to come back to the bedsit and shut the door on the rest of the world for a few hours until it was time for the theatre again.'

Lincoln made a mental note to track down the former PC Bradman. The more he thought about it, the more certain he became that Darbyshire *knew* Vaughn had been murdered.

The clue was in the title of the podcast he never got to complete: *The Death of a Pantomime Dame.*

CHAPTER 64

Even though it was late in the afternoon and growing dark, a café near the railway station was still serving Sunday lunch, ambushing Lincoln with the evocative aroma of roast beef and potatoes. He strode past it and shoved open the door of the cab office.

A middle-aged woman hunched behind the desk looked up. 'You want a cab? It'll be a wait. They're all out.'

'Beryl Amos?' He showed her his ID, but she scarcely glanced at it.

'Not you as well!' She cranked herself round in her well-worn swivel chair. 'Why's the world and his wife so interested in me all of a sudden? First that archivist chap comes in here, then Chris Darbyshire, then that woman from the library.'

In the absence of another chair, Lincoln perched his behind on the corner of her untidy desk.

'What did Chris ask you about?'

She poured herself a capful of coffee from her flask. 'He said he'd found *evidence* that someone was cooking the books at the theatre while I was accounts clerk there. Accounts clerk? General dogsbody, more like.'

'But you dealt with the accounts, didn't you?'

'Among other things. I'd only just left the Tech when I started there and didn't really know what I was doing. I suppose that's why Bill Burnett took me on. I did as I was told.'

'What did Bill tell you to do?'

'I had to count the box office takings every day and he'd tell me what to put down in the account book. It was always recorded as a lot less than the actual takings. Then, when I recorded what we paid for things – the electric, costume hire, salaries – I had to write it down as *more* than we actually paid out. It would look like we had less money in the bank than we did. Bill said it was a way of paying less tax.'

Lincoln wondered how she could have been so naïve, but then she had been eighteen and fresh out of college. 'How did you keep track of it all?'

She took a sip from her little plastic cup. 'Two account books, one red, one blue. The actual amounts went in the red book, the altered ones went in the blue.'

'And you didn't suspect anything?'

'Not at the start, no. Bill made it sound so logical. But then the penny dropped.'

She'd started work in the theatre office in July 1990, she said, typing letters, filing paperwork and answering the phone, making teas and coffees.

'After the first couple of weeks, Bill started to get a bit... *suggestive*. Making comments about how I looked and what I got up to with my boyfriend.'

'Must've made you feel uncomfortable.'

'Damn right! I'd have walked out, but I needed a job and there wasn't much around. I thought if I didn't rise to it, he'd give up.'

'But he didn't.'

'And it wasn't just him. Mitch was always hanging around the office, telling me I was doing it wrong, playing with my hair, hiding my pens, messing my papers up. Thought he was being clever, but he was just being a dick.'

'And you couldn't say anything because he was the boss's son.'

'Exactly. When the end of the month came and there

was no pay packet on my desk, I took it out of petty cash, put it down as expenditure on stamps. I know, it was wrong,' she said, holding her hands up. 'But I was so pissed off. Like the stupid kid I was, I thought I'd got away with it and did it again a week or so later. But Bill was biding his time, the crafty bugger.'

'And how long did he "bide his time"?'

'Another two weeks. He catches me as I'm about to clock off one afternoon, says he wants to discuss something, and I think, *Oh shit*!'

She broke off to pour herself the last dribble of coffee from her flask. Lincoln saw her as both this dowdy forty-something woman and as an unworldly but spunky young girl.

'He says he knows I've been doing a bit of "creative accounting" with the petty cash so I won't tell anyone about the two account books, will I? And that's when I realised it was dodgy, not just to fool the taxman.' She swivelled her chair away as a call came in, someone who'd been waiting "simply ages" for a cab and would call another company if it didn't turn up in the next five minutes.

'Suit yourself,' Beryl told the woman. 'I can't control the traffic. Or the weather.' She slammed the phone down and swivelled back. 'It wasn't the taxman he wanted to fool, it was Mr Vaughn. But what could I do? He'd have sacked me if I'd said anything. Spread the word that I'd been stealing from petty cash.'

'You were caught all ways.'

'Damn right! But then, just before Christmas, Mitch cornered me in the office as I was packing up to go home, tried it on with me, hands up my jumper, pushing himself into me. He'd been drinking, but I wasn't gonna put up with him thinking he could do what he liked just because of who he was. So once I'd shoved him off me, I photocopied pages from both account books and left them in Mr Vaughn's pigeonhole anonymously.'

'A brave move.'

'Or a stupid one.' She gazed at the phone as if willing it to ring, but it stayed silent.

'What happened next?'

'First week of January, I came back from lunch one day and Mr Vaughn and Bill were having a huge row. Couldn't make out what it was about, but money came into it. Something about a house. How Mr Vaughn felt betrayed. A day or so later, he was dead. Bill paid me two months' salary, handed me my cards, said he'd give me a good reference. Made me promise not to tell anyone about the two account books. Our little secret, he said, like me dipping my fingers into the petty cash.'

'So you left?'

'Had no option. And I kept thinking – if I hadn't sent Mr Vaughn those photocopies…' She sniffed loudly. 'Somehow or other, Chris Darbyshire had got hold of them and wanted to know what I could tell him. Told him what I've just told you.' She looked away again. 'It was funny seeing those account pages after all that time. I'd forgotten what nice handwriting I had.'

'Beryl, would you be prepared to make a statement? Write down what you've told me to make it official?'

'What, and have Mitch Burnett set his legal team on me? I see him on the telly and my skin crawls, but I'm not stupid. I know which of us has got the power – and it's not me.'

CHAPTER 65

'It's years since we had a bonfire with proper fireworks.'

Cody turned, startled by the sound of a familiar voice. 'Mitch. Long time, yeah.'

'Not since before Mum died.' His brother sat down next to him on the bench overlooking the playing field. The public fireworks display was coming to an end and the crowd was beginning to drift towards the exit to beat the rush. 'She was always afraid we'd set ourselves on fire. And then when she wasn't there to fuss, we stopped anyway.'

'Long time ago.' Cody shifted a little farther along the bench. Mitch always made him feel overwhelmed, as if he was stronger and bulkier than he really was, but he couldn't put off seeing him any longer, not if he was going to find any peace of mind. Meeting here, before Mitch went back to London and before Cody's family flew back to Boston, seemed the best they could manage.

Mitch looked around. 'Didn't you bring the kids along?'

'Courtney's taken them to get a hot drink from the van down there.'

'They'll be a while. There's a long queue.' Mitch raised a cardboard cup to his lips. 'Shit coffee, too, once you get there.'

Cody could've done with a warming drink inside him. The rain had eased off two hours ago as the display was getting under way, but now there was a keen wind and his mac wasn't thick enough. He envied his brother the thick tweed coat he was wearing, even if it did remind him of the itchy tweed coats they'd had at St Luke's, the private school Cody had loathed but that Mitch had loved. 'When are you off to France?'

'A week tomorrow. A series on the last months of the Great War. Bloody harrowing, I can tell you. The Somme last year was bad enough.'

And yet you love it, Cody thought. You love every earnest appeal to the camera, every dramatic fact you reel off.

'Who had Chris Darbyshire killed? Was it you, Mitch?' He kept looking straight ahead, but he sensed his brother's shock at the question.

'Me? Come on, Cody, what do you take me for? How can you ask me a question like that, sitting there watching the fucking fireworks, asking me if I've had a man killed?'

'Was it Nate?'

'Nate? You haven't seen him lately. The guy's a wreck. All he cares about is making his bloody daughter famous.'

'Remember those photos you took of me? Of me and Nate?'

Mitch wouldn't look at him, his gaze on the fireworks instead, the finale a messy volley of rockets, as unsynchronised as the rest of the display. 'These guys should've quit while they were ahead.'

'Guess it's not something you can rehearse. Either you let your fireworks off or you don't. Those photos, Mitch, the ones in Vaughn's scrapbook. What happened to them?'

'How would I know? I thought all that stuff was long gone, but someone must've found it when they cleared his place and hung onto it.'

'What else is going to turn up, d'you think?'

Mitch shrugged. The whole bench jolted. 'What did the police ask you?'

'They asked about the stuff in the scrapbook and was I surprised Vaughn killed himself.'

'What did you say?' Mitch finished his coffee and crushed the cup. Dropped it at his feet.

'What *could* I say? It's hazy now, nearly thirty years later.'

'Suicide, though. A shock, wasn't it?'

'Not sure what I thought at the time.' Cody could feel his brother's eyes on him now. 'I was more worried about Mum and how much longer we'd have with her.'

Mitch was silent for several minutes, then said firmly, 'I still think he killed Bob Greenaway. He was there, doing drama in his school. He knew that Harry guy with the market stall and Harry was a mate of that Kelly creep who ended up in jail. Just because Vaughn didn't fancy *you*, doesn't mean he didn't go after Bob.'

'He *did* fancy me, but he was honourable enough not to act on it.'

Mitch sniggered. 'Have it your way.'

They watched the crowd heading towards the exit.

'Did they ask about Dad?' Mitch turned up his collar and pulled his scarf over his chin, probably afraid someone would recognise him and pester him for an autograph or a selfie. 'The police. Did they ask about Dad?'

'No. Why would they?'

'Vaughn told people Dad was stealing from him. It was all crap, but it's rumours like that…'

'Who cares now, Mitch? They're both dead.'

'*I* care. *Eloise* cares. She took over from Dad. She doesn't want people thinking he was a criminal.'

That was rich, given the way their father had blagged his way through life, getting backers for poor productions, conning punters into paying good money to sit through crap. Cody summoned up the courage to ask a question he'd wanted to ask for a long, long time. 'Where did you go that night, Mitch, after we finished the show?'

'Which night? What are you talking about?'

'The night Vaughn died.'

'Courtney!' Mitch stood up and called out to Cody's wife as she and his sons climbed the slope towards them. 'How *are* you? And my gorgeous nephews. My, how you two have grown.'

Cody stood up too, suddenly wanting to shield his family from his own brother. If only he and Mitch had been as close as his own sons were.

'We haven't seen you in ages,' Courtney said as Mitch hugged her.

'I should keep in touch better.'

'No, we should come over more often. As it is, we're only here till the end of the week and then it's back to Boston.'

Mitch turned to him. 'You're off again?'

'Courtney needs to get the boys back home before they miss any more school.' Cody reached for his wife, pulling her protectively into his embrace. 'I'm staying on.'

'Maybe when I'm back from France...' Mitch punched him lightly in the shoulder. 'We must meet up again, yeah?'

He hugged Courtney once more, ruffled the boys' hair, embarrassing them both, and hurried away.

Courtney slipped her arm through his. 'Wasn't it great to see Mitch again?'

'Sure.' Cody watched as his brother, despite his best efforts, was waylaid by a gaggle of fans. 'It's always good to catch up.'

MONDAY 6TH NOVEMBER

CHAPTER 66

'Thanks for agreeing to see me at such short notice, Roger.'

'No worries. I know how it is.'

Lincoln followed Roger Bradman into his lounge and sat by a picture window that overlooked a field of black and white cows. 'Nice view.'

'Yeah, well, they're about to start building in the field next to that one and then I expect the farmer will sell this one too, so we're enjoying it while we can.'

Marie, his wife, disappeared into the kitchen to put the kettle on. A rotund ginger cat came to investigate the visitor, quickly decided Lincoln could be trusted and settled down on the sofa, pressing itself against his thigh.

Roger explained that he'd been out of the police ten years now and worked on security solutions for small businesses.

'Covers all sorts,' he said. He dropped a glossy brochure on the table next to Lincoln, who felt obliged to flip through it. 'Building security, CCTV, vehicles, digital. Now, what did you want to know about Vaughn? You said you were trying to clarify a few things.'

'You were the officer first on the scene that morning. How much do you remember about it?'

'My first dead body,' Roger said cheerfully. 'Like they say, nothing prepares you, does it? But poor old Vaughn, that was particularly gross.'

'Why?'

'He was hung up in an alcove in the corner of this tiny little flat. Dangling on the end of a stripey scarf, his legs bent. Made me think of one of those string puppets, you know? It was upsetting, the sight of him, his tongue sticking out… And the smell… Well, you'll have been to a few crime scenes, won't you? I don't need to tell *you* what it's like.'

'No doubts that he'd killed himself?'

'Is that what this is about, people having doubts?' He sat up straighter.

'Well, it's just that…'

'Because I've always wondered, but no one would listen to me.'

'What did you wonder about?'

'He'd had company, you could tell, an empty mug by one armchair, a half-full mug by the other. Not a lot to go on, admittedly, but the way the chairs were facing each other, he'd obviously had a visitor. But when my sergeant turned up…' He shook his head, tutting. 'See, in those days – as you'll remember, I'm sure – the attitude to gay men, it was different to how it is now. My sergeant said maybe Vaughn had been entertaining another fella and they'd fallen out. The other fella left and Vaughn was so upset, he hanged himself. He said, best not set any hares running, going looking for whoever he'd had there. Could be a man who doesn't want people to know he's gay.'

'I suppose that wasn't such a strange attitude, twenty-odd years ago.'

'No. The doctor who came, a doddery old chap, confirmed Vaughn was dead and went off again. They took the body away and that was that.'

'Nobody wondered about the two mugs?'

'Someone put them in the sink out of the way. I wish to this day that I'd bagged them up so someone could've checked them for prints, but I was just a new uniform seeing my first dead body. Who was going to listen to me? And my sergeant wanted it all hushed up, squared away, no questions asked.'

Marie came in with cups of coffee, a plate of biscuits. 'Help yourself. Homemade.'

They were still warm from the oven. Lincoln took two.

'Did anyone interview neighbours?' he asked. 'Other people in the house?'

'The next-door neighbour heard a car pulling up outside number thirteen late that night, between ten-thirty and midnight, a biggish man driving, middle-aged. The girl downstairs heard a bit of a ruckus in Vaughn's flat around the same sort of time – which was unusual, she said, because he was always very quiet. The pathologist gave Vaughn's time of death as around then – eleven to midnight. That's why I've always wondered: did we sweep it under the carpet when we should've taken it more seriously?' Roger spread his hands. 'But that's how it was back then. He was gay, invited someone back and things turned sour. Best not to dig too deep. Different times.'

Lincoln bit into a biscuit and it seemed to melt on his tongue. 'Delicious.' He drank some coffee. 'Did Chris Darbyshire get to speak to you?'

Marie gasped. 'God, that was awful, wasn't it? You'd only spoken to him a day or two before that, hadn't you, Rog? He was here, sitting where you are now, Inspector.'

Without thinking, Lincoln looked down at the sofa, at the ginger cat dozing next to him, oblivious.

'That's right, and then we went off to Tenerife, didn't know what had happened until we got back. Terrible.' Roger shook his head sadly. 'I told Chris I'd always felt it was unresolved somehow. Unanswered questions. And he gave me the chance to get something off my conscience.'

'Oh?'

'There was a coat, an overcoat, left on the sofa. Tweed, good quality. And it was way too big to fit Vaughn.'

'You think his visitor left it behind?'

'Who else?'

'What happened to it?'

'My sergeant said to take it.'

'Take it? What, take it back to the station?'

'No, to take it and keep it.'

'But it was evidence of someone else being there.'

Roger chuckled. 'Yes. And that's what he didn't want. Wanted to keep it simple. No second mug, no coat left on the sofa.'

Lincoln found it hard to believe, but not impossible. As Roger had said, different times. 'What happened to this overcoat?'

'I kept it for years in the back of the wardrobe. Scared to wear it in case someone knew where I'd got it from. Stupid, eh?' He laughed ruefully.

'Anything in it to identify the owner?'

'Damned if I can remember. Nothing obvious. I slipped it into one of those suit covers and hung it up behind everything else in my wardrobe.'

'You don't still have it, do you?' Lincoln mentally crossed his fingers.

'Nah! I was still living with my mum and dad then. Didn't get my own place for another year or so. Left it with them.' He must've seen the disappointment in Lincoln's face. 'Sorry. Shouldn't have mentioned it.'

'No, that's okay. You don't happen to remember who did the post-mortem?'

'Not the usual chap, I remember someone saying. The weather was bad that week and he couldn't get there.

There'll be records, won't there? It's not *that* long ago.'

'Any other reason why you doubted it was suicide?'

'The clothes rail. It must've been six foot up and Vaughn was only five-eight, five-nine. Couldn't think how he'd strung himself up there without standing on something. But there wasn't a chair or a stool anywhere near. And then I thought, the landlord must've moved things when he got there, checking Vaughn was dead, trying to get him down. And my sergeant…' He shook his head.

'Told you not to worry about it.'

'More or less.' Roger took a deep breath. 'It'd be a relief to know someone was looking into it now. I won't say it's troubled me all these years, but what has always been at the back of my mind is, did we do right by him?'

CHAPTER 67

Lincoln returned to Barley Lane, more sure than ever that Vaughn had been murdered. But by whom and why? There was no reason to assume his killer was someone connected to the theatre. But why else did so many leads take him to one of the Board Treaders, Bill Burnett or his daughter Eloise Gilbert?

A heavily built, middled-aged man had been seen going into the house where Vaughn lived – a description that would fit Bill Burnett, but that wasn't enough. The armchairs drawn up towards each other, the mugs that Roger Bradman had noticed, all suggested Vaughn knew his visitor, had spent time talking to him – or her – before the atmosphere changed. Or had a third person turned up?

So many unanswered questions.

His laptop pinged with an incoming email from the Digital Forensics Team. At long last, the data from the tracker on Leanne's car. He skimmed through it.

'That's strange,' he said.

Pam looked up. 'What?'

'The day after Darbyshire's body was found, Leanne drove all the way to Tisbury, to Standish's Farm. Was she taking his laptop to Jessica, d'you think?'

'But Jessica asked me if we'd found it. Why would she do that if she'd got it back? Maybe Leanne drove over there, lost her nerve and came away again without calling at the house. She must've felt pretty bad about getting involved with Chris, about what happened to him.'

'Or Jessica's lying.'

'Shall I go over there? I'll tell her we know Leanne was there, see if she still tries to deny it.'

'Okay, do that,' said Lincoln. 'See what she says.' The laptop was crucial to the investigation and finding it would be a huge breakthrough.

After Pam had gone, he told Woody what he'd learned from Cyril Carter and Roger Bradman.

'Reckon Vaughn could've been strangled first,' Woody said. 'Then strung up to look like suicide. Shame about the coat. That could've had DNA traces on it.'

'It probably ended up in a charity shop years ago.'

'But you're thinking it was Bill Burnett who was there with him?'

Lincoln nodded. 'Beryl Amos was in the theatre office when she heard them arguing, only days earlier. Bill could've gone round to Vaughn's to patch things up, or to finish the argument off, once and for all.'

'And if Darbyshire was killed to protect Bill's reputation…'

'Then we're looking at one of the Burnetts.' He didn't want to stick his neck out and guess which one, but his money was on Mitchell.

'So now what?'

Lincoln headed for the kettle. 'We still haven't traced Craig Newton and until we do, we're not going to find out who was behind this.'

Craig had kept in touch with Tawny Howell via a burner phone, but if they could get a warrant to track his personal mobile, they could see where he was and who he'd contacted.

'I'll talk to the DCI about getting a warrant,' he said. 'And then maybe I should go over to Presford Motors, see if his number two there can give us a clue. Coming with me?'

Brian York recognised Woody as he and Lincoln approached the reception desk at Presford Motors.

'If you're looking for Craig, you won't find him here. And if *I* knew where to find him, I'd gladly tell you because I'm looking for him too and we could go and beat him up together. He's taken a load of dosh out of the business account and I won't have enough to pay the lads at the end of the week. If his dad knew what he was getting up to…'

Lincoln told him, briefly, that Craig was suspected of paying someone to kill Chris Darbyshire, but that he, in turn, had been paid by someone else.

'Any idea who that could be, Brian?'

York shrugged hopelessly. If he knew anything that would get Craig into trouble, he'd probably be only too ready to reveal it. It was clear that his loyalties lay with Dave Newton, not his son.

'Have you ever seen him with this woman?' Woody showed York a photo of Eloise Gilbert.

York shook his head. 'Nah, that's not his girlfriend. Fifi, he calls her. Posh type. Fuck knows what she sees in him. That's what happens when you use your phone to find yourself a date.'

So they'd got that wrong, had they? The well-off older woman Craig was seeing *wasn't* Eloise after all.

'Do you know where Fifi lives?'

He shrugged. 'No, but… Hang about, there was a number for her scribbled on the pad in his office.' A minute later, he emerged with a mobile number and Lincoln rang it.

'Fenella Brooks, here. Hello?'

At Standish's Farm, Jessica was adamant that she

hadn't seen Leanne the day after Chris Darbyshire was found dead.

'I've never even met her,' she told Pam. 'She certainly never came here. She wouldn't have dared.' She hugged herself as if she felt exposed and unsafe. 'Annie came, though. I let her take his papers away, all the stuff that was in his office.'

Pam recalled the neatly shelved box files, the early chapters of his ghosted autobiography of Lydia and the photos of the actress as a young girl. Leave it, Lincoln had told her, so she'd left it. But might they have missed something? Was it safe with Annie Darbyshire?

'But no,' Jessica said, hugging herself tighter, 'that Milner woman definitely wasn't here.'

Disheartened, Pam was about to get in her car when she had an idea. She climbed the iron staircase that led up to Toby Hale's flat. When he came to the door, she turned her phone towards him, displaying a photo of Leanne.

'Do you recognise this woman, Toby? She drove here the day after Chris's body was found. Did you see her?'

'When was that?' He frowned uncertainly.

Pam stepped over the threshold into his living room. 'Thursday the twenty-sixth. In the afternoon. Were you here then?'

'Are you sure she came here?'

'A hundred per cent.'

He must have realised there was no point denying it. 'You've come for this, I suppose.'

He crossed to a cupboard on the far side of the room and pulled out a blue carrier bag. 'She wanted to give it to Jess herself, but I didn't want Jess to see it, to see *her*. So I took it and told her to get lost.'

Pam took the bag and peeked inside: the missing laptop. She could've told him how much he'd hampered the investigation, how much quicker they might have been able to act if only he'd come forward sooner, but what was the point? It was enough that, at last, she had it.

'I tried to get into it, but I don't know the password and I doubt if Jess does. I wouldn't even want to ask her.' He edged Pam towards the door. 'He was going to help me with my writing. Now what am I going to do?'

'I expect you'll find someone else to help.'

'Wait, there's something else.' He went back to the cupboard. 'She brought this back too, but I didn't want Jess to see it.'

He retrieved the overcoat Chris must have left behind when he got out of Leanne's car and went into Coronation Gardens, moments before his death.

Pam draped the coat over her arm and, with the carrier bag in her other hand, hurried down the metal staircase to her car.

CHAPTER 68

Chris Darbyshire's laptop was sent off to the tech team, to be dealt with as top priority.

'Well done, Pam,' Lincoln said, standing at the whiteboard as the rest of the team assembled. He felt more positive than he had in days. 'Let's hope they can get into it.'

At last, Darbyshire's discoveries would be revealed.

'Our chief suspect is now Mitchell Burnett.' He tapped the TV personality's photo, in pride of place on the board. 'His personal assistant, Fenella Brooks, is Craig Newton's girlfriend – the older, well-off woman Tawny Howell told us about. I think we can assume that when Mitchell was looking for someone to shut Darbyshire up, she suggested Craig.'

'I wasn't expecting Mitch to be the one behind Chris's death,' Pam said. 'Was he so ashamed of the way he and the other Board Treaders baited Vaughn?'

Lincoln shook his head. 'No, I think he was afraid Darbyshire had proof Vaughn was murdered.'

He went on to explain how, through talking to Cyril Carter and Roger Bradman, he'd got a fair idea of what had happened that January night in 1991.

'Bill Burnett and Vaughn were heard arguing about money in the days before Vaughn's death,' he said. 'I think Bill drove round to his flat on the Saturday night to talk to him, reason with him, smooth things over. Something went wrong, the encounter turned violent and Vaughn ended up dead. Bill was a big chap, well able to string Vaughn up and make it look as if he'd hung himself.

Mitchell must've found out what happened and has been trying to protect his father's reputation ever since.'

'How did Mitchell pay Craig?' Dilke asked. 'We should be able to trace the payments.'

'Unless he paid him cash.' Lincoln tried to imagine the popular presenter and the rough-and-ready car salesman meeting somewhere to exchange a fat brown envelope. More realistically, he guessed the transaction was carried out through Fenella.

'Do we bring her in?' asked Woody.

'We need more evidence that Mitchell's behind this. If we close in on him too soon, he'll set his legal people onto us and we won't get anywhere.' He turned to Pam. 'Any luck finding Sherilyn?'

'Not so far,' she said. 'I'll call Valerie Bancroft, see if she's heard from her. By the way, Annie's got all the stuff that was in Chris's office at Standish's Farm. Jessica let her take it away.'

'What stuff?'

'Those box files, early chapters of his book about Lydia. We had a quick look through it, remember? We decided it wasn't relevant.'

'You mean *I* decided it wasn't relevant.' Lincoln had to admit he might have been wrong. He phoned Annie to ask if he could come round and take the box away.

'I'm in school,' she said. 'You've caught me in my break. Lydia's at the house, though.'

Lincoln welcomed the unexpected chance to talk to the elderly actress again, hoping she'd be more forthcoming face-to-face than she'd been over the phone. 'How long has she been with you?'

'Since Saturday evening. She won't admit it, but I think she's afraid to be on her own in London while all this is going on. I'll let her know you'll be coming round.

The box is in Chris's study. Sorry, I've got to go.'

When someone knocked on the side door of the Old Farmhouse, Lydia guessed it was Inspector Lincoln. She pushed Annie's tabby cat off her lap and brushed herself down. She swept her hands through her hair and licked her lips, hoping she didn't look as washed-out as she felt. She'd spoken to the inspector on the phone when she'd still been in London and was curious to know what he looked like.

But it wasn't a detective who opened the side door and erupted into the kitchen, it was Sherilyn.

'Auntie! Molly said you were here, but I thought she was joking.'

Oh dear, Sheri had been so pretty once. Even though she'd seen recent photos of her niece, Lydia was shocked by how strange she looked in the flesh. Freakish. All her natural beauty had been lost.

'Why would Molly joke about something like that?'

'Oh, you know Molly. She likes to make things up.'

Lydia felt she hardly knew her youngest niece. When Molly had dropped in on Annie yesterday, she'd sat staring at Lydia for minutes on end, answering questions in monosyllables and volunteering nothing at all.

'She's a bit starstruck,' Annie had whispered when Molly was out of earshot. 'She's heard so much about you, but I suppose you've only seen each other a few times.'

Now, Sherilyn slipped out of her big, quilted coat and headed for Annie's fridge.

'Too early for a quick one, Auntie?' Without waiting for an answer, she pulled out a bottle of wine and filled a large glass she'd plucked from the cupboard. 'Why aren't you in London?'

'I needed a few days away after all that's happened. Chris getting killed and then Orlando.'

Sherilyn carried her glass across to the sofa, where she stretched out without even bothering to take her boots off. 'You must've wondered who'd be next.'

'Can you blame me? Vaughn was murdered, I *know* he was. And Chris was on the very brink of finding out who killed him. He'd been talking to Orlando the day he died. And then Orlando was killed too.'

'Orlando was an accident,' Sherilyn said, draining her glass. 'No one was meant to *kill* him.' She pushed herself up and, unsteady on her feet, headed for a refill.

'What?' Lydia tried to unravel the meaning of her niece's words. Was she involved somehow? 'What were they *meant* to do, then?'

'Get the fucking scrapbook, that's all. But they couldn't even do that.'

The scrapbook. Lydia could see it in her mind's eye, the ring binder Vaughn had filled with photos and letters. "My evidence", he'd called it, after those stupid Burnett boys tried to catch him out. And after all he'd done for them, for their father…

'Is this down to Eloise, Sherilyn? Eloise protecting her bully of a father?'

Sherilyn banged the bottle down on the worktop. 'Eloise? She's got nothing to do with it. This is…' She broke off as if she knew she'd already said too much.

So if not Eloise, then who?

'Anyway, Auntie, I'm off to Spain, away from this bloody awful weather. Don't you hate autumn?'

'I rather love it. It means that Christmas is on its way. Pantomime season.' Lydia hugged herself, saddened to think how the memory of Vaughn had been sullied by those mean little Board Treaders. Not Sherilyn, of course.

She wouldn't have been so cruel, but those boys…

'So what do *you* think happened to Vaughn, Auntie?'

This again! She'd phoned Lydia over a week ago now, asking the same questions: what had Chris found out? Had he got proof that Vaughn was murdered?

And when Lydia had told her that Chris didn't like to talk about his writing until he'd finished it, Sherilyn had sounded sceptical, as if she suspected Lydia of withholding something from her.

Her niece's probing had left her unsettled, so when Inspector Lincoln had phoned last week, Lydia had played things down, acted the silly old woman, pretended she must have made a mistake. So what if Chris had found out the truth? It was too late now. It would've added spice to her life story, but that wasn't going to get written now, was it?

'Did you ever think Bill was involved?' Sherilyn returned to the sofa, wine slopping.

'It crossed my mind. Especially after that massive row they had. We all heard it.'

'When the Tannoy got left on.' Sherilyn giggled. 'That was *so* funny!'

'Stealing from someone is never funny, Sheri.'

'Bill wouldn't have *stolen* from Vaughn. They were running the theatre together. Eloise says…'

Oh yes, Eloise says. Sherilyn and Eloise had been besotted with each other since they were teenagers, a strange relationship between girls who were so different from each other and years apart. Since then, though, Eloise had always been ready to bail Sherilyn out of whatever scrapes she got into – which had been many and various. But what was in it for Eloise?

'Did Annie get Chris's laptop back?' Sherilyn asked.

'I've no idea.' Wouldn't it be at his new girlfriend's

place? He'd never told her much about this Jessica except that she lived on a farm. Lydia had visions of her milking cows or herding sheep.

Sherilyn craned forward, peering at her. It was obvious now that she was drunk. Had been drunk when she'd barged in, but hiding it well, until now. Her breath stank of stale booze.

'So why did *you* think Vaughn was murdered, Auntie?'

'Why? I'm not sure I can put it into words.'

Lydia had always thought, had always *known* he was murdered because he wasn't so unhappy that he'd have killed himself. And how on earth could he have strung himself up from that stupid clothes rail? Yes, there was a stool of some sort nearby, but it didn't seem nearly tall enough for him to stand on and tie his scarf in a noose. And that was another thing. He'd always been so useless with knots. His shoelaces were forever coming undone.

But did Lydia know *who* had killed him? She'd always thought it must have been Bill, except for one thing.

There was a knock at the side door. Sherilyn sat up and dumped her glass down on the floor.

'Are you expecting someone, Auntie?'

CHAPTER 69

Lincoln knew he had too little evidence to bring in Mitchell Burnett, but he was unsure how to gather more. Would there be anything of value on Darbyshire's laptop? Would Sherilyn be a reliable source of information? Even if she knew what had gone on the night Vaughn died, would she risk upsetting her 'best buddy' Eloise by implicating Eloise's father? If only they could track her down!

He'd asked Pam to keep checking Sherilyn's social media posts, in case they revealed where she might be. But apparently she'd posted nothing for days.

'But I'll browse back through her Instagram feed,' Pam said. 'See if there's anything useful there.' After a minute or two's browsing, she tutted impatiently. 'How come she's worked her way through a succession of desirable-looking men without actually marrying any of them? She can't want to settle down.'

Breeze chuckled. 'Can you see any man managing to keep Sherilyn under control? She's off her head a lot of the time and when she's not, she's pulling stupid stunts to get herself in the tabloids.'

'That sounds like sour grapes, Breezy.' She grinned across at him.

He grinned back. 'I'm happy with my Rosie. *She's* the sort of woman I want to settle down with.'

'Oh look, here she is at HarCon in September. Loads of photos.'

Lincoln came over to look at her screen. 'What's HarCon?'

'It's a convention for fans of *Harbinger Hollow*, that silly kids' series. They held it in Camden Town this year.'

He recalled Nate Newton mentioning it. A children's TV series that still had fans willing to pay for selfies with its once-teenage stars.

'But look. Who's that?' Pam pointed to a photo of Sherilyn, Nate and Mitchell with a fair-haired man Lincoln initially thought was Cody, until he zoomed in on the man's face. No, not Cody. Younger, with sharper features.

'That's Philip Brooks.'

'Fenella's brother?'

He nodded, surprised that Mitchell's odd-job man would have been accorded the privilege of attending HarCon with him. Or was he more than just the odd-job man? Philip was gazing at Mitchell, unaware that his attentiveness was being caught on camera.

'You think he's part of all this?' Pam waved at the whiteboard.

'I doubt it, but let's see what we can find out about him in case we've missed something.'

Lincoln looked up at the whiteboard, wondering what to make of Pam's discovery. He'd suspected that, if Mitchell was involved with anyone, it was Fenella Brooks. Until they'd found out that she was Craig Newton's girlfriend, Fifi. Was Mitchell's attachment to *Philip*, rather than to his sister?

'Hey, isn't that Craig Newton?' Pam paused at another of Sherilyn's Instagram posts: Fenella, Philip, Sherilyn and Craig enjoying a drink somewhere out of doors back in the summer.

'An interesting foursome.' Lincoln tried to fit it all together. 'So if Sherilyn is mates with Craig…'

'And Philip is mates with Mitch…'

'Maybe it's *Philip* who's been Mitchell's middleman, not Fenella.'

'Philip Brooks has got a record,' Breeze said. 'I just checked. He and Craig have both got convictions for possession and it's common knowledge that Sherilyn's been an addict off and on for years. Maybe that's what brought them together – drugs.'

'But where's Craig now? That's what I want to know.' Lincoln stared hopelessly at the man's photo on the board. Only a short time ago, he'd been feeling optimistic about pinning Darbyshire's murder on Mitchell Burnett, but now he wasn't so sure.

Where to go from here?

And then a call came in. A patrol had spotted Craig's 'borrowed' SUV at a service station on the A303 near Popham Airfield. According to staff, it had been there since the previous day. Might he have flown out to join his father in Spain hours before the car was first noticed?

Lincoln's spirits plunged lower still. 'Keep up the search for Sherilyn,' he told Pam. 'She's not allowed to drive – not that she'd let that put her off if she could get her hands on a car. But check with local taxi firms, see if anyone's taken her anywhere in the last couple of days. I'm going over to Annie's house to talk to Lydia and to see what's in Darbyshire's box of stuff.'

CHAPTER 70

Barbury Theatre was quiet. There was no evening performance on a Monday so Jed Chamberlain was overseeing rehearsals for this year's pantomime. Not *Jack and the Beanstalk* but *Through the Looking Glass,* a departure that might not bring in the crowds the theatre could expect for, say, *Aladdin.*

While Jed was going over lines with Terence, the Red Queen, Cody went down to the dressing room the Board Treaders had occupied during the run of *Jack and the Beanstalk.* They'd had to share it with both halves of Dame Spriggins's cow so it had been cramped and uncomfortable, adding to his misery over Mitch's plot to trap Vaughn.

All last night, he'd replayed yesterday's encounter at the firework display, recalling Mitch's reaction when Cody asked him if he'd had Chris killed. His shock had seemed genuine enough, but Cody knew his brother was hiding something. Mitch *had* gone to Vaughn's flat the night he died. And so had their father.

Even after that showdown, when Vaughn had threatened to tell Bill how they'd tried to set him up, Mitch had still insisted that Vaughn was responsible for Bob Greenaway's disappearance.

'I *know* Vaughn's the guy Bob was seen with,' he'd said. 'It all adds up. He did workshops at his school just before Bob disappeared. Vaughn's the older guy he was seen with, I bet. Hey, little bro, how d'you think he'd react if I came out and accused him?'

'You can't do that, Mitch. He'd go straight to Dad and you'd be in deep shit.'

After Christmas, their father and Vaughn had seemed to be constantly at odds with one another, creating a strained atmosphere backstage. One day, the Tannoy got left on and their voices blasted out in the dressing rooms, much to the delight of the Board Treaders, too naïve to understand the implications of discord within the management.

'We should've broken even by now,' Vaughn had fumed at full volume. 'We've had record takings for this panto, yet we're losing money hand over fist. You're not being straight with me, Bill. I *know* you're not. I've seen the accounts.'

The Tannoy had been hurriedly switched off, so they didn't get to hear their father's response.

Had Vaughn been in a bad mood because Cody had betrayed him? Could Cody put things right?

On the first Sunday of the new year, unhappy that Vaughn felt he could no longer trust him, Cody had decided to go and see him after the performance and explain everything. Tell him how the nude photos and suggestive letters hadn't been his idea. But he wasn't quick enough. Vaughn had already left the theatre by the time Cody had finished changing. He'd have to go to his flat, talk to him there.

It was late. Apart from one or two hands clearing up, the only people left in the theatre were his father and Mitch. He'd let them think he'd gone home alone.

He'd slipped quickly along the passage to the stage door – only to see Mitch ahead of him, quietly letting himself out, turning his overcoat collar up, not wanting to be seen.

Cody had followed him. All the way to Inkerman Terrace. On the corner, he'd hung back, guessing his brother was heading for number thirteen too. To confront Vaughn or to apologise?

The terrace was a short, one-way street, so Mitch would have to come back this way. It was freezing and Cody's anorak couldn't keep out the bitter cold of that January night. The ground was getting slippery and snow was forecast. He'd walked up and down under the railway bridge at the bottom of the road, trying to keep his feet from going numb.

After about fifteen minutes, a familiar car had slowed beside him. His father's Montego. Had he come to fetch him home?

But Bill hadn't seen him, hadn't stopped. Instead, he'd turned into Inkerman Terrace. Cody had hurried after him, pressing himself close to the garden walls and hedges to keep out of sight.

The car had parked outside number thirteen. Why was his father going to see Vaughn? To resume their earlier argument or to explain himself? How would he react when he found Mitch was already there? Would he think Vaughn had invited him?

Cody had waited under the railway bridge for another twenty minutes, his hands and feet going numb. A police car had cruised past him, window wound down.

'All right there, son?' the cop had shouted across.

'Fine, yeah, just walking home.' Cody had shrugged himself deeper into his anorak and begun to stride back towards town.

He'd reached home a few minutes ahead of his father and Mitch. His mother had called out from the bedroom, where she was resting, surrounded by all the paraphernalia of her illness: the oxygen tank and the tubes, the pill bottles and the lidded water jug.

He'd gone in to say goodnight, wishing he could hug her, that she could hug him, but it was difficult when she had so little strength left. Instead, he'd taken her hands and rested his head on them.

A month later, she was gone.

For a long time, he'd blamed himself for Vaughn's suicide, but then he'd come to realise that his father or Mitch – or both of them – must have murdered him that night. Why else had Chris Darbyshire had to be silenced? But who had ordered the silencing? Mitch or Eloise?

What had Chris uncovered that had lain secret all these years? Cody would find no answers here.

He called a cab, told Jed he'd see him tomorrow and went outside to wait on the theatre steps, planning what he'd say when he got there.

CHAPTER 71

'Eloise!' Sherilyn stumbled across Annie's kitchen to greet her friend. 'What are you doing here?'

Lydia had never been fond of Eloise, a bully like her father, desperate to be as tough as her brothers – or that's how she'd seemed thirty years ago. God, how she'd aged!

'I've come to see *you*, actually, Lydia.' She didn't bother to sit down, standing at the head of the table as if delivering an ultimatum, smart in her sharp suit and fancy-collared blouse. 'I want to know all about what Chris was working on.'

'He was writing my life story. That's all I know. He went a little off-piste with his research into Vaughn, but he didn't share anything with me. And, as I explained to Sherilyn, he was superstitious about discussing his work-in-progress.'

'Was he going to blame my father for what happened?' Eloise's dark eyes flashed. Why was she directing at Lydia the anger she could no longer direct at Chris?

'Darling, I really don't know. You'd have to ask Chris yourself. Except, of course, you can't, because someone had him killed.'

'You're looking at me as if you think *I* had something to do with it.'

'Well, if the cap fits.' Lydia sat back in her chair, wary of Eloise but unable to resist provoking her. The thought that this woman might have ordered Chris's murder made her physically sick.

'That's unfair, Auntie.' Sherilyn rounded on her. 'Eloise doesn't know anything about any of this.' She staggered a little as she turned, nearly losing her footing. Lydia felt pity for this woman who had once been so lovely, with such potential, now reduced to an artificially enhanced bimbo.

How insecure she must have felt, growing up, never thinking she was pretty enough, slim enough, sexy enough. Lydia had had to endure the same feelings of inadequacy but, in those days, there was little one could do about it.

'Then who was behind it, Sheri, if it wasn't Eloise?'

'It was Philip.' Sherilyn looked from Lydia to Eloise and back again. 'Philip Brooks. Mitch's boyfriend. He did it for Mitch. Not personally,' she added, her words slurring. 'He went to Craig and Craig found some kids who'd do it cheap. And Lenny helped.'

'Lenny?'

'He works at the theatre. My little spy. Told me he'd seen Chris there with his girlfriend and I told Craig. Serves him right.' She sat down heavily on the sofa, knocking over the half-full glass she'd left on the floor. 'I think I'm drunk,' she said, smiling weakly as she slumped sideways. 'How'm I going to fly like this?'

'What d'you mean?' Eloise crossed the room in three strides, shoving her upright. 'You're flying somewhere? When? Who with?'

Sherilyn could hardly keep her eyes open. 'Craig. Spain. Going to Spain. He knows someone. Aeroplane.' She tried to push Eloise away. 'Should go home and pack.'

'You can't fly anywhere like that, dear,' Lydia said, still processing the news that Mitch had a boyfriend. Although, she shouldn't be surprised. 'I'll make you some coffee.' She rose and crossed to the sink, hoping she could remember where Annie kept the coffee. All these cupboards looked alike.

She spun round at the sound of a slap. Eloise was standing over Sherilyn, who had a hand up to her face.

'Shit, Elle, that hurt.'

'It was meant to. Where the fuck do you think you're going with Craig? He's a crook, Sheri, a conman.'

'Who's Craig?' Lydia looked round from filling the kettle.

'Nate's cousin,' Eloise snapped. 'Her bloody dealer.'

'Oh, that silly Nate.' Lydia reached for some mugs. 'Did Simeon really fall off the stage by accident? I've never been sure.' Except she did know. Vaughn had known and told her. Nate had wanted Simeon's part in the panto and he'd wanted Mitch to himself.

'Nate pushed him,' Sherilyn said, rubbing her face. 'Why did you hit me, Elle?'

'Come back to Gilbert's. You can stay there as long as you want.' Eloise held her hand out, but Sherilyn pushed it away.

'I said, I'm going to Spain. With Craig.'

'And I said you're not.'

When Lydia looked round again, the glint of metal caught her eye as Eloise grabbed a knife from the block on the worktop and held it close to Sherilyn's face.

'I wouldn't do that, Eloise,' she said calmly, although her hands were shaking. 'If Sheri wants to fly to Spain, I think you should let her.'

She had to accept that her niece, the one who'd always been her favourite, was a criminal. Sherilyn had been part of the conspiracy to take away a man Lydia had loved like a son, a man who was going to restore Vaughn's reputation and prove what she'd always known. That Vaughn had been murdered and his death had been covered up by the police as well as by the bastards responsible.

She looked into Sherilyn's drunken, distorted face and knew that if only she had the strength she'd had a few years ago, she'd kill her herself and take the consequences.

Now she could only watch in disgust as Eloise launched herself at Sherilyn, who kicked out at her, grabbed her hair, her jacket, the collar of her blouse as she tried to fend her off. The women tussled, grunted, shrieked, swore.

And then a rat-a-tat-tat at the front door made everybody freeze.

Lincoln walked in on a scene of chaos as Lydia fluttered ahead of him into the big kitchen of the Old Farmhouse.

'Perfect timing,' she cried. 'I thought she was going to kill her.'

Sherilyn lay stretched out on the sofa, eyes closed, a trail of fresh vomit down the front of her T-shirt, the smell so acrid, he nearly gagged. A thin trail of blood snaked down her neck from an apparently superficial wound below her ear. At the other end of the sofa sat a dishevelled Eloise, a small kitchen knife in her hand, her face blank.

'What the hell's been happening here?'

'There was a bit of an argument,' Lydia told him. 'And Sherilyn's had way too much to drink.'

He knelt down by Sherilyn. 'She'd be better off sitting up,' he said, but when Eloise didn't respond, he gently lifted Sherilyn himself. An image of Tim Anderson flashed through his mind, a knife driven into him by the young mother he was trying to help. Lincoln kept his eyes on Eloise and the knife in her hand. She didn't move.

Sherilyn groaned and opened her eyes. 'Need to go with Craig,' she managed to say. 'Fly Shpain.'

'You're not going anywhere.'

Lydia was hovering. 'I'll find you something to change into, dear,' she said. 'Annie will have plenty you can get into.' She glanced at Lincoln and rolled her eyes. 'It shouldn't have come to this.'

'Put the knife down, Eloise.' He stepped nearer, ready to grab the knife from her if she tried to hurt Sherilyn again, but she gave it up without a fuss, not even looking at him.

He cautioned her and called for a car to take her to Park Street. He called for paramedics for Sherilyn – a patrol car could come later. While they were waiting, Annie arrived home with Molly.

'Oh God!' She rushed across to Lydia. 'What happened? Are you okay?'

'I'm fine,' her aunt said, though her voice quavered. 'I had to lend Sherilyn one of your tops.'

Annie looked across at her cousin and then at Lincoln. 'Can someone please tell me what's going on?'

'That's such a cliché, dear,' her aunt said, sinking down at the kitchen table. 'But I may be the best person to tell you.'

CHAPTER 72

Mitch's house was on an unlit village street, while the house itself, the Old Forge, was bright with lamps in the porch. Cody climbed up from the road, two steps at a time, to his brother's front door. Someone had been clipping the Virginia creeper and left reddish-orange leaves lying on the ground like open palms.

'I know you were there that night,' he said, as soon as Mitch opened the door to him, scrapping the preamble he'd rehearsed on the way. 'At Vaughn's. I saw you. You and Dad.'

'And you've known this all these years and done nothing about it?' Mitch strolled across to the hearth, stepping carefully over the huge, skinny hound that was stretched out in front of the fire.

'I didn't know how to.'

'But you do now?' Mitch picked his phone up off the mantelpiece. 'You want me to call the police, turn myself in?'

'You could've turned Dad in. Instead, you let everyone believe Vaughn was suicidal. Let them think he was so ashamed of what he'd done to one of us, he'd killed himself. All people remember now is that he hanged himself, the rumours that he was a paedophile. And that's not fair, Mitch, because you know it's not true. It's not true because, between us, we made it up and made his life hell. And then Dad killed him.'

Mitch sent his phone flying across the room into the wall, making Cody flinch and rousing the dog, which scrambled, alarmed, to its feet. 'We didn't make it *all* up, little bro. He was all over you all the time *and* he abducted Bob and made him disappear. How many other boys were there? You asked me last night at the fireworks and I told you: I don't know who had Darbyshire killed, but it wasn't me, so just…'

A door opened behind him and a fair-haired man appeared, casually dressed in camo cargo pants and khaki T-shirt, like an off-duty commando.

'Phil, meet my brother. Cody, this is Philip. His sister's my PA.'

And what was Phil to Mitch? Cody wondered. Did this mean what he thought it did, the guy being here this late in the evening?

'So what happened that night? You and Dad went to Vaughn's flat and you found him hanging there? Was he dead when you got there?'

Philip took a step forward. 'Be careful what you say, mate. You go accusing people, that's going to get you into a lot of trouble.'

Mitch stomped across to retrieve his phone from the corner where it had landed. 'Why dredge this up now, Cody? Just when everything's going right for both us, for Eloise. What's the good of going over this now?'

'Chris Darbyshire was killed because of what he was writing about,' said Cody, refusing to back down. 'The police have already arrested the people who killed him and it won't be long before they find out who paid them to shut him up. If you had anything to do with it, Mitch…'

'The police won't make the connection,' Philip said with confidence. 'They're not clever enough. And once Craig gets to Spain…' He stopped abruptly.

'Who's Craig?' Mitch faced him squarely. 'Phil, who the fuck's Craig?'

CHAPTER 73

A patrol car took Eloise to Park Street and a paramedic arrived on a motorbike. While Sherilyn was getting checked over, watched by Annie and Molly, Lydia led Lincoln upstairs to Darbyshire's old study.

'This was my bedroom when I was a girl,' she said, switching the light on and drawing the curtains. 'Annie's wasting all this space. She's wasting this house, rattling around on her own. It costs a fortune to heat. There's the box.'

Lincoln began to empty it onto Darbyshire's desk: papers, photographs, the photocopied account pages Beryl Amos had told him about.

'I hadn't realised how much stuff Chris had taken away from my flat,' Lydia said, a little crossly as she watched. 'I gave him free rein, of course, but some of these things… Oh Lord, our last panto together!' She picked up some glossy publicity photos. 'I was Ermintrude, the giant's mother. Look at that frock. A crinoline with polka dots all over it. And look at Vaughn, in something even more absurd. However did we manage to do a song-and-dance routine in those costumes?' She dropped the photos back onto the desk before Lincoln could look at them.

Annie came into the room. 'The paramedic's checking her for concussion,' she said. 'But the cut's only superficial. God, it's cold in here!'

'What can you tell me?' Lincoln asked Lydia, who had pulled out the office chair and sat down. 'You said downstairs…'

'I was the one who found Vaughn's body first,' she said

with a sigh. 'I just didn't report it and I know I should've done. I'd gone to his flat when he didn't show up at the theatre and there he was. I thought at first that he'd killed himself and I looked for the scrapbook that he'd got so obsessed with, because I thought, well, if the police had found it, the way they might have misinterpreted it...' She glanced at Lincoln apologetically.

'Yes,' he said. 'I understand.'

'But when I got back to my digs, I went over and over it in my mind and I just *couldn't* believe he'd killed himself. He'd get low at the end of a run, we all do, but never *that* low. And after that row he'd had backstage with Bill over the money, and Bill being the way he was... And there were two mugs on the floor, the chairs drawn up as if he'd had company. I was so sure they'd realise he'd been murdered. Only they didn't. It was all tidied away. Suicide.'

'Couldn't you have come forward?' Annie said. 'If you were so sure someone else had been there?'

'I'd left it too long, darling. And I was afraid it would beg more questions about what was going on behind the scenes. But I always regretted not speaking up for Vaughn at the time. And then along comes Chris, keen to write my story for me and I saw my chance. He'd done investigations for his documentaries. He knew how to dig. Maybe he'd be able to find out what really happened.'

'Only it ran away with him.' Annie shook her head as she looked down at the array of photos and papers her husband had accumulated.

Lincoln spotted some photos that were certainly *not* of the pantomime. Were these the nude photos that Cody had been so anxious to reclaim? In one of them, he and Nate looked as if they were getting it on. In the other, Cody was sitting in a chair, touching himself, a look of ecstasy on his young face. Before either Lydia or Annie noticed them, Lincoln discreetly slid the photos off the desk and into his pocket. Yes, it was wrong, but…

'Sherilyn kept saying she was flying to Spain with someone called Craig,' Lydia said. 'But I think she may have missed the plane.'

It was late when Lincoln got back to Barley Lane. Everyone had gone home except Pam, who was sipping peppermint tea from her Royal Albert teacup.

'I tried to call you,' she said as he headed for the kettle. 'I got a call from Rocco, Craig Newton's stepson.'

He checked his phone. He'd somehow managed to turn the sounds off – all of them.

'Sorry, Pam. What did he say?'

'His mum got a text from Craig. He was on his way to Spain but Zelda wasn't to tell anyone. She tried to phone him, but the number was dead. He'd used a burner phone.'

'We guessed that's where he was heading,' he said, resignedly. 'And he'd left the SUV across the road at Popham Services. He must've known someone who'd fly him out on the quiet. Well done, Rocco. Not sure he's going to be seeing his stepdad again any time soon.'

As he restored the sound settings on his phone, Lincoln noticed he'd missed three calls from the same mobile number: Cody Burnett.

Lincoln called him, wondering why he'd tried to get in touch.

'I went to see my brother this evening,' Cody said, 'because I thought he'd paid to have Chris Darbyshire killed.'

'That's quite an accusation,' Lincoln started to say, but Cody interrupted him.

'Chris thought he'd got proof that my dad killed Vaughn. It made sense it was Mitch who wanted to shut him up, only…' He paused to take a deep breath. 'There was this guy there tonight. Phil. He lives right next door. When I accused Mitch, Phil said something about a guy called Craig and…' He exhaled sharply. 'It all came out. You lot think it was Mitch who paid to have Chris killed, but it wasn't – it was Phil. My brother didn't know anything about it.'

'*Phil* paid Craig to have Chris killed? But why?' Lincoln thought back to the slim, fair-haired man, half of Brooks and Brooks, "Mitch's maintenance team".

'He did it for Mitch. Phil thought that's what he wanted.'

TUESDAY 7TH NOVEMBER

CHAPTER 74

It had taken nearly two weeks, but now they knew who had arranged Chris Darbyshire's murder. Philip Brooks.

Lincoln had gone to the Old Forge first thing and arrested him, much to the consternation of Mitchell Burnett, who had first harangued them and then tried to pull Philip away.

'Please, Mitch,' said Lincoln, standing stolidly in front of him. 'Don't make this any worse.' He waited until Mitchell stepped back, defeated.

Fenella, who lived at the other end of the village, arrived for work to see uniformed police officers leading her brother down the steps to a waiting patrol car. Bewildered, she rushed into the Old Forge to find out what was going on.

'Don't say a word.' Mitchell paced the living room, hugging himself, his head bent. 'Wait for my solicitor to get here.'

But she wanted to talk, and Lincoln and Woody were ready to listen.

Phil had a drug problem, she explained. That was how he met Craig. He'd met Sherilyn too, another of Craig's regular customers.

'I met Craig on a dating site,' she said. 'I didn't know then that he knew Phil. He was good company, a bit rough around the edges but…hey! You only live once.' She sat on the sofa, watching while Mitchell paced. 'I haven't actually seen him for a while. We'd run out of things to say to each other.'

But, Lincoln thought, the connection had been made.

Philip wanted to protect Mitchell from Darbyshire's revelations and he'd found the man who could help him.

'We'll need statements from both of you,' he said. 'Come to Park Street later today, please.'

'Have you arrested Craig?' Fenella asked.

'Not yet,' Lincoln said. 'If he tries to get in touch with you...' He gave her his card, though he doubted that her erstwhile lover would try to make contact. Craig was probably in Spain by now, flown out in a light aircraft by someone who owed him a favour.

Had he really planned to take Sherilyn with him? Probably not.

Once more, Lincoln found himself at Park Street, where Sherilyn had been charged with conspiracy to commit murder. He guessed that, like Eloise, she'd be released on bail – which might mean she'd have to live with Martin and Valerie for a while. He didn't envy them having her as a house guest.

He sat across from her in the interview room. What a long way she'd fallen, but she would surely bounce back, the darling of the tabloids. Now, though, she looked rough after a night in a cell. Eloise had left her with a black eye and bruises. A large plaster covered the cut on her neck and, by her own admission, she was nursing the hangover from hell.

She told Lincoln what he already knew: that Philip had paid Craig Newton to have Darbyshire killed because he'd believed that's what Mitchell wanted.

'I suppose I kind of brought them together,' she said sheepishly. 'Dunno how much Phil paid Craig, though. He never said.'

'What part did Eloise play in all this?'

'She didn't. She was worried about what Chris was

going to say about her dad, but she could've got through it like she's got through everything else.'

'Didn't she want to protect Bill's reputation?'

Sherilyn flicked her false nails. 'That bastard never deserved her loyalty, the way he treated her when she was a kid. That's why we've been such good mates.'

'He treated her badly?'

'He was strict with the boys too when they were kids, but as soon as Elle turned twelve, thirteen…' She sniffed. 'He abused her every which way. I was the only person she could tell. That's why we've always been close, why she's always been there for me, like she owed me one. But now I feel like I've let her down.' Tears brimmed in her eyes and she wiped them awkwardly away. 'I've let everybody down, haven't I?'

Lincoln was pulling into the car park behind Barley Lane when he saw a familiar figure approaching: Roger Bradman, carrying a suit cover over his arm.

'Glad I caught you, Jeff,' he said, beaming. 'Look what I found.'

Lincoln let him in the back door, not daring to hope.

'You know how it is,' Roger went on, following him into the incident room. 'Couldn't stop thinking about this after you came round. Went round Mum's on the off chance, and what d'you know? There's that overcoat, hung up at the back of the wardrobe in my old bedroom, next to my dress uniform and my little sister's wedding dress from twenty years ago.'

He unzipped the plastic cover and pulled out a tweed overcoat, good quality, if a little musty after nearly thirty years in the back of a wardrobe. Bill Burnett's coat, left behind after he'd murdered Vaughn.

Lincoln opened the coat and there, stitched along the

top of the inside pocket, was a name tape.

'I must've seen that at the time,' said Bradman, 'but the name meant nothing to me then. Mitchell Burnett. I probably thought it was the brand name. Well, you would, wouldn't you?'

CHAPTER 75

Lincoln and Dilke took their seats across from Mitchell Burnett and his solicitor, John Gage.

'My client has prepared a statement,' Gage said, laying a two-page printed document on the table between them. 'So there's no need to question him.'

'That's not how it works.' Lincoln pushed the document back towards the two smartly dressed men. 'Not here, anyway. Not in this case.'

As his solicitor began to protest, Mitchell patted the man's arm.

'It's okay, John. Let's do it your way then, Inspector.'

'As you know, we arrested Philip Brooks this morning and he's been charged with conspiracy to commit murder. What's your relationship to him?'

'He's worked for me for the past four years and his sister's been my PA for even longer.'

'Nothing more than a working relationship?'

'We're friends, too.' Mitchell lowered his gaze to the table, evasive, but Lincoln decided against probing any deeper.

'Did you know he paid Craig Newton to have Chris Darbyshire killed?'

'God, no! Not until last night. You really think I'd have sanctioned something like that?'

'You're saying Philip acted on his own initiative? Why would he do that? Did he have some personal issue with Chris?'

'Phil thought he was protecting me. He knew I was worried about what Chris was going to say in his podcast, but I didn't ask him to do anything, I promise you I didn't.'

Lincoln paused. Did he believe him? The phrase "plausible deniability" came to mind. But was he being unfair? He didn't like Mitchell, was all too ready to think he must have known what Philip was doing, but where was the evidence?

He laid a photo on the table: Philip, Nate, Sherilyn and Mitchell at HarCon in September.

'Was this when you found out that Chris was investigating Vaughn's death?'

Mitchell nodded. 'Sherilyn's little sister, Molly, told her Chris had found out what happened to Vaughn and was writing a true-crime podcast about it. I was afraid he was going to implicate my father. Phil must've seen how anxious I was about that, but never in a million years would I have asked him to kill someone for my sake or for Dad's.'

'Were you worried that Chris was going to write about the honey trap you set for Vaughn?'

He cleared his throat, embarrassed. 'Of course I was. You've seen the photos. You know the way we tried to catch Vaughn out. I'm not proud of any of that, but I know what Chris would've done – made the most of anything salacious because that's what sells, a bit of sleaze, a bit of scandal. I was worried about how he'd interpret what he found.'

Lincoln laid two photographs on the table. One was of the original Board Treaders: Sherilyn looking innocent and unspoilt, Simeon with his blond curls, Mitchell and Cody with their matching silver ID bracelets. The other photo was of a tweed overcoat.

'Do you recognise this coat, Mitchell?'

He leaned forward, peering at it, then took his glasses

from an inside pocket and slipped them on. Heavy-framed, they made him look scholarly. 'I had one like that when I was at St Luke's.'

'What happened to it?' Dilke asked.

Mitchell exchanged a look with his solicitor before admitting, 'Er…I lost it. Towards the end of the run of *Jack and the Beanstalk.*'

'Left it somewhere?'

'Someone took it off the peg at the theatre, mistaking it for their own, I suppose.'

'So another St Luke's boy took it?'

He nodded. 'I suppose so, yes.'

'There were other St Luke's boys in the panto?'

'Only Cody.'

'You're saying your brother took your overcoat by mistake? And left his own there instead?' Lincoln frowned at him in disbelief. 'He's a lot smaller than you, isn't he? Wouldn't he have realised he'd got the wrong coat?'

Mitchell shrugged, once more glancing across at Gage. 'I don't know.'

'This coat was in Vaughn's bedsit after he was found dead, along with evidence suggesting he'd had a visitor that night. It's *your* coat, Mitchell. It's got your name in it. How do you think it ended up there the night he died?'

'Um… Maybe Cody took it by mistake, was wearing it when he called on Vaughn. It was *Cody* who left it behind, not me. He was trying to frame me.'

'Frame you for what, Mitch? If he wanted to frame you for Vaughn's murder, why would he go to the trouble of staging his suicide? And all on his own.'

Mitchell had no answer to that. He took his glasses off and rubbed his eyes. He sighed heavily.

'Okay. Yes, it was my coat. And yes, I left it there.' He ignored Gage's obvious agitation. 'All I wanted was for

Vaughn to admit he'd had some part in Bob Greenaway's death, that was all. I wanted to know where Bob was buried.'

'You were close to Bob?' Dilke leaned in, his voice gentle.

'Yes, we were close. He hadn't made many friends, moving from place to place, one foster carer after another. We used to hang out together until he went back to Swindon.'

Dilke went on, 'So when you heard he was missing and you knew Vaughn had taught at his school, you suspected that Vaughn had done something to him?'

Mitchell nodded. 'There were so many coincidences. Vaughn knew that Priest guy and we all knew *he* was a pervert.'

'And Vaughn was paying your little brother a lot of attention, wasn't he?' Lincoln put in. 'How did that make you feel? Jealous?'

'Don't be ridiculous! It was sickening, the way he fawned over Cody. Why would I want that sort of attention?'

'Tell us what happened that night.' Lincoln sat back, letting him take his time.

'I went there to confront him, but he invited me in, offered me coffee. We chatted a bit and then I asked him about Bob. He said he hadn't seen him since his last drama workshop. Why did I think he'd had anything to do with him disappearing? Did I think all gay men were perverts? Wasn't I taking a risk, calling on him on my own if I thought he killed teenage boys? And then he said I seemed *unnaturally* concerned about Bob. Was that it, that I was *in love* with him? And…' He lowered his head. 'I snapped. I didn't mean to kill him, for Christ's sake! I just wanted him to shut up.'

Putting his head in his hands, Mitchell sobbed silently.

'A middle-aged man was seen entering the house around that time,' Lincoln said at last. 'Was that your dad, Mitch? Was that Bill?'

'Yes.'

'Why was he there?' asked Dilke.

'He'd come to talk to Vaughn about the money.' Mitchell fished a cotton handkerchief out of his pocket, wiped his eyes, blew his nose. 'They'd argued earlier. Vaughn had threatened to pull out of the theatre, make Dad pay him back at least some of what he'd put into it. Dad couldn't let him do that. He'd come to reason with him, ask for time to repay him.'

'But he never got the chance, did he?' said Lincoln. 'Vaughn was already dead when he got there – because you'd strangled him.'

Mitchell lifted his head, his face flushed, his cheeks wet. He nodded.

'Then you and your dad made it look as if Vaughn had killed himself,' Lincoln went on. 'Putting you in the clear and letting your dad keep the money.'

'Only you left your coat behind.' Dilke patted the photo of the smart tweed coat. 'And you couldn't go back for it, could you?'

Mitchell shoved the handkerchief back in his pocket. 'I knew stuff had been taken from Vaughn's flat after he died. I was afraid Chris had got hold of my coat, or something else that put me there that night. But I didn't want anyone to get *killed* because of it. I was prepared to pay to shut him up – but not like that.'

'Only Philip didn't understand that, did he?'

'I swear to you, I didn't know. And then yesterday…'

'Yesterday?'

'Cody came to see me last night. He knew I went to

see Vaughn that night. He more or less accused me of having Chris murdered and that's when Phil said…' He broke off to take a deep breath. 'Phil admitted he'd paid Craig to… to get it done because he knew I was worried about what might come out. Oh God, if I could take it all back!'

'We never have that luxury,' Lincoln said, closing his folder. 'We can rewrite history, but we can't change what *really* happened.'

CHAPTER 76

'Christ knows what we can charge him with.' DCI Claire Connors sat at her desk with her head in her hands. 'How old was he when he killed Vaughn? Seventeen? Too young to have been charged as an adult then, too long ago to charge him with anything now that a good counsel won't get him out of. He could plead manslaughter, self-defence, blame his dad, dee-dah-dee-dah.'

Lincoln nodded, guessing that trying to charge Mitchell Burnett with Vaughn's murder would not be a good use of resources.

Phil had acted because he'd thought Mitchell's father had committed the crime. That Mitchell was desperate to protect Bill's name. Who else knew that Mitchell had been there that night? Only Cody, it would seem – and Roger Bradman. But did either of them know for sure that Mitchell was the killer or did they both assume it was Bill?

'Karen Bolitho's not going to leave it alone, is she?' Lincoln said. 'She'd risk legal action if she tried to use the material in the scrapbook, but that won't stop her trying to find out what really happened. Knowing her, she'll dig until she finds what she's looking for. Mitchell's not going to get away scot-free.'

'Shamed in the pages of *The Messenger*?' Connors's lips twitched into a smile. 'That's punishment enough.' She leaned back in her chair, stretched her arms over her head and yawned. 'I am so fucking tired. The last two weeks…'

He grinned at her. 'Tell me about it.'

'Good work, Jeff. I'd better ring DCS Youngman, give him the good news.'

'The tech team got into Chris's laptop,' said Pam as Lincoln walked in the door at Barley Lane. 'Notes he made when he talked to Orlando Snell and Lydia; research into various people and events to do with the theatre; and a draft outline of the podcast. Not much else. Seems as if he was only in the very early stages of putting it all together.'

Lincoln was bitterly disappointed. He'd hoped Darbyshire's laptop would reveal all that he'd found out before he was killed, including the proof that Vaughn's death was murder not suicide. Or maybe he never did have proof, convinced instead by Lydia's insistence that Vaughn wouldn't have killed himself, relying – as Lincoln so often did – on gut instinct. He'd been so much less of a threat to any of the Board Treaders than they'd feared. Such a pointless death.

Lincoln settled at his desk to start on the paperwork, but he hadn't got very far when he heard someone knocking on the street door. Breeze went to open it, returning with a man in his early forties, not very tall, his hair thinning on top, curly at the sides. One eyelid drooped a little, but he had a cheerful, open face.

'I think you've been looking for me,' he said, accepting Lincoln's offer of a seat. 'The name's Bob Taylor, but I used to be called Greenaway.'

He'd loved the drama workshops at school in Swindon, Bob said, and was sorry that Hamilton Vaughn taught there only for a short time the summer he'd turned sixteen.

'I'd been in the Board Treaders in Barbury for a few

weeks, but I was a foster kid from Swindon and they all seemed a bit stuck up. Felt like I didn't belong.'

'But you were friends with Mitch Burnett, weren't you?' Lincoln said.

'He was the only kid who took any notice of me. Same age, both mischief-makers. Even after I left Board Treaders, we'd meet up, hang around the bus station and the park – you know what lads that age are like. But then I got sent back to Swindon, never saw him again.'

'And then you went missing.' Lincoln laid a file on the desk – the case file that Tim Anderson had got hold of, a case his father had never forgotten. 'You want to tell us what happened?'

Bob looked sheepish. 'I was bunking off school a lot. No interest in the lessons and things weren't great at home. One Friday, when I should've been in school, I saw this guy who used to hang around outside the school gates some days in his van. He had a stall in the market, cheap shit and imported fags. Harry. Harry Priest. We got chatting, he offered me fags and lager if I'd go in his van with him. I wasn't stupid. I knew the score. So I went with him, did what he wanted but then…' He looked down at his hands. 'His wallet was lying there in the footwell, bulging with notes – he didn't even know he'd dropped it. When he was cleaning himself up, a bit distracted, I grabbed the wallet and jumped out the van. Scarpered without looking back.'

'Then what did you do?'

'Hitched a lift to London, dossed down different places, did odd jobs – not all of them legal – and went on from there. There was six hundred quid in that wallet, gave me a good start. Changed my name, got respectable.' He grinned. 'I knew people were looking for me, but I couldn't go home, could I? Didn't think Mum and Dad would want me back after what I'd done. Wasn't sure they'd want me back, full stop. They were always fighting, usually about me. Figured they'd be better off without me.'

'So you never went home?'

'Couldn't see the point. And the longer it went on, the harder it got. How could I show up after five years, ten years, fifteen?'

'So why show up now?'

'Because of Chris Darbyshire. See, the first Christmas I was away, I felt kind of guilty. In the New Year, when I was living in Stoke Newington, I wrote to Vaughn, care of the theatre. I knew he was doing the panto so I was sure the letter would reach him. Wrote and told him I was okay, still alive if anyone asked.' He grinned again. 'Never heard anything back. And then, of course, I found out he was dead. Didn't know if he'd ever got my letter.'

'So how…?'

'Chris found that letter among some papers in a flat in London where he was staying. God knows how it got there! He did some detective work and tracked me down a few weeks ago. He was doing this true crime thing about the theatre and the Board Treaders. Asked me if I'd take part because I'd been a mate of Mitch's and I'd known Vaughn.' He sighed. 'To my shame, I said no. And then I saw Tim Anderson was dead. The news report mentioned his dad and I remembered he was the detective leading the search for me at the start. And I thought…' He looked up, a rueful smile on his face. 'I thought it was time I showed up.'

CHAPTER 77

'I'll be going back to the States at the end of the week.' Nick Chance dumped a bottle of Talisker single malt on Lincoln's desk. 'I thought this business with Cody would keep me here a lot longer, but maybe it's for the best.'

'Shame we couldn't have seen more of each other. You haven't met Trish or seen the house.'

What would Nick have made of the Old Vicarage, though, still far from finished? And would Trish have taken to him? Probably not. She'd never known Nick the mischief-making schoolboy, the music-loving teenage daredevil, the freewheeling twenty-year-old. And in truth, it was hard for Lincoln to believe the man standing there now had once been all of those.

'Before I forget, Jeff, Nell sends her love. She was asking if you knew your sister's husband had died. His obituary was in some literary magazine she gets.'

'No, I didn't know.' Lincoln had met Reg only half a dozen times, if that, because Ruth's visits to England were rare. Reg had been a lot older than her, a laidback Chicagoan with a passion for trains that Ruth didn't share and a love of Shelley's poetry that she did. 'When was this?'

'August. Ruth didn't tell you?' Nick looked surprised.

'Not sure she's got my phone number. Which reminds me – how did you get hold of it?'

'Nell has it. She got it from Andy, the guy Cathy…' Nick broke off.

'Andy Nightingale.' The man who'd taken Cathy away from him. He and Andy had reached a kind of peace now, which is why they'd exchanged phone numbers, but it still seemed strange to think of Andy being in touch with Cathy's best friend (and bridesmaid) when Lincoln wasn't. Then he thought about Andy having to go through the address book after Cathy was killed, a task Lincoln had been spared, although it might have brought him some sort of closure.

'Nell would love to hear from you,' said Nick, probably trying to make him feel better.

'Nell was a good friend to Cathy.'

'Thanks for these photos, by the way. Cody will be grateful.' Nick tapped his pocket, the nude photos of Cody and Nate safely secured.

'But don't tell him how you got hold of them,' Lincoln said. 'Or maybe just burn them.' He was on his feet now, striding round his desk to give Nick a hug, not wanting to let him go, taking the past with him. He doubted if they'd ever meet again.

And then Nick was gone.

Lincoln picked up the bottle of Talisker, not a whisky of which he was fond. He'd keep it anyway. You never knew when you might need it.

Towards the end of the morning, he got a text from Trish:

Can we meet lunchtime? The Two Starlings at 1pm?

The Two Starlings was a wine bar across the street from the library, but he'd never known her to drink there, except at Christmas time with colleagues. Why the urgency?

A few minutes after one, he walked into the low-ceilinged bar with its loud carpet and black beams. There were only two other drinkers there, talking quietly against a subtle background of classical music. With a cup of tea in front of her, Trish was sitting at a corner table, looking unhappy and tense.

He guessed she'd got bad news about her father.

'What's up?' he asked, setting his Coke down.

'Dad's been to the doctor's.' She fidgeted with her cup, lifting it up and lowering it again without drinking. 'It's something to do with the crystals in his ear.'

'Crystals?'

'In the inner ear. There are crystals that can get dislodged and upset your balance. That's what's happened to Dad. He's got to do exercises to get the crystals back to where they ought to be.'

'Exercises?' He had visions of Ted Whittington embarking on a fitness regime.

'Head movements.'

'But that's good, isn't it? You were afraid it was Parkinson's or something.'

'That's not all.' She stared fixedly into her untouched tea. 'I'm pregnant.'

He froze. 'Pregnant?'

'Stop repeating everything I say! Yes, I'm pregnant.'

Time slowed. His heart pounded in his chest. 'You're sure?'

'Yes, I'm sure.' She picked up her cup in both hands and took a sip from it. 'What am I going to do? I can't give up work. How's Kate going to feel with a baby in the house?'

He had no answers. He was still trying to make sense of her news. He reached across the table to her, but she dumped her cup down and hid her hands in her lap.

'You aren't on your own, Trish. We're in this together.'

'God, that sounds so corny.'

'What do you want me to say? "You're on your own, sweetheart, we're finished"? Of course we're in this together. Unless...' he grinned. 'You're telling me it's Steve's.'

To his relief, she burst out laughing, dispelling the tension and making the other drinkers look across at them. 'For heaven's sake, Jeff, you *know* it isn't.'

'When? How far on? Sorry, I'm making a mess of this.'

'About fourteen weeks. It'll be due late April, early May.'

He couldn't think that far ahead. 'Have you told anyone else?'

Trish shook her head. 'And I'm not going to, not until after the first scan. Just in case.'

He reached for her hand again. This time she let him take it in his.

'It'll be fine, Trish. *We'll* be fine. I'll get the house sorted out, finish the decorating. Put more carpet down. That little room next to the big bedroom – that'd be perfect as a nursery and…'

'Stop!' She was laughing again. 'Slow down. One thing at a time. Just promise me one thing.'

'What's that?'

'That you will at least think about getting a television.'

When he got back to Barley Lane, Lincoln took a last look at the whiteboard.

'So, Bob Greenaway wasn't missing after all.' He peeled the schoolboy's photo off the board and chucked it onto his desk. 'At least, he was missing, but by choice.'

Pam picked the photo up and stared at it. 'So Mitchell killed Vaughn for nothing.'

'That's the tragedy. Kid Detective turned vigilante. Aren't most murders pointless, when you think about it? What does anybody gain, really?'

'You sound a bit down, boss. You should be celebrating.'

'Celebrating?' He thought about Trish's news, which

still hadn't sunk in yet. Had Pam heard about it?

'Closing the case,' she said. 'Three cases. Two of which weren't even ours.'

'Four cases, including Ritchie Payne.'

Yes, cause for celebration indeed, but he just wasn't feeling it.

'What about the overcoat?'

'Mitchell's?'

'No, Chris's. Should I take it back to Annie?'

He picked up his car keys. 'I'll take it. I need to tell her what's happened, anyway.'

Annie took her husband's overcoat out of Lincoln's arms and hugged it to her.

'Thank you,' she said. 'I'm grateful for all you've done.'

'How's your aunt?'

'She's settling in quite nicely here. She's better off here than up in London and it's not as if I haven't got plenty of room.' She laid the coat carefully over the back of a chair. 'So she was right all along, wasn't she? About Vaughn?'

He nodded. 'But I hope she doesn't think what happened to Chris was *her* fault.'

'I suppose it was, a bit.' Annie sighed. 'But then, he wouldn't have enjoyed what he did if there'd been no excitement to it, a bit of a risk. That's how he was. Thank you for bringing his coat back.'

TUESDAY 7TH NOVEMBER

CHAPTER 78

Tim Anderson's funeral was held at Hilperton, on the edge of Trowbridge. Lincoln drove up there on his own, feeling like an interloper until Aileen, his widow, greeted him as if he was an old friend, introducing him to her in-laws and her toddler son, Arthur.

'I left the baby with my sister,' she said, 'but I didn't want to keep Arthur away. Thank you for being there for Tim. He was a bit out of his depth to start with, but you made him feel he was doing okay.'

She took his hand in both hers and smiled at him sadly before moving on to speak to the other mourners.

Arthur, in miniature dark suit and tie, hair neatly combed, ran in and out of the pews as everyone filed from the church after the service. Lincoln watched him, amazed by the little boy's energy and resilience. He would go with his family to the interment and Lincoln would make his way home.

Dusk was falling as he approached Barbury. Christmas was little over a month away and in less than six months, he'd be a father. The thought terrified him. How could he be sure he wouldn't make a hash of it? How would he know what to do?

'You just get on with it,' Woody had told him when he'd shared his doubts. 'You learn as you go along. Are you and Trish, y'know, going to get married?'

Trish and Kate would be moving into the Old Vicarage in the New Year. They'd agreed on that much. But getting married?

'I don't want to do anything hasty,' Lincoln had said

with a grin. 'I'm not one to rush into things.'

When he got back from the funeral, an answerphone message was waiting for him. The caller had a faint but noticeable American accent, her voice both familiar and strange.

'Hi, Jeff, it's me. Ruth. Your sister. Thought I'd give you a call, catch up on all your news. It's been too long. I'll try you again tomorrow.'

In Chris's study at the Old Farmhouse, the room that had once been her bedroom, Lydia Bancroft sifted through his box of papers, reading again the opening chapters of her life story and wishing that he'd had a chance to finish it. What would Annie do with this box now, she wondered? Into it, she slipped Mitchell Burnett's silver identity bracelet. She'd found it on the floor of Vaughn's bedsit, not far from his body. To think, if she'd left it there for the police to find, things might have turned out differently.

Or maybe not.

Leaving the box where it was, she turned out the light, shut the door and went downstairs to where Annie and Molly were waiting for her.

ACKNOWLEDGEMENTS

This book has been a long time in the writing and I'm grateful for all the help and support I've received during its creation.

In particular, I must thank Frome Writers' Collective for ongoing encouragement, Dea Parkin and Fiction Feedback for a constructive critique, Alison Shakspeare at Shakspeare Editorial for proofreading and typesetting (and the rest!) and the team at MoreVisual for the cover design.

I'd also like to thank Bristol and Bath Crime Club, an informal group of writers, readers and reviewers, and especially Steve (SJ) Richards for his advice and guidance.

Last but not least, my thanks to John, who's had to put up with me all this time.

ABOUT THE AUTHOR

Nikki Copleston has written five previous novels featuring Wiltshire detective Jeff Lincoln. Her stories have won awards and she is an active member of Frome Writers' Collective. After a career in local government in London, she moved to Somerset in 2012 to write full time.

A keen photographer, Nikki takes her inspiration from the landscape of the West Country, although her novels reveal the darker side of life in rural towns and the countryside. She lives in Wells with husband John.

For more information, go to her website at www.nikkicopleston.com

THE DI JEFF LINCOLN SERIES (IN ORDER)

THE PRICE OF SILENCE

When popular businesswoman Holly Macleod is found strangled in public toilets on the outskirts of Barbury, DI Jeff Lincoln assumes she's fallen victim to a violent Peeping Tom. But as he sifts through the details of her life, he uncovers one mystery after another. A car abandoned at the crime scene belongs to Leo Goldsmith, a family man from London with no apparent connection to Holly or to Barbury — and now he's disappeared.

Lincoln and his team must find out who Holly really was and why she came to this Wiltshire market town. Was Leo Goldsmith an innocent witness to her murder — or her killer? Lincoln soon starts to suspect that the attack on Holly that dark October night was anything but random — but who would want her dead?

The Price of Silence is the first book in the DI Jeff Lincoln series.

WHAT READERS SAY:

"What a complex plot, but very well thought out! Even though there is a large cast of characters, each was well-defined with their own balance of attractive and repelling sides, something that's not easy to achieve. Lincoln himself is very sympathetic – a 'good copper' who persists – but one who is all too human. I really liked the way the plot unpeeled, suitably messy as real life tends to be. And just when you think you've cracked it, the author throws something else in. Recommended."

"Great quality & a fantastic read."

A SAINTLY GRAVE DISTURBED

When archaeologists Beth Tarrant and Josh Good excavate a ruined chapel at Barbury Abbey, they don't expect to uncover a modern mystery too…

Finding the tomb of a medieval abbot would mean a lot to Beth. Fifty years ago, her grandfather was forced to abandon his own search for the tomb, but nobody knows why. Can Beth finish what he started?

As one incident after another threatens to sabotage the dig, Detective Inspector Jeff Lincoln is called in. When a bungled burglary at the museum turns into murder, he finds a shocking link to a case he's already investigating.

A Saintly Grave Disturbed is the second book in the DI Jeff Lincoln series.

WHAT READERS SAY:

"This book really grabs the reader's attention from the very beginning and continues to pull you in the whole way through. Perfectly paced with believable, engaging characters, an exciting storyline and lots of clues dotted throughout."

"Flawlessly written."

"If there's one thing I love, it's a book that you can read in one sitting…the book is so brilliant that I was late for a meeting because I became so engrossed in the story!"

THE SHAME OF INNOCENCE

Stage-struck teenager Emma Sherman is found

dead on a Wiltshire golf course — no witnesses, no suspects. Detective Inspector Jeff Lincoln gets little help from Emma's neurotic mother, but he's sure she knows something. When explicit photos of Emma are found hidden in an abandoned summer house, Lincoln's sure they hold clues to her murder. But who was the photographer, and why doesn't Lincoln's boss want him to find out?

Days later, another teenage girl is brutally murdered, her body dumped in a country lane. The disappearance of a third teenage girl makes Lincoln realise he's facing a more dangerous enemy than he first imagined.

The Shame of Innocence is the third book in the DI Jeff Lincoln series.

WHAT READERS SAY:

"Keeps you entertained and curious right to the end."

"I was hooked from start to finish. A definitive 5* from me."

"Fast paced, with several threads of the story woven together to a clever conclusion. Gritty, and hard reading at times, but I promise you won't be able to put this book down."

THE PROMISE OF SALVATION

When little Yazmin Fletcher's bones are discovered in Wiltshire woodland twenty years after her disappearance, DI Jeff Lincoln promises Sonia, her mother, that he'll find out what happened to her. His efforts are hampered by his new boss, though, who'd rather he investigated an incident at the country club.

But then local aristocrat Hugh Buckthorn dies, apparently in a bizarre sex game, although Lincoln suspects murder — and he's soon proved right. Once a headline-grabbing playboy, Buckthorn had become a respected art historian, returning to the family seat of Greywood Hall with plans to restore its fortunes. But who wanted him dead?

Searching for Buckthorn's killer, Lincoln and his team at Barley Lane uncover a trail of fraud and deception going back decades. And then Sonia decides to take the law into her own hands...

The Promise of Salvation is the fourth book in the DI Jeff Lincoln series

WHAT READERS SAY:

"What an amazing story. This is the first book I've read by this talented author and will be reading more. DI Lincoln is so well written he becomes real. There is such a strong plot with so many dodgy people ...who to believe?? It's gripping and very hard to put down. Loved it."

"The complex plot – with an additional mystery elsewhere – heads up several blind alleys and has the reader occasionally yelling 'No! Not that!' before it all becomes beautifully resolved. A very enjoyable read."

A STRANGE AND MURDEROUS AIR

Ramsay Keiller is found dead and Jill Fortune has disappeared. Was Keiller still working for the government, even in retirement – or was he working against it? Was piano teacher Jill simply in the wrong place at the wrong time? Fifty years after his blues band made the Top Forty, Dan Swann is still causing ripples – but not with his music. He has a message for the world, but the world isn't listening.

DI Jeff Lincoln needs to fit the pieces of this puzzle together, but he's in a different police station, with a team he doesn't know, and a member of his own team is in trouble. Can he solve this case before it's too late? A story of revenge and conspiracy, regret and retribution, against the backdrop of Salisbury Plain.

WHAT READERS SAY:

'I loved this book. Great characters and brilliant plot which were superbly woven together.'

'Very possibly the best in the series – well constructed, well observed and no lack of drama. Recommended.'

'Deeply satisfying.'

Printed in Dunstable, United Kingdom

76390110R00272